BEASTS OF BEARING — ISABELLE TÖRNQVIST

BEASTS OF
BEARING

ISABELLE TÖRNQVIST

Publisher: BoD · Books on Demand, Östermalmstorg 1, 114 42 Stockholm,
Sverige, bod@bod.se
Print: Libri Plureos GmbH, Friedensallee 273, 22763 Hamburg, Tyskland

ISBN: 978-91-8080-934-4

CHAPTER 1

Vicente

"What's this guy's body count, anyway?" Vicente tried to sound dismissive, like he wasn't concerned about the matter at hand, but anticipation brewed bitter in the pit of his stomach.

"Confirmed? One hundred and five. Suspected? Merciful, I dare say around four hundred kills for sure." Broker discarded his smoldering cigarette before clasping his rifle again.

Even though night fell hours ago, the heat hadn't yet lifted. It pressed against the stone walls of the tower like a second skin, damp and inescapable. Vicente could feel it in his clothes, in the back of his knees, under his collar: the kind of warmth that soaked into bone and made your patience sweat out through your pores.

The capital's biggest avenue sprawled below them, lit in scattered oily torchlight, and from their hide within the tower, they had a perfect view of its entire length. Vicente scanned the windows of the buildings that stood sentinel across the street for any sign of movement. "Right. Keep your eyes peeled, Officer Broker. The assassin's window of opportunity is about to close."

Broker huffed. "You'll address me as 'Sergeant.' The rangers are part of the military, not the police."

A collective, muted chuckle escaped the six other rangers.

"My apologies, Sergeant Broker," Vicente said. This marked his inaugural mission with them. He could not afford to make a mistake.

Below, the procession of trade caravans made their way up the tree-lined, white-stoned boulevard. The crowd moved like syrup around it: slow, dense, thick. Lord Pascal, positioned at the forefront—and wrapped in too much silk and wool for this kind of climate—had successfully undertaken secure passage from the nearby village. However, the lord was not yet safe; all the murders attributed to the assassin had occurred in the city, not in the countryside.

"Protecting this swine is not a task for the rangers," Sergeant Broker grumbled. "And thanks to us, he will undoubtedly indulge further tonight at the queen's court, growing even fatter."

"Lord Pascal will die here in just a few moments," Vicente said.

"Then what the fuck are we standing around here for?"

"The only way to catch Far Cry is to have him reveal his location—which he will, once he takes his shot."

It was Pascal himself who had divulged the truth of the bounty placed on his own head. The mystics of the quorum had accepted the mission to protect him, driven by the slim chance of apprehending the assassin. Thus, they had assigned Vicente the job. Unbeknownst to Pascal, his commitment to this cause would demand his life.

Vicente was the one who had suggested it, his most daring gamble yet: sacrifice one lord, in order to capture the assassin that had terrorized the city for months. When the plan had been approved, he had felt confident, proud even, but now, the stinging taste of doubt prickled the roof of his mouth.

"You never know," Broker said. "The bastard might miss." Then he laughed under his breath, already certain the assassin wouldn't.

The tower creaked, not often, but just enough to remind them that they were very high up and very unwelcome. Vicente exhaled and leaned against the battlement, binoculars slick in his hands. His curls stuck to his forehead. The sea was a smear of black on the horizon, its gusts barely reaching them.

Vicente's investigation had revealed Far Cry's modus operandi: the criminal would hide within one of the tall buildings that afforded a vantage point and unleash his lethal snipe on

Pascal from there. But placing soldiers nearby would only force him to find another spot to strike from or delay his attack. Hence why Vicente decided to post himself and the rangers in the tower of the Tal Miril university, where their view encompassed all potential locations. Each ranger held binoculars to their eyes, keeping watch. The trap was set. Now, they could only wait for Far Cry to strike—

A single gunshot shattered the tranquility, violently jolting Pascal from his horse. Screams pierced the air as he, already unconscious, slammed into the ground.

"Where?"

"Location twenty-four C, top floor!" one of the rangers responded.

Vicente hesitated. "You're sure?" A six-story building, seven hundred yards from Pascal. *How is that possible?*

"Positive! Move out, now!"

Sergeant Broker stepped away from Vicente. "Do your thing, mystic."

Vicente downed a potion of Stormwater; the one entangled to the receiver he had planted in building twenty-four C. He opened the tunnel. The force of it hurled him into space, tearing him away from the tower.

The instantaneous transition left him breathless. Endorphins flooded his senses, momentarily obscuring his thoughts within a swirling vortex of euphoria. He didn't know why teleportation felt so wonderful, but he embraced it with open arms. It was like settling into a hot bath when freezing and sore after a long day of chopping wood in the winter. Relaxation seeped into every part of his body.

As the disorienting rush of transportation subsided, Vicente found himself deposited within a new chamber, its air heavy with dust and the lingering scent of abandonment.

"Where the fuck did you come from?"

Vicente stared down the barrel of a rifle. He resisted the impulse to raise his hands in a show of compliance. "I'm a mystic, and I suggest you drop your weapon before I'm forced to hurt you." Gradually, his vision adapted to the darkness, revealing a pair of hazel eyes looking back at him. What immediately struck him about the man was his small stature, and his youthful face hinted at an age not exceeding twenty summers. He was even younger than Vicente.

Far Cry, garbed entirely in shades of beige to camouflage himself amidst the desert-toned buildings, stayed motionless and his firearm remained trained on Vicente. Vicente had been given a gun he didn't know how to use, but there was no way he could draw it before Far Cry would pull his own trigger.

Vicente met his eyes, steadfast, trying to sound convincing when he said, "I'm only here for the initial arrest. You have a better chance of making your escape once I've handed you over to the police officers. You saw what I can do."

Far Cry glared at him, sizing him up. Of course he couldn't make sense of what had just happened; how could he? Seeing Vicente teleport would make any sane man feel fear.

Slowly, Far Cry lowered into a crouch. He placed his rifle on the floor, releasing his grip.

Though the original plan merely entailed stalling, Vicente recognized an opening. Given Far Cry's small build, Vicente had the physical advantage.

He aimed a kick at Far Cry's face, but the man threw himself backward, nullifying the impact. Vicente surged forward, slamming him to the ground, adrenaline giving him the strength to hold him down.

Vicente had also been equipped with a pair of handcuffs, for the purpose of detaining the assassin until the arrival of the rangers. He fastened the cuffs around Far Cry's wrists, binding them together behind his back.

"Bastard," Far Cry barked, "I was yielding."

Vicente pulled him to his knees. "They're on their way, just sit tight." Through the window, he saw a crowd forming around the murder scene far off in the distance. Vicente stared, struggling to make sense of what Far Cry had managed to do. *Seven hundred yards.* "How did you do that?"

"I was about to ask you the same thing."

Vicente looked back to where he had appeared, where the other glass vial with the receiving end of the Stormwater had stood. Now it lay discarded in the tower he and the rangers had been in a minute ago. The two entangled vials had been substituted with each other through a quantum tunnel, and Vicente had merely been pulled with the liquid.

"I'm afraid I can't tell you; that's a state secret. Nevertheless, take pride in the fact you forced the government to resort to employing a mystic in their pursuit of you. You're an amazing sniper; why not use your abilities for a nobler purpose than of a hired killer?"

Far Cry remained silent.

Vicente steadied his breathing as he took in his surroundings. A bow and a quiver full of arrows were leaning against one of the walls. He had no doubt Far Cry carried other weapons, and if he had a knife on him, Vicente couldn't turn his back. As he picked up the rifle, Far Cry's jaw tightened. A subtle reaction, but Vicente noticed. A tell, maybe. But he let it slide.

The firearm appeared unremarkable, resembling the standard-issue weapons wielded by the military. It was a simple bolt-action rifle, made of wood and metal. "Your gun lacks a scope," Vicente pointed out. "How did you accomplish such remarkable marksmanship without one?"

"Fuck you."

Undeterred by the response, Vicente squatted down before the kneeling Far Cry. "Why don't you use a scope?"

"None of your business."

"Who paid you to kill Lord Pascal?"

"Fuck me, you ask a lot of questions."

Seven hundred yards. A sniper hitting a target from that distance was unheard of, and yet here was Far Cry, a malnourished, young civilian with no military affiliation. Why hadn't he joined the army? And how, in the Merciful's name, had he avoided the draft in the first place? Curiosity burned through Vicente like a fever, growing into agitation. Questioning Far Cry wasn't his job; he was well aware of that. But, to Vicente, indifference was an illness, and he could never get comfortable remaining in the dark. "Tell me your name."

Far Cry snorted. His nose bled from the fight and he looked a bit dazed, blinking hard, once. "*That's a state secret.*"

Vicente couldn't stomach feeling belittled, but anger sat comfortably on his shoulders like a well-worn coat. Frustration became rage, an emotion much easier to harness.

He seized the assassin's chin. "I am a mystic. You have surely heard tales of the formidable might exerted by the mystics of the Sensis Quorum, but I assure you, my power surpasses theirs."

Far Cry's eyes fixed on Vicente from behind the veil of his black bangs. "Is that supposed to impress me? Besides, you'll have to hand me over to the police at some point. Once those lazy motherfuckers let their guard down, I'll slip right past them again, and come for you when you sleep. Then I'm going to gut you from throat to dick."

Finally, some information: he had been arrested before. He must have a rap sheet, then. And from there, they would be able to trace the evidence and find the person who had ordered the bounty on Pascal's head. Though, that wouldn't be Vicente's job. He was almost done with his.

Vicente took in the sight of him. Black hair, a pale complexion, sharp features, dark lashes. Dark enough for him to take note of it.

Far Cry tipped his head backwards, trying and failing to pry his chin from Vicente's grip. "You have a death-wish, pretty boy? Get your filthy hands off me."

Vicente didn't let go. Beneath warm skin, he felt the subtle tremors, the honed fury in Far Cry's body as he struggled to free himself. Vicente could mark this mission down as a success; the quorum would be proud of him. The victory wavered before him now, though, empty and dull. His curiosity was still unquenched, a greedy vice that couldn't be satiated.

The sound of people rapidly ascending the stairs reverberated through the concrete walls, drawing Vicente's attention to the soldiers' imminent arrival. He stood. "Perhaps the rangers will prove more successful in coaxing information out of you."

Shock drained Far Cry's face of all color. "The rangers? You said you were working with the police."

"My apologies, I get them mixed up—"

Far Cry sprung from the ground and bolted towards the nearby window, the one he had fired out of. Vicente lunged, latching onto the metallic chain of the handcuffs before Far Cry could swan dive to his death like a lunatic.

Vicente hauled him back to the center of the room. "I wouldn't do that if I were you."

"If you were me," Far Cry said, "you'd rather die than be in their custody."

The door slammed open with such force the wood cracked against the wall. The rangers burst in, weapons raised and steady. When they saw Vicente had things under control, they lowered their guns.

The men erupted in a cheer, an outpouring of exultation and relief. Meanwhile, Far Cry shrank into himself, rounding his shoulders, head bowed, retreating as far as Vicente's grip would allow.

"Iver Vasiliev." Sergeant Broker grabbed a fistful of Far Cry's hair, raising his drooping head. "How I've longed to get my hands on you. Couldn't come up with a better nickname?"

Iver sneered at the sergeant, but the fire in his eyes was slowly dying. "Fuck you, Broker."

Vicente kept his expression neutral, refusing to let the surprise show on his face. All this time, the rangers had known the identity of the Far Cry assassin? His skin crawled, the air heavy with a pervasive *wrongness*, like the unsettling scent clinging to the sick. Was this part of a broader deception? And if so, how deeply did it extend; did the queen know?

Iver fought and struggled. The rangers maintained their firm hold, escorted him out of the room and seized his rifle as a token of triumph.

One of the rangers patted Vicente on the back. "We finally caught Far Cry. Nice work, mystic."

Vicente could only nod. He felt childish then, watching as the rangers led Iver away and identifying the sensation as akin to being robbed of a prize.

*

A week later, the queen summoned Vicente. During his years with the quorum, he had made himself quite familiar with the Arkensaali palace. But the regal hall still took his breath away, every time. The vaulted ceiling was so high he half-expected clouds to gather beneath it. Golden filigree intertwined with gemstones glimmered against the blue expanse, creating the illusion of a starlit sky.

At the heart of the chamber rested the very epitome of supremacy: the throne. The polished ebony glistened like a moonlit lake, accentuated by patterns of silver tracing the lineage of the Rhys dynasty. And on it sat the queen herself, Leandra Rhys. She reminded Vicente of the sun: radiant and everlasting, unbearable in its dazzling intensity, and dangerous when exposed to for too long. The fire in her fed itself. She had ruled since before Vicente's birth, and given the power burning within her, she would likely continue to rule for many years after his death.

Vicente was a little taken aback to see Indra of the Sensis Quorum seated next to the queen. When his eyes met Indra's, she gave him a small nod. The demigod Otter, Lyska, was at her feet, smoking its pipe. Lyska rarely left the quorum's archives. Something was up.

Vicente took in the assortment of individuals. Nobles, dressed in fine attire marking their privilege and influence. Soldiers of the Tactics and Assault Operations Team—also known as the rangers—bore the distinctive markings of valor on their chests. Some faces, those of Tal Miril diplomats, Vicente recognized. These were his colleagues. This could only mean a diplomatic mission was on the table; a job of such importance it necessitated the input of the quorum and their bonded demigod.

Vicente sensed the weight of expectation hanging in the air. The reason for their shared summons was being kept a secret. Nothing like this had ever happened before; at least not in the seventeen years he had studied with the quorum. He took his place in the crowd, feigned indifference settling into his expression with well-rehearsed ease.

When Queen Leandra rose from her seat, the assembly fell silent. "There's an unfortunate situation forming in the small town of Llyr, and it needs to be dealt with immediately. Since the bandit raids in the area have come to an end due to Bruvran and his company's... *interference*, land is now available, and two clans are at each other's throats over it. The Llyrians won't be keen on Arkensaal's intrusion, but it's in our interest that this conflict be resolved quickly."

At the mention of Llyr, it clicked for Vicente. Llyr's relationship with the capital had been unstable for the better part of a century. It could be described as 'shaky,' at best. At its worst, Llyr's leaders had been persistently seeking any excuse to spark a civil war against the central provinces.

The queen looked around at the people gathered. "This mission demands discretion; I will not send a crowd. Only those who are unquestionably suited for this assignment should step forward."

Naturally, she didn't want this operation to look like Arkensaal deployed an entire brigade to deal with the Llyrians: they would interpret it as an act of aggression. Sending an agent of the crown that was both a diplomat and able to hold their own in a fight would be ideal. Few fit that description, and Vicente was one of them.

Vicente would be lying if he said he wanted to return to Llyr, but he still had much to prove in his career. This could be the opportunity he had been waiting for. Yet the mere thought of setting foot in Llyr again immediately filled him with sickening nerves. Ambition and reluctance warred in his chest. He had left Llyr at eight years of age and hadn't been back since. Sometimes he forgot why; his thoughts skipped on the memory of it. Going back, would it open old wounds? But the only other person who knew what Vicente had been through was dead. Vicente was sure of it, as he had been the one to kill him.

Vicente moved forward, his steps echoing off the marble floor. "If it please, Your Majesty. I volunteer my humble assistance."

Queen Leandra tilted her head to the side and her long, inky hair fell over her shoulder. Her eyes narrowed. "You may approach."

He did, discreetly pulling on the hem of his shirt to straighten it out. Behind him, the rest of the assembly stayed quiet. He could sense them watching him, and it made him feel claustrophobic. "My name is Vicente Lamor. I am a mystic in training and a diplomacy student at the Tal Miril university."

"Ah, the mystic," she said as she recognized him. It shouldn't have been difficult, as he was also the *only* mystic student—the very first the quorum had been allowed to tutor—but he reckoned she was a busy woman. "Let's hear your proposal," she said.

"It's true the people of Llyr won't be glad about outsiders meddling. I was born there, raised there until I was eight. They might not consider me an outsider and thus heed my advice." *Might.* He sounded too unsure; he shouldn't have said that word.

"I've been informed you're the one who brought the Far Cry assassin to justice. An impressive feat." The queen remained standing as she spoke to him, like they were on equal footing, and Vicente tried his best not to be nervous about that.

"Thank you, Your Majesty. He now fears my mystic abilities, as he should."

A small lie. The queen didn't need to know Vicente wasn't actually aggressive or dangerous. He could protect himself, and that was all he needed, really.

"Your mystic powers, do they render you a skilled fighter?"

He looked over at Indra, still seated by the throne. She looked intently at him, nodding subtly.

She wanted him to exaggerate and convince the queen. Vicente opened his hands. "I do lack any military training, but my skills as a mystic are very unique," he embellished, injecting a little confidence into his voice.

"Your Majesty, if I might interject?"

Queen Leandra's harsh gaze softened when she spotted the source of the question in the crowd. "Please, approach."

Marcia Jadanza stepped up next to him. The sun shining in from the tall windows painted her black skin with a golden glow. She was in her early thirties but didn't look a day over twenty-five, and whenever Vicente tried to point out how beautiful she was, she'd swat him in the back of the head.

"You need an experienced diplomat for this mission," Marcia said. "Me and Vicente are familiar; he is a dear friend of my wife's. I too was born and raised in Llyr. I volunteer my time and effort as well, at the disposal of Your Majesty."

The corners of the queen's mouth lifted ever so slightly. "I was hoping you'd step up to the task, Lady Marcia."

Marcia and Vicente exchanged looks. She had promised to bring him on a job, and it was long overdue; she would let him take the lead on this one.

"The rest of you are dismissed," the queen announced, relieving the others of the stress of having to decline the offer to be sent off to the god-forsaken countryside.

"Will you dispatch part of your queen's guard to accompany us?" Marcia asked once the crowd had left, leaving only the three of them and Indra in the throne room.

"No, this is too sensitive." Queen Leandra looked Vicente up and down. "You said the Far Cry assassin respects your abilities, which I have also grown to suspect during his time in our custody. I have therefore made the decision to send him with you."

"Pardon?" Vicente said before he could stop himself.

The queen furrowed her brow. "I'm sending my best diplomat to Llyr. Marcia will need protection, someone other than a mystic. Besides, this mercenary fears only you, Mister Vicente. He's displaying an impressive level of disregard for authority. You'll domesticate him. I want him back broken... manageable."

Apprehension prickled under Vicente's skin just then. After cooling down from his encounter with Far Cry, anger gave way to embarrassment as he reflected on his temper flaring beyond his control. His pride still ached, and he didn't want to meet Far Cry again, but he was not about to disagree with the queen. Despite the existence of the High Council and the quorum, Queen Leandra had the final say. She always got what she wanted. "As you wish, Your Majesty. Forgive me for asking, but what's in it for him? He'll just be going back to jail. He'll save himself the trouble if he simply rejects."

"If this mission is a success, he will be pardoned of his crimes. He's too skilled of a marksman to be locked away in prison."

"He'll join the Tactics and Assault Operations Team then, or the queen's guard?" Vicente asked.

"Like I said, he's proved to be non-compliant and refuses to listen to orders. Thus, he'll be sent to war, some remote location where he can't do any harm to anyone except our enemies. He won't be made aware of that until after the mission is completed, though. Promise him his freedom; that should suffice."

His skill would still be lost, then, in the fruitless war with the neighboring countries. It had been going on for decades and was a waste of manpower and talent—but aside from the members of the Sensis Quorum, Vicente seemed to be alone in thinking that— because the realm of Ōeken hadn't gained any ground since the war had started.

"I must thank you for your service, Mister Vicente," Queen Leandra said. "That assassin has been quite the thorn in our flesh for some time now."

Indra rose from her seat and stood by the queen's side. Her white hair was braided today, and unlike the days spent in the archives, she wore modest clothing to protect herself from the sun she was so unaccustomed to. Only a small glimpse of her teak-colored skin showed at her wrists. "This couldn't have come at a better time, Leandra."

Queen Leandra cocked an eyebrow. "Is that so?"

"My sisters of the quorum and I suspect the Stag demigod is located in Llyr, and we need Vicente to travel there to either refute our suspicions or to set it free." Indra was almost giddy with excitement when she turned to him. With a hideous fixity, she locked her unnaturally dark eyes onto him, like a wolf staring down its prey. "Your mission to Llyr will work as an excellent guise for finding the Stag and unleashing it."

Vicente gritted his teeth. He was surprised and a little worried by Indra's boldness, openly sharing her objective in front of the queen, effectively derailing her carefully plotted plan. But the quorum had always been just that: bold, sometimes excessively so. And it *was* indeed perfect: Arkensaalis were otherwise not allowed to cross the borders into Llyr. This was the first time the attempt at bonding with another deity, like the Otter Lyska, had been realistic.

Queen Leandra clasped her hands. "Indra," she said and Vicente internally cringed, "I need not remind you what will happen if the tentative trust between Arkensaal and Llyr is broken. I will require Mister Vicente's complete focus on the task."

"Queen of humans," Lyska roared, overloud, splintering the air. Everyone else fell quiet when it spoke.

The Otter walked over to them slowly on three legs, using the fourth one to lift the pipe out of its mouth. Water flowed from where it placed its feet, welling up with such force it cracked the marble floor. "Your god Eldvittra demands that you wage war. Unleashing the Stag will bring us one step closer to achieving equilibrium, and with it in your arsenal, the war will be won by you. I insist you let Vicente fetch the Stag for me."

What Lyska didn't understand, was that Eldvittra—the god of war—demanded *war*, not victory. The queen knew this. It had taken Vicente years to grasp this, and a few years on top of that to accept it. However, gods were egotistical by nature, and Lyska would most likely never comprehend. It wanted its family back, and nothing else mattered.

Vicente was, perhaps, selfish as well. Above all else, he desired to bond with the Stag, to prove to everyone he was equal to the mystics of the quorum, to free himself from their curse, and to escape the constant heat from both the quorum and the queen. Lyska amplified the powers of the members of the quorum. Vicente could only imagine what the Stag could do for him.

The queen scowled, but didn't protest. She couldn't. "Very well. Fine. You'll do this as well, Mister Vicente. But people outside the capital despise mystics; you must keep your abilities to yourself."

Queen Leandra oversaw the balancing act of the needs of her people, the greed of the High Council and the will of Eldvittra. It was a delicate and dangerous job, and her inane idea of stability was constantly being threatened by the ambitions of the quorum: permanency or development? Conservatism or progress? Deference in the face of the gods, or harnessing their powers? Vicente, as a mystic diplomat, was uniquely positioned at the intersection of these two worlds.

But he had plots of his own. He was walking a separate tightrope, carefully playing both sides to survive. The Stag was the only force that could tip the scales. With the Stag by his side, the quorum could no longer pit him against the queen. This was his chance to break free from his role as a pawn in their struggle for power.

Vicente bowed to her, hopeful that this was the last time he did so. "As you command, Your Majesty."

CHAPTER 2

Marcia

Marcia shielded her eyes from the glaring sun as she and Vicente stepped out of the gondola that had taken them from the airborne island where the palace and the seat of government, Arkensaal, sat. Relief washed over her as she set foot on the ground; being that high in the air always left her feeling a bit uneasy.

"The assassin's papers will be ready tomorrow," she said. To be allowed to leave the capital, the criminal would have to take on another identity. If only the queen had assigned them a soldier instead, they wouldn't have to jump through so many hoops, but alas, they all had to suffer the whims of her royal highness.

Vicente raked a hand through his hair, pushing his brown, almost black, loose curls from his forehead. "What about Daiyu's?" The beard that grew only along his jawline and above his upper lip was shorn short: he had taken extra care to groom himself for the audience with Queen Leandra. It was quite endearing.

"If she agrees to come, I'll request that the university fabricate some expedition to Llyr. That should be enough to allow her to leave the capital."

The plaza in front of the palace was a blister of polished white stone and rust-red banners, fluttering listlessly. Around the edges, crowds ebbed and flowed: petitioners, tradesfolk, and students in diplomat's black or engineer's blue, all dabbing at their foreheads. Zeppelins passed overhead in a low drone, cutting between the spires of government buildings that had names longer than their foundations were stable. Marcia looked up at one of the airships. It was most likely heading to the frontiers with a load of freshly minted soldiers.

Vicente looked up as well. "Queen Leandra likes you; you should ask her if we can borrow one of those. Can't say I'm looking forward to riding for a week straight."

Marcia huffed. "It will be far from a glamorous trip; Llyr doesn't even have electricity yet. If you want to take a shower in the next few months, you'll have to go to the nearest military base."

The roadblocks around the royal heartland, the unkept roads and the laws prohibiting civilians from leaving the capital all filled the same purpose: a way for the government to keep its population from travelling and exchanging information, to make it easier to conscript new soldiers, and to fend off any potential uprisings or revolutions. She could understand why it was done. Eldvittra, the god of war demanded, well, war. It sure caused their jobs as ambassadors to be an unnecessary pain, though.

Of course, she and Vicente had the diplomat's benefit of free travel. But that didn't mean this mission would be easy. "Queen Leandra was right, you know; you need to be careful out there. They don't take kindly to mystics." It was the fact it was in his blood, that he was born with it, that made it taboo: some people considered mystics to be tainted by the horned god.

Vicente shared one of his charming smiles and hooked his arm with hers, the tawny brown skin of his forearm warm against the inside of her wrist. "Don't you worry about me," he said, his voice containing that tiny hint of playful mockery again, "I'll behave."

*

After Marcia and Vicente parted ways, she headed to the university for a quick word with the dean of the science department. Naturally, he approved her request. Then she entered the Tal Miril lecture hall, which was filled with laughter from the students. It made her smile, witnessing the effect her wife had on every student she took on. The Order of Tal Miril had founded the biggest university in the capital, which was were Daiyu—as well as Marcia and Vicente—were employed, but today, her auditorium was occupied by children; most likely in an attempt by the school to entice the new generation into pursuing an academic career.

Daiyu pushed her glasses further up the bridge of her nose. "Let me remind you that chemistry is like any lovely relationship: complicated, full of surprises and occasionally explosive!"

Giggles rippled through the room. Students exchanged amused glances as Professor Daiyu scribbled formulas on the chalkboard with a flourish.

"Now, let's talk about the noble gases," she declared. "They're like the introverts of the periodic table, never wanting to interact with anyone else. It's as if they have their own exclusive club, where only a select few are allowed in. So, if you're ever feeling bad for choosing to be alone, just remember even atoms can be a bit antisocial."

Marcia watched fondly as her wife continued to guide the students through the intricacies of chemical reactions, injecting humor into each concept to keep their minds engaged. The lecture hall's tall windows stood wide open and the fans whirred at full strength, sending papers fluttering across Daiyu's desk in gentle protest; but the heat held fast, unmoved by their efforts.

As the class ended, one student lingered. "Can I ask you something?"

"Is it about homework?" Daiyu asked as she packed her bag. "Are your teachers giving you a lot? You know, when you move on to higher studies, there won't be as much. Professors don't really care about stuff like that."

The young girl smiled. "No, it's alright. I wanted to ask you: Is it possible to make schorl in a lab?"

Marcia had heard questions like that before, usually asked by people from the villages scattered across the crown-administered prefectures. She had to stop herself from rolling her eyes. There was only one use for this mineral.

The girl wrung her hands nervously. "I need some, but I can't afford it."

"There's tons of it in the Crooked Mountains; you could find some there." Daiyu stooped down to the student. "But you won't need any. The mystics here in the capital are not going to hurt you."

"My mom told me to always keep some under my bed." The girl's cheeks flushed, and her eyes grew wide. "She said it keeps mystics away. She allowed me to come here only because I promised her."

Daiyu smiled at her. "Schorl works, but it requires a lot to be effective. Like, *a lot*."

Marcia did roll her eyes this time. Daiyu wasn't the most sensitive one. "Actually, the dangerous mystic is leaving the capital for a few months," she said. "You'll be safe."

The girl gave her a quick nod before hurrying out the door to catch up with her classmates.

"Where's Vicente going?" Daiyu wore a billowy, button-down shirt tucked into the hem of her trousers. A chain was threaded through her wedding ring, allowing her to wear it around her neck and freeing her fingers from any expensive mistakes in the laboratory.

Marcia reached out her arm towards Daiyu, and the smile drawing on her face made so much fondness bubble up inside Marcia, to the point she almost choked on it. Daiyu twirled once before grabbing her hand. Marcia wrapped her in her arms and drew a deep breath of her scent. Even though she spent her time cooped up in a lab with chemicals, she smelled sweet and floral. "We received a mission from Arkensaal. We'll be heading out in a few days."

"Such short notice. Does it pay well?"

Marcia snorted. "Not really, but there are redeeming qualities to it."

"Well, you've always been too easily tempted."

"You'll never guess the circumstances."

Daiyu groaned. "Please don't make me guess. You know I can't keep up when you talk about what you do for work."

Tucking a loose strand of hair behind Daiyu's ear, Marcia let her fingers linger just a moment longer than necessary. Daiyu was beautiful like teenage rebel years. Her eyes had a certain gleam to them, something that dared you to keep up or be left behind. Sometimes Marcia had to take a few seconds to settle in the thought that Daiyu was really hers. "Funny that, coming from you," Marcia said.

"You should attend my classes sometime; you might learn what too much acid does to your teeth."

"Had you been my teacher during my early schooling, I might've actually paid attention."

"Is there something off about this assignment? I feel like you're avoiding the topic."

"Well, for one, I'll be travelling to Llyr."

Daiyu wriggled from her embrace, eyes darting over her face to spot any hints of worry. "You're ready to meet your father again?"

Marcia took her hand, stroking her thumb over her knuckles. Though Daiyu took great care of herself, nothing could hide her red fingers, the burns she'd suffered from being a bit too excited in the lab. "It doesn't bother me any longer; he has no influence over my life."

"What if he tries to make you follow through with it?"

"No laws nor scripture support his claims; marriage trumps the vow of engagement." Her father's arrangement on her behalf had no standing, not when she was legally married. The contract she and Daiyu had signed years ago—acknowledged by both divine and legal authority—stood firm, impervious to her father's will.

"I'm hearing I have no competition in Llyr to fear," Daiyu said.

"Well, at least not that of a man."

Daiyu slapped her shoulder. "Hey!"

"Maybe you ought to join me, make sure I don't get tempted. I have already spoken to the Dean: you can do some fieldwork while we're there. They have hot springs."

Daiyu scrunched up her nose, contorting her face in this incredibly adorable manner she always did when she was trying her best not to smile. "You know, you have this weird habit. You did the same when you asked me to marry you: you never ask outright."

They had been married for years, but from time to time, Daiyu did something that brought forth a surge of affection and memories within Marcia. She looked just like she had done the day Marcia proposed: her black hair in a messy ponytail, questionable stains on her lab coat, and her thin eyes—halfway hidden behind fingerprint-smudged glasses—made thinner by her brilliant smile. "Is that a 'yes'?" Marcia asked, echoing the question from that day.

Daiyu sighed, stalling her answer for a long, fraught moment as she tried to act hard to get. "Fine, I'll tag along. But when we return, can we—"

Here we go. "Honey…"

"—get a baby?"

Marcia fought to keep any hints of irritation from her tone. This was supposed to be a happy topic, but Daiyu had been nagging about it for weeks. "It will take us some time to find a suitable donor."

"We could at least get the process started."

Marcia admired Daiyu for wanting to go through pregnancy. She had told her that she had this deep yearning for it, something Marcia had never experienced. For the longest time, she thought something was wrong with her for lacking this desire. Still, as an adult, she didn't know whether this missing piece in her derived from within her heart or originated from defiance against her father trying to force her onto that path. Perhaps it was fear deterring her. She didn't know, and it didn't matter, in the end. Daiyu was the one who wanted it.

"We'll see when we get back."

CHAPTER 3

Vicente

Under the merciless glare of the sun, Vicente, Marcia and Daiyu waited in the sweltering heat beneath Arkensaal's floating palace. High above, the gondolas swayed lazily from the palace's upper docks. Within those heights, Iver was parleying with the queen. Most likely, she was assuring him her offer of a pardon was legitimate—lying through her teeth all the while.

Daiyu stood beside him in the shade of a column, hair already escaping her braid in delicate wisps that clung to her neck. A cart passed by, selling sticky-sweet dates. She bought some and offered one to Vicente. "This guy the real deal?"

"Sure is." Vicente spat out the pit of the date, watching as a giant beetle the size of his foot marched past. "Though he has indeed proved to not be keen on higher-ups telling him what to do." He tugged at one of his cuffs as damp, hot air congealed against his skin.

The sun spilt molten gold into the crowded plaza. The city around Arkensaal wasn't built so much as amassed: tiered in layers of ancient stone and stubborn ambition, stretched along the bay like a cat sprawling belly-up on hot marble. Three million souls packed in tight, fighting for breath between salt air and the steam of urban life. Vicente had his life neatly packed in a bag by his feet. Being away from the coast during peak summertime would be torturous, and they wouldn't be leaving Llyr until the mission was a success, but it would be nice to get a break from the crowds.

"I've only heard bad things about Llyr," Daiyu said. "Please tell me they have tasty food, at least."

"I've always said that the best thing about Llyr is that you don't have to go there."

"Well, that's not true anymore." Daiyu licked the stickiness from her thumb. "Are you alright with going back?"

Bone-deep panic struck Vicente immediately. It was a primal, instinctual fear. A fear of being found out, of losing everything he had built, earned and the potential he hadn't reached yet. But Daiyu didn't know, he had never told her. He hadn't told a soul about what happened to him and what he had done in Llyr. All she knew was that his circumstances there had been awful enough for him to leave it all behind. She was just acting friendly, showing concern. *Calm down.*

Vicente leaned his hip against the stone planting trough. "Is Marcia?" He asked instead, but his voice stuck in his throat. He cleared it without much success.

"She says she doesn't mind, and I believe her. Her father can't do shit to us. Do you have family there still?"

Heart-shaped petals from roses drifted to the ground, perfuming the air with their sweetness. The aroma mingled with the saffron and cinnamon wafting from a nearby tavern. Vicente's memories of Llyr were blurred; a gray and cloudy cataract, somber, and void of color or scent. To his child self, Llyr had seemed lifeless. Returning didn't trouble him, but the thought didn't bring him any joy, either.

"You know, I'm actually not sure," he said. "Not that it matters." He wouldn't visit his mother; he hadn't received any letters from her since she had let the Sensis Quorum take him to the capital. Perhaps that was a good thing. He wanted to leave his childhood behind, to cut all ties to what happened, to erase all evidence of it. And it had been: the past had been buried under years of a great life sitting on top of it, concealing it. Shaking off the panic was a skill he was well versed in, and so he did it again.

Marcia, who had been tending to the horses, came to join them. "What's taking him so long?"

Vicente could tell she was anxious by the way she held her own hand. She too had left Llyr amid less-than-ideal circumstances. "What, can't wait to get up on that horse?"

Daiyu noticed it too and tried to distract her. "I've heard some scientist made an engine that can be powered by steam. Imagine using that to travel, instead of on horseback."

"The government would never allow that. Not for us non-military, anyway." Vicente looked over at the four horses waiting patiently. For most, transportation difficulties posed little concern. The villages, towns and cities outside the core royal dominion operated under clan rule, though technically within the monarchy's jurisdiction. Ruling clans retained authority in key areas, including the choice to exempt their people from conscription, making enlistment voluntary. This autonomy discouraged many from venturing beyond the protective boundaries of clan-controlled territories. "Who is the ruling clan of Llyr? Are we running any risk of conflict if they oppose our upcoming decision?"

"Llyr has no ruling clan, only minor ones." Marcia looked at him and blinked. Slow and heavy. "That's why our queen is sending diplomats, Vic."

Vicente bit his tongue. History, not current politics, was his academic forte. To become a skilled ambassador, he'd need to bridge that gap. Charm alone wouldn't suffice when navigating disputes.

"There is something I must run by you, though," Marcia said, eyes cast downward. "Queen Leandra told me to favor the Errani clan; those who want to turn it to farmland."

Vicente had hoped to play this fairly, but instead, they would have to act as puppets of the monarchy yet again.

"Don't argue," she said before he could get a word in. "The High Council demands it, there are some Arkensaali nobles who are looking to make a fortune on the trade this enables. Besides, we could feed an entire army with the soy grown from those acres."

Vicente wasn't sure he'd ever get used to the unfair ways the game of politics was played, but for now, he was nothing but a cog in the machine. "Yes, ma'am."

"Marcia… there's something I need to tell you, too," Daiyu said. She scuffed her foot over the gravel, hands burrowed deep in the pockets of her trousers. Her expression was one of shame, of embarrassment.

Marcia frowned, concern consuming her face as she looked at her wife. "What? What's the matter?"

"Ever since I first met you, you've given me this special feeling in my tummy. I can't contain it any longer…"

Marcia's eyelids fluttered with annoyance. "Stop."

"I'm falling in love with you."

"Stop it."

Vicente smiled. The two of them were so different. When he had first introduced Daiyu to Marcia, he wasn't sure they would get along, but by the end of that year, they had gotten engaged. To this day, he takes credit for this impeccable match.

Another gondola descended from the palace. Iver stepped out of it, flanked by two police officers. One of them took the handcuffs off his wrists. He didn't immediately run; whatever the queen had said must have worked.

Daiyu approached Iver, a bounce to her step, and reached out her hand. "I'm Daiyu, nice to meet ya!"

Iver hesitated before shaking her hand. His rifle and bow were strapped to his back. It shouldn't have surprised Vicente—after all, Iver was joining them to 'protect' them—but it still made him uncomfortable to see him armed.

Marcia's tone was cold when she spoke. "I'm Marcia Jadanza and I will be holding on to your new documents of identification. They will get you past the roadblocks and keep you safe in Llyr. You are now Iver Russo, by the way."

It was a common family name in the countryside, and the identification papers falsified on the queen's orders detailed how Iver was born in one of the small settlements in the lands surrounding Llyr, giving his cover-story at least some degree of verisimilitude. No one would care to check if it was true.

"Couldn't have given me a fancier one?" Iver said.

What Iver said was disrespectful, and Vicente wanted to shut that down immediately, but he hesitated. Beneath the scowl on Iver's face, Vicente picked up on signs of fear. The tightness in his brow, the way his eyes darted from him to Marcia to Daiyu. He looked like a wild dog, snarling, hackles up like he wasn't yet fully convinced Vicente wouldn't attack him. Their previous encounter had sparked a dynamic between them, an unspoken recognition of power. Iver believed Vicente was dangerous, and Vicente knew Iver actually was. Besides, cornering a frightened dog would only invite retaliation.

Marcia 'tsk'-ed and sat up on her horse.

Vicente handed Iver the reins to one of the horses. "She's yours. Have you ever ridden before?"

Iver's stance had a lightness to it, an intrinsic balance, like a bird on a laundry line. He gently patted the horse's snout. "What's her name?"

"I'm not sure; I didn't catch it," Vicente said. "Don't even know what my own horse is called. We got them just now."

Iver clicked his tongue. "You don't know the name of your own horse? Makes me sick. Do you have no respect for the innocent beings beneath you, in your care?"

A wave of contempt rolled off Iver, so palpable Vicente half expected to look down and see it lapping at his feet. He fought the urge to step away from Iver in alarm. "Maybe not horses, but I do have a reputation for being very gentle to people underneath me."

Iver whipped his head around to glare at him. "What the fuck is wrong with you?"

"Don't worry," Daiyu said in a singsong tone. "He's like that with everyone."

The four of them set off on horseback, passed through the gates of the capital without issue and headed westward. They wouldn't reach Mariemoor before nightfall, so they would have to pitch their tents in the wilderness.

*

When the sun gave up on them and the sky blushed with hues of pink, they stopped for the day.

"We'll make camp here," Iver said after inspecting the clearing. The woods stood just beyond the edge of it, dark and crowded, full of the sort of trees that could conceal anything or anyone. Vicente disliked how close they were to the forest, but if he had to use words like "scary" to explain his discomfort, then he would rather not.

He dismounted his horse, feeling the weariness settle into his muscles. Daiyu displayed signs of fatigue from the journey as well. Marcia was as stoic as ever. She moved like a soldier, methodical and precise, as she set up their campsite and ordered Daiyu and Vicente to 'get out of her way.'

By the time night fell, their tents had been pitched and their horses fed. Gathering around a crackling fire, they partook in a modest meal. Little conversation had taken place throughout the day, and Daiyu now made an attempt to remedy that. She was talking, animatedly, about copper sulfate reactions. Or maybe wasps; Vicente had stopped paying attention four sentences ago.

Iver… well, Iver brooded. Sat a little too far from the flames, like he didn't want to be associated with them.

"Why don't you tell us a bit about yourself, Iver?" Daiyu asked. "The rest of us know each other quite well already."

She stared at him in amiable silence. Iver's response was a withering glare.

Daiyu's smile only widened. "You're a grumpy one, aren't ya?"

With a huff, Iver got up and walked off, away from the light of the fire.

Something cold settled in Vicente's gut as he watched him disappear into the trees. If Vicente was to stay out of harm's way, he needed to win Iver over. Vicente prided himself on his ability to make friends with anyone, invariably spotting at least one redeeming quality in the people who crossed his path. But he found he didn't like Iver in the slightest. Once the initial curiosity had subsided, he saw him for who he truly was: a violent criminal without depth or anything else to offer. Vicente would have to feign friendliness, which was distasteful, but in this case, he couldn't really be bothered to care about his morals. They had always been a bit shady, anyway.

"He thinks I'm dangerous," Vicente offered, pulling his cloak tighter to shield against the coolness of the night. The kick to Iver's face, that particular detail, he chose not to share.

"Now, wouldn't that be something," Daiyu mused. She peered into the dark shrouds of the trees where Iver had escaped to. "You think it's enough to stop him from running from us?"

"He saw me appear out of thin air. That's all he needs to know about me." Perhaps some mystics could be dangerous given the proper training. But Vicente could only open tunnels to either move himself or objects he had entangled. There was nothing harmful to it, but Iver didn't need to know that—not after vowing to gut Vicente like a fish.

"I'd like to know more about him, though," Marcia said. "He seems a bit young, don't you think?"

She was right about that; he couldn't be older than twenty. "I doubt he'll tell us anything. The officers said he had no paperwork, only his rap sheet as the Far Cry assassin."

Marcia looked at the flames, swept up in the enthralling effect fire had on most people. "Undocumented?"

"Likely going under a fake name." Vicente didn't think anyone with those skills could be that low-born. He must have learned from someone skilled; military or police.

"Don't you think this puts us in danger, Vic?" Marcia said.

Daiyu shrugged. "He seems like a nice guy."

Marcia playfully jabbed her in the side with her elbow. "You think everyone is nice."

Still, Vicente couldn't wrap his mind around why the queen thought it would be a good idea to send Iver with them. Outside the city walls, he was an even greater flight risk. "Your suspicion is warranted, Marcia. We all need to stay vigilant."

The horses were tethered twenty feet away, heads bowed, occasionally stamping at the dry ground as if to remind everyone that they were prey animals with opinions. Iver would have to steal one of them to escape, but even if he managed to do that, he still wouldn't be free. There was a reason all his murder-scenes were located inside the city walls: every road out here was surveilled by police. First, he would have to steal his papers from Vicente or Marcia, and Vicente didn't even want to juggle that scenario in his head. Out here, they would have to sleep in shifts.

Daiyu wiggled her eyebrows at Vicente. "You'll kill him if he tries anything, am I right?"

He chuckled, suffocating the panic, and bumped his shoulder to hers. *She doesn't know. Calm down.* What if someone in Llyr recognized him? He tried so desperately not to think about that.

With the crackling flames reducing to dying embers, Daiyu and Marcia retreated to their tent. Vicente remained awake, sitting in quiet contemplation, gazing out at the vast expanse of the plains, which had now been swallowed by darkness. Only the moon offered a gentle illumination. Iver had yet to return.

Vicente grabbed a vial of Stormwater he had prepared beforehand and threw it into the small collection of trees. He had already entangled that one with another vial of Stormwater; the sending component. He drank it, then opened a tunnel to the receiver and ended up a few yards away. The sensation coursed through his veins, an intoxicating surge of adrenaline that ignited every fiber of his being. Familiar and exhilarating, a sweet symphony of ecstasy he willingly succumbed to. A moment of pure bliss, where he relished the euphoria only this could evoke. The feeling couldn't be replicated by any other means; neither alcohol nor sex made him feel as delightful. The high was like the thirty second rush of pleasure after an orgasm; but it lasted for hours.

"Freaky motherfucker."

Startled, Vicente's head snapped upward, where he discovered Iver perched on a tree branch, his legs swaying nonchalantly in the air, almost childlike.

"Getting a good view from up there?"

There was a pregnant pause before Iver finally responded. "Good enough," he answered with derision and contrariness. Knife in hand, its glint catching the moonlight, and a slender stick clutched firmly in his other, Iver shaved off slivers of wood.

Vicente cleared his throat. "Where did you learn to shoot like that?" His eyes traced the lines of the rifle in his lap. The weapon wasn't intended for the pursuit of game but crafted for military purposes. Could it be that it was pilfered at some point, or perhaps there existed a black market where such weapons found their illicit trade? Was he always a murderer, a thug? "I suppose you weren't in the army; you don't seem like the type."

Iver narrowed his eyes, watching him for a long, careful moment before speaking. "Why? Because I don't sit or come like a dog?"

Vicente bristled, but couldn't help also being impressed by Iver's talent for needling him in exactly the right place. "Because you're not acting like a team-player. Is it too much to ask, I wonder?"

"You kicked me in the face after I surrendered. What do you expect?"

Vicente navigated the edge of the clearing, his gaze fixed on Iver in the tree. "I expect you to follow orders. You'll get paid, won't you? Apparently that's all it takes to shift your moral compass."

"Getting paid with my freedom is not payment; freedom is my right."

"You don't think murderers should be locked up? Pray tell, are you delusional or just dumb?" Not only was Iver unruly: he was entitled as well. He had committed crimes that rendered him deserving of cruel treatment; he had murdered Lord Pascal that day, and many others before.

Iver stabbed the knife into the branch he perched on. "Listen here, mystic-cunt—"

"'Mystic-cunt'? Ah. Astute. Really rolls off the tongue."

"Look, the people that hired me are the ones who should be behind bars. I'm just—"

"Just what? A tool? A dog? Then shut your damned mouth and come back to camp, like a good little—"

Vicente's next step caught on something that swiped his feet from under him. He slammed to the ground before getting torn skywards, upside-down. As he found himself suspended there, the world around him span, his perspective abruptly inverted. Blood rushed to his head, creating a pulsating rhythm.

"That was very satisfying to watch," Iver said, again carving away at his stick.

Vicente tried to get his bearings as he dangled. "Did you put this trap up?"

"I'm no hunter."

"Well, did you notice it?"

"Of course I did."

Vicente had no doubts about that. "I'm guessing it was beneath you to offer me a warning?" Iver was determined to hurt him, then. Surely, he was longing to get his revenge on Vicente for capturing him. "You won't get your freedom if I'm killed."

Iver merely shrugged his shoulders. However, he suddenly sat up straighter, as if having noticed something. "Speaking of hunters..."

Vicente heard them too: voices quickly approaching from the woods to the east.

Iver pulled his legs up under him, crouching on the branch. "They could be harmless."

"Let's not gamble. Stay quiet."

Seconds later, a group of men entered the clearing. They were armed with bows and knives, already drawn.

"My sincere apologies, gentlemen," Vicente said. "I seem to have destroyed your trap. Quite a stealthy one at that; I didn't notice it until I was in the air."

"You drunk or something?" Their eyes scanned him cautiously, going over his fine clothing and capital demeanor.

"Just very unobservant, I'm afraid. Plus, it is dark."

One of them, a lean man with a full, blond beard, stepped closer. "I've noticed. What are you doing here, in the dark?"

"Taking a leisurely stroll before sleep. Heading to Mariemoor but set out a bit too late, you know how it is."

"Where's your stuff?"

They were not going to let him go. If things became violent, Iver would pick up on the fact that Vicente couldn't use his tunneling powers to fight, and the whole plan would go awry before they'd even arrived in Llyr. "If you'd be so kind as to help me down, I'll invite you over to our campsite, treat you all to some of the finest wine this side of River Zinat—"

"You'll be staying right there," the bearded man snapped. "How many in your party?"

How many people to discourage them, yet remain believable?

"Eight of my comrades are sleeping on the other side of this clearing. I'd rather not wake them." He needed to tell them as much as possible, prattle on, to make them believe he was the type to give out sensitive information. And any good lie had elements of truth.

"Comrades? Y'all military or something? That's why you're heading to Mariemoor, I suppose. Why are you this close to the capital this time of year?"

"Indeed, we are army men," Vicente said. "Well, not me. I'm just a diplomat, Tal Miril-trained. But the boys, they talk. We're transporting some, ah, delicate cargo. Says he's quite vicious. Horrid affair."

"Who is?"

He made sure to speak loud enough for Iver, a few yards away, to hear him. "This mystic we're escorting. Weapon of mass-destruction and all that." He forced a bitter laugh. "Don't wake him. He'll blow this whole clearing to smithereens, and Arkensaal won't be happy if they found out he went off. They'll probably execute any survivors to keep this sensitive operation on the down low."

The thug blinked lazily. "You are a liar, aren't you?" He turned to his companions. "Over that hill, and stay quiet."

Of course, Blondie hadn't bought it, but there was no need. That story was not for him, but for Iver.

An arrow buried itself in the thug's back and he yelped. Another twang from a bowstring, and arrows whistled through the air as the other thugs ducked down.

Vicente tossed one of his receiver potions to the ground, drank its entangled sender component out of another vial, and stepped through a tunnel to where the other vial landed. He turned to the bearded man. "You wish I was lying."

Vicente heard the metallic sound of a rifle being cocked. The thugs raised their hands above their heads. Iver didn't show himself—a good call.

Vicente pointed in the direction they came from. "Get the fuck out of my sight."

With their hands still in the air, they all fled.

Iver descended the tree, rifle in hand and bow slung on his back. "You should've blown them all to pieces; I wanted to see it."

Vicente brushed the dirt from his pants, trying to hide his disgust over Iver's remark. "Queen Leandra made her orders clear: keep it quiet. If the Llyrians find out about me, they won't let us set a foot in their town, let alone accept our counsel." He reluctantly accepted that this might be the last time he could step through a tunnel, at least for a while.

CHAPTER 4

Marcia

Unlike most towns, Llyr wasn't nestled along a river. Instead, it sat at the fringes of the mountain range, drawing its life force from the springs in the Crooked Mountains by use of aqueducts. The heat this far inland was suffocating, and Marcia yearned for the tang of salt-kissed air and the refreshing caress of the ocean breeze.

As they traversed the stone bridge, the arches of the aqueducts came into view. They weren't as tall as Marcia remembered. The realization made her temples pinch. What else had the passage of time manipulated in her memories? She felt, suddenly and inexplicably, exhausted.

They continued deeper into the town, passing through a market square—or rather, a gathering of stalls—its calm atmosphere a stark contrast to the capital's vibrant bazaars. People in the crowd turned to stare at them as they moved past.

As they rode into the courtyard, which was a dreadfully familiar path, Marcia saw her father waiting in front of the town hall. Seeing him this soon upon arrival was expected: he was the prime minister of Llyr, after all. But to her surprise, she felt nostalgia. She hadn't seen him since she'd fled Llyr at the age of fourteen.

They all dismounted their horses, and Daiyu, Vicente and Iver introduced themselves.

"Your rooms are ready for you, in the Sunfire Rest." Prime Minister Renato Jadanza smiled warmly at her. "I'm glad to see that you are well, Marcia. 'Ambassador,' I should say. Would you join me for a drink this evening?"

"I would love that," she lied. Nevertheless, it would be beneficial to talk, to find out where he stood in the matter of their mission.

Marcia took the lead to the inn. She still remembered where it was. In small towns like this, things rarely changed. The Llyrian prefecture was home to about seven thousand people and most of them lived in this town, but it was in the farmland surrounding it that the real value of Llyr lay. Losing this relationship would be a terrible blow to the capital.

A giant dragonfly, the size of an adult's forearm, tried to land on Iver's head and he swatted it away. "Piece-of-shit insects."

"Do you know why they're that big?" Daiyu prompted. "They didn't used to be, a millennia or so ago."

"I bet you're about to tell me," Iver said.

"It's the elevated oxygen levels in the air. Humans didn't evolve to handle this much. That's why some people have developed allergies to it. It makes some insects grow huge."

Iver said nothing.

"While the ambassadors work," Daiyu said at Iver, "Would you like to go do some chemical experiments with the water in the hot springs? I read they're full of hydrogen sulfide and smell like rotten eggs—"

"No."

"Okay."

Daiyu was trying her best, but she also didn't need a second person to hold a conversation. She was frantic, smitten again, the way she got sometimes when she met new people, barely letting anyone else get a word in edgewise. She placed her trust generously, in abundance and without discrimination, and Marcia didn't have the heart to take that away from her. All she could do was protect Daiyu from any potential fallout.

The inn was in the western part of Llyr, surrounded by pastures of grazing sheep. It all looked so picturesque, deceivingly so, that it made Marcia's stomach roil.

The heat was somehow worse in Llyr, and Marcia's blouse was already sticking to her back. It was probably because the town was in a valley. Around them, terrace gardens spilled down the hillside in rows, alive with figs and lavender and the smell of worked soil. Whitewashed walls curved along the slope, stacked in mismatched layers, as if the town had grown by sheer stubbornness rather than planning.

A man stepped onto their path. His black, coiled hair was thinner, his jaw wider, but she still recognized him.

"Lady Marcia," Falco said. "You look well." His smile was shy.

They had been best friends once, but when his father proposed the match and hers accepted, he asked her to consider it. That was the deepest betrayal: revealing that he had never truly known her at all.

"You as well," she managed, realizing she should probably say something.

Falco's eyes darted between the members of her party, but he didn't introduce himself. "I'm working at Lord Ottone's apothecary. You should stop by sometime, chat about the old days."

She nodded and he went on his way, disappearing around the corner of the butcher's shop where sun-faded red pots hung from the windows, all overflowing with herbs and flowers.

Vicente put a hand on her shoulder. "I must say, I've never seen you that awkward before."

Marcia swallowed around the lump in her throat. She had expected to see Falco again, just not this soon. "He was my, uh, fiancé."

Daiyu slapped her hand to her chest, feigning exasperation. "You had a partner before me?"

"Only in the ways that don't matter."

*

After she had settled into her room, Marcia met with her father at the Harvest Heart Tavern across the road from the inn. As the afternoon progressed into evening, more and more Llyrians trickled in. A few bards were playing and singing. The melody was unfamiliar to her, but the topic of the song was less so. The lyrics told the story of a particular assassin who could shoot the head of a needle miles away: Far Cry. He was a legend here as well. If only they knew what a little runt he actually was.

"Both clan leaders say the land used to belong to them," Renato Jadanza said. "But nobody knows, because it was under siege for almost a hundred years. It has turned into an infected conflict; I fear it will tear this town apart."

"Who do you think has the stronger claim?" Marcia asked.

"You'll learn more about their cases during the meeting tomorrow," he said, as if avoiding the question. "Lord Eloy wants to turn it into farmland, and I have found most of the citizens support him on this quest. Strengthening our trade with the capital will bring prospects to us."

As with all her diplomatic missions, Marcia needed to tread carefully. Disappointing the High Council of nobles in Arkensaal could end her career, and frankly, even her life. Such was the reality of life in the realm of Ōeken, and she had long since accepted it. She took comfort in knowing the Llyrians would be pleased if the capital got what it wanted: awarding the land to Eloy. But her role also entailed convincing the Llyrians that her actions served their interests. It was her duty to ensure they believed the decision was rooted in historical facts, not merely the will of the High Council. "Me and Ambassador Vicente will dig through the archives and find out who owned the land before the bandits took it."

Renato gave her a small smile. "You are so grown up now, Marcia. Life in the capital has treated you well, I assume?"

"It has, yes." Speaking with him again, after all these years, was awkward to the nth degree. She had spent more years without him than with him, and to be sitting across the table from him and attempting to have a casual conversation had her feeling like a snake trying to wriggle back into shed skin.

He held his mug of wine with both hands, shoulders slumped. He almost gave off the aura of a concerned father. Then he started talking again. "I heard about an interesting practice you have in the capital."

Marcia finished her watered-down wine in one swig. "Which one would that be?"

"It voids a marriage."

Marcia stifled a sigh. Showing frustration would only make it worse. "Divorce is not recognized in the eyes of our Lord, the Merciful Eldvittra."

"I'm prepared to make an exception."

She wasn't surprised to hear that. In her experience, even the most devoted tended to disregard the scriptures whenever they saw fit. "You would need both parties to consent, and in our case, neither of us does."

He held up his hands. "It was merely a suggestion. I just needed you to know that even the worst mistakes can be remedied, if only somewhat."

"This discussion is over."

She rose to her feet in the narrow booth, and Renato stretched an arm out across the table. "You are an adult, and you must recognize that you have responsibilities as my daughter. Your engagement with Falco still stands. He has been waiting for you, hasn't even considered taking on another bride."

She had sympathy for Falco, she really did. They had both been fourteen when it all was arranged, and he had spent the last seventeen years holding out for her. "There are many more who share our family name."

"But we are the head of the clan. You and I." The expression on his face was a pleading one. That was how he usually got to her: by making her feel sorry for him. He was a lonely, pitiful single father, bearing the sole responsibility for Llyr and his only daughter, and all he wanted were some grandchildren. *Woe was he*. In the past, it worked. It didn't anymore.

Marcia stepped out of the booth. "Then I guess our bloodline ends with me. Good night."

*

"Honey?" Marcia rubbed the sleep from her eyes, for a few seconds not knowing where she was. It was a new room; they were in Llyr. She left the warmth of the bed to find her missing wife.

Daiyu was standing in the washing area in front of a mirror. Why she chose to watch herself do it was almost as incomprehensible to Marcia as why she chose to harm herself in the first place. But Daiyu couldn't stop the urges, no matter how valiantly she tried to control it.

"It's alright, my sweet thing." Marcia grabbed a clean towel and wrapped it around Daiyu's upper arm.

Daiyu's cheeks bore stripes of tears, and blood streaked her arm. "I'm sorry." Her voice sounded strange, like she was a million miles away and in a different time.

"No need to be sorry, it's okay. Let me get that for you."

They sat on the floor as Marcia cleaned and bandaged the fresh wound. In the past, Marcia had begged Daiyu not to harm herself, had screamed at her for it, had even tried to ignore it. Nothing ever changed. This was a journey Daiyu needed to traverse alone. No matter how much she wanted to, Marcia couldn't carry this burden for her.

"Nightmare?" Marcia asked softly.

Daiyu rubbed her eyes. "You know, I can still taste the air. The blood. The screams, I can still hear them."

They returned to bed, Marcia engulfing Daiyu in her arms and placing soft kisses on the back of her neck. She put her hand on Daiyu's stomach, touching the thin scars there. She wished she could alleviate some of her pain. Daiyu kept her past a closely guarded secret, only sharing fragments of it from time to time.

They stayed like that for a while, listening to the cicadas chirping in the darkness outside. This was all she needed, she realized. With Daiyu in her arms she was invincible, no problem was unsolvable. How lucky she was, to have happiness in her embrace, to have it be someone physical and tangible. The only

threat to their peace was Daiyu's haunting memories, and Marcia
knew from experience those would fade into oblivion with time.

"How did it go with your father?" Daiyu asked.

"It went well."

"You tell me if he gets too pushy. I'll gladly kick his ass."

Marcia snickered. Daiyu always felt the need to care for her,
even when she was in a state like this. They were each other's
protectors. She pulled Daiyu closer, pressing their skin together
like she could fuse with her. "I heard them sing about the Far Cry
assassin in the tavern. Picture me this: we pay Iver to snipe my
father, I take over as prime minister and head of the clan. We force
everyone except women who love women to leave."

Daiyu laughed with unrestrained glee and rolled over to face
her. "Llyr would have an even smaller population." Then she
kissed her, and Marcia remembered their first kiss. It was more
teeth and noses mashed than anything else, but since then, they
had familiarized themselves with each other's features: the curves
of their jaws and cheekbones, the arcs of each other's noses.

"We would invite more of us from the capital and the other
villages," Marcia suggested.

"What about children?" Daiyu asked. There was more to the
question.

Marcia was uncertain, had always been, but for the moment,
she wanted nothing more than for Daiyu to have everything she'd
ever wished for. "Oh, we would have so many tots running
around, you'd have to be careful with your every step."

Daiyu kissed her again, this time with hunger.

"You sure you're up for this?" Marcia asked.

"Nothing like post-crying sex."

Marcia found her mouth again, drinking her kisses as she
moved to be on top of her. She slid her hands up her torso, taking
the shirt with her as she touched her ribs, her breasts. She lost
herself in the curves of her body and in the softness of her skin.
She removed her underwear and sat back to savor the sight as
Daiyu arched her back and reached her arms above her head.
Knotted heat spasmed in the base of Marcia's stomach. Daiyu

melted under her touch as Marcia spread her legs wide and caressed the soft skin of her inner thighs.

"All mine," Marcia whispered before diving in for another kiss. Daiyu wrapped her arms around her neck, pulling her closer, suddenly cut loose.

Marcia's fingers found the heat nesting deep within her wife. Daiyu moaned into the kiss as Marcia pleasured her, hands tangled in Marcia's hair.

Sex with Daiyu was like meditating. Marcia was always worried, always thinking and twisting ideas, but with Daiyu in her arms, the world disappeared. Nothing else mattered.

CHAPTER 5

Vicente

"You are Llyrian, correct?" Prime Minister Jadanza was speaking to Vicente but kept eyeing the warriors in front of him. The sun had reached its zenith, and it was so damn hot there were mirages wavering on the horizon.

"Though I was born here, my connection to this lovely town wanes beyond that, I'm afraid," Vicente said and clasped his hands behind his back, mirroring PM Jadanza's stance.

"The blood of our ancestors flows through your veins, Ambassador." It sounded almost like a welcome. "You might not have heard about our fine warriors, trained by the hero Bruvran himself," PM Jadanza declared with pride, despite his own limited involvement in their training.

An assembly of twenty-two soldiers were lined up, their arsenal boasting swords and tautly strung bows with quivers full of arrows. Moments before PM Jadanza called them over, they were target-practicing on bales of hay.

"No doubt they do an excellent job at protecting Llyr," Vicente said. "You still suffer the attacks of bandits?"

"Well, no. The audacity of bandits has been effectively quelled by the exploits of Bruvran and his company." PM Jadanza looked at Vicente, picking up on the unspoken query lingering in his silence. "Our warriors serve a crucial role in, well, dissuading even the notion of invasion from ever materializing in the minds of thugs."

Meaning, these twenty-two soldiers had no purpose. *What a waste of resources*. Out here, there were no generals giving orders; the prime minister solely controlled the militia, and he had yet to give them any tasks.

Vicente looked back at Iver, who was trailing a few feet behind. "My friend here is an excellent marksman, skilled with the bow as well. He might show them a thing or two."

Iver, armed with only a bow today as he must have left his rifle in his room, didn't seem pleased with Vicente's bid. If they were to be trusted, any and all of them, they needed to make alliances, extend olive branches. Conflict was dangerous.

One of the female warriors said, "Thank you for your offer, Ambassador Vicente. Though I see his bow is rather primitive. Unfortunately, we make use of more refined instruments."

The anger practically vibrated off Iver. "A weapon doesn't need to be advanced to get the job done. Keep running your mouth and I'll fucking—"

Vicente interrupted him before he could spoil the meeting. "Sorry, I didn't catch your name, Miss...?"

PM Jadanza looked fondly at her. "This is Sergeant Celia, trained in archery by Helio themself."

Celia shook Vicente's hand. "I was a hunter when Helio took me under their wing. I thought I knew everything there was to know, but they had me rebuild my skills from the ground up."

The tale of Helio, one of the five heroes of the Bruvran Company, had spread like wildfire, and Vicente pondered who the better shooter was: Helio or Iver. Iver had quite a reputation himself, though not as positive. Naturally, Vicente wouldn't dare bring it up: revealing that Iver was the infamous Far Cry assassin would be detrimental to their diplomatic mission.

Vicente couldn't help but notice that the woman was beautiful, with brown skin and pitch-black hair spilling out from underneath a silk scarf draped over her head. He smiled back at her. "You must be formidable as well, then. Perhaps you could show me your skills, clue me in on some techniques?"

A blush reached her ears. She brushed her fingers over the polished wood of the bow strapped to her chest. "I would love that, Ambassador."

Vicente knew he was handsome—a few independent sources had assured him of the fact, and his own observations confirmed it—and he had no qualms about using it to his advantage. Forming friendly relationships with the locals was essential. "I look forward to it."

With that, the soldiers were dismissed, but Sergeant Celia joined them to go back into Llyr's center. The dusty road between the training field and the town lacked shade entirely, and it was too hot for small talk.

Llyr squatted like an old cat in the sun, unbothered by the heat because it had known worse and wouldn't give you the satisfaction of a complaint. The place was seven thousand people's worth of crumbling stone and fading grandeur, dressed in sun-bleached stucco and chipped mosaic tiles that might've once told stories but now whispered only of disrepair and generations too poor or too fed up to care. The streets were shaded only by dusty olive trees, linen awnings, and the occasional miracle of a vine still clinging to life.

Still, the town had charm. Everyone here had that look in their eye: too tired to rush. Appointments dissolved into conversations, errands meandered into detours, and anything that couldn't be done today was clearly something that had never needed doing in the first place.

As Sergeant Celia and PM Jadanza walked ahead toward the town hall, Vicente lagged behind to speak privately to Iver. "Your small mind only has one track, doesn't it? I know murder excites you, but would it hurt to keep it in your pants for one interaction?"

"*Murder*," Iver mocked. "Do you even know why Pascal had a bounty on his head?"

"I apologize if I gave you the impression that I care."

"Fuck you."

Vicente scoffed. "What, you're going to tell me he deserved it? Like that would somehow make you a hero. You don't kill out of passion; you kill for money. There are few worse than you." The words slid from his lips like acid, so bitter in his throat he nearly choked on them. In just one year, Iver had taken the lives of *at least* one hundred individuals, and during one of his busiest days, he was the culprit in fifteen murders. How does a person kill once, then pull themselves together quickly enough to do it fourteen more times before even sitting down for dinner? Iver forced Vicente to accept he couldn't befriend everyone. Iver was the exception, an outlier that threw Vicente off-kilter, because how could he possibly find common ground with someone built for violence and bitter indifference.

Vicente and Iver met up with Marcia who guided them toward the town hall for the council meeting. The sweltering heat outside seemed a distant memory as they entered the cool sanctuary. On the dais stood a table, large enough to seat all the members of the committee: nineteen, now that Marcia and Vicente joined in their roles as ambassadors.

Marcia whispered to him, "You take the lead on this one." She wanted him to practice, and he was grateful for the opportunity.

A white man in his forties with sandy blond hair and a scraggly beard approached them with his hand outstretched. "Name's Ottone Cronin." *Cronin.* He was one of the stakeholders regarding the disputed land. He made the effort to approach them first, a smart move.

Cronin was dressed entirely in silk: an embroidered vest the color of overripe cherries clung to his narrow frame, stitched with little golden suns that winked when he moved. Around his neck, he wore a white cravat pinned with a garnet brooch. His shoes— soft, polished things—seemed more suited for salons than small-town streets, and Vicente couldn't help but wonder how many innocent mirrors had been forced to reflect that much self-satisfaction in a single outfit.

Next, a young man of dusky skin and lean muscle offered his hand to Vicente. "I'm Eloy. It's a pleasure to meet you, Lord Vicente." Eloy Errani's eyes were wide, mouth slightly agape, and he looked like he was completely overwhelmed.

Vicente shook it and, as kindly as he could muster, said, "I'm not a nobleman, Lord Eloy; 'Ambassador' will do."

"Shit. Sorry. My apologies."

Eloy was surprisingly young for a clan leader. If Vicente had to guess, he'd place him at twenty-one, maybe two. He wore simple, durable clothes; clean, but obviously meant to be worn while working outside. From these details, a picture formed in Vicente's mind: Eloy was raised to tend to his family's fields. His parents died unexpectedly and recently, leaving him in charge. He was a fish out of water, so to speak.

"Nothing to worry about, my Lord," Vicente said. He lowered his voice, just for Eloy to hear, and continued, "a word of advice for the future: greet Marcia first. She outranks me; I'm just a diplomat in training."

Eloy nodded and said in a fevered whisper, "got it. Thank you."

The other council members introduce themselves as Eloy rolled out a map of Llyr. The parchment depicted the expanse of the prefecture, detailing every plantation, all the creeks and each grazing field.

"The land has been cleared since the Bruvran Company executed the bandits ruling the Crooked Mountains." Eloy pointed to the terrain surrounding the remnants of old Tal Llyrie: the ruins of the original settlement. "My clan's property surrounds the land that is now free. All that lies within this span rightfully belongs to my clan, a heritage woven into Llyrian history."

Indeed, his grounds encircled the disputed land. "And what is the intended usage of the land," Vicente asked, "if it is granted to your clan?"

"We will use it for farmland," Eloy said, not meeting his eyes, "to grow soybeans. The soil on my clan's land is not nutritious and only good for growing grass, hence why most of it is used to feed our cows. But the knowledge about how to cultivate soy has been passed down in my clan for generations. I know this land is ours."

Vicente had no doubt Eloy worked the fields himself. He would make sure the land was put to good use, and it was in the best interests of the realm if Vicente and Marcia appointed the area to him. Arable farmland was hard to come by, and the war being waged at the country's border wasn't gaining any ground. But that argument wouldn't resonate with the Llyrians; they had their own goals in mind.

"Lord Ottone?" Vicente prompted.

Ottone had his arms folded over his chest as he looked at the map. "A claim of proximity is not a good one, cattle-farm prince," he declared, projecting his voice for all to hear. "In my family, tales of that area have been passed down through two generations. The elders in my clan all say it's theirs."

"And what will you use it for?"

Ottone bit the edges of his moustache with his bottom teeth. "It's hard for you… people of the capital, to understand, but we have special medicine here. Potions that can heal even those on the very doorstep of death."

It was intriguing, naturally, but he was right in that the esteemed nobles of Arkensaal would wrinkle their noses at such statements. Vicente looked over at Marcia, and she nodded. "We would like to see the medicine in person, and the effects of it."

Ottone scoffed. "If the opportunity arises, you're free to do so. Let's pray it doesn't."

Vicente, terminally curious, didn't appreciate how Ottone tried to evade his request. "I understand you're considerate of the wellbeing of your city-men, but we cannot take this claim at face value, without proof."

"What would you suggest—that we harm someone to prove the medicine's potency?"

Vicente shot Marcia another look and she frowned at him: *stop that.*

"How are the potions manufactured?" Vicente asked instead.

"Ambassadors, you are welcome to join me in my apothecary," Ottone offered, halfheartedly. "My clan and I would use the land for plantations of the necessary herbs; a lot is required, after all. Then, we can expand business to supply the entire realm, bringing huge profits to Llyr."

Ottone made it sound so easy. But if he was speaking the truth—if he had somehow invented a potion that could heal—his plantations would be under attack from thieves the second word got out. "And how will you be protecting your land? By employing the militia?" Vicente possessed only a scant knowledge of the Cronin clan, a diminutive lineage lacking any notable artillery.

Ottone raked his bottom teeth over his moustache again. "That won't be an issue; the raiders have all been dealt with."

"There are still thugs around, especially in the mountains," Iver interjected, scowling at them from the corner of the room where he'd decided to plant himself.

"We'll keep our land safe," Sergeant Celia said to him. "Bruvran and his heroes may have left, but they trained us well. Don't you worry."

Iver sauntered over to them, taking stock of Celia as he did. "I saw your warriors at target practice. Who are you protecting Llyr from; scarecrows?"

Out of the corner of his eye, Vicente noticed Marcia sitting up straighter. She tapped her finger on the table twice: *abort*. She was telling him to make Iver stop immediately.

Had there not been witnesses, Vicente would've already barked at Iver to shut up, but he didn't have any experience handling a situation where someone on his own team— supposedly—was derailing the negotiations.

"Would you rather have us practice on living things?" Celia kept a forced smile on her lips.

"Doubt you'd hit a moving target no matter how hard you tried," Iver said, tilting his head to the side. "I saw you all carry your quivers on your backs. How do you expect to run like that?"

The corner of her mouth twitched as she struggled to maintain her cordial expression. "We shoot long distance, standing still."

"That's why you also line up your arrow to the left of the bow while firing with your right hand, I'm guessing." Iver clicked his tongue. "It's too many unnecessary movements, it's too slow. You would've known that had you seen actual fighting. Archery should be as natural as throwing something, not this convoluted shit you're doing."

Vicente had no idea how to handle such contrariness. He pressed his teeth together against a string of insults, hating the little bubble of anger coming up in the back of his throat like bile.

Sergeant Celia walked slowly around the table, arms still crossed. "What's your problem?"

"My apologies, Sergeant," Vicente said, voice stern. "Please don't mind him, he is tired from our travels—"

"Not as tired as her warriors are, apparently," Iver sassed.

Celia finally angered and stepped up to Iver, standing toe-to-toe. "Do not speak ill of my men."

Iver's face remained neutral. He was either genuinely unfazed, or very good at concealing whatever he might have been feeling. "Or what?"

"Or I'll kill you, piece of—"

Iver charged at her, swiftly tackling her to the ground. She was at least a head taller than him, but he took her down like she weighed nothing. Two other warriors tried to get involved in the fight. Iver moved at an incredible speed and attacked with chilling efficiency. He swung at one of them, fist hit the man's jaw. The man tumbled to the floor. Then Iver drew his knife.

Something fierce and furious crested in Vicente's chest all at once, but he couldn't make any obvious threats that might alert the others to his mystic abilities. "Iver, you'll be pardoned for your outburst only if you stop this right now."

Iver paused, picking up on the hint. He scoffed, sheathed his knife, and raised his hands over his shoulders in defeat. There was something so sarcastic in the way he did it, it only made Vicente angrier.

While the elderly members of the council stared in shock as the soldier got back on his feet—holding his jaw in pain—Vicente said to them: "Never mind Iver; he's nothing but a mercenary. Our sincerest apologies—"

"Ambassador Vicente," Marcia said, "get Iver out of here."

Iver had just cost Vicente the experience the meeting would've given him. His hand clamped around Iver's shoulder, and he shoved at him to start walking. *Fucking nutjob.*

"That's it, dog, know your place," Celia muttered under her breath.

Iver bared his teeth at her, seething with a rage Vicente couldn't identify. "What was that, bitch? Say that a little louder for me."

The council members and the stakeholders took their seats again as Vicente pushed Iver to the exit. He wouldn't disrespect Marcia by going against her orders, but he strained his ears to hear the rest of the conversation.

"How do we proceed?" Ottone asked.

Marcia said, "We will search through the necessary documentation and historical archives to see which clan has the strongest claim to the land. Then Ambassador Vicente and I will deliver our final verdict."

Vicente practically dragged Iver back to his room in the Sunfire Rest. The door shut behind them and Vicente let go. "Merciful. You really want to be executed, don't you?"

"Just keep any soldiers away from me." Iver was like a feral animal.

"Well, that's a bit pathetic. I'll do no such thing. Are you a child in need of protection?"

"Fuck you."

"Yeah, yeah, fuck me." Vicente stabbed Iver's knife into the soft wood of the wall. "I'm keeping the knife. This won't happen again, or so help me, I will strangle the last, breathless whimper out of your throat."

"Don't you dare touch me again," Iver said. His eyes flickered to the knife, stuck in the wall, then back to Vicente. "Look, *Ambassador*, I was told this whole operation could go sour real quick, and my job here is to ensure that no harm comes to any of you three. I'm not sure you know how these things can go, but those people need to know we're capable, enough so they won't even *think* of trying anything."

Vicente did understand. After all, it was the same ruse he was using with Iver. But if the Llyrians feared them too much, they wouldn't be able to negotiate with them at all.

But Vicente, also, didn't quite believe him. Something about Iver's behavior set off Vicente's alarm bells. His gut told him Iver genuinely wanted to harm him, and he could only be grateful Iver seemed to value his freedom more than revenge.

Iver gestured to the window. "Llyr has *trained soldiers* at their disposal. And since you can't come forward as a mystic, it's up to me to be the bad guy and have you *pretend* to be the good one."

Iver had put more thought into this than Vicente had ever expected. He was playing the role of a vicious bodyguard, who would kill anyone if Vicente and Marcia allowed it. This would persuade the townsfolk to never cross the ambassadors. "You're just pretending, is that it?"

"It's not pretending. I'm threatening them. Just let me do my job."

Vicente leaned against the wall and crossed his ankles, calming down a little. "And you want us to reel you in, make it seem like we can control you. Then why are you so pissed?"

"In the future, just tell me to stop and I will." Iver walked over to the door and yanked it open. "Don't put your filthy hands on me again." Then he exited and slammed the door shut behind him.

It was a good plan, one that would've been made even better by being communicated properly. Iver might not have been as erratic as he portrayed himself to be, but Vicente still needed some way of more reliably keeping him back, other than the threat of consequences.

He placed Iver's knife on the desk and took off the thin silver chain he always wore around his neck. Then he began the entanglement process. Using his mystic ability, he could control the energy level of every particle in the necklace, as well as in the knife. This allowed him to excite them until they reached a boiling point invisible to the naked eye. Then, he looped through all possibilities in this micro realm, until the particles became entangled and existed in a so-called superposition. No matter the distance put between the knife and the necklace, they would remain tied together—entangled—and could be substituted with each other one time, once Vicente used his abilities again to open a quantum tunnel between them. This was the power of the Stag, a force the quorum desperately sought to unleash but could not, bound as they were to the Otter. Vicente trained for this purpose. If he succeeded, the quorum could justify teaching an army of mystics, shifting the balance in the established distribution of power, in the current political and cultural order, that had smothered Ōeken's progress for centuries. If Vicente succeeded, Ōeken might grow powerful enough to win the war and end a *centuries* long stalemate, that was only upheld for the financial benefit of the already wealthy elite.

The arrangement was faintly nerve-inducing.

After he was done, he put the necklace back around his neck. If push came to shove, he would need quick access to it.

He knocked on Iver's door, the room on the other side of the hallway. The door yanked open, and Vicente damn near had a heart attack. He handed the knife back.

Iver accepted it without hesitation. "You change your mind fast."

"You'll make better use of it than I. But please, try to dial the hostility back a few notches. Do you think you can manage—"

Iver closed the door in his face.

CHAPTER 6

Vicente

Vicente and Marcia, in their roles as diplomats, were the only ones to receive access to Llyr's historical archives in the basement of the town hall. No one had touched these books since the raids. Few had the authority to do so.

Vicente estimated at least a hundred books. Nothing that compared to the vast library in Tal Miril, but it would be time-consuming nonetheless.

Some of the shelves stood empty, proof of the raiders' success. "Looks like they got their hands on a lot of it." It was a pity; the archives contained local stories that were now lost forever.

Marcia dropped her bag on one of the wooden chairs. "Who in their right mind burns books?"

Vicente understood the thugs' ambition; if they were from the Llyrian area, chances were someone might have recognized them and documented it.

Marcia plucked a worn volume from a shelf and handed it to Vicente. "Let's begin with anything that mentions the clans." It was a testament of Llyr's ancestral lineages. The words, penned in fading ink, held the names of all newborns a century ago.

Hour after hour, they searched for any fragment of evidence holding the potential to tip the scales in favor of one clan over the other. Each page turned resounded hushed, rustling in the otherwise silent room.

A sobering truth gradually descended, cloaking his spirit: nothing was written about which clan owned the land before the siege. This would be a lot harder than he'd expected.

*

Vicente had left the comfort of his room to check on the commotion, and now he wished that he hadn't. The sun crested the horizon, casting long shadows across the street. The whispers of a gruesome discovery swept through Llyr, and the townsfolk crowded the road outside the Sunfire Rest.

The Llyrians stared powerlessly at the lifeless body of a girl, about seven years old, that lay sprawled on the ground.

Iver appeared by Vicente's side. "Why the fuck were people screaming?"

Vicente ticked his jaw, his stomach twisting into one awful, confused knot. He had seen dead bodies before, but never one belonging to someone so young. Witnessing the effects the loss of life had on the living always made him feel weak and small, like a child. "Are you that accustomed to death that you lack any basic human compassion, or are you just dumb?" He asked Iver for a second time.

Iver said nothing, blinking in the morning sunlight that sliced across his face at an angle, eyes now turned to the victim. His bottom lip went white from the force of his teeth.

Vicente approached Sergeant Celia, who was crouched down by the girl's head. "I offer my sincerest condolences," he said mildly, uselessly. "Who is she?"

Sergeant Celia didn't turn to face him. "Her name is Natalina," she whispered. "One of my soldiers found her in the bushes, discarded like trash. What kind of wretched monster would do this?"

Murders were uncommon in such a small, close-knit community as this. The idea that the Llyrians would suspect Vicente and his crew struck him, a mistrustful thought, but nonetheless possible.

One of the orphanage staff members showed up. She was a devoted sister of the worshippers of the Merciful Eldvittra, who helped tend to the sick and took care of the temple. She walked as fast as her old body would allow her, hands already raised in the air, but then pressing them to her own chest once she saw the girl. "Where is her necklace?" She searched the ground, shoving people out of the way in her haste to locate it, gesturing frantically at her own neck. "A chain with a silver pendant, *Natalina* is engraved on it. Please, help me look! Please! Oh, my sweet girl."

Vicente swallowed around the sea urchin in his throat. So, the girl was an orphan, possibly of war. Anyone from Llyr could be drafted, since they had no ruling clan to dispute the orders from the capital. An unfortunate fact for Llyr, but not so easily fixed: a ruling clan needed to be a descendant of the royal Rhys clan, and no offshoot of the Rhys clan would ever consider moving here.

"She was strangled," said Iver, who had stationed himself by Vicente's side again.

Sergeant Celia looked up at him, eyebrows high on her forehead and a pleading look in her eyes. "How can you tell?"

"May I?" When Sergeant Celia reluctantly nodded, Iver knelt by the body and lifted her chin. There was the faintest bruising on her throat, just below her jawline.

Vicente took another, more careful look at the body. The soles of the girl's feet were dirty, and blood had dried into flakes around several small nicks in the thick skin. Though she was an orphan, it didn't seem like people of her standing went without clothes or shoes here. She didn't look unkempt otherwise, she wasn't malnourished.

She had the same type of bracelet, crafted from sticks and twine, that some other children wore. He had never seen anything like it before, but it didn't seem strange when others were wearing it too.

Quite a lot of twigs of the bushes she had been found in were snapped, and the grass had formed a cradle for her, her final mark upon the world, where the earth had made space for her.

Coins were strewn around the grass and on the street. Worthless enough that no passers-by had picked them up; or perhaps the gold and silver coins had already been taken?

Vicente figured she had been somewhere safe and had to flee unexpectedly, because she had fled barefoot. The murderer had chased after her, there had been a struggle where she dropped her money, and they killed her in blind rage. Once the killer had calmed down somewhat, they realized what they had done and threw her body in the bushes to hide their crime.

He wondered if it had been a traveler, someone not native to Llyr. People of only a few select professions were allowed to travel, but that still left thousands of people in circulation. The road between the capital and the north was well trafficked. A passing merchant could have done it and disappeared before sunrise.

But the girl was barefoot. She must've been with a person who she trusted enough to be alone indoors with.

He stole a glance at the people gathered. Some looked to one another, searching for answers or signs of guilt. Others exchanged glances of sympathy and compassion. The prime minister was nowhere to be found.

Atli, the town's blacksmith, took a step forward in his stead. "A tragedy has befallen us. We cannot allow this heinous crime to go unpunished. Let us seek the truth and bring the perpetrator to justice, for the sake of the departed and the safety of our community."

Murmurs of agreement rippled through the crowd. The people dispersed, each undertaking their own role in the search. Some scoured the area for any signs or clues that could lead them to the culprit, scanning the surroundings with grim determination. It was all so pitiful and helpless. Llyr had nothing that even resembled a police force, decades behind in the development of security and safety nets Vicente just then realized he had always taken for granted. *But if I can find the Stag and end the war, I might be able to fix that.*

The holy sister, with the help of the blacksmith, carefully lifted the body of the girl and began carrying her away, possibly towards the temple. Despite the tragedy, the weather was almost offensively lovely. Sunlight draped the street in warm gold, the kind that usually softened hard edges and made the world feel kinder. Today, it only made everything worse. Bougainvillea spilled off balconies in reds and purples so lurid they looked like dye; too vibrant, too alive, as if the town couldn't be bothered to dim itself, even for death.

Iver walked away from the scene. Vicente watched as the people gave him a wide berth, like he was a shepherding dog among sheep. Iver had gotten what he wanted: people left him alone after his outburst. Soon enough, everyone in Llyr would've heard about it.

Vicente approached Sergeant Celia again. To avoid suspicion, he didn't want to speak about the murdered little girl, as a perpetrator would likely prod for information, but he felt the need to address it. It would be malicious not to offer his advice. "Things like this don't happen here, do they?"

Celia looked in the direction the sister and the blacksmith had gone. "Not during my lifetime. I'll ask my mother when I get home, see if she remembers anything like this happening before. Who would do such a thing to a child?"

A flash of fear short-circuited his brain. He grappled for reasons to feel safe and listed them out, like talking himself down from a nightmare: he was seven years old when it happened. No one knew. There was no evidence. And if there was, even if everyone found out, they would take Vicente's side, because the man he killed was the type that hurt children.

Seven thousand people were quite a lot, but after spending most of his life in the capital, Vicente found he had to remind himself of that. Even in a crowd, the risk of running into his mother was slim. If she was even alive still. The risk of her recognizing him was even lower. The possibility that someone else would, was nonexistent.

Vicente cleared his throat. "It's of no comfort, but where I'm from, these things happen frequently. There is always a reason for it, and where there is a motive, there are clues. Who will take charge of the investigation?"

"I assume PM Jadanza will. He's got us through a lot before."

"I've heard positive remarks about Jadanza," Vicente lied. In truth, the only knowledge he had about him came from his daughter, Marcia. "He must be a great leader for the community."

"The elections are just for show. The seat at the head of Llyr belongs to a Jadanza. It has been that way for generations."

Vicente found that the best way to get information out of someone was to feign ignorance. "I take it a son of his will pick up the mantle after him?"

"PM Jadanza has no sons, only an unwilling daughter." She tightened her clutch on the bow across her chest. "Lord Ottone Cronin has made it clear he wants the position. For the first time in centuries, another clan will have to lead Llyr."

*

With the weight of the news still fresh, Vicente summoned the crew to his room, and he retold all the information he knew. A moth circled the oil lamp, and the shadow of its wings flickered massive against the walls.

"Why would you call me here for this?" Iver snapped. "I was there when they found her, I know what happened."

"We need to have each other's backs," Marcia said. "We're together in this."

Daiyu uncorked a bottle of wine and poured each of them a glass. Marcia finished hers in one swig, and Vicente did so too. He needed this frivolity, to ease the tension in his muscles. Even though it was disgusting in comparison with the wine available in the capital, the alcohol still had the same effect.

Iver placed his glass on the floor, still untouched. "It's not a big deal. Kids turn up dead all the time."

Vicente had little hope the townsfolk would ever find the killer. It was most likely a merchant passing by, because if the murderer lived in Llyr, they would've done a better job of covering it up. No, the people of Llyr could do nothing but grieve, and the only thing Vicente and his crew could do was to show sympathy— which Iver wasn't doing. "Maybe in the capital, but not here, not like this." Although he knew about Iver's past, his ambivalence still made Vicente's stomach turn. "Seeing as your only concern is for yourself, let me tell you this: they might suspect *we* had something to do with it. Understand? I can explain it to you, but I can't understand it for you, Iver." He turned to Marcia. "You're thinking it too, right? We only just got here, it's suspicious."

She nodded. "Maybe I'm being too distrustful. No matter what, we should try not to get involved in any of that mess. Let's stick to our tasks."

It sounded like she was trying to convince herself. Vicente had always found Marcia hard to read. Her face was in a constant state of rest, stoic and neutral. Had she considered aiding the locals in their pending investigation regarding the murder? Vicente sure had, but that wasn't why they were there.

Daiyu pulled her black hair up into a ponytail. Her clothes bore the stench of rotten eggs, an oddity not yet explained. "I'm impressed you figured out the cause of death, Iver. How could you tell?"

"None of your business."

They continued to drink, a foul wine from grapes grown locally. Vicente missed the red Rinkai wine, and the sparkling white only produced in the Vale. Nevertheless, he let the buzz of the alcohol sweep him downstream. It made him less eager to open a tunnel. He still craved the euphoria he got from it, of course, but he wasn't going to let a simple urge jeopardize his job.

This was their fifth night in Llyr, and the first time they'd had any time off to relax. Vicente felt utterly wrung dry. He had expected nostalgia and grief to hit him once he saw the familiar streets and buildings again. As such, he had mentally prepared himself. But the murder of the little girl triggered a feeling of helplessness he couldn't have anticipated. Feelings he thought he had buried long ago reared their ugly heads, and he was craving

Stormwater to remove all the restlessness dancing under his skin. Alcohol was a weak substitute, but it would have to do.

Iver stayed with them, but he neither drank nor participated in the conversation. Vicente could tell, out the corner of his eye, that Iver was watching him. There was something dangerous in the way he took stock of others, preternaturally observant, a recognition of his surroundings and the people around him that spoke of guile.

When Vicente finally turned to confront him, Iver asked, "You drunk yet?"

Vicente was indeed intoxicated, but didn't dignify the question with a response. An uneasy churning started in his stomach.

Just past midnight, they all went to their own rooms. Iver was the last to leave. While the door was still open, he twisted the key. He felt the bolt of the lock, wiggled it, before unlocking it again and leaving.

He was checking if it was easily breakable.

Vicente sobered up quickly after that. He locked the door and placed a chair in front of it. Not that it would do much to keep it closed, but maybe the sound of it scraping across the floor would alert him if Iver decided to break in.

CHAPTER 7

Vicente

Two boys shrieked as they ran past Vicente and his crew, up the hill towards the temple. Vicente envied their energy.

The last sliver of the sun dipped beneath the horizon, and the air was velvety with dying warmth. Eloy had invited all of them to the temple, and Iver had come with them even though he looked bored out of his mind.

"What's with the twig bangles all the kids are wearing?" Iver asked.

Marcia waved the cloud of dust out of her face, caused by the kids' feet kicking up sand. "They're children. Children do weird things."

"I am so excited," Daiyu said, pausing at every word.

The constant shrill chirping of grasshoppers and cicadas grew louder as the sun set. Though the temple was the first structure to be built, it was a far walk from Llyr's center, and sweat was already running down Vicente's back.

"You're a scientist, you've never seen someone get their blood drawn before?" Vicente asked and smacked a mosquito that had landed on his forearm.

"Of course, but this is *religious* blood-drawing," she said. Then she laughed in a way that sounded half-crazed. "I wish we did stuff like this in the capital!"

"If you're gonna get all riled up about this thing, I'm not going," Iver said with a warning, but continued to walk with them.

An overwhelming need to defend her washed over Vicente. He was a little jarred by the feeling's intensity and the abruptness of its onset, but still... "She's right; this is very exciting. It's an honor to be invited. Maybe if you spent less time sneering at things you don't understand, you'd see there's value in this." Vicente had no real interest in watching Eloy's daughter getting baptized; he had come to watch the other people, the adults. If he and Marcia wanted their decision regarding the land to be received well, they needed to prepare the people, and to do that, they needed to investigate them, map out the key players and work on them.

"I'm sure participating in their blood-sacrifice is going to aid your investigation," Iver said. "Tell them to ask the Merciful to figure out who the land belongs to while it's here, and save yourselves some time."

Marcia barked out a laugh at Iver's expense, but quickly stifled it.

Vicente, however, ran with it. He smiled through his words. "You do understand that this is a ceremony of cultural significance, right? That we are going there to get to know the people of Llyr, not to actually commune with the gods? Please Iver, you're not pretty enough to be *this* dumb."

Iver clicked his tongue. "You're not listening. You think watching them do a ritual they've done a hundred times is going to let you see their true colors? Like this ain't something rehearsed? Especially since the murder. Do you really think attending a staged event will be of any use to you, two agents of the crown, to gauge them?"

"Rehearsed behavior still tells us something," Vicente insisted. "No matter how hard they try to put up a façade, there will always be cracks." It was also good practice for diplomats to immerse themselves in the local culture. It garnered trust, which made their jobs so much easier. "Besides, in the wake of a murder: don't you think declining this invitation would seem suspicious? Hypothetically—that means 'in theory,' in case you didn't know the word—if we had something to hide, wouldn't we want to not be under scrutiny? The congregation would notice our absence, and think we were hiding something."

Iver brushed a spiderweb off his shoulder with more force than necessary. "People don't think like that."

"Well, say they do, and we told them our dear Iver was too cranky to attend the baptism of a little child, they would think—"

"Well, say *I* was the one who killed the kid, and knew you well enough to reason like that, wouldn't I want to act like a little bitch to you so you wouldn't suspect me? What now?"

Vicente blinked. "Well…"

"You see how when everything becomes a hypothetical, it doesn't fucking matter?" Iver said.

Daiyu snorted behind them, ducking to avoid a low-hanging olive branch and nearly walking straight into the back of Vicente.

Vicente decided not to engage anymore. He was too tired for an argument, anyway. He and Marcia had spent all day in the archives where the windows wouldn't open fully due to the grilles, and despite the late hour, the air outside was still the temperature of tepid tea.

They ascended the temple stairs. Inside, the scent of incense and burning candles filled the hall. The columns rose high above them, casting shadows across the stone floor. It was already crowded.

Vicente took a lap around the hall, leaving Iver to stew in his own misery, Daiyu to jump out of her own skin with excitement, and Marcia to try to contain her.

The temple was centuries old, built during a time when the realm worshipped the entire pantheon, not just Eldvittra. This was evident from the idols standing by the altar. At the forefront stood the likeness of the god of war, a fox engulfed in flames. Flanking it were the Usurper gods: Delta the crane, goddess of crops; the Gambler, god of fate and unpredictability, depicted as a cat—a portrayal Vicente had never seen before—and the Horned God of death in its familiar goatlike form. There was also Curiosity as a raven, Themyr the snake, goddess of justice and law, and Rage as a jackal. Had these statues been in Arkensaal, they would've been demolished years ago.

Vicente watched as the priest prayed over Eloy, his wife and his daughter. The congregation asked Eldvittra to watch over the baby girl as the priest pricked her finger and captured the beading blood in a vial of glass. She cried, of course, loudly, and the sound reverberated and bounced off the stone walls of the temple. The priest placed the vial of her blood on a shelf above the altar, where hundreds of others already stood. The vials remained there until the person's death. If they perished in battle, their family could bury the vial, a stand-in for an unrecoverable body. Thus, the temple held only the blood of the living. Vicente's vial still stood there.

Once the ceremony ended, Eloy's wife served drinks and food in the courtyard in front of the temple. Eloy stayed inside, and Vicente threaded his way through the departing crowd to join him at the altar. "Congratulations," he said.

Vicente's eyes scanned the shelves behind the altar, and when he didn't find what he was looking for, the relief that washed over him was the sweetest sensation he had felt in days: his mother's vial wasn't there. She was dead and had been buried. A tension he didn't know he had been carrying started to seep out of his shoulders.

Eloy tucked his hands into the pockets of his simple coat. "I didn't think you'd come."

"It is a joyous occasion; I am honored to have been invited to share it with you and your family, as your lovely daughter is accepted into the arms of the Merciful." As Vicente spoke, he watched Eloy's reaction. Eloy's eyes flickered to the blood vials and the smile growing on his face was sardonic.

Based on this, Vicente decided to change tracks. Take a risk. "Even though the ritual is a bit... over the top."

"I'm expected to sit back and do nothing as they draw blood from my daughter, watch her cry to appease a god." Eloy chuckled, but the sound was humorless. "Oh, and the god of war will descend upon us if the vials are destroyed or tampered with. Isn't that right?"

"Right." This was the story the public believed. Few knew the true purpose behind the quorum of mystics' secret introduction of this practice into rural village culture over two centuries ago.

"The promises made in this temple," continued Eloy, "it's all a farce, isn't it?"

"You don't believe in it?" Vicente asked.

"I believe in survival. I believe in doing what's necessary to protect my people. But gods and old rituals?" Eloy had a far-away look on his face. "No. I stopped believing in those when my parents died."

Vicente understood the sentiment more than he cared to admit. He noted the lines of weariness etched into Eloy's features. This was a man too young to carry the burdens he did. Vicente could take advantage of that. He winced at the fact that this was where his mind went first, but in his role as a diplomat, it was expected of him. Besides, all he did was for the good of the community, in the end.

"Frankly, I'm not a pious man myself," Vicente said, sharing some personal information, making him more likable to Eloy, "but I do believe there are some valuable lessons to pull from the religions curriculum."

"And what is that?"

"That effort is rewarded eventually. Maybe not as late as the afterlife, but it often comes later than we'd like. Meanwhile, we fight tooth and nail, and it seems like nothing is working. Then one day, we look around and realize we're not just surviving; we're living."

He could hear Eloy swallowing thickly.

"Lord Eloy, this ritual might not curry the favor of the Merciful, but it did have an effect: look at the people who gathered here this evening for her. By continuing this practice, you have pleased the people of Llyr, and they'll continue to hold your family in their hearts. They will protect her."

"Thank you. I really hope you're right."

In the light of the murder, Vicente too hoped he was right.

"Your blood is here too, isn't it?"

Vicente pointed at his vial. *Vicente Lamor* was written on it. The brown label had begun to peel. Even though he didn't live here anymore, he needed the vial to remain at the altar: if it didn't, his connection to the Stag would fade, and he would lose his deal with the quorum. Only he, the quorum and the queen knew this of course, but no one in Llyr would dare to tamper with the vial: the Merciful itself would kill those who did. According to the quorum's planted lies, that is.

"I've always loved travel." Eloy gave him a wan smile. "Or at least the idea of it. How did you end up moving to Arkensaal?"

Traveling was prohibited for those without approval. Vicente needed to stay close to the truth. "An Arkensaali merchant passing through Llyr noticed my intellect. When my family fell on hard times, I was allowed to go with her to the capital to study."

"You're a lucky man," Eloy said, "and I'm sorry to hear about your family. This was seventeen, eighteen years ago, wasn't it? Such a shame we didn't know each other then; my family would've helped you, I'm certain."

Vicente cleared his tightening throat. "Nothing to worry about."

"Do you have family here still?"

"I do not." Vicente took a tentative step away. "If you'll excuse me, I heard they were serving crawfish outside. I haven't had one in years; they aren't very popular on the coast."

Eloy paused for a second, but then nodded. "Of course. Thank you for the words of wisdom, Ambassador."

Vicente made his way through the now empty hall. The scent of food came in on the breeze allowed through the open temple doors.

His heart raced, and he drew a few shaky breaths. The feeling was hard to identify, but it contained a sharp streak of panic familiar to him by now. He felt disproportionately vulnerable after Eloy had brought up his background. But it was in the past. *No one knows.*

Seventeen years ago

Vicente's father had died when he was very young. In fact, Vicente had been so young he didn't even remember his father. His mother never remarried, and never had any more children. Once Vicente was old enough to attend school, she submerged herself in her work as a seamstress. For many years, it was just the two of them. Things were okay. Sure, they struggled from time to time, mostly with the financial aspect, but things were generally good.

Life got better when Father Fulvio came along. They would have meat in their meals again. There was wine on the table once more. Vicente's mother would laugh again, which was odd, as Father Fulvio wasn't a very jovial person.

Vicente always did what Father Fulvio told him to do. He respected his authority, the knowledge and influence he had as a priest, the wisdom he possessed as an older gentleman who had spent his youth serving in the Llyrian militia. Father Fulvio commanded respect. There was a certain reverence required when Vicente spoke to him.

The first time Father Fulvio ordered him to join him in the bedroom and lock the door after himself, he did. It never occurred to him to refuse.

That first instance opened the floodgates. The abuse grew more frequent, more sinister. By the time Vicente was seven, he killed Father Fulvio. Vicente hadn't planned it; he simply snapped one day and shot the man with his own revolver that he kept in the drawer of his bedside table.

Vicente didn't feel any guilt about it. He was the only one who knew it, but Fulvio was a bad man, and he needed to die. What Vicente felt was fear—fear he would be caught and executed for what he had done. So, when the townspeople of Llyr found the body and attributed it to a robbery gone wrong, Vicente stayed silent.

His mother didn't snap; she decayed. It was a slow unraveling, so gradual Vicente couldn't pinpoint when her once comforting scent started to spoil into something foul. A soft shuffle broke through his thoughts. The girl at the desk behind him leaned forward, her presence now more intrusive, her breath audible as she took in a sniff. Vicente braced himself. "You stink, just like your mother," she whispered. The teacher didn't hear her.

Blood surged under Vicente's skin. He spun around in his chair, the side of his fist hitting her in the jaw, and she tumbled sideways to the floor with a shriek. He was on top of her, pinning her shoulders down with his knees and punched her in the face, over and over, until the teacher reached them and pulled him off her.

The girl sat up and blood gushed from her broken nose. She put her fingers to her face and when she saw that they came away bloody, she started wailing uncontrollably, tears rolling down her chin.

Vicente stared at her, fists still shaking with rage, feeling a strange mix of impending doom and envy as their classmates and the teacher consoled her. Vicente would be punished for this. She wouldn't be. If only he could cry like she did, all dramatic and pathetic, then maybe they wouldn't all hate him so much. But seeing her having her tears dried only fueled his anger. There was nothing else there. He could reach into the well inside him where tears resided, and it was empty, it made his throat close and eyes sting, but his hands came back clutching nothing.

It didn't matter. It had always been easier to be angry.

The teacher took Vicente home, where she spoke to his mother for a few minutes in private before leaving again without ever saying a word to Vicente. She didn't even look at him. She just looked at the drained wine-bottles cluttering the dinner table, at Vicente's unwashed and urine-soaked bed sheets piled on the floor, and left.

His mother came out of the bedroom and stared at him. He glared back. The rage in her eyes matched his own, like two storms spinning in different directions and canceling each other out. A sort of quiet, static chaos formed when their pupils aligned like matching bullet-holes in walls. In tandem. He could see all of her and she could see all of him, and she knew. She knew what Fulvio had done to him and it was all the more reason to hate her, to pay back the suffering she had bestowed upon him. *You made me*, he thought. *Now live with the consequences.* Had there been only hate between them, it wouldn't have been so bad. If only there had been terror and no love, instead of both. What a gruesome bond they shared.

She pointed at the scattering of uncooked rice by the stove. "Kneel."

He did. It never occurred to him to refuse.

For five hours he kneeled on the rice. Pressed against the wooden floor, the hard grains dug into his skin. The pain in his skin transferred to his muscles and to his joints, wandering from his knees to his calves all the way down his feet, until he lost all sensation in his legs.

Night fell. The darkness crept in. It was raining outside, an ice-cold autumn rain. The drops tapped on the windows.

"You can get up now," his mother said.

Vicente slowly got up. He couldn't feel his feet.

She was already halfway through another bottle of wine. "I don't know what to do with you, Vicente," she said, and she sounded so sad and frail, as if she was just on the verge of shattering. "It must be exhausting for you, too. To be so angry all the time."

He didn't know what to say, so he said nothing.

A knock broke the stillness. Vicente's mother moved to open the door, her steps unsteady. She peered outside, then let out a strangled sigh of relief.

Standing on the threshold were six women, their expressions calm and self-assured. Each had tan skin, braided hair as pale as winter light. Their eyes were completely black. Vicente had never seen people like this before; they were beautiful in a way that felt almost unreal, like figures stepping out of one of his mother's stories.

One of the women inclined her head. "We are here about a requested exorcism."

Vicente's mother held the door open wider. "Please," she said, desperation creeping into her voice. "I don't know what to do with him. I can't handle him on my own."

The women came inside, crossing the threshold with silent, graceful steps. Water dripped from their cloaks.

"He beats up the other children at school," his mother continued, "wets the bed every night. He argues, yells. There are evil spirits in this boy. You must help him. Please."

The woman lowered herself to Vicente's eye level, her gaze warm but piercing as she studied him. Her face was kind, a gentle smile playing at the corners of her mouth. "I am Indra. And you are?" Her eyes shone with something like understanding, something like pity.

Vicente swallowed, wary of the stranger but unable to break away from her gaze. "Vicente Lamor."

"Vicente," she repeated, as if tasting the name. "A strong name." She extended her hand. "We're going to help you. Will you come with us?"

Vicente didn't want to. He wanted them all to leave. He didn't accept her hand.

"Take him," his mother pleaded.

With a nod, Indra stood and motioned to her companions. Vicente joined them outside. He didn't have a choice.

The gentle shower had graduated to a full-blown downpour. Water seeped through his clothing. He was freezing to the bone. They walked in a silent line to the temple of Eldvittra, the women flanking him like guardians. His mother didn't come along.

The spires of the temple stretched infinitely upwards, the peaks of them hidden in the dark or perhaps even in the clouds. Vicente followed them inside, dumbly, like a sheep ready for slaughter.

Aside from them, the temple was empty. They gathered in front of the altar. Vicente looked up at the hundreds of vials. Like all children, Vicente had his drawn when he was brought into the protection of the pantheon and received his name.

He took a shallow breath. He was shaking uncontrollably now. What did an exorcism entail, he wondered. This was it. The old him would die here, tonight. Either he came out on top, or he didn't. Both options were fine with him. The heave of his shoulders was arrhythmic as he breathed viciously.

"We are no priestesses of Eldvittra," Indra said and removed her hood. "We serve a demigod: the Otter. It lives in Arkensaal, our realms capital, and it would like to meet you. Do you know why, Vicente?"

He shook his head.

"Because like us, you have the blood of a mystic," she said. "We are the mystics of the Sensis Quorum, and we want you to join us, to train with us."

He knew who they were. Six mystics, the most powerful people in the world. They were all centuries old, staying on earth like ghosts, never aging, never dying. He should've been scared, but he wasn't. Everyday, he would dream of being taken away from here.

"Let me show you." Indra found the vial with his name on it. She picked it up from its place at the altar.

Something vanished inside Vicente. It was sudden and it was crushing, like the fog of sleep going away in an instant when he heard his mother running down the hallway towards him. His young mind couldn't interpret what it was, it wasn't an emotion nor a sensation. It was more akin to an instinct. Like a shock of freezing water after dying in the desert.

As soon as Indra put the vial back on the altar, it came back. It was primal and it was powerful. It was bone deep. It had been lying dormant.

"What was that?" he asked.

Indra lowered herself to his level again. "Ever since the six of us discovered that there were more mystics in the realm, we've been working hard to find them all. A mystic without training is a fragile thing, and the High Council of Arkensaal wants that to stay so. We are a threat to the status quo. With training, you will be, too." Indra grabbed his hands, motherly. Her skin was warm. "We organized this religious practice to find *you*, Vicente. Placing the blood on a temple altar allows us to find your mystic tethers, and allows you to tie to your own demigod. Who is it you feel?"

"The Stag," he said. He had felt it in his dreams. He had seen the beast when asleep. It had been calling for him, for all his life. He hadn't known how to listen for it, but now he did.

Indra looked up at the other mystics. "Good. The Stag, we cannot get for ourselves. You must be the one who attaches to it. When you bond with it, like we have bonded with the Otter, you'll be one of the most powerful people in the world."

Vicente was vibrating, some wild beast caged within, lashing against its bonds. "Let's find it now."

Indra smiled. "You are not yet strong enough, Vicente, but we will train you. I promise you this. Come back with us to Arkensaal and realize your true potential."

"I'm ready."

"One thing, first." She stood, slowly unfolding herself to her full height like a sunrise. "Your current fragility is our greatest threat. This is not a fault you are to blame for, but you must do all you can to mitigate the risk to your life."

"How?"

Again, she took his vial of blood down from the altar. Vicente wanted to scream in pain. "We are family, Vicente; all your enemies are also ours. Your enemies are the nobles sitting around the queen's table, the ones that make up the High Council. We must make it so that if harm comes to you, then that will make us, the other mystics, even stronger. They would never hurt you then, do you see? They would never risk increasing our powers."

She cut her finger. The blood beaded on the thin line. "I will add my blood to your vial, and if you were to perish, then I would gain your powers. Your tether to the Stag would be inherited by me. This way, we will ensure that the nobles in Arkensaal will never harm you. It's the only way to protect you: if they hurt you, they empower me."

He nodded, sealing his fate. "Okay."

She smiled. Then she let her own blood drip into his vial. "Your blood is a precious thing. This is where our powers lay, and they can be stolen from you. If someone consumes your blood, they will take your powers. But as long as your bond to me stays in this temple, you will be immune to this threat."

CHAPTER 8

Iver

When Iver awoke from his nightmare, he was stiff like a corpse. He lay there, breathless and frozen, while the waves of terror washed over him as he tried to discern what was real and what was part of the nightmare. He was not locked up, being tortured. For now, he was somewhat safe.

Blinking burning eyes into the dim light of the early morning, he stood too quickly, then stumbled. Shaking hands grabbed the sink and he dry-heaved into it, stomach empty and constricting, snakelike. *I'm okay. Get a fucking grip.*

It wasn't always this way; some nights were worse than others. The "worse" seemed linked to stress, as if a tense day bled into restless, haunting nights, but he could never be sure. At times, it felt cruelly random, as though a good day was a sin to be punished, paid for with nightmares.

Good days were sparse and far between, but he held onto them, let himself hope. Then, the terrors slammed into him, reminding him he was stuck on this path, that he was a dog on a leash tied down to a train track.

Despite feeling inside-out and wanting nothing more than to stay in bed and ruminate on his own misery, he went down to the first floor of the inn for breakfast. He decided to leave his rifle in his room. The Llyrians feared him enough as it was. But the bow and his quiver, he brought with him.

The air was rich with saffron, cumin, cinnamon, and the intoxicating aroma of garlic and onion sizzling in olive oil. He sat by the window with a bowl of golden rice, topped with tomatoes and peas—a dish he much preferred to the seafood-heavy fare of the capital.

He didn't do it on purpose, but he again found himself in the same room as Vicente. A section of the dining hall had been cordoned off, where a cluster of children sat in front of the arrogant ambassador.

All the children wore identical bracelets: wool-twine and leather cords wrapped around twigs. Birch sticks, if Iver had to guess. He wouldn't have given a shit, if it weren't for the fact that all the kids had one—including the murdered girl. Unless every child under ten in Llyr was part of the same friend group, it had to be some cultural practice Vicente and his crew had overlooked. And whenever someone Iver worked with didn't know all the details regarding a job, it was always up to him to pick up the slack.

Iver peered out of the corner of his eye as Vicente started reading to the kids.

The queen had ordered him to kill Vicente. That's why he was there in the first place. He wasn't privy as to why the queen wanted Vicente dead. The reason didn't matter to Iver though; if he succeeded, she'd pardon him, clear his charges, and set him free. As soon as he had his chance, he'd take it. When that chance would arise, he didn't know, and it made his stomach roll around like a cartwheel. He had no idea how that bastard's magic worked, which meant catching him off guard was essential. Shooting him from a distance wasn't an option: if he missed, Vicente would vanish and reappear, alert to the threat. Iver knew he had only one shot. And truthfully, nothing would feel better than driving his fist through Vicente's smug face.

There was one thing he needed to do first, though: get Vicente's blood vial out of that temple. Again, he didn't know why. He just did as the queen asked, like a good little servant. He had to wait until the day's services were over, because he wouldn't want the Llyrians to see him tampering with their religious paraphernalia.

To kill some time, Iver naturally decided to snoop around and to stalk Ottone, the man with the strange healing potions.

Ottone was easy enough to find; the man walked the streets of Llyr like a stray cat and stopped often to chat with townsfolk who crossed his path. Iver kept him in his peripheral vision as he feigned interest in the gray Grandpa's-beard-moss hanging from the trees, in the shopwindow of the seamstress, and the open workshop of the blacksmith. Hours ticked by just like this, and as the sun climbed higher, the scent of baking earth rose on the light breeze. Iver's garments mirrored the earth's natural tones, merging with the sandy landscape. Ottone didn't spot him once.

Ottone's journey through town ended at one of the taller buildings in the southern parts of Llyr. He knocked on the door, and Prime Minister Jadanza opened it.

Iver stood back and observed the windows. Soon enough, he saw Ottone again on the third floor, drawing the curtains shut.

Iver went to the back of the house, where vines of ivy and wisteria snaked their way up the wall of it. There were no people there, but he needed an excuse for climbing the wall, in case anyone noticed him. He wasn't used to all of this. Before Vicente had shown up and blithely turned his life upside down, Iver made sure he was seen rarely and never for long. He hated working out in the open like this.

He picked an arrow from his quiver and shot it upwards, and it stuck to the soffit of the roof. "Whoops." He waited a few moments to see if there were any reactions from inside the house. When there were none, he scaled the wall. The house was brick, and in the grooves between the stones, he found enough purchase to climb.

This time of year, most windows were left unlocked and cracked. After checking that the room was void of people, he swung the window open fully and jumped inside.

Particles of dust lingered in the air. The room appeared to be some sort of storage space; numerus chairs were stacked on top of each other and lined the walls, boxes and crates cluttered the floor.

The door to the room where Ottone and PM Jadanza were, was ajar. Iver quietly walked up to it and listened, balancing on the balls of his feet.

"In the eyes of our Lord Eldvittra, she is married," said Ottone. "Albeit to another woman."

"I will never understand why the priests in the capital allowed such a thing," said PM Jadanza. It sounded as though his mouth was full of something, like he was eating. Iver heard the clink of metal against ceramic. "But it's official, and I can do little about that. And any babe born into that house will be no heir of mine."

"You wouldn't have had this problem, had you taken on a new wife."

PM Jadanza scoffed. "And have her die when birthing me one, too? I would've been left rearing two children, all by myself."

"This will not be the death of your clan."

"I am the oldest, not my brother. His line is not the true one to continue gracing this land with our blood."

Ottone sighed, sounding defeated. "Is there any way you could convince Marcia to be impregnated?"

"And leave me with a bastard as an heir? Don't be ridiculous."

Iver tried his best not to get pissed off on Marcia's behalf. She had been quite rude to Iver, but maybe that was to be expected when her father was this type of person. Maybe being a stuck-up shithead was a family-trait.

"I understand your frustration, Renato," Ottone said, "but back to my original point: you need to address the public and—"

"And tell them what? Whenever there is a dispute regarding land, Arkensaal will put their noses all up in our business, I can't stop them from interfering. It is out of my hands."

"And see what happens when they come: a little girl is dead."

Iver was still on the balls of his feet. He ignored the way his heart hammered, ignored the way his legs itched from how much he wanted to bolt.

"You cannot prove it was any of them—"

"I know that when Arkensaali people come, terrible things happen," Ottone said. "As prime minister, you have a duty to make sure no more agents of the crown set foot in our town."

*

After managing to slip out of the house undetected, Iver went back to the scene of the crime. It had been left intact—aside from the body not being there anymore, of course. Iver had noticed something that day, and he wanted to confirm it. Unfortunately, it looked like he was right.

The coins hadn't been dropped near the body: they'd been deliberately placed. It looked so staged, he was surprised no one else had picked up on it. Maybe no one besides Iver really cared, maybe the rest of them were too jaded to bother. Vicente, in his drunken state, had insisted the murderer wasn't from Llyr, because then they would've done a better job of covering it up. Only Iver seemed to recognize that the body had been left there as a threat *to them*, but that the staged details were subtle enough not to be meant for outsiders to understand.

He looked closely at the coins, careful not to touch or disturb them where they lay on the gravel. The culprit had intended for this to look like someone had dropped them in a panic. But they were all different value, different currencies, old and new, some foreign, some local, and they were spaced in a way that formed an irregular curve around the body. In Iver's experience, trying to replicate randomness was difficult for a person, because patterns were so intrinsic to people. This was intentional, staged randomness. No one dropped coins like that by accident.

Iver fished out the notepad from his backpack and quickly sketched the patterns of the coins. Then he walked backwards a few steps to take it all in. He tried to figure out the story the culprit had wanted to tell, and what they had wanted to hide.

He saw two reasons for staging the crime scene: to cover up the true motive, or as some part of a ritual. But the first reason didn't make any sense. The kid was like seven years old; why would she carry coins in a currency that wasn't even valid in Llyr?

And if the intent was to make it look like a robbery gone wrong, why would the murderer leave money behind? Either the murderer was incredibly stupid, or that wasn't the reason at all. The coins were so obviously not the property of the victim, that there was no possible way the murderer had placed them there to serve as an explanation for why the girl had been killed.

No, this was ritualistic. This looked like some occult shit. Combined with the weird bracelets the kids wore, it gave Iver chills.

He made his way back through the town center, now heading for the temple to finally steal Vicente's blood and maybe talk to anyone who knew the murdered girl. Talking to the kids was the only way. Had this been in the capital, he would've found some hookers or drug dealers who knew the underbelly by now. Here in Llyr, the underbelly was unfamiliar, hidden in a way he wasn't used to.

He walked up the raked gravel walkway towards the temple. Llyr was in a valley, where the Crooked Mountains boxed it in on one side, and woodland on the other. The forest was so thick it looked to be in perpetual darkness, and the temple was close enough to it that Iver could hear the occasional cry from a bird of prey. A meadow created some distance between the temple and the wilderness. The bugs buzzing over the tall grass caught the light of the setting sun, and they lit up like little specks of golden orbs floating in the air.

It was dark and quiet inside the temple's main hall. A multitude of silver sensers hung from the rafters of the low ceiling, and the smell of burning incense was suffocating. He was alone in there, and the sound of his steps against the stone floor bounced off the walls. In his twenty years of living, he had never managed to figure out why all places of worship insisted on being so goddamned creepy.

The vials were lined up on the shelves. *Vicente Lamor*, one of them read. He took it and pocketed it, and put in its place a vial of pig's blood. Having been there a few nights before turned out to be beneficial: it gave him the idea to replicate the label. Now they looked identical. Not that anyone would've noticed: people rarely registered the details.

He steadied his breathing and looked at the fake vial, trying to forget he had the real one in his pocket, as the best way to appear inconspicuous and innocent, was to believe himself he actually was. Now, he had in his possession the blood of a mystic. If he decided to drink it, he would steal Vicente's powers and gain his ability to teleport. Iver wouldn't do it, though. For one, he'd need training from the quorum, and they grossed him out. And two— the biggest reason, frankly—doing so would be absolutely disgusting and he'd puke the second the blood hit is tongue.

No, Queen Leandra had told him he needed to do this first. Weren't it for this vial, Vicente would've been killed years ago by some affronted nobles, but this was the first time in decades agents of the crown were allowed to enter Llyr.

Now, he could finally kill Vicente.

"Don't touch those."

Iver turned on his heel to find a boy standing in the doorway of the main hall. "I'm not touching them. Mind your own business."

The boy didn't leave. "My name's Jairo. What's your name?"

"What did I just tell you?" When Iver pushed past him, he noticed the silver pendant hanging around his neck. His name was engraved on it. *Disgusting.* Was this how the holy sisters remembered the orphans' names?

Iver walked back outside, and the boy followed him. The sun had set, but the sky was still bright, and the ungodly heat had yet to relent. Iver smelled cigarette smoke. A group of teenagers had set up camp at the edge of the forest, sitting on the trunk of a fallen tree.

The boy, Jairo, continued to gawk at Iver with owlish eyes. "How old are you?"

"Grown."

"But you're so short."

Iver blinked slowly. The other orphans housed in the temple were also out and about, but they were kicking a ball around in the trampled section of the meadow. They seemed busy. Iver would have to talk to this one. "What's that bracelet you all have?"

"Natalina made it up." Jairo looked at the bangle of twine and twigs on his own wrist and started fidgeting with it. "It's to protect us from the monsters in the woods."

"There are monsters in the woods?"

"Yeah. They eat you and take your bones."

Weird kid. "What do the monsters look like?"

"I don't know. No one's seen 'em."

"Then how do you know there's monsters?"

"Gabriel died there, so they told us not to go there anymore. Probably a monster that took Natalina, too."

Something cold spread in Iver's chest. The girl wasn't the first victim, and the other murder had happened recently enough for this eight-year-old to remember it. Why had no one said anything? "Who's Gabriel?"

Jairo pointed at one of the girls chasing after the ball. "Sam's little brother."

"Doesn't seem like a very hungry monster," Iver said. "I mean, two kids are not a lot."

"A bunch has gone missing, too. They were probably eaten whole, that's why no one is talking about it."

So, kids *were* going missing here. But why didn't anyone mention that when they found Natalina? Why were they trying to hide it? "Was Natalina in the woods often?"

The boy scrunched his nose. "I told you; we don't go there anymore."

"I see a shit-ton of kids there right now."

"Yeah, but grown-up kids aren't scared."

That was accurate. Stories of monsters only served to spook little kids, not teenagers, into obeying. Whoever planted the story had wanted the small ones to stay out of the woods and—given the ages of Natalina and the other boy—these were the killer's target. Spreading a rumor of monsters in the forest would attract teenagers to go there, maybe even young adults, and that wouldn't keep the woods secluded enough to hide shit there.

The murderer wanted his targets to stay in the town, probably for ease of access. The bodies of the ones who had gone missing were probably used for something occult, similarly to Natalina's. The killer sought small kids, orphans, and had done this before. Iver would find no luck asking the adults about it, because for whatever reason, they didn't want anyone to know. Perhaps it was because of what Ottone had said: they didn't want the capital to interfere.

"Very clever," Iver muttered, mostly to himself.

Jairo smiled. "They say I'm very clever, even though I'm so ungainly."

That was an adult talking. "Who said that to you?"

"Would you like to play with me?" Jairo asked.

"You ain't got friends your own age or something?"

"No."

Oh. Iver sighed, hard. "Fine. Just this once, though. You shouldn't be talking to adults that you don't know."

Jairo beamed at him and plopped down smack-dab on the terrace, right next to the door of the temple. He pulled a pouch from his pocket and emptied out its content: dice clattered over the stone.

Iver sat down too. "You'll have to go easy on me, I don't know any games."

"Don't worry. I'm really, really clever, and really good at explaining things."

Iver barely paid attention as Jairo described the game, instead he studied the boy, tried to figure out how to formulate his questions. Jairo didn't have any friends, he was the right age, he was too social with strangers: there was a huge risk he was next.

It turned out to be a simple numbers game, one Iver had played before—with prostitutes in the capital. It was called poker dice, and didn't make any sense without bets. Jairo never brought up any bets, and he called it 'guessing game.'

Iver played along, though it was creeping him out. On his turn, he picked up the dice made of bone and rolled them. "Who taught you how to play?"

"Nobody," Jairo said with a smile.

"They told you to keep it a secret?"

"Not the game, I'm allowed to play it with anyone."

It was Iver's turn again. He could play this game in his sleep. "But that you've been meeting with them. Did the tell you to keep that a secret?"

Jairo said nothing. His smile faded, fell off his face slowly then all at once, the same way the sun set in the desert.

Anger and disgust filled Iver's entire ribcage. Getting information from Jairo was so easy, it infuriated him that no adults in Llyr had addressed the problem yet. "Do you do strange things? Like rituals?"

Jairo stayed quiet for a while and turns passed between the two of them, until he said, "I'm not allowed to say."

"Listen, you shouldn't—"

"You won." Jairo looked at him with anticipation, mixed with a little disappointment that he bravely tried to hide.

"Okay?" Iver didn't know what to do. He didn't know how to talk to kids, or how to get them to talk. If he brought this up to the holy sisters, would they hear him out? Would they even care, or did they already know?

"You have to take your price, dummy."

"What's my price?"

"You decide. It can be anything."

Iver's skin crawled. "Fine. Give me a die." Without a full set, Jairo would have to find another, less eerie game to play.

Jairo rolled one over to him. Iver took it and put it in his pocket, the same one he was carrying Vicente's blood in. He really needed to get back to the inn to hide it.

They both stood. Jairo looked happy. Iver felt sick to his stomach.

"Can we play again someday?"

Iver hurried down the steps of the temple. "No. You shouldn't be playing with adults." Fortunately, Jairo didn't follow him.

Darkness had fallen when Iver returned to his room in the Sunfire Rest. He removed the label with Vicente's name from the vial and hid it in his travel bag. He wouldn't destroy it yet.

He picked up the die too, and held it up to the light cast by the lantern on his desk.

Iver reeled. He actually took an involuntary step backwards.

Like most dice, it was made of bone. This one hadn't been refined though, barely polished, and it looked too much like a bone he had seen before. A human tarsal bone. A foot-bone.

That's it. This was getting too fucked-up to keep to himself.

He tried to walk calmly to Vicente's room. If they followed patterns, like people usually did, then they would all be there.

They were, but they weren't sitting in a circle and drinking and talking smack. Instead, Vicente looked like he was one step away from losing his mind. He paced around the room like a wolf in a cage.

"Vic, please calm down," Daiyu said.

"What's going on?" Iver asked.

"Someone's stolen my blood from the temple."

Shit. Could Vicente sense it, or something? The queen had not warned him about that. "So?"

"Did you do something with it? Iver I swear to the Merciful—"

"The fuck would I do that for?"

"Where have you been, then?" Marcia asked.

"I've been talking to the kids at the orphanage. Turns out another child died a while back, and a bunch more has gone missing."

Vicente whipped around to face him, already snarling, dawning fury evident. "So you were at the temple."

Iver folded his arms over his chest. He was chewing on his lip, because he had little patience for getting accused of wrongdoings. Especially when he actually was the right person to blame.

"Did you see anything weird while you were there?" Marcia asked. She took the unlit cigarette from between her teeth. "Anyone going into the room where the altar is?"

"Yeah, loads of people; it's a temple. Look, did you hear what I said?" Were none of them going to acknowledge the information he had shared, that Natalina wasn't the first child found dead? Once again, Iver was shouting into the void. If he pressed the issue, they would ridicule him, pick apart every observation he had made and conclusion he had drawn, and then laugh at him. *I'm not doing this again.*

Vicente sat down on the bed and put his head in his hands. "You have no idea what this means, Iver."

Arrogant, rich, high-born prick. "No, and I also couldn't care less." Iver hated feeling this way: feeling stupid. As a kid, he had been smart, but there was never a way for him to use it, and that wasn't his fault. He had excelled in math, but without an education, there was nowhere for him to go; every door was slammed in his face. In the end, he turned his math skills toward becoming a sniper. It was survival, not choice.

Daiyu rubbed her fingers over her eyelids under her glasses. "We should go to the temple. Maybe someone saw something, and we can get the vial back. Or you can just make a new one? Yeah, we can baptize you right back into your freaky deal," she concluded and snapped her hands down to her hips.

Vicente stood. "Doesn't work like that. Let's go."

Iver's anxiety settled a bit as they began the trek to the temple. If Vicente could see the fake one still standing there, maybe he could get the idea of theft out of his mind. Who knows, the deal could've expired, or something. With blood magic and all that inexplicable, fucked-up shit, there was a multitude of reasons for triggering whatever sensation Vicente was feeling. *Right?*

The moon hung low in the sky and rimmed the treetops with a dull edge of light. Vicente walked briskly, like his ass was on fire, and Marcia kept pace with him, but Iver couldn't be bothered.

Daiyu fell into step with him. "How many children?"

"Sorry?"

"How many more children have gone missing?"

"Dunno; kid didn't say." He cleared his throat without meaning to. "He'd been told not to talk about it, and I didn't want to prod too much in case I spooked him, you know, it must've fucked him up a bit, his friends just, being killed like that…" He trailed off, letting his voice fade into silence once he realized he was rambling. It was strange not to get interrupted, to not have the other person on their toes, antsy to jump in and speak over him.

Daiyu nodded. "That was smart, to let him offer up whatever information he was comfortable with."

"Yeah…" *I should give her the die.* She was a scientist; perhaps she could figure out if it was human bone or not. But most dice were made of bone, that wasn't suspicious. Had Iver really seen enough skeletons to make the distinction himself? He was probably freaking out over nothing, because why would the killer make dice out of his victims and hand them out to random children?

"I'm a bit surprised, actually," Daiyu began, smiling awkwardly, "that you—that this bothers you."

"What, that I care about kids being murdered?"

"No offense, but you're a mercenary. I didn't expect this."

Iver wanted to get pissed off—he usually was, he had a short fuse—but there was no hint of accusation in Daiyu's tone.

A friend of Iver's had called it 'cognitive dissonance': that they could kill for money and still consider themselves good people. There was always a reason, an excuse, and everything could be explained away. It was unpleasant to be confronted by it, but Iver was getting better at assimilating the truth. "So just because I'm a horrible person, I can't do good things?"

She smiled at him, genuinely. "Touché."

"I hate to say it, but we need the police here."

"I think you're right. I'll talk to Marcia, have her try to convince her father to send a message to Arkensaal."

"He might not agree. They don't want Arkensaali people to come here."

"It's the only way. Courier birds are so expensive, we'll need his approval. I know it's difficult, but please trust us. Marcia will take care of it."

They reached the temple and stepped into the darkness ten paces behind Marcia and Vicente. The prayer room was otherwise empty of people and candles still burned around the altar, offering sparse light.

Vicente raked his fingers through his hair. "See, I fucking told you. Someone took it. I can't believe this."

What? Iver walked up to the altar—to the sound of Vicente loudly and publicly losing his mind—and his unease was replaced with utter bewilderment.

The vial of pig's blood with Vicente's name on it was gone. Someone had come in after Iver and stolen the fake one.

What the fuck?

CHAPTER 9

Vicente

"What are her ailments?" Vicente glanced at the older woman. "Aside from the injury, of course." The sore on her wrist didn't look too bad, albeit a bit red. But she was wrapped in a blanket, despite the pressing heat.

Various herbs tinged the air inside Ottone's apothecary with a pungent scent. Every surface, from the desks to the shelves, was cluttered with jars, notebooks and other equipment Vicente recognized from visiting Daiyu in her laboratory.

"She caught a blight while working the rice fields," Ottone said. "Symptoms are headache and a fever."

"Could it be fatal if left untreated?" Marcia asked.

They were all speaking about the woman like she couldn't hear them, which made Vicente uncomfortable, but he, Marcia and Daiyu were all eager to see the supposed healing potion in action, and they needed to have full knowledge of the relevant parameters.

Daiyu had dragged Iver along as well, and he was now standing with his arms folded over his chest, hip cocked and glaring at them with mild frustration. Vicente decided he didn't want to invite Iver anymore, and made a mental note of broaching the subject to Marcia whenever he got the chance. They didn't need Iver: no harm would come to them in Llyr. Queen Leandra's real ambition was for Vicente to break Iver's spirit. He wanted to serve her in most regards, but he wouldn't do this. He would return Iver unbroken, wild and thrashing, and he would be sent off to the frontiers where he'd surely go down in a blaze of glory.

"Considering her age, yes." Ottone grabbed a sealed bottle, opened it and poured it into a cup that he handed to the woman. Without hesitation, she drank the whole thing.

"How long does it take?" Daiyu asked, looking with her hands as usual, grabbing bottles and swirling the liquids around to inspect them.

"It varies," Ottone said with a tone Vicente couldn't decipher. Was he disappointed? Nonchalant?

"Sometimes it requires a second or third dose. But it always works. I need to do some more testing, of course." Ottone put the back of his hand to the woman's forehead. "Today, we are lucky."

And before their eyes, the sore on the woman's wrist healed, leaving behind a faint scar.

This was not mere medicine; Ottone had perfected the art chemists and doctors had given up on years ago, deemed impossible to perform. Vicente's head started swimming. His mouth went dry.

Ottone's eyes gleamed. "My potions are the real thing, as I have proved. They are brewed from rare herbs, and they mend wounds, cure ailments, and restore vitality to those on the brink of the abyss. If my land is rightfully handed back to me and my clan, I will farm these herbs and begin a large-scale production of my potions, creating a big enough stock to supply the entire realm."

Marcia gently tapped Vicente's elbow.

"We will take your claim into consideration," Vicente said after wetting his lips. "Thank you for your demonstration, Lord Ottone."

Daiyu stepped up to the woman. "May I feel your forehead?"

The woman nodded.

Daiyu did. Her head whipped around to look at Vicente, and the excitement in her eyes had been replaced by a fierce intensity he wasn't sure he wanted to see. "Her fever is gone! Could I join you when you work, Lord Ottone?" she blurted out. "I'm a chemist myself. I'd like to see how it's done."

Vicente felt Marcia stiffen next to him. Did she think Ottone would take offense?

But Ottone's eyes lit up, just like Daiyu's. "Why, yes! I would be honored, Professor. I have no one else to share my progress with."

Ottone's potions would serve the realm well, but the queen had expressed her wishes clearly: the land should be appointed to Eloy Errani. But this could save countless lives from the war that killed so many and left so many orphans. This could change the culture of the realm. Would there still be honor in death once it could be so easily avoided? Would that entice the capital, or did they want to protect the status quo, the war they worshipped that had been going on for so long there was no one alive to remember peace? If Vicente's suspicions were correct—that the conscription of that many soldiers were partly because the population had to be culled as it outgrew the bounds of the country—then these healing potions would be of no interest to the High Council.

Vicente tried to reel in his excitement. He had only seen the potions work once, and Ottone had hinted that they were unreliable, unpredictable. They needed more data. But this was worth pursuing, he decided.

"If Marcia and Vicente find that the land belongs to the Errani clan, could you not just plant your herbs on some other land?" Iver asked.

Vicente knew the answer, but most people—unless they were employed by the government or in agriculture—didn't.

"The land out here that is not already cultivated is not arable," Ottone said. "The sand has taken much of it."

The sand dunes moved with the wind, demanding more land every year. The queen's decision was understandable, yet Vicente couldn't drop this opportunity.

They thanked him and left the laboratory, leaving Daiyu behind.

Iver looked over his shoulder. "She's a bit of a weirdo."

It surprised Vicente to hear Iver initiate conversation. It knocked him backwards a little. Still, only he and Daiyu's other friends were allowed to call her weird. "I admire Daiyu for her unyielding clarity of vision regarding her goals."

Marcia and Vicente stepped out into the sunlight, but Iver stopped outside the door. Marcia went on ahead, towards another grueling session of digging through Llyr's archives. Vicente stayed. "Having ambitions is important," he said. "As long as they don't harm anyone else, I suppose."

"What the fuck are you talking about?" Iver said, glaring at him through the fall of his bangs.

Vicente clasped his hands behind his back, drinking Iver's distress greedily, letting it feed his own stillness. He feigned interest in the potted plants around the porch; orchids of different colors and windmill palms that rattled softly whenever the breeze made a half-hearted pass through the shaded veranda. "I was just talking out to the ether, seeing what energy comes back to me."

"She's going to be alone with him."

"I simply adore how you state the obvious with such a sense of new discovery."

"Aren't you worried about leaving her there? You don't know him."

Was Iver testing him? It sure sounded like it. "Has violence decayed your brain? Why would Lord Ottone harm her?"

Iver sucked his teeth. "You talk a lot of shit for someone who sleeps down the hall from someone like me."

A knife sat in the holster strapped to Iver's outer thigh; the same knife Vicente had entangled with his necklace. If Iver attempted anything, Vicente could get a hold of that knife in an instant.

"By all means, try it." Vicente leaned down and forward, into his space. "I'll gladly crush your face."

Iver didn't flinch. "Be my guest. It was never of use to me anyway."

Vicente 'tsk'-ed. "Don't say that. I doubt you ever had any issues with the ladies."

Iver finally backed up, his expression stormy. "Why are you like this?"

"I have tried being cordial with you, but you seem determined to get on my last nerve. Now, get out of my sight."

Maintaining his smokescreen of confidence resulted in Iver acquiescing, and Vicente felt like a beast ready to pounce as he watched him leave. He reckoned Iver wanted him dead, and since a murderer was running loose in Llyr, Iver might deem that as enough of a cover story to follow through. Vicente wondered, did Iver picture killing him? Did he fantasize about slitting his throat? As the Far Cry assassin, he had been untouchable: no one could bring him to justice. And then Vicente showed up.

Someone had stolen Vicente's blood from the temple, and he suspected Iver was the one, but couldn't be certain. Because why would Iver steal it? There was no way he knew what it meant, because if he did know, then he would've drunk it already and Vicente wouldn't still be a mystic, which he was: he had entangled his dinner last night just to make sure.

What this did mean, however, was that if Vicente were to die now, then his established ties to the Stag wouldn't transfer to Indra. With this theft, their contract was voided. Everything, all his progress, would be lost. He had always been mortal, but this somehow made him feel one step closer to death.

Trying his best not to panic about this, he walked beneath the colossal arches of the aqueducts, relishing in their shade. Purple and blue wisteria climbed their way up them, curling around the pale stone. Beyond the shade, Llyr buzzed with late-afternoon energy: vendors calling out the last of their offers, the clatter of carts over uneven cobbles, children darting between alleys with olives in their fists and no shoes on their feet. A woman leaned out of a second-story window to shake dust from a rug, shouting a half-hearted scolding at someone below. The scent of frying onions and sweet vinegar drifted in from a nearby stall, undercut by the briny tang of sheep and sun-warmed stone.

He heard the blacksmith's metal clang well before he arrived. Atli, a blacksmith and part of the Llyrian council, was bent over a barrel of water, quenching a piece of metalwork that had already suffered through the forging process.

"You've lived here long?"

Atli awarded him a single glance and then returned to his work. "Born and raised. My family has lived here for generations."

'Atli' wasn't a Llyrian name; it was northern. Either his parents hadn't been particularly traditional, or they had immigrated at some point, but Vicente decided not to ask. "I don't suppose your grandparents ever told you who farmed the land around the ruins of Tal Llyrie?"

"Unfortunately, no."

Atli resumed his hammering. Vicente was losing him already. He felt stupid. Once, he belonged here, and it was tough to be confronted so abruptly by the fact it was no longer true. To gain some social currency, he said, "what about stories of the fortress of Tal Llyrie? I've read about the grand rotunda at its center, but I assume text cannot do it justice. I was told it was even more magnificent than the soaring towers of Arkensaal."

"My maternal grandfather, bless his soul, remembered seeing it before it got burned to the ground. He said it reached the sky." Atli shook his head. "The memories of a child."

Atli was exactly what one expected from a blacksmith: thick arms, weathered hands, and a face lined by age and the heat of the forge. His hair and beard were long and black, streaked here and there with silver, framing a face that looked as sturdy and dependable as the metal he worked with. Vicente noticed the way Atli's gaze lingered on the people who passed by his shop, his eyes softening whenever he greeted a neighbor or nodded to a child. He wasn't just a blacksmith; he was a caretaker, a pillar in his community. That quiet, unspoken dedication told Vicente everything he needed to know. A man like Atli valued loyalty and tradition; and Vicente could twist that sense of duty to get exactly what he wanted.

"You know, I read something similar." Vicente embellished; the fortress was indeed magnificent, but nothing could reach the sky like Arkensaal did. "They said Llyr would never survive, being located so far from any lake or river. But challenges make people smart. I have never seen anything like these aqueducts before." This was truthful. They were a symbol of mankind's ability to harness nature for survival, as they channeled water from the mountain springs to nourish the town below.

"I don't suppose your books told you which clan the land belongs to?"

Vicente enjoyed it when conversations went his way. "If you could choose, what would you prefer?"

Atli set his hammer down and dragged his wrist over his forehead, wiping the sweat from it. "I'd prefer it if Arkensaal took a step back and let us Llyrians decide. Let us vote."

"I understand you care a lot about your community, Mister Atli."

"Ambassador, that would be an understatement." A faint smile graced his face just then, and Vicente knew he had him right where he wanted him.

"You know what a vote would do to your community?" Vicente said, frowning to show concern. "It would create conflict, breed resentment. Whoever you don't vote for will despise you if they find out. But if you let me and Marcia decide, you could resent us instead. And believe me when I say, Mister Atli, both Marcia and I have Llyr's best interests at heart."

*

After a long day of work, the crew went to the Harvest Heart for dinner and drinks. The tavern was crowded, but the bustle only added to its cozy atmosphere. Smoke curled from the hearth, thick with the scent of charred rosemary and slow-cooked lamb. The table groaned under clay dishes of blistered flatbread, bowls of stewed lentils and chickpeas soaked in spiced oil, fire-roasted squash slick with honey, and goat cheese rolled in cracked pepper and ash.

Iver had decided to join them for dinner, for reasons Vicente couldn't begin to fathom. He said nothing as he picked at the bread like it owed him money, drinking just enough to look like he belonged, but never enough to relax. And Vicente hated how much space that carved into his mind, how much of his attention bent toward reading this man.

"I'll be working with him in the apothecary," Daiyu said. "He's going to show me how he makes them."

Vicente refilled his own cup with a little more force than necessary, sloshing dark red onto the table, and pretended not to notice. "How did he come up with it?" It was baffling to him that Ottone had managed to produce healing potions. Llyr didn't even have any universities. "Did he tell you if he studied with someone?"

"Probably some old-fashioned trial and error," Daiyu said. "That's how we chemists work: you take what nature offers and try to mix it all together. And without the restraint of censorship and Arkensaal breathing down his neck, chances are high he came up with the formula all on his own."

Vicente always felt left out when he was reminded of this. Had it not been for the government's iron fist, how advanced would their country have been by now?

"I heard about a new technology developed in the Vale," Daiyu continued. "They called them 'regenerative tissue patches.' They were these small, bioengineered patches that, when applied to an injury, used nanotechnology to close wounds and stimulate tissue regrowth. They literally knitted the skin back together on contact."

"That's amazing."

Daiyu shoveled another bite of food into her mouth, but that didn't stop her from talking. "A few years ago, a coworker of mine made a drug that removed the need for sleep. Then Arkensaal caught wind of it, destroyed all his documentation and threw him in jail. It was probably for the best though; because of that medication, his bowel-movements went haywire."

"Honey, please shut up," Marcia said. "Not while we eat."

She picked a more appropriate topic. Iver didn't say a word. But once they had all finished eating and moved on to drinks, he still didn't leave.

Vicente tried to rest his mind. The low simmer of the alcohol was enjoyable. Marcia could drink for hours without showing any signs of intoxication. Daiyu was the opposite. Iver and Marcia watched as she befriended every party in the tavern. Vicente watched them watching.

He studied Iver closely, subtly, trying to read something, *anything*, from the way his eyes followed others, the way he held his body. But his face was illegible.

CHAPTER 10

Marcia

As Marcia's eyes grew weary from the strain of reading, she leaned back in the creaking chair. "Found anything?" Every day, they spent at least eight hours in the archives, inspecting mind-numbing documents about price-fluctuations and the weight of all newborns fifty years ago.

Vicente scrubbed a hand over his face. He looked wrung out. "Nothing yet."

"We'll stop for today. We don't want to rush through all the fun."

Vicente clambered to his feet. "How about a drink?"

Marcia stood and stretched. "I was hoping to exchange a few words with Sergeant Celia. Besides, you'll just get me so drunk I can barely stand, and I want to keep up the professional appearances."

"I wouldn't do that to you. I'm not a student anymore."

She squeezed his elbow fondly. "To me, you'll always be my student."

"Daiyu told me you're looking to replace me, find someone more suitable to mother."

It didn't surprise her Daiyu had told him—those two shared everything—but it still threw her, just a little. She had been hoping to sideline the topic while in Llyr, but now, all her doubts came rushing back. "She's jumping the gun a bit. But yes, we're considering trying for one."

She and Vicente parted ways, and she decided to take the long way through the town, as she tried to remember when the feeling had first wrapped around her neck like a vice. She wondered if she could raise a child, mold a life and give them everything they deserved. Or would she pay the trauma forward? Would she hurt her child unknowingly, unintentionally, like her father had her? Doubts crept in, whispering in her ear, urging her to play it safe.

The adventure would be amazing but brutal. Could she balance out the strain that growing and birthing a baby would put on Daiyu's body? Could she make it up to her, be thankful enough as she gave up a part of herself to give them a child, for bearing an impossible weight both in mind and body? The idea of not owning her own body terrified Marcia, and she projected that fear onto Daiyu, even though she had assured Marcia that the prospect of pregnancy was exciting to her.

Marcia walked along the dusty pathways through Llyr. In the heart of it, structures of modest stature, no more than four stories high, stood shoulder to shoulder. As she ventured forth, the gaps between the buildings widened and their architectural complexities gave way to simpler forms, revealing the quieter outskirts of the town.

The warriors were sparring when Marcia arrived. In the wake of throwing each other to the ground, clouds of dust hung in the air over the open field.

"Ambassador Marcia!" Sergeant Celia called out and ran up to her. The white scarf protecting her head from the sun, once pristine, was now marred with streaks of rusty sand. "Have you come to join us in training?"

Marcia chuckled and waved her hand. "Wouldn't that be a sight. No, I have come to ask about the investigation. Seeing as there are no police here in Llyr, will you be taking charge of it?" The murder of the girl was unfortunate in many ways. She had initially vowed not to get involved, even though she wanted to offer her aid, but the fact of the matter was that the incident would take the focus off her and Vicente's job, which was a problem.

They needed all the available resources at their disposal; she didn't want to stay in Llyr for longer than she had to.

"We have not received any word of it from PM Jadanza," Celia said.

Though Marcia felt extremely apprehensive about it, she entertained the thought that the best course of action might be to send a message to Arkensaal about the event, and request help from the police. Other than the fact it would get that mess off her plate, it would cast her and her party in a better light in the eyes of the Llyrians, making the crew look less suspicious as possible culprits. "Jadanza is the one to give you orders?"

"As prime minister, yes," Celia said. "If you were to step into your role as your father's successor, the militia would take command from you next. Though I understand that won't be happening. Your father is left with no successors."

This was not a conversation Marcia wished to have, but it was expected, as she had asked questions of her own. "He made his bed," she said, because she would no longer bear the burden of making up for others' missteps. She refused to be handed difficult situations and be robbed of resources. Navigating through impossible conditions, with available assets dangling just out of reach, was something she'd had enough of.

She decided then: she would ask the Arkensaali police to send officers.

One year ago

Marcia immersed herself in reviewing a briefing document when an Arkensaali staff member approached. The young woman, Harin, had a manila folder clutched to her chest. "The emissary from the Vale of Rayon Vostok is waiting for you in the Red Parlor."

Marcia glanced up, arching a brow. "He is? How long have you kept him waiting?"

Harin flinched. "My apologies, Ambassador. He arrived sooner than expected."

Marcia sighed, setting the paper aside. "I sure hope the prime minister isn't with him."

"He's currently on a guided tour of the Akashika cathedral," she replied. "Emissary Karl agreed it would be best for you two to go over the details before the Prime Minister meets with Her Majesty."

"Some happy tidings. Walk with me. Vicente, you too."

Vicente looked up from his corner of the room, where he'd been flipping through the draft of the queen's speech. He rose without a word, falling into lockstep beside her as they moved through the palace's endless corridors.

The palace was alive with movement: staff rushed past carrying either trays or armloads of documents, their expressions a cocktail of harried focus and ingrained decorum. A pair of courtiers argued in hushed tones over a map spread across a marble bench, while a cluster of maids debated the placement of a floral arrangement.

Marcia's pace was brisk. Only three years ago, she had held Harin's role, darting between nobles and diplomats, juggling urgent tasks with impossible deadlines. Now, the difference in their stations wasn't lost on her, nor was the knowledge of how quickly things could change.

"Her Majesty has a dinner scheduled with the Prime Minister for seven o'clock tonight," Harin said. "The attack is the fifth point on her agenda."

"That won't do," Marcia said. "We'll have to move it up."

"I'll see what I can do," Harin said and peeled off down a perpendicular corridor.

"Where do you want me?" Vicente asked as they neared the Red Parlor.

"Sit off to the side," Marcia instructed. "Introduce yourself, but then just listen in."

"Anything I can help with?"

"We must be out of that room before the PM gets here. No one can see us. If we run on for too long, fabricate some meeting and remind me of it." Negotiations between ambassadors *before* the world leaders met with each other weren't exactly protocol.

"Sure thing," Vicente said. "Are you going to ask the Vale to back off?"

"That is not my job. We trade information and favors, that is what we do, what you need to become a specialist in, Vic."

"You're risking a lot by talking to the emissary like this."

He was right, and Marcia was aware of that. But she needed to know what they knew, and most importantly, what they didn't know. "The whole world is propped up on a bartering system. Goods and services are traded for each other, everything comes with a cost, and everything has a price. The question is, how much are you willing to pay to reach your goals?"

The heavy double doors of the Red Parlor loomed before them. With a steadying breath, Marcia placed her hand on the brass handles, pushing them open.

The walls of the Red Parlor were painted with a warm crimson, and wainscoting ran along the lower halves of them. A richly patterned carpet stretched across the floor, muffling footsteps, and an array of high-backed chairs and settees, upholstered in deep red velvet, were arranged with an almost mathematical precision around a low mahogany table. Emissary Karl was seated at it, with a half-finished drink in his hand. *Damnit, Harin.*

"Ambassador." Emissary Karl rose to his feet as they entered, offering a handshake to Marcia.

Marcia gave a polished smile. "Emissary Karl, what a pleasure."

She settled into her chair, her notes resting on her lap. She didn't need them; they were merely there to lend weight to the conversation, to ground it in the hard evidence she had memorized down to the punctuation. "I understand Prime Minister Tapani took the mention of possible Vostok involvement rather harshly."

"That would be the understatement of the year," Karl replied, his mouth curling acerbically. "Ambassador, he took the accusation as a declaration of war. Against my advice, he is already bolstering Vostok defenses. He expects retaliation in one form or another, either from Arkensaal itself or from agents of it."

"Her Majesty did not lob a formal accusation," Marcia said.

"The Arkensaali queen is well aware the eyes of the realm turn to wherever her finger points." Because of Harin's mistake, Karl had been sitting there waiting for Marcia and been allowed to stew in his own thoughts and frustrations for a while now.

"Then let us see where the evidence points, shall we?" Marcia shuffled the papers on her lap, looking down for a second, pretending to read. "Sixty-four hours ago, a unit of three hundred infantry soldiers unknowingly marched into a field riddled with subterranean explosives. Two hundred and twelve are dead, the remainder maimed and clinging to life. Most are still in surgery."

"I know this," Karl said, his voice quieter but no less resolute.

Marcia pressed on. "That field is under the Vale's jurisdiction. But that hasn't always been the case, has it? I'm told you call it 'the Ruby Field' in the Vale because the fight over it once turned it into a lake of blood."

Karl nodded tersely. "I know."

"The University of Tal Miril has examined the few landmines we managed to recover. Their findings? These devices are like nothing the Arkensaali military has ever seen. Nor are they Rinkaian, Daegunese, Shirinian, or Elathian. That leaves Llyr: a prefecture whose main exports are grain and beef, whose literacy score is a ten on a scale that reaches five hundred, and which lacks universities altogether—or the Vale of Rayon Vostok. A subnation with six universities and a military budget comprising twenty-five percent of its gross domestic product—"

"Ambassador," Karl interrupted, leaning forward. "I understand the numbers. The Vale understands the numbers."

Marcia arched an eyebrow, her silence inviting him to continue.

Karl's expression hardened further. "We don't make landmines. Today, the prime minister will request access to all the data your investigation collected. With that information, he intends to prove that these weapons were not built in the Vale."

The Arkensaali police would never share their findings, they had never done so in the past, but she couldn't tell him that. "As a state within the Ōekenese borders and under the monarchy's rule, we expect your full cooperation in the upcoming inquiry."

"And as a state in the queen's arms, the Vale expects her protection from any insurgent retaliation." Karl's voice dipped, eyes darting to Vicente in the corner, and said, "Marcia, even if it turns out the attackers were from the Vale, you must realize they did not act on our behalf. There are currents—powerful ones— pushing for an independent Vale of Rayon Vostok, but no such forces, to my knowledge, would ever attack the queen's soldiers to achieve it. And Prime Minister Tapani sure as fuck wouldn't have green-lit something like this. Not with the election coming up next spring."

The election. *Shit.* Horror dropped flat in her stomach. She had forgotten about that. A two-year relationship with Prime Minister Tapani, built on hard-won negotiations and delicately worded treaties, now teetered on the edge of collapse. If this escalated further, it could all fly out the window.

"That remains to be seen," Marcia said. "In the meantime, Arkensaal wishes that the Vale step down their efforts to posture. We do not want to see an escalation."

"Neither do we," Karl replied. "But Queen Leandra cannot lob a formal accusation against the Vale at dinner tonight. People are outraged, Marcia. They will seek revenge. Prime Minister Tapani has an obligation to protect all the lives in the Vale."

Marcia rested her hands on the papers in her lap. "I understand your concern. But as you say, the families of these soldiers are angry, and they want answers."

Karl didn't flinch under her gaze. Marcia held it, while the tension between them remained a thread pulled taut, threatening to snap. But he was right: the crown had more to lose in this matter.

Marcia softened her tone. "I will admit Her Majesty made a mistake when she spoke of the Vale in this context. It was a misstep, and I will do what I can to stop it from happening again. But the Vale must understand that tensions are high. Stepping back now will save lives, not just in Arkensaal but within your borders as well."

Karl's lips pressed into a thin line, his fingers drumming briefly on the armrest of his chair. "I'll do what I can to ease tensions," he said. "But the Prime Minister's first priority is to protect our citizens."

"As is ours," Marcia replied. "Let's not allow fear to guide our actions."

Marcia and Vicente left Emissary Karl in the Red Parlor. Staff moved briskly around them, heads down, intent on their tasks. Marcia barely noticed. Her mind was already on what came next.

"We need to give the queen an efficient brief that makes her feel like she's in control," she said, her tone clipped.

"I think Emissary Karl was right, Marcia."

Marcia didn't break stride. "I know."

Vicente kept pace. "Can you convince the queen?"

Marcia would try, but she wasn't hopeful. Leandra tended to plant her heels in the ground, and when she did that, Marcia had no chance of persuading her otherwise. "I will do my best, but we must prepare in case I fail. If she accuses the Vale tonight, PM Tapani will lose the election, and we lose our foothold in the north. Find me the leader of the contending party and invite him to Arkensaal. Keep it on the down low; I don't want PM Tapani to catch wind of this."

"On it," Vicente called over his shoulder as he left her side, probably heading straight for the House of Parliament.

When Marcia entered her office, Queen Leandra was seated at her desk, her gaze fixed on the cityscape visible through the arched windows. She didn't turn around.

Confessing to having met with the emissary before their meeting would create problems of its own, but Marcia didn't have much choice. "I have spoken with the emissary from the Vale of Rayon Vostok. The statement from the Vale remains the same: they weren't behind the attack."

"Bullshit," Leandra said flatly.

"They say that our investigation will prove the weapons weren't built in the Vale. They're asking for more time and further restraint on our end."

Leandra finally turned to face her. "I don't care where the weapons were built. The Vale has plenty of reasons to assault us. Of course, they won't take the blame: they're only concerned with causing as much bloodshed as possible."

"Good point," Marcia said without conviction, wondering why the queen even bothered to accept council when she had already made up her mind. "Still. They are asking that you don't mention the Vale in the context of the attack at dinner tonight."

"I have hundreds of angry families marching the streets below. I need to tell them something."

"The Vale fears retaliation."

Queen Leandra's face shone with ire, with such intensity it left Marcia feeling nauseous. "I'm not planning on bombing them, are you?"

"Not from us, per se," Marcia replied. "They have an election coming up. If Prime Minister Tapani appears to be damaging the bonds between the Vale and the capital, he'll lose it."

Leandra shot to her feet. "Oh, for fuck's sake." She began pacing around the room, a clear sign they were nearing the time when Marcia had to get the heck out of there. "Don't do this to me, Marcia. Not you too. The goddamned quorum is already nagging at me about how the Vale didn't do it, but they're refusing to show proof or offer a better explanation. And frankly, I don't believe them. My soldiers died on land that belongs to the Vale. The Vale means to tell us someone else snuck onto their land and dropped bombs on an entire battalion, without their knowledge?"

Marcia exhaled quietly, her gaze dropping for a moment. She had pushed as far as she could. Leandra wouldn't budge. Once again, Marcia would have to let herself—and everyone else—be bludgeoned into submission by the queen's unflagging selfishness. But it was for the greater good. The monarch was the glue holding the realm together, and where her advisors couldn't steer her right, they were there to salvage the scorched earth left behind in her wake.

The system would make up for this misstep. The system would regenerate. It was almost invincible.

"The bombs were not dropped, Your Majesty," Marcia said, her voice quieter now. "The unit walked in on subterranean anti-personnel weaponry. They had been buried in the ground."

Leandra froze, mid-step. "Landmines?"

"Yes."

"Holy Merciful." Queen Leandra was quiet for a moment, her mind clearly racing. Then she turned back to Marcia. "Rewrite my speech. Remove all mentions of the Vale of Rayon Vostok. Just keep the sorrows and prayers."

"What's happening?" Marcia asked, heart thumping.

She began pacing again. "The Vale didn't do it."

How could she possibly have known that? The only way for her to rule out the Vale, was if she knew who the actual culprits were. Marcia got the feeling she did. "What are you not telling me, Your Majesty?"

Queen Leandra recomposed herself, masking the cracks with a veneer of authority. "You were right. We can't escalate the tensions between Arkensaal and the Vale. We can't lose Tapani as the PM and our hold on the north. Rewrite the speech. You're dismissed."

Marcia bit down on the inside of her own cheek. Restraint was her most useful tool. *Don't rock the boat.* Did she really need to know what the queen knew in order to get her job done, or was she simply curious? Not that it mattered: Leandra wouldn't tell her, and that was a certainty. They had been through this dance before.

"Of course, Your Majesty."

CHAPTER 11

Vicente

After another week of digging through the archives, they finally found something of interest. As the heat subsided and the light outside faded, Marcia spoke, startling Vicente. "Look at this."

A hand to his chest, Vicente stood behind her, looking over her shoulder. The paper she held was creased, like it had been folded many times. He read the smudged ink—or at least tried to. "It's gibberish."

"I think it's code. All these pages are written in the same way." She handed him the stack of papers that she had piled up in front of her. "Take a look, please. My eyeballs are burning."

She was right. Every loose page followed the pattern of a letter, making it plausible they had been encrypted. "We would need some sort of key to read them." He considered who might've found it necessary to encode their correspondence; there were no dates scribbled on the sheets, but the parchment looked to be at least a hundred years old: around the same time the bandits began their reign over the mountains. The rebels would have reason enough to obfuscate their messages.

Marcia groaned as she rose from her seat. "Let's finish up for today. We wouldn't want to miss information due to exhaustion."

Vicente folded one of the letters and pocketed it. "I'll try to decipher it tonight," he said as he and Marcia stepped outside. "You think we'll ever find anything? The most useful stuff has probably been pillaged in the raids."

"If we don't, we'll have to settle this the old-fashioned way." Marcia stretched her back, joints audibly popping. "I don't oppose Queen Leandra's request: another soybean farm would be good for the Llyrian economy."

"I would have to agree, Ambassador Marcia." Eloy was standing at the landing of the stairs. "The realm cannot continue to supply itself with only one plantation."

Vicente wondered how much Eloy had caught, though he doubted he would attempt something foolish. Besides, there was nothing to do about it; Eloy had already overheard them. "It will be up to which clan has the stronger claim over the land." Vicente ascended the stairs, stepping into the fading but warm sunlight. The shrill calls of swallows filled the air above as they flew from their nests underneath the roof tiles.

"Naturally," Eloy said with a smile. "Have you found anything? I would aid you in your search, but unfortunately, I'm not permitted inside."

"Nothing yet," Marcia admitted. "However, we did come across documents that look to be encrypted." She seemed to trust Eloy instinctively, and Vicente trusted her gut more than his own.

At Marcia's nod, Vicente produced the letter and handed it to Eloy. "Does this look familiar to you?"

Eloy frowned as he scanned it. "I'm afraid it doesn't."

It wasn't until then that the idea struck Vicente: the archivists at Tal Miril might've encountered a similar code before. And even if they hadn't, their mathematicians would certainly be able to decode it. "Marcia, we should send this back to the capital, have our colleagues at Tal Miril take a look at it."

Her eyes lit up with excitement. "Genius, Vic. They'll crack it in no time."

Vicente had once heard that the military's radio transceivers allowed real-time communication over great distances. Moments like this made him wish they weren't restricted to military use. "My Lord, you have birds here, yes?"

"I'll show you to the couriers first thing tomorrow," Eloy said. "Our feathered friends don't do well travelling in the dark."

Vicente would rather have sent it off immediately but couldn't refuse his offer. "I would appreciate that very much, Lord Eloy."

"Hopefully you'll find enough evidence to settle this dispute," Eloy said. "This whole ordeal has turned into a bit of a mess. In the end, we all want what's best for Llyr."

"We will make every effort to reach a fair resolution," Vicente replied as they parted ways.

He and Marcia walked through the market square as they headed back towards the inn. Soldiers of the militia dotted the streets. They surveyed the crowd, pretending to be some sort of police force. He doubted Llyr had problems with petty theft. Seven thousand people were far too many to know personally, but he figured they must all recognize each other, at least to some extent. How could anyone risk committing crimes in a place like this?

Vicente had stolen once. His mother hadn't gotten them food in over a week, and he was so hungry. What was it that he stole?

He shook his head to rid himself of the invasive memory. This was how his memories poked at him: diffused and in the wrong order. Jumbled, absurd.

As Vicente and Marcia neared the inn, they crossed paths with Prime Minister Jadanza and Ottone.

Marcia drew a breath when she saw them. "Perfect, I needed to speak to my father."

"What for?"

"I've decided. Come with me."

Marcia approached the two men and exchanged a few pleasantries, before getting to the point: "Father, I wanted to let you know that I'll be sending a message to Arkensaal, requesting the help of the police in the matter of the murdered little girl."

Vicente sensed she had been growing restless by her father's lack of action. He was relieved by her decision: if people suspected Vicente and his party, they needed an unbiased mediator at the helm of the investigation.

"Absolutely, do as you must." PM Jadanza nodded eagerly. "You have my endorsement. We are ill-equipped to handle this issue by ourselves."

*

After hours of attempts to decipher the letter, Vicente decided to send the message despite the darkness. With no one on the streets to ask for directions, he still managed to find the tower where the ravens perched. A thick band of stars arced across the sky, and the birds were all sleeping. He hesitated to wake them. Birds like these were expensive, and Llyr's economy wasn't great. He could argue Eloy had given him permission to send one, but if anything were to happen to the bird en route, he could get himself and Marcia in big trouble.

"Trading secrets or something?"

The sudden voice startled Vicente and his pulse pounded in his ears as he turned to face Iver, standing on top of the parapet. "Would you kindly stop sneaking up on me?"

Iver nocked an arrow, pointed it towards the dark void where the forest lay, and let it loose. "I was here first. Why are you up?"

"I needed to send a message. How about you; early bird?"

Iver looked him up and down, like Vicente had offended him. "What's it to you?"

Vicente scoffed and shook his head, suddenly aware of how tired he truly was. "Just making conversation." Below the tower, Llyr slept silently, save for the occasional bark of a dog echoing through the streets at irregular intervals.

Iver 'tsk'-ed before turning back to face the darkness beyond. Then, he surprised Vicente by offering a response. "Late, rather." He nocked another arrow, drawing the string taught. He kept both eyes open as he let it loose. When he focused, his face looked too severe for his age.

"So instead of going to sleep at a reasonable hour, you decided to waste arrows?"

"I'm practicing, you thick fuck."

Vicente stepped closer to the battlement, peeking through the regularly spaced openings to get a better view of the forest below. Indeed, Iver was firing at—and hitting—a small tree stump. "Remarkable," he breathed.

"Suck my dick," Iver replied automatically. Then he shut his mouth, like he just then realized Vicente had paid him a complement. When he spoke again, Vicente could tell he was making a deliberate effort to limit his usual tone of resentment. "With the rifle, I could hit something double the distance away."

Did he just brag? It was almost endearing, in an off-putting and unsettling kind of way. Maybe the correct term would be 'humanizing,' or even 'embarrassing.'

Vicente decided to repay the favor and refrained from addressing that first part of Iver's statement, to keep this rare conversation civil. "Then, why aren't you using that?"

"Bullets are expensive."

"Could I try it? The bow, I mean." The words just slipped out of Vicente's mouth before he could stop them. He braced for the incoming retaliation.

But Iver didn't unleash a tirade of insults; instead, he said, "I'll let you, if you show me how your mystic powers work."

For a moment, he wanted to. He was proud of what he could do. But he had been ordered to abstain from using them at this job. Besides, Iver couldn't be allowed to know Vicente wasn't a real threat. "I'm sorry, but I can't do that. Queen Leandra would find out."

"Hm. You want to please her, yeah?"

"You speak as if you know me." Iver was right, though. The High Council wished for Vicente and the quorum to fail, and the queen defended them when she could. Despite planning to remove himself from the power struggle and dick-measuring-contest between her, the quorum, and the High Council, Vicente still wanted to be on her good side and maintain a working relationship with her.

Iver threw him a guarded look. "I know people like you. You're all the same."

"Is that so?"

"Humans are extraordinary bad at making up new shit. We always follow patterns. I just happen to be good at spotting them."

"Sounds like you're very clever, Iver. Maybe you should've pursued academia instead of murder."

Iver kept giving Vicente these shifty, wary little looks from beneath his lashes. "Being excellent at math doesn't help you if you can't even afford food."

"You—" Vicente had to take a breath to stifle his laughter. Even he, who had been the best in his cohort at university—his statistics professor had called him a 'prodigy'—would never describe himself as 'excellent' in math. "You're saying you're good at math? At seeing patterns?"

"Yeah." Iver sniffed, shrugged his shoulders. "Used to be, at least."

"Could you decrypt something like this?"

Vicente handed him the letter. Iver didn't realize he was teasing him, and Vicente was starting to feel bad, was beginning to feel a twist of guilt. Just a little one, though.

Iver looked it over. "I need some paper to write on, but sure. Looks like a shifting cypher."

"What?" Vicente had gotten ready to mock him, but the feeling died instantly. "What does that mean?"

"The letters have been shifted forwards or backwards in the alphabet." When Vicente only gawped at him, he elaborated. "See this three-letter word that is reoccurring, 'sgf'? That's probably a 'the', which is the most common word in correspondence. The consonants have been shifted to the letter before it in the alphabet, and the vowels to the letters after. If this is true, then this, 'bs,' really means 'at,' which—"

"You are amazing." Vicente felt bad. Merciful, did he feel bad. "Please, come with me. I need your help."

Iver followed without hesitation. They made their way to the town hall in the rock-cut, urban core of Llyr. It was there the handiwork of Llyr's founders was most pronounced, as buildings seamlessly merged with their stone-carved façades in the cliff. The stairs were long and winding, and they too had been sliced into the rock.

"I'm not allowed inside the archives," Iver reminded him as they reached the door to the cellar.

"No one will find out." Vicente opened the door for him, and with some reluctance, Iver followed. Vicente locked the door behind them. If they hurried, they might finish the decoding before anyone else woke up. "You should know what a privilege this is. As a child, I begged a guard to let me inside, but he wouldn't allow it."

Iver's eyes scanned the bookshelves. "You're from here," he said, a mix between a statement and a question. "I wouldn't have pegged you for a hick."

Vicente cleared the table and laid out the different letters. "I left Llyr quite young and grew up in the capital."

"Your parents didn't love you or something?"

Annoyance prickled Vicente's skin and he pressed his teeth against a sigh, but ultimately decided not to pick a fight; he already knew where that would take them. "I was a rowdy kid. My mother believed I needed an exorcism, so the holy sisters here contacted their counterparts in the capital. The women of the Sensis Quorum intercepted the correspondence and came to my aid, pretending to be high priestesses and vowing to straighten me out. Instead, they made me more of a heathen by teaching me mysticism."

"Exorcism? You were that much of a shit?"

Vicente blinked back the venom. *Don't fall for it.* "I was... not treated kindly. I acted out quite a bit."

He could tell by the look on Iver's face that he wanted to provide a snide remark, but he ultimately kept his mouth shut. Perhaps he didn't know what to do with himself when someone didn't rise to swallow his bait.

Vicente sat down with a stack of blank sheets of paper. The task was daunting. He counted fifty-three letters that needed to be translated. He began writing down the alphabet. "A shifting pattern, you said. Consonants to the letter before, vowels to the one after."

Iver must have realized what Vicente planned on doing for the next hour, but still didn't leave. He sat awkwardly on the edge of his chair, like he was unsure of the space he was allowed to occupy. "Because the alphabet begins with a vowel and ends with a consonant. So that idiots who have to write down the alphabet in order to remember it won't get confused if they try to move the last letter forwards, or the first one backwards."

Idiot? The word drove into Vicente's pride like a thorn. He took a calming breath, but it was a long time before his brain actually picked up the words on the page he was staring at. *Idiot.* The thorn wormed its way deeper each time he thought about it.

He worked in silence. The first light of dawn spilled through the slim windows by the ceiling. As he decrypted the twenty-first letter, he found what he was looking for. "Listen to this:

Four men were lost in the battle near the ruins of Tal Llyrie, six more wounded. We claim victory. Lord Dimitrios Cronin bargained for the life of his family; this was granted. Lord Dimitrios Cronin bargained for his land; this was rejected. Glory for those that ride with Dominus Estra."

Iver, who had abandoned his seat after five minutes and had been pacing around for the last hour or so, leaned over his shoulder to get a closer look. "Who wrote that?"

The warmth of Iver's breath on the shell of his ear raised goosebumps on his arms. He was so close Vicente could smell him: citrusy soap and warm skin. It was quite lovely. Vicente cleared his throat. "Estra was the leader of the mountain clans a hundred years or so ago; this was written by the raiders at the time."

"Why are these letters here?"

"They intended to make Llyr their next settlement, before the Bruvran Company drove them off." Vicente turned to face Iver, which thankfully caused him to take a step back. "This means the land belonged to the Cronin clan. Ottone has the stronger claim."

"That just made your job a lot easier."

"Unfortunately, it doesn't. Queen Leandra wishes to see Lord Eloy Errani appointed owner of the land. We cannot tell a soul about this until I've consulted with Marcia."

Iver cocked an eyebrow. "Perhaps I'll tell everyone about this; ruin your life."

There was something else in Iver's tone then, and suddenly, Vicente realized he was joking with him. "Perhaps I'll wrestle you to the ground again, before you get the chance."

"You'd have to trick me into surrendering first, and I won't fall for that a second time."

Vicente looked him up and down, pinching his eyebrows in contemplation. "I could probably take you on in a fair fight."

Iver physically recoiled from his gaze. "Listen here, bookworm, you don't know how to fight. Using magic isn't the same as fighting."

Vicente knew he was wasting precious time during which he could be bringing his findings to Marcia, but the conversation was interesting. He found himself warming up to Iver's odd sort of sarcasm and his filthy, irreverent language. "Sounds to me like you're very eager to prove your point—"

Someone pulled on the door from the outside, but it didn't budge. Vicente heard the jangling of keys.

Iver mouthed, *Marcia?*

Vicente shook his head and held up the key; they had only been given one.

He pocketed the translated letters. From the pouch hanging from his belt, he took two sender potions and handed one of them to Iver. Iver's eyes went wide. Vicente drank the contents of his vial, urging Iver to do the same. Iver drew a breath, then drank it.

Vicente grabbed his hands, forming an electric circuit through their bodies. This would allow him to bring Iver with him as he teleported. He invoked the tunnel to open, and they appeared in his room where he had his stash of receiver potions.

Iver gasped as if arising from underwater, then looked around in wonderment. "Fuck me. What the fuck did you do?"

Vicente shut his eyes, reveling in the afterglow that only he could feel. Euphoria crept in, slow and viscous like honey, filling all the crevices of his mind, righting all the wrongs to ever have existed in his thoughts, be that imaginary or perceived. It coated every nerve, every inch of his skin. He felt it in the seams of his closed eyelids, like hot water when sinking below the surface in a bath.

Vicente shouldn't have been using his powers in the first place, but he'd had no choice: Iver wasn't allowed inside the archives, and Vicente could be punished for having let him in. But still, disappointment with himself took root deep within: he had made a promise to the queen, and he broke it without a second thought.

There was a knock at the door and Vicente went to open it, leaving Iver to get his bearings and process what had just transpired.

Marcia stood outside the door to his room. She folded her arms over her chest. "Vicente, did you go to the bird tower last night?"

"I did. Why?"

She shifted her weight from one leg to the other. "Something happened."

*

When Marcia, Vicente and Iver met up with PM Jadanza, the tower he and Iver left mere hours ago was now a crime scene. Slick, black feathers in pools of darkened blood covered the stone floor. Vicente had never realized how much blood was in a raven; they were always so light, despite their size.

"It's going to take months before new birds are fully trained." There was a sheen of sweat on PM Jadanza's face, and he took a handkerchief from his pocket to dab at his forehead. "People are worried enough as it is, I don't want to add any fuel to this fire. I'll say the birds all fell ill, and if you could keep this to yourselves…"

"Of course, father," Marcia said.

Vicente turned to PM Jadanza and swayed a little, still high from travelling through the tunnel. "We'll try our best to find this animal abuser, I promise you." He regretted saying it the moment the words left his lips. Using his powers always made him feel confident, sometimes too much so.

Marcia shot him a disapproving look. She offered her condolences to PM Jadanza and then dragged Vicente out of there. They hurried down the stairs and went back outside.

"Poor birds," Iver muttered under his breath.

This had disconnected them from the capital: now, they couldn't reach Tal Miril, which put them in an even more sensitive situation. Vicente wasn't worried, not yet. But why would someone kill all the courier birds? Obviously it was to cut communication, but why? Did it have anything to do with their investigation or had this something to do with the murder? Something was brewing beneath the surface, and he wanted to know what.

Marcia finally let go of his arm. "Would you stop trying to get involved with issues that are not ours to solve? You're acting weird—have you just opened a tunnel?"

"Why would anyone want to sever Llyr's contact with the outside world?" Vicente asked, choosing to ignore her question.

It was the wrong choice.

Marcia grabbed him again, stopped dead in her tracks and fixed him with a stare. "Vicente Lamor, look at me. Have you been using Stormwater?"

Her eyes were huge. Dread coiled in his stomach. Even in his addled, drunken state, he felt the fear of her impending castigation pressing down on him, tightening his chest. She was his friend, but she was also his boss.

He steeled himself and met her eyes. "I was ordered not to. I would never break that promise, Marcia. I've been working all night, I'm exhausted and that's why I messed up a little back there and I'm sorry. It won't happen again, I swear it."

Her gaze searched his face. The tension across her shoulders eased. "Alright."

Vicente held back the irremediable need to smile. He was too good at hiding that he was high, always had been. He had never lied to Marcia before, and wouldn't make it a habit, but this time it was necessary. He couldn't let it slip that he had allowed Iver into the archives. "Now, I'd like to know what you think."

Marcia threw a furtive glance back at the tower and lowered her voice. "I think whoever killed that little girl wants to stop us from reaching out to the police in the capital. I told Lord Ottone and my father I'd be contacting Arkensaal about it just yesterday. Either it was one of them, or they unknowingly informed the killer. Now, would you please drop it? Maybe this is a sign we should be focusing on our mission."

*

As they ate dinner, Vicente recounted what he had found after decoding the letter. The inn's dining hall was sparsely populated, but they kept their voices low just in case. Marcia was unhappy with the news but agreed their job was not yet finished.

When sunlight faded to candlelight, Vicente retreated to his room, still euphoric from stepping through the tunnel. He sank onto the bed and his entire body relaxed. The sensation would pass in a few hours, and he wouldn't feel it again until he opened another tunnel. He had asked the members of the quorum many times if they ever experienced the same effects, but they always said no. Perhaps this was something unique to the Stag.

He felt sorry for them, missing out on what was, by all accounts, the greatest feeling in the world. It was a softness under his skin, like a warm silk blanket, softer than anything he had ever encountered in real life, enveloping him just beneath the surface. It was a level of comfort he'd never known before Stormwater. Everything was alright, everything was peaceful. His problems felt distant, and those that mattered were manageable. And the best part? His mind was completely quiet.

There was a knock at the door. Vicente unlocked it and, to his surprise, found Iver on the other side. Iver only stuck around when he was forced to do so and left the crew at every opportunity. Iver coming to Vicente was odd.

"Is this a bad time?" Iver asked, keeping his gaze averted.

"A bad time for what?"

Iver shook his head absentmindedly, still speaking more to the doorframe than to Vicente. "I just... need to talk to you."

Vicente swung the door open and stepped back to let Iver inside, staggering a little as he did: the pleasant emptiness in his body made him feel weightless, and he tried to move his legs faster than the laws of physics allowed him.

Iver closed the door behind him and, to Vicente's disbelief, turned the key. The sound of the lock was cacophonous in the silence of the room. Drawing a deep breath, Iver leaned his back against the door. He appeared to be unarmed. The holster on his thigh was empty. His hair was damp, like he'd just bathed, and he avoided looking Vicente in the eye.

Vicente stepped forward again. "Unlock the door." Worry spoke to him as a distant echo, muffled by the pleasant honey-like substance in his brain.

"I promise, you want it locked for this."

"I doubt it." Vicente was in front of him then, Iver at least a head shorter than him.

Iver finally looked up at him through his eyelashes. He lifted his hands to his own chest and undid the top button of his shirt. His fingers were shaking slightly.

Vicente's heart raced. He watched in a semi-lucid rapture as Iver undid a second button, then a third. Then his hands rose to Vicente's collar, and he pulled him down, pressing their lips together. It was an innocent kiss, perfunctory in its execution. Their faces remained only an inch from each other, so close he could see Iver's pupils dilate.

"Why'd you stop unbuttoning your shirt?" Vicente asked. *What am I doing?* This was all too out of character, but it intrigued him: he wanted to know where this was going. Besides, he was already teetering on the brink of his own sanity.

"I thought you'd want to do it," Iver said, voice wavering.

Something in Vicente's stomach flipped over at the suggestion. He began undoing the other buttons but got distracted when Iver leaned his head back with a thud, exposing his throat. Vicente traced kisses down the column of his neck, caressed the skin of his lean abdomen. Vicente's hand felt big and clumsy pressed against his chest, feeling the quick rise and fall of it. Desire bled into his mind until it usurped control.

Vicente hadn't had sex since the night before they left the capital, and he had been too busy to realize just how pent up he was. It had been ages since he had slept with a man; not that he had a preference either way. He desired men, women and adults who were both or in-between all alike, as long as they were beautiful and smart. Iver was attractive—Vicente had noticed that pretty quickly—but it had taken him longer to figure out that Iver was clever.

Vicente slid Iver's shirt down over his shoulders until it fell to his elbows. He kissed Iver's collarbone, teeth scraping along the skin, head buzzing and empty, and grabbed at his crotch.

Iver's breath hitched, and he snatched Vicente's wrist, viper quick, stopping him. Vicente looked at him questioningly, ready to back off. Iver hesitated for a second before kissing him on the lips again, tentatively, like he didn't know how to.

He wants to take it slower. Vicente didn't mind. He took Iver's chin in his hand and turned his face up, then kissed him deeply, slowly. A proper kiss. The soft velvet of his tongue made Vicente's head spin. Iver was truly beautiful. His body was like parchment with swatches of black ink. Something about Iver's foul, crass nature had fascinated him, captured him, and hadn't yet let go. Perhaps if Vicente attacked his desire with urgency, he could convince himself it wouldn't result in any sort of feeling, that having sex once would settle his curiosity.

Iver pushed him off again, licking his kiss-swollen lower lip. "The bed?"

Dark exhilaration thrilled up Vicente's spine. He was getting whiplash from how Iver was acting but walked him over to the bed, ripped his own shirt off and undid his belt. No matter the risk, he was ready to do whatever Iver asked of him, determined to not let this opportunity go. He would like to try Iver—so very desperately, in fact.

"Lay down on your back, I want to ride you."

Vicente did as he was told and Iver straddled him, bent forward and kissed him again, with the same reticence that stoked Vicente's curiosity to a fever pitch. With his mind going blanker by the second, Vicente held Iver's hips and ground into him. Scowling, Iver made a dissatisfied noise and sat up again. *What does he want, exactly?*

Iver unbuckled his own belt. He reached behind himself to remove his belt from the loops of his pants. Which was strange... A knife was in his hand and he dove forward, pressing the point to Vicente's throat. "You disgusting—"

Vicente grabbed the chain around his neck and forced the quantum tunnel to open. The knife appeared in his own hand, blade in his palm, slitting the skin of his fingers.

The necklace was now in Iver's hand. He tossed it aside. "You absolute motherfucker—"

Vicente wrestled him off, pinning him to the mattress. His heart hammered and embarrassment crept over his skin. *Should've figured this was all an act.* Had he not been high, he might not have fallen for Iver's scheme. Iver must have noticed that Vicente was acting weird when they went to the bird tower, and seen it as his opportunity to strike.

Vicente threw the knife to the far side of the room. A thin trail of blood ran down his shoulder from the wound in his neck where Iver had pressed the blade. "That was quite convincing. You've done this sort of thing before? You want to ride me—I mean, really?"

Iver made a furious sound through his teeth. There was a terrible, frustrated blaze in his eyes. "I had to fucking get you when you weren't expecting it, didn't I? Mystic bastard."

"I'm surprised it took you this long to attempt getting revenge. It was overdue enough to be an insult at this point." Vicente was holding him down by his shoulders, and now he pushed down even further. Embarrassment turned to anger, spreading and catching. He hoped the wire-tension in his jaw looked like rage, not pain. "Don't do this shit again. I told you, I don't want to be forced to hurt you."

With those words, Iver stopped struggling, but glared at him like *he* wasn't the one who had tried to kill *Vicente*. "Let me go. I won't try it again."

"Now, how do I know that?" Iver might not have been as clever as Vicente had believed, then. Perhaps it was wishful thinking. If he did kill Vicente, he was unlikely to escape with his life, and that would truly be a shame. The distance at which Iver had sniped Lord Pascal was impressive. Vicente would hate to see such talent go to waste. *Just to get his revenge. Idiot.*

"You'll manage to stop me even if I do, I assume." Iver smashed his elbow to the side of Vicente's head, knocking him to the floor. He jumped over him and grabbed the knife, holding it up towards Vicente like he was afraid he might pounce on him.

Vicente propped himself up on his elbows, head pounding. "That knife listens to me now; it won't be of any use to you." That wasn't true. The teleportation of entangled objects only worked once. If he wanted to do it a second time, he'd have to do the entanglement process again.

But Iver didn't see through his lie. He dropped the knife again and left.

CHAPTER 12

Iver

From his place in the meager shade of the fig trees, Iver counted twenty-four children engaged in carefree play outside the temple. Their laughter rang through the air in a melody of mirth. To the right of the playground was a holy sister who bore a more subdued demeanor. Her golden hair swayed in the breeze as she hung bedsheets on a clothesline. A second sister came out of the temple, carrying her own basket of laundry.

Iver moved close enough to hear them speak but still stuck to the shadows. It wasn't a restricted area; he could pretend to be going to the temple for a visit. Also, the two women hadn't noticed him yet.

"Jairo wet the bed again," the blonde sister said. "That's the third time in a week."

"Maybe we should have a doctor come look at them? I mean, seven bed-wetters in a group as small as this? There must be something going around, a virus perhaps."

"They're copying each other, that's what I think."

The sister clicked her tongue. "Don't say that."

Iver moved closer. If someone was hurting the children, he wanted to know. Then, he could do something about it. Vicente and Marcia thought he was stupid, but he was the only one who seemed to notice that weird shit was going on in Llyr. If he was the only one that could save the kids, well, then he would do his duty.

"Natalina had nightmares, and now all of them do? They want attention, that's all. I just wish they wouldn't pee in their beds to get it."

The sister put her hands on her hips. "Maybe we should send a message to Arkensaal, ask for a priestess to perform an exorcism?"

The shriek of a child interrupted their conversation. In the meadow, a girl straddled over a boy, punching him in the face. She couldn't have been older than nine, yet she was beating him with the ferocity of a wild animal. Her knuckles were smeared with blood by the time one of the sisters pulled her off him.

The boy sat up, face bloody, and bawled.

"Young lady, what are you doing?" The blonde sister shook the arm of the kid in her grip. The girl stared up at her with a snarl. The look on her face, the look of a feral beast, left Iver feeling physically ill.

As the women had their backs turned to the temple, a boy appeared in the doorway and slipped out unannounced. He hurried down the pathway, passing by the orchard without spotting Iver, or being spotted by the sisters.

Iver decided to follow.

He didn't need to keep much distance; the boy never looked back. He followed him across the tan hills that rose in lazy folds, crowned with dry shrubs that looked like they were praying for death. Lizards skittered between sun-bleached rocks, and the soil crackled beneath Iver's boots; bone-dry, the kind that split if you so much as looked at it wrong. As they drew nearer Llyr, dust gave way to packed earth, then to the uneven cobbles of the outer streets, where the houses were low and fig trees leaned over stone walls. The boy didn't glance back once.

For a third time that day, Iver questioned what the fuck he was spending his time on. If everything had gone according to plan, Vicente would've been dead by now, and Iver would've been on a horse on his merry way back to the capital.

But then, someone stole what they believed was Vicente's blood from the temple. This had changed his trajectory entirely, upending his plans. Of course, he already knew Vicente was useful: the government wanted him assassinated, and powerful people wished to rid the world of other powerful people. Iver was always on the hunt for these individuals, getting a feel for them. None of them, so far, had been influential in the way he sought.

But some Llyrian had figured out that Vicente was a mystic, and if that person valued Vicente's blood enough to steal it, then they intended to channel his mystic abilities for themselves. Vicente was more valuable than Iver had first realized. This failed attempt at stealing his powers certainly wouldn't stop them from trying again. If Iver didn't secure Vicente's powers, either as a tool or in the form of an ally, then someone else would. This route was worth exploring. If it turned out to be a dead end, then he could just kill him. Because now Iver knew a little bit more about how Vicente's mysticism worked.

That was why Iver had tested him that night, when Vicente had been off his rocker. Seducing him had been uncomfortable but easy—he could tell Vicente found him attractive by the way he looked at him—and doing so had told Iver several things: opening tunnels wasn't taxing or difficult to Vicente, he reacted quickly, and even when he was drunk, horny and in danger, he kept his head about him. Vicente didn't burn bridges due to anger, not when there were more benefits left to reap. He recognized that Iver was still more valuable to him alive, and didn't kill him or tell the others about what he had tried—not very hard, but still tried— to do. There was *potential* allyship to be found in a person like that.

He trailed the boy to Ottone's apothecary. Customers crowded inside. The shopkeeper, Falco, greeted Iver before returning to unpacking boxes. Iver was good at going unnoticed, and as a couple of other patrons left the shop, Iver ascended the stairs, following the boy's path. He reached the landing and peered into the hallway of the second floor. There was one closed door on the right, and the child was gone. The other two rooms were unoccupied and used for storage. He went into the first one and retreated into its shadows.

After only a few moments, the door across the hall opened.

"The letter is of no use for me in the laboratory. Bring it here." It was Ottone's voice. "I have told all of you to deliver my messages *here*. Perhaps you ought to clean your ears?"

"Yes, m'Lord," the child said. This was followed by the sound of pitter-patter of one set of small feet running down the stairs. Iver heard the door close again. Was Ottone using the kids to run errands for him?

For a few minutes Iver remained hidden, listening. He wasn't nervous—he was made for this, after all—but this was different from the capital. The capital was home to over three million people, and Llyr to about seven thousand. There were more social gaps and crevices in Arkensaal, more people to blend in with, aiding his anonymity. But here? If anyone saw Iver doing something shady, then everyone would find out.

The door to the chamber opened again. This time, a set of heavy footsteps descended the stairs and Iver crept to the door and peeked around the corner just in time to spot the back of Ottone's head.

Iver never heard the door lock. He waited for the front door of the building to slam shut before he went across the hall to the door. He tried to open it but couldn't. The door stayed in place like it had been locked after all.

He crouched down and pulled out his lockpicks, peering at the keyhole in brass underneath the handle. He selected his tools, then slid the slender metal probes into the keyhole and began to manipulate the tumblers. But as his pick met resistance, a jolt coursed through his fingers and up his arm. It felt almost like a static shock. Was it booby trapped? As far as he knew, they didn't have electricity in Llyr.

Iver abandoned his attempt and went down two floors, to the laboratory. The door to it was wide open, which he found strange, as this was where Ottone worked. He kept the door to his office locked and rigged, but not the door to his workshop where he stored all his rare ingredients and brewed his healing potions?

The air inside the basement was thick with the scent of dried herbs. There was a single window, sitting so high up on the wall it almost touched the ceiling. He watched people's shoes pass by on the street, their movements briefly interrupting the light and causing the prismatic reflections from the glass bottles and crystal vials on the walls to flicker.

Iver investigated, eyeing each dark nook between desks and crates. There was a door, nestled in between two tall bookshelves, and it was closed. However, it wasn't locked.

Cold air welled from the room, like something in there radiated freezing temperatures. He had never experienced anything like it. It was like the opposite of standing close to a fire. He went inside, and his heart sank.

A white shroud covered what looked to be a small body lying on the marble slab. He had seen corpses before, but they always announced themselves, there was always the smell of them before the sight of them reached his eyes. But not this time, the air bore no stench of death. He hadn't expected to find a dead person. This felt unfair. He wasn't ready.

Lockers lined each wall of the cold room. They were all closed. Just to the side of him, next to the door, was a cluttered table, as well as a chair with a knitted sweater draped over the backrest of it. The raised stone slab sat in the center of the room. He couldn't pick up any smells at all, and there was nothing in there that could logically explain why it was so cold.

After a few shaky breaths, Iver's feet unstuck from the floor. He ignored the way his heart pounded, ignored the way the hair on the back of his neck stood on end, and walked closer. His breath formed a visible mist. He pulled the sheet back from the body's head.

It was Natalina. She hadn't been burned yet. It had been fifteen days since her passing, and they had not yet cremated her. The low temperature in the room must have slowed down the decomposition significantly, because she didn't look too different from when she had been found. There were only subtle changes.

Her skin had marbled, the lace-like veins in her face had darkened and her cheeks bore a gray, greenish tinge. There was something underneath her eyelids. Something hard, flat and circular. Iver held his breath as a shiver slid down his shoulders. *I'm sorry.* He put his thumb on her paper thin, ice-cold eyelid and pried it open. *I'm trying to help you.* A coin. A copper coin had been placed under her eyelid; it was sitting on top of her sunken, cloudy eyeball. He could only assume the situation was the same in the other eye.

"What are you doing?"

Iver's chest seized up. He hadn't even heard the footsteps, but he only had himself to blame for that. This was too much for him, and it was starting to show.

Ottone was standing in the doorway, waiting for a response. He didn't look happy.

Iver pushed her eyelid back down over the coin. "Sorry. I just…"

"I suppose it looks strange to you." Ottone strode inside and stood on the other side of the body. "We do things a bit differently around here."

"What will happen to the coins when she's on the pyre?"

"We don't cremate our dead in Llyr, we bury them in the earth." He looked down at the child. Gently, he brushed a knuckle over her hair. "From earth we are born, to earth we shall return. As Llyr's chemist, it has fallen on me to prepare them for their final journey."

It did look strange to Iver. The Merciful Eldvittra, the god of war, demanded they should all be returned to the flames. But maybe it wasn't that suspicious. Eldvittra also decreed that everyone fight, and hardly *everyone* did. The precepts were strict, but they were observed with a certain leniency. "What are the coins for?"

"Why do Arkensaali people put flowers around the funeral pyres?"

"You're saying it's for decoration?"

Ottone nodded. "I use special herbs to preserve the bodies for a while, to give the family some time to grieve. We normally don't wait this long, but I've been asked to keep her like this to aid with the ongoing investigation." He looked at the girl again. "The people I take care of usually aren't this young."

What a strange thing to say. Ottone kept explaining why the body was here, even though Iver wasn't questioning it. It was suspicious how hard he tried to not appear suspicious. "Was she too running errands for you?"

Ottone smiled at him. One of those strained, joyless smiles. "We have our own ways here in Llyr. We might not have universities here, or noble clans for the less fortunate to marry into, but that does not mean our lives are unimportant. We work the earth, we feed ourselves, we take care of each other. I teach the children to serve their community, which is all that matters. I don't expect you to understand. You are individualists in the capital. You believe everything is within your control, and yours for the taking."

"So, what shapes our lives then, if not ambition or choice?" Iver asked. He had gotten a read on Ottone already: he was the preachy kind, an old man who thought he was smarter than everyone else, and saw it has his duty to lecture the stupid.

Ottone sighed, his eyes fixed on Natalina's body as if speaking to her, not Iver. "Ultimately, it is the whims of fate that decide. You people in the capital, you think everything can be mastered, held tight in the palm of your hand if you're clever enough, strong enough. But life isn't so orderly. No, life's a storm, a whirlpool dragging you under and spitting you out where you least expect it. We don't get to choose the currents. All we can do is learn to ride it, to harness what fate offers us, and make our peace with it. We've seen the tides turn too often, watched as the earth takes and gives without reason. It is everywhere you look: when it rains, who gets sick, which younglings fall in love, which pregnancy results in a miscarriage or in a new life, who lives, who dies. It's all chance, it's all random, it's all a…"

…coin toss. The pit in Iver's stomach expanded.

"…a stroke of luck, good or bad," Ottone concluded.

Iver shuddered. He hadn't noticed how cold he was getting. "You have given me a lot to think about, Lord Ottone. I have to get back to my crew, but… thank you."

"Any time, Iver." His smile was all sweetness and superiority, polished to a gleam and utterly insincere. "*Mister* Iver, I should say. Forgive me, you just look so young."

Iver made a hasty exit. He had seen enough. The static-shock-door, the freezing room, the die crafted from human bone, the abnormal burial practice, the coins, the proselytizing. Ottone was dabbling in the occult.

CHAPTER 13

Vicente

"He'd gone completely white, couldn't stand up so he was just lying there in the grass, and the blood was gushing—"

"—Alright!" Vicente squeezed his eyes shut against the onslaught of vile imagery. Daiyu had an eye for detail, and it served to everyone's detriment. The odor in the stable, the cigarette in his mouth and the nicotine already in his system—on an empty stomach, no less—didn't help with his brewing nausea.

Daiyu had this half-crazed look in her eyes, and she sounded far from concerned. "It looked ready to fall off. I swear, I could see bone—"

"Spare the fucking details," Iver snapped. He was listening with a bored expression on his face, the one he typically wore when he wasn't simmering with anger, but he did look a bit paler than usual. "For fuck's sake."

Daiyu continued telling the story: "I was carrying a bag-full of potions, because Ottone never knows how many it's going to take. Poor farmer couldn't sit up, so we poured it down his throat. Three doses in: his foot is back to normal. Can you believe it?"

If Vicente hadn't seen firsthand the healing potions working, he wouldn't have believed it. It shouldn't have been possible. Yet, it somehow was.

The stable floor had smatterings of bird poop everywhere, and when he looked up at the rafters above, he spotted multiple bird nests. *That explains that.* As much as he wanted to skedaddle, Marcia was supposed to arrive any minute now.

Iver was standing in the archway to the stable, leaning against it with one shoulder. Daiyu had invited him, and even though Vicente didn't want him there, he couldn't refuse him without giving her a reason—and he was not about to tell her what had happened between him and Iver the other day.

"Well, his foot wasn't *completely* back to normal," Daiyu continued. "He had scars where the plow had sliced him. It looked like an injury six months into the healing process. I wanted to take a sample of the scar tissue, but they told me it was an *inappropriate request*."

Vicente snorted. After all, Daiyu was a scientist, always acquiring data, no matter the tactful or social ramifications.

"I can't imagine why," Iver said. He threw Vicente a look.

Vicente immediately averted his gaze. If things were tense before, that was nothing in comparison to now. He would prefer to forget about their intimate encounter entirely, would like to forget about the soft heat of Iver's mouth, his weight on top of him, about the sensual way Iver had tipped his head back—Vicente jerked himself away from the intrusive memory. *Stop that.*

Iver squinted into the afternoon sun. "Here she comes."

Marcia was walking briskly across the market square, threading her way through the slow-moving crowd. She looked deeply unhappy.

Bracing himself for the worst, Vicente took the cigarette from his lips and handed it to her. "What's the verdict?"

Marcia accepted it and took a drag. "My father put in an order for new ravens, and like he suspected, it's going to take them *months* to train them."

"Well." Daiyu sighed. "That's it, then."

They were in desperate need of guidance from Arkensaal. The land appeared to have belonged to Ottone's clan in the past, but the queen's orders had been clear: grant it to Eloy's clan. Before they let anyone in Llyr know what they had found, they needed to consult with the High Council of Arkensaal.

They had concluded that Daiyu should be the one to go to the capital with the news and ask for advice. If she could return with some ravens or pigeons, they would be able to establish a line of communication to Arkensaal. If not, then she had a few of Vicente's receiver potions of Stormwater tucked in her bag, and they could send messages that way. Vicente was grateful Daiyu had volunteered; he needed Marcia here. Marcia was the one least excited about this: it would take Daiyu two weeks to make the journey.

With a smile on her lips, Daiyu sat up on her horse. "I'll be quick, I promise."

"Be safe," Vicente said. Having Daiyu travel by herself was too dangerous, so instead she would be accompanying a group of farmers part of the way as they made their deliveries to Mariemoor. The arrangement did little to settle his nerves.

They stepped out into the sun together, then Marcia led Daiyu on her horse through the market square towards the road. Could she handle it if they ran into robbers? This was a bad idea, but they needed to be able to communicate with Arkensaal and Tal Miril.

Above him, a whistling duck landed in the water in one of the aqueducts, causing some of it to spill over and splash onto the ground. They had been in Llyr for no more than twenty days, and they were already sending someone home. But the queen must understand that they couldn't operate under these conditions. Marcia was her most trusted diplomat, she wouldn't veer from the plan without a reason or a shift in circumstances that left no other choice. The queen couldn't castigate them for that.

"Vicente." Iver nodded towards the other side of the market.

PM Jadanza was waving his hands, stopping Daiyu from crossing the bridge leading out of Llyr.

"Damnit." Vicente jogged over to them, and Iver followed.

PM Jadanza wore a pained smile, all teeth and breath. "Ah, Ambassador Vicente, I was just telling Professor Daiyu that, sadly, I can't let her leave."

"And why is that? My Lord," Vicente tacked on, a second too late.

"The three of you are under investigation and will not be allowed to leave Llyr for the time being. Perhaps Iver should go in your stead, Daiyu?" PM Jadanza suggested. He was wringing his hands, looking so flustered Vicente felt an inexplicable urge to grovel. He wouldn't, though.

"Under investigation for what; the murder?" Vicente asked. Why was it only them, and not Iver? By all accounts, Iver should've been their prime suspect. He was the mercenary. The dangerous one. Even the way he carried himself and looked at others spoke of the violence he was capable of.

"Would you mind explaining why that is?" Marcia asked, calm as ever.

PM Jadanza waved his hand, like he hadn't just offended all of them. "No need to worry; most who were in town during the crime is a suspect. So are you, Mister Iver, but we do deem you more likely to return. Seeing as you are a mercenary and not yet paid and all…" he said, trailing off.

Vicente didn't buy that excuse: as far as PM Jadanza knew, Iver could make a living anywhere in the realm. It didn't make any sense. Did they really think they could stop them from leaving? And with no tangible evidence, no less.

Marcia placed a hand on Vicente's elbow, as if she could tell he was going to start arguing. "Thank you, father. We'll stay put."

Daiyu climbed down from her horse as PM Jadanza left them. Her smile was gone. "Could I sneak out during the night?"

Marcia's gaze traced the PM's departure. "We're complying with their wishes."

There was another reason Vicente needed to talk to the capital: his search for the Stag. He didn't want to mention it in nervous times like these, but Marcia knew about it, of course, and Daiyu and Iver were aware of it. But without birds, he wouldn't be able to continue his quest: the quorum never taught him *how* to bond with the Stag. "We need to—"

"Don't argue with me on this, Vic. This is still a diplomatic mission, and we are not here to cause a ruckus or make enemies. We'll make do without Queen Leandra's assistance."

Vicente stepped in front of her, stopping her from walking away. "They're prepared to let Iver leave, of all people. Our supposed protector."

Alarm bells were going off in Vicente's mind. Putting them in a position where Iver was the only one allowed to leave was basically an encouragement to have him do so. Even though Iver was the violent and suspicious one in their crew, the prime minister was in support of him leaving.

"You think we're in danger?" Marcia asked.

"It's a possibility." Vicente had seen no other threats directed at his crew, but he couldn't shake the feeling.

Or... maybe he had. Maybe it wasn't Iver who had stolen his vial of blood, after all.

"Let's go somewhere more private to talk," Marcia suggested.

They untacked and stabled Daiyu's horse before venturing out onto the hills sprawling just behind the Sunfire Rest. Continuous cicada song serenaded their journey through the yellow grass, so tall it reached Vicente's waist. With no shade in sight, the temperatures soon had his clothes glued to his skin. A warm breeze dragged itself over the field and left nothing cooler in its wake.

"I don't want to dismiss your concerns or minimize your feelings," Marcia said, glancing over at him as they walked. "But I think you might be worrying over nothing. You've got this instinct for picking up on danger, which I know makes it hard to relax. If you say it's a possibility, then we'll be cautious, but we won't jump to conclusions."

"Should we really be here for this?" Daiyu said, gesturing to herself and Iver.

"Yes, this applies to all of us: we're a team," Marcia insisted. "These jobs can be difficult at times, but I don't want you to be frightened. You must remember that, during missions, we are agents of the crown, and we are under the queen's direct protection—"

"We're a team?" Iver interjected. "Sure doesn't feel like it."

This absolute bastard. Vicente couldn't believe it. *Iver* had tried to kill *him*, not the other way around. Was he teasing him? Not only had he figured out that Vicente couldn't tell the others about it, but he was rubbing it in his face too. Vicente shoved his hands into his pockets to hide that he was clenching them into tight fists.

He refused to tell Marcia and Daiyu about Iver's attempt on his life, because if he did, he would also have to admit he had opened a tunnel and was high when it happened. Aside from the mystics of the quorum, Marcia was the only one who knew about the effects Stormwater had on him—and she hated it. She couldn't understand that it was worth the risks. Though she had no qualms about scolding him for being too paranoid, she despised the way he acted when all his worries melted away.

"I'm sorry I've made you feel that way, Iver," Marcia said. "I wanted to keep you at arm's length given your background, but I must trust in the queen's judgement. She decided to send you with us, and you are a vital part of this crew. I will do a better job at making you feel included and appreciated."

An unguarded look flashed across Iver's face: his eyebrows lifted, and his lips parted as though he was about to say something. The vulnerability was only there for a second before he quickly dropped his gaze to his feet in an attempt to hide it.

"Now, if everyone is feeling safe and not in danger," Marcia said, voice getting a little sterner, "let's talk strategy. We won't receive any guidance from Arkensaal. We'll keep our archive-findings to ourselves and let the Llyrians vote."

"They might vote for Ottone, and then the High Council will be very unhappy with us, Marcia," Vicente said.

"Can't you just lie and tell them you found evidence that the Errani clan owned the land?" Daiyu suggested.

"They would want to see proof of that," Marcia said. "We have searched through everything in the archives and the only thing of value was a letter suggesting the land might've belonged to Ottone's clan before the siege. With a vote, we still have a chance of it going our way."

Vicente remembered what he had told the blacksmith but agreed that this was the best option. "If we're going to stop Ottone from getting the land, we need to figure out who everyone will be voting for and sway them if needs be." To give the capital what they wanted, Vicente and Marcia would have to manipulate the key players in Llyr to see the benefits of giving the land to Eloy.

"You could trash Ottone's reputation," Iver offered with a shrug.

Vicente didn't want Iver's insane input, but he did his best to keep his true feelings far from his face. "That's not what I had in mind."

"It's not a terrible idea," Marcia said kindly, shielding her eyes as she looked toward the west. The sun was beginning its descent, setting the hills aglow in rust and gold.

"Honestly, that would probably be the way to go," Daiyu said. "Ottone is a pillar in his community, you'd have to build Eloy really tall to outshine him. But trashing Ottone could be easy, he is a very strange person once you get him talking…" She lapsed into silence, her voice fading into the hum of cicadas and the hush of the settling evening. It was always staggering when she aborted a rant of her own volition.

She had been working with him for a couple of days; if anyone had dirt on Ottone, it would be her.

"Anything you've noticed, Daiyu?" Marcia coaxed.

Daiyu stayed quiet for a few seconds. "The healing potions he gives to patients… they're always sealed. With wax."

"What's the significance of that?" Vicente asked.

"It strikes me as odd, is all. He didn't use any component that would oxidize or be altered by being in contact with air, in any way. Why seal them? It was all boiled, put in sterile vials, the natural preservative of the honey… but why seal the lid with wax? I've never actually seen him seal them, which means the liquid has all cooled down by the time he does it, which messes up the whole process of creating an airtight environment—"

"To prolong their shelf-life, maybe?" Vicente interjected.

"Did you hear what I just said? It can't possibly be for the purpose of preservation. It has to be something else. Ottone has also never shown me the entire procedure from concoction to finished product. I've seen him brew, and I've seen him give potions that heal a person, but never straight out of the beaker, you know?"

Iver held up a hand. "I don't get it; you don't think he's brewing the potions when he's with you?"

"There might be a secret ingredient needed, one he doesn't want me to know about," Daiyu said. "I mean, there must be. Some sort of newly discovered plant or new technology. The ones we use aren't even that rare. Now that I think about it, he's just mixing herbs and spices. We're basically making tea in there."

Iver frowned and looked her up and down. "You're a scientist and it took you this long to notice that he's brewing tea?"

A blush spread across Daiyu's cheeks. "I put it together eventually, didn't I? Look, that man can *talk*, and I have been a bit too focused on what happens after the patient drinks it."

For once, Vicente agreed with Iver. "I'm sorry, Daiyu," he said, "it's just a little shocking—"

"No, no, I love this. I love looking like an idiot."

Vicente fought to keep his frustration in check. He had trusted Daiyu to uncover the secret behind the potions, but all along, she had been kept in the dark and hadn't even realized it.

"We need to figure out what Ottone's doing," Marcia said. "We all agree on that."

For a few moments, they all stood in silence, watching as the red sun sunk behind the lonesome cypresses in the distance.

"I'll go," Iver offered. "Spy on Ottone a bit. I can stay hidden, just observe."

Marcia shook her head. "You shouldn't go alone. You might not understand whatever you uncover."

"I'm not dumb, asshole," he snapped.

"I didn't say you were, Iver. *I* shouldn't go. I wouldn't make sense of it either. Vicente should go with you."

"Wouldn't it be better if Daiyu tagged along?" Vicente doubted Iver would try to kill him again so soon, as he knew Vicente would see it coming. But that didn't mean Vicente was about to give Iver another opportunity.

"Let's not forget ourselves," Marcia said. "She's here for fun, the rest of us are here to work. You have some basic-level knowledge about chemistry; that should be enough to at least have you remember the important parts of what you see. It's best if you go, Vic."

Four years ago

The capital bloomed with spring, budding flowers saturated the air with their scent and Vicente could hear the hum of activity from the bustling streets of the capital's center all the way from Tal Miril. He walked across the university quad, his satchel slung over one shoulder, beside Nari.

"Did you read about the landslide in Elath?" she asked.

"I have a plan." From his mentor, Marcia, Vicente had gotten the details of the event, and he had formed a strategy he was sure was going to work. He was going to save everyone in Elath: those trapped beneath rubble and those caged inside because of the damaged roads.

Spring was his favorite season. The lawn had just been cut and it smelled wonderful, though he could go without the mush of freshly cut grass sticking to his shoes. Despite that, small clusters of students dotted the quad, buzzing with academic vanity and overconfident minds. A flock of yellow ring-necked parakeets nested noisily in the crown of a flowering elm, their screeches more learned than most of the debates happening below.

Nari rolled her eyes but kept a playful smirk. "Such a hero."

"Of course," Vicente replied. "Next, I'll develop a way to use my tunneling ability to get water for irrigation to farmlands. Who knows, maybe even create a system to scatter fertilizers more efficiently. No one will go hungry when I'm done." He could be open about his mystic powers to his peers: no one would hurt him, no one would dare to steal from the Sensis Quorum. He was the quorum's future, and everyone knew that.

They passed under a couple of flowering cherry trees, and their petals drifted down like snow. "Always so optimistic."

Vicente grinned. "You don't think I could do it?"

"It's not about whether you could do it," Nari said thoughtfully. "I don't think the problem is that there isn't enough food in this country. There's plenty to go around. Greedy people just don't want to share."

He stopped and turned to face her, his brows knitting together. "That's crazy talk."

She laughed, the sound light and carefree, and tugged on the front of his jacket to pull him closer.

Vicente kissed her and the world fell away for a moment.

When they broke apart, her smile lingered, her fingers still clutching the fabric. "Same time tomorrow?"

"See you then."

Vicente and Nari parted ways, and he went to his home with the quorum in the Arkensaali palace.

The Sensis Quorum resided within the palace complex, their quarters as imposing as they were isolated. Silence greeted Vicente as he entered through the doors.

Six shallow pools dominated the hall. Before each pool stood a member of the quorum. The sisters all carried themselves the same way: their postures were rigid, like they were afraid to bend, to not stand tall for even a second. Their eyes fixed on the water, which rippled with the energy of their scrying.

Vicente boots echoed against the tiles as he approached the nearest pool. None of the mystics acknowledged him. Their focus was absolute, their gazes locked on the shifting images forming in the pools. Of course, Vicente couldn't see them, but once they had told him what they saw.

He sank into one of the chairs, his gaze flitting between the mystics. This was their work, their constant vigilance: gathering information, spying from a distance.

Indra spoke, her voice low and gravelly. "The shipments from Rinkai are delayed again. If they don't arrive within the week, we'll be in a worse position than anticipated."

Another mystic, a woman named Elira, responded without looking up. "The delay is deliberate. The Rinkaians are testing our patience. They think they can gain leverage."

Vicente's brow furrowed. They were always discussing leverage: who had it, who didn't, and how to tip the scales. It was exhausting.

"Anything new on Elath?" Vicente asked.

A few of them glanced his way, brief and sharp, before turning back to their pools. It was Elira who answered, her tone clipped. "Nothing we didn't already suspect. The landslide has caused utter devastation."

Vicente's stomach tightened. "How many dead?"

Indra's raised her hand to silence him. "Enough questions. You're here to observe, not to pry."

The reprimand stung, but Vicente said nothing. His optimism felt distant here, smothered by their cold efficiency. He was exhausted by all the red tape, but for now he would watch, listen, and wait.

Indra tore her attention from the pool. She rolled her shoulders, stretched her neck. The sisters were all hundreds of years old, but apparently, they could still get sore muscles if they worked too hard.

"What is Arkensaal's plan for the disaster?" Vicente asked.

"If it has not yet happened, then we cannot see it."

"Not very useful, then."

"We can see back one millisecond, or as far back as prehistoric times. Anything in the realm of history, anything that dwells in the past, we can—"

"Alright, I get it."

"You should be studying, Vicente," she said. "If you want to know what will happen in the future, then you need to be ready to bond with the Stag once opportunity arises."

"And when I find it, then what do I do?" For years now, Vicente had studied the laws of the Stag, in books only a mystic could see the text in. Bonding with the Stag, like the quorum had done with the Otter, was a necessity—but they refused to reveal how to do it.

Indra didn't budge. "When you locate it, you must reach out to us first, before you proceed."

"You could tell me now."

She clasped her hands in front of her chest. "We have shared with you most of the things you need, but I can't share this with you yet. You have to understand: anyone with mystic blood can bond to the Stag, this privilege is not reserved for those who have studied the texts. If others capture you and torture you, you mustn't have this knowledge in your possession."

The Otter, Lyska, took the pipe from its mouth. "Is it too much to ask, Vicente, that you listen to your elders?"

Vicente groaned.

"If the Stag was to fall into the wrong hands, we cannot trust it will be brought to me," Lyska said. "I have been separated from my siblings, the *parts* of my *soul*, for centuries. Surely you can marshal enough patience to wait for this piece of information until the right time?"

Why the Stag would refuse Vicente was also a mystery: the demigods couldn't move around on earth unbonded. All the quorum members were bonded to the Otter, and in turn for teaching them more mystic tricks, it was allowed to roam freely. As the demigods' goal was to be united again, he didn't understand why the Stag would say no to him. "If anyone with mystic blood can bond with the Stag, then why do I need to study?"

"You are the future of mysticism, Vicente," Indra said. "You must become successful enough to prove to the government that there is a reason for them to allow us to train more. For centuries, they opposed the practice of mysticism. But seventeen years ago, the High Council allowed..." Indra slowly raised up a single finger. "...one to be trained." Then she pointed at him. "You. You were born with a great power, Vicente. But true influence doesn't come to those born for it, it comes to those who would do anything to achieve it."

"And you all have authority?" Vicente questioned. "Then why aren't you doing more to help the people?"

"We have limited sway," Indra said. "Even if the passage of time can't claim our lives, death can still come for any of us six sisters. Accidents, assassinations. We are burdened by a weakness that the rest of humanity—that the monarchy—isn't: we cannot reproduce, we cannot multiply, we cannot ensure a future. Our only way to do that is through training more mystics. Training you."

"And when will I be allowed to show the council what I can do?" Vicente said. "The disaster in Elath is a perfect opportunity. I have a plan." This was what he wanted to use his mysticism for: helping the world. But instead, the quorum used him as something to posture with. Once he bonded with the Stag, he would be as powerful as the quorum, and his deal with them would be broken. The sisters of the quorum knew this, of course, but they believed they had his loyalty. To an extent, they did. He would aid them in whatever matters aligned with his own ambitions.

Indra said nothing.

*

Shadowing Marcia, he was allowed to join in on the briefing the ministers had with the queen. All the members of the High Council were seated around the table, together with Queen Leandra, Marcia and a few emissaries from Elath. Vicente stood behind them, with the secretaries and people in training.

They droned on and on. When time finally came to discuss the landslide in Elath, Vicente held his breath: first, he needed to know what their current strategy was. Many had been killed in the disaster and vital infrastructure was disabled. His own plan was simple: send him there. He would entangle the rubble blocking the roads and go to a field or a lake and open tunnels, thus moving heavy debris and large quantities quickly. It was perfect.

"I'll send my company to Elath," Lord Gian said. "I can spare eight hundred horses. My men will work in shifts, moving rock, trees and waste from the streets. I have received estimates that it will take about two weeks. The beleaguered aid workers in Elath will thank Arkensaal for this."

"Excellent, Lord Gian," Queen Leandra said.

Two weeks? That was too long: many more would die trapped inside the ruins during that time. Vicente rallied some courage and spoke up. "I have a suggestion."

No one even spared him a glance.

"Not now," Queen Leandra said without looking up as she jotted down something in a notepad.

For fuck's sake. "It's a good one. I promise."

Only then did people pay attention. Old nobles turned around in their seats to glare scornfully at him.

Queen Leandra looked up, too. "I'm sorry, who are you?"

"Vicente Lamor, the mystic in training."

A minister on the High Council, who was sitting next to Marcia, spat at his feet. "Mystic witch."

"Meeting adjourned," Queen Leandra called. "Please have a seat, Vicente Lamor."

Vicente told her about his plan, emphasizing that they didn't have two weeks. People were dying right now.

"I understand your concern, Mister Vicente, I really do. As queen, I'm walking a never-ending tightrope. The needs of the people, the greed of the noble clans, and the commandments from the Merciful Eldvittra are all at play here. The quorum fought very hard with the High Council to get the approval needed to train you. Scores of people in Arkensaal wish to see you fail and see an end to this project of theirs."

Vicente hovered on the edge of movement, gripping the armrests so tightly his fingers were turning white to stop himself from standing. "But I could do this."

"And I don't doubt that. But what if you make a mistake? What if you forget to take one minor aspect into consideration, and someone gets hurt as a result?"

"People are already dying," he said. "People who still have time will die because medical personnel can't reach them, but I could help." *If you all would just let me.*

"Natural disasters are not the scene for trying new methods, Vicente. We need tested, reliable systems, we need to do it the way we always have."

Vicente had tested his plan—of course he had—and he knew it would work. He wouldn't have suggested it otherwise. He was prepared to show her and the High Council a demonstration if they would just *let* him. "You could put me in charge of one road, a small one. Let me try it. If I fail, then you can go with your approach."

"And what if you succeed; what then?"

"Pardon?"

Queen Leandra leaned back in her seat, absentmindedly spinning her pencil between her fingers. "I'll clue you in on something, Vicente, something about how the world has organized itself. Say your way works perfectly; it's efficient, speedy and safe. The citizens of Elath would rejoice, and the rest of the realm would hear all about it. The next time another disaster rolls around, the people would expect you to do the job again."

Vicente expected her to say that his workload would be unmanageable, but he had a solution for that too: allow the quorum to train more mystics. They would have no other choice. Mystic children would then be saved from abuse, like he had been. Additional funding would be directed to the studies of mysticism, and they would all learn more about the world. Increased knowledge, better prospects. Society would flourish. Medicine, history, architecture, agriculture, transportation; all these fields would benefit if they could just get the resources to train the people with mystic blood.

But that was not what Queen Leandra said.

She pointed to the door. "If we give the assignment to you, that means Lord Gian doesn't get it. If you get the work done so much more efficiently, then he's out of a job—and the same goes for everyone who works for him. That's four hundred people, who suddenly have no way of supporting their families. Also, Lord Gian now owns one thousand useless horses, who cost a lot to feed. He would have to slaughter them, and a thousand horses out of the equation is enough to affect the prices of grains in the Rinkai prefecture. Lady Evelia has worked tirelessly for months to stop the fluctuation of those prices. That's why she would never *allow me* to give the job to you."

Vicente couldn't believe it. Had his girlfriend been right, after all? Was it the greed of the influential who stopped the world from progressing? He wanted to say something, but couldn't conjure a single word.

Queen Leandra stood. "I'm truly sorry, Vicente. But the fact of the matter is this: introducing mystics to the workforce would shatter our economy like a pane of glass."

CHAPTER 14

Vicente

When Vicente returned to the inn after dinner, the door to his room was wide open. With blood pounding in his ears, he went inside. The room was in disarray. Stormwater and shards of glass covered the floor. His potions had all been smashed.

He opened his drawer and found that his bag with components had been left untouched. They were not rare ingredients, and he could likely buy them in Llyr, but at least the intruder had spared him that hassle.

Careful not to cut his fingers, he collected the labels from the destroyed bottles. One receiver was missing. He knew which one it was: he had entangled it with a sender potion that morning.

Vicente gritted his teeth against a groan of frustration. Iver hadn't joined them for dinner—was he the one behind this? If he was, he was only making the situation harder for himself, but at this point, Vicente honestly wouldn't put it past him.

Iver's knife was still where Vicente had hidden it, tucked between the bedframe and the mattress. Just like Marcia, Vicente had a copy of Iver's forged identification documents, and he always carried them with him. Surely, Iver didn't break in with the hopes of stealing them? This could've been a simple display of dominance from Iver's side. Did he want to tell Vicente that he was in constant danger from multiple sides? Or had Iver finally figured out how Vicente's tunneling powers worked and decided to try and sabotage him?

He stomped over to Iver's door and knocked. Destroying his potions could have been an attempt at taunting Vicente. Had he done this now because he knew they weren't allowed to leave Llyr, and had no way of contacting the capital? Or was this his way of showing Vicente he rejected Marcia's claim that they were a team?

When Iver opened the door, Vicente snapped. "Did you break into my fucking room? Someone picked the damn lock."

Iver scoffed. "I'm not the only one who can do that, you know. Why would I go inside your nasty room?"

"To steal your papers and get your knife back." It had to be him. He had reason enough to do it, a clear motive for trying to render Vicente defenseless. Despite the risks, Iver was going to attempt to murder him.

Vicente needed him to know he was still capable. He saw only one way of doing that.

He let out a sigh of frustration and slumped his posture a bit, pretending to cave. "I'm sorry, I shouldn't have thrown accusations at you. It just pisses me off. Someone broke in. All my potions have been destroyed."

Like usual, he was unable to read Iver: he remained stony-faced as Vicente complained. It was eerie how little Vicente could gauge in their interactions. It looked like Iver's entire focus was on him, he looked like he absorbed every little detail he came across—and couldn't care less about what he saw. His attitude was like a paradoxical mix between complete awareness and total indifference.

Iver tipped his head to the side. "Can I see?"

He looked unarmed. However, he had carried concealed weapons before. But this time, Vicente wasn't high. He would keep Iver at a distance, and if he lunged at Vicente with a knife, he could probably stop him. "Come have a look."

They went to his room and he closed the door behind them. A flash of the memory of Iver kissing him struck him, but he shook it off.

Iver looked at the glass on the floor. "This could be bad, Vicente. You think whoever broke in knows you're a mystic?"

Vicente considered it. Many people were born with mystic blood, but it was only useable after years of studying with the quorum: only after rigorous training did one become a mystic. Very few things about Vicente would indicate to others he had received this education. "No. The only known mystics are those of the Sensis Quorum, and their powers don't work anything like mine. I'm the only one like me."

"Then why did they destroy your potions?"

"They must've suspected they were important in some way. But from this alone, there's no way they know about my abilities." Around the realm, people knew *of* mysticism, but not what it looked like. Legends had formed regarding the quorum, and people knew about their capability to peer into humanity's past and lift forgotten technologies from it, but that was the extent of what they knew. And those tales certainly didn't mention any connection between mysticism and potions and teleportation.

Iver raked a hand through his hair. "Good. Well, shit, does this mean you can't do your little magic trick anymore?"

That was the question Vicente had been waiting for: he was going to show Iver that he wasn't reduced to helplessness just because of a few broken bottles.

He took his component bag from the drawer. In it were the jars containing the material he needed. He lined the jars up on his desk: calcium, phosphorus, potassium, sulfur, salt and magnesium, as well as other trace elements. "Do you know what these make up?"

Iver shook his head.

"They are ingredients that make up a human body. I mix it with water so I may consume it more easily, but it doesn't fil any function. I call it *Stormwater*."

The reason for that name, he kept to himself. During a storm, rain—or any form of downpour—flowed into lakes and rivers or drained into the earth, replenishing the groundwater. Using his Stormwater made him feel just that: replenished.

"There has to be more to a body than that," Iver said.

"There is: oxygen, carbon, hydrogen and nitrogen are the main materials, but all that can be found in the air around us." Vicente felt almost giddy telling him about his magnum opus. It was rare for him to have the chance to teach anyone about it: everyone permitted to know about Vicente's mysticism already understood how it worked, because he couldn't shut up about it.

Iver's expression was still unreadable, but he was obviously curious. He tore his eyes off the jars and looked at Vicente. "Why do you need ingredients for a person?"

"Because when I teleport myself, I am actually creating a new copy of my exact being from the Stormwater and from the air around it."

Iver's eyes widened for a moment, and Vicente heard one quiet but sharp intake of breath. The reaction was over in a second. Had Vicente dissuaded him from trying anything again? Did he understand now that bringing a mystic to heel wasn't as simple as he'd thought?

"So, to answer your question," Vicente said, "no: I can still do my little magic trick. All I need are these ordinary, accessible ingredients to make more Stormwater."

"But how does it work?" Iver asked. "Do you teleport as soon as you drink it?"

"No, only when I've invoked the tunnel to open."

"Tunnel?"

Vicente fished two unused glass bottles from his bag and held them up between his index fingers and thumbs. "I do something called 'quantum entanglement': these two vials will be opposites of each other. On a molecular level, they exist in a superposition. That means that two opposing concepts are true at the same time. It's a sort of oxymoron: both spinning up and down simultaneously…"

Iver frowned so deeply that Vicente understood he had lost him, and so he brought the conversation back to the important details. "So, when I open a tunnel, I don't actually step through it, but all the possibilities collapse into two, where I—as I have drunk the sending potion—am made anew from the components of the receiver potion."

"...Are you teleporting or not?"

"The physical matter isn't what's being teleported; it's the data. The molecules we consist of are not all there is to us, they are just a part of the picture. Through the tunnel, I'm transmitting the information about how I'm constructed, aligned, which way my particles are tilted."

"Particles can be tilted?" Iver held up his hand before Vicente could elaborate. "Wait, I don't care. So, can you make a human? Like, a whole new person?"

"There are other ways to make more people, you know." Vicente was a little amused by Iver's line of thought. "But no, I cannot. I can't create new data, only transport existing information."

"How did you move my knife? You dipped it in your drink first or something?"

Vicente allowed a smile to dawn on his face as Iver's resolve to be miserable and uncooperative began to wear away. Receiving genuine-sounding curiosity from Iver was a welcome surprise. "The Stormwater is only to relocate myself. It was a sidestep I developed, as I need to have physical contact with two objects to entangle them, and simply touching my own hand doesn't work."

Questions kept pouring out of Iver's mouth, and Vicente could tell he was trying—and failing—to sound unimpressed. "You can move anything?"

Vicente figured a demonstration was in order and took a seat at the desk. He placed a pen and a mug in front of him, touched his fingertips to them both and began the entanglement. He forced the particles of both objects to become entangled with each other, aware it might look odd to Iver: the process was invisible to him. From his point of view, Vicente sat there and did nothing.

But Vicente could feel the tension building in the objects, like the resistance in a rubber-band the more it stretched. When he opened the tunnel, that tension would release.

It was heavy, and the strain only grew as the tautness increased. It had taken him years to master this skill, but by now, the muscles in his mind were honed. Objects with greater mass were heavier and took longer to entangle, as you'd expect, but he had no doubts he would soon be able to entangle anything.

It reached a point where the pent-up force locked in place, like a joint hyperextending. "Now, the pen and the mug are entangled, and I can open a tunnel between them."

"If you say so." Iver's mouth set in a hard line. He even pursed his lips a little. Did he think Vicente was messing with him?

Vicente opened the tunnel and, in the blink of an eye, the pen and the mug switched places. The event was silent; the air around them didn't even move.

This wasn't the first time he had shown Iver his powers, but the other times had happened so quickly and without explanation. He half expected—and half wanted—Iver to marvel at it, but he didn't.

"That's fucked up," he said instead, in an oddly conversational tone.

Vicente smiled as he looked up at Iver. "This is the power I have gained from studying the laws of the Stag. Only gods can grant magic like this."

Iver shook his head again. "Why do you need the Stag then, if it has given you magic already?"

Vicente felt his own eyes gleam as he turned back to the desk and began mixing a new potion of Stormwater. "The Stag's teachings were partially transcribed by mystics centuries ago. There used to be scores of mystics, and they were all under the tutelage of the three therianthropic demigods: the Otter, the Stag and the Bird. But for reasons unknown to us, this trinity was forced apart, and the Stag and the Bird vanished. But if I can find the Stag... well, we believe it will bring great power to the realm. But since my blood vial was taken from the temple, I can't sense it anymore. Finding it is going to be hard." Vicente's connection to it, the strange pull he had felt all his life, was missing.

"How would the Stag give power?" Iver asked, ignoring Vicente's remark about his blood. "Would it fight?"

"Yes it will, until we can unite them both with the Bird. During that period, as the Stag holds all the knowledge of the future just as the Otter is the keeper of all knowledge regarding the past, we will learn more about the world, about what is to come." Vicente shook his head. "Our government's only priority is the war: developing new weapons and sending people to the frontlines to die," he said, aware of the vulnerability the statement held, but exhilarated and fueled by dreams of creating a better world. "It has stunted our entire society. Think of how many geniuses have died on the battlefield, holding guns instead of pens because that was their only path in life. Imagine how many brilliant minds have starved to death before the age of two because they were born in the wrong part of the country. Imagine how many poets never learned to read or write because we couldn't afford to send them to school. The Stag might not be able to win the war by fighting in it per se, but with it in the quorum's arsenal, they would gain more influence over the realm."

Vicente knew he was rambling, but Iver hadn't stopped him yet. Either he was interested in what Vicente had to say, or he was studiously ignoring him. He was too nervous to look over at Iver to check. "If we manage to find the Stag, we will have proven to the queen and the High Council and the *people* that there is a future in mysticism, and they would be forced to let us train others. In turn, more people would be educated, more universities founded. They keep this war raging because Eldvittra demands it, but if we focus on learning more about the world, we might come up with a solution to the war and finish it. Instead of evolving, we are stuck in old tracks. But if we—if *I*—can prove this effort to be fruitful, more people will get the chance to learn, to get an education. Instead of bowing our heads to the god of war and letting thousands die—"

Vicente finally turned to face him, and his voice cut off abruptly. Iver looked at him in a way he had never seen him before. At some point during Vicente's rant, Iver's usual expression of animosity had melted away. He looked relaxed, in awe, almost wistful. The eternal tension had seeped from his shoulders. His lips were slightly parted. He wore the sleeves of his shirt pushed up, and Vicente noticed the finely tuned muscle of his forearms, the veins on his hands making their way up to his elbows. His irises were black in this light. *He really is beautiful.*

Something fluttered in Vicente's chest, something unfamiliar. He felt remarkably exposed, like he had been stripped bare, being on the receiving end of a look like that.

Vicente's fervor evaporated so quickly it pulled the air from his lungs. He was too surprised, and too embarrassed by how disproportionately perturbed he was—for Merciful's sake, Iver was just *looking* at him—to continue the conversation.

After a few moments of unnerved stalling, Vicente cleared his throat. "Anyway, it's getting late. You should go back to your room. Get some rest."

Iver lowered his head as his gaze dropped to the floor and when he looked back up again, his scowl had returned. He gave Vicente a curt nod. "Alright. Good night."

"Good night."

Vicente felt stupidly and unaccountably sad as Iver closed the door on his way out. He had achieved his goal: Iver now knew Vicente could make potions easily; destroying them would do nothing. Even if he hadn't been the culprit, Iver had to be wary enough to keep a respectful distance. It couldn't be helped. He had shattered what tentative respect was building between them when he had decided to try to kill Vicente.

But even so. Iver had looked like he wanted to continue talking. And Vicente wanted him to stay.

Damnit.

He knew what this was. It was the restless need to tunnel.

When in the capital, in his usual habitat, he was better at staving off the craving. There were things he could do, methods to use, to quench it somewhat; nothing was as good, but they came close. Those tools were alcohol, tobacco and sex. He would layer them, replace them with each other, as soon as the effects of one grew dull he'd swap, all to settle the itch. It would work for a while, until it became unbearable, and he had to open a tunnel. But it worked, he had a system.

But here in Llyr? The wine was terrible, he had to ration his cigarettes, and there was no one for him to sleep with. He couldn't trust the Llyrians, and they didn't trust him. Iver coming onto him had caused him to snap. Now, he wanted nothing more, and when he couldn't, it made the desire to open a tunnel grow another set of teeth. The need to have sex with someone was so bad it hurt. He wanted to have sex with *Iver* so badly it felt like another pain alongside the rest. But he couldn't, he wouldn't take that hit to his pride just to satiate an irrational, physical need, and so his only choice was to use Stormwater.

CHAPTER 15

Iver

"What if you get the dosage wrong in your Stormwater?" Iver whispered. "When you mix all your ingredients for a human?" Iver hadn't slept, kept awake by a thousand questions grinding in his head.

The forest floor beneath them was dry as ash, but the ferns surrounding them had somehow survived the burning-hot summer and gave them enough cover to stay out of sight.

"You might lose or gain a microgram of iron in your body," Vicente said. He wasn't looking out to the fields, but at Iver. Out of the corner of his eye, he could tell Vicente was smiling. Iver gritted his teeth. *Why was he smiling?* It made him feel awkward, the way Vicente was grinning like he'd gotten Iver all figured out. He had been subject to Vicente's uninterrupted scrutiny all day. It left him feeling like an idiot.

The sun was way past its zenith, and they had spied on Ottone's land since dawn. So far, nothing looked out of the ordinary. From their location in the woods, they watched as farmers harvested lavender from waist-high bushes, ginkgo from the orchard, and chamomile daisies from the meadows; as well as other plants, the names of which Iver had never bothered to learn. They had been doing nothing else.

Iver rolled his eyes as Vicente shifted his weight again; laying on his stomach on the ground for hours mustn't be something he was used to. Two small twigs had found their way into his curly, dark-brown hair, and Iver had no idea how he had managed to do that. Outside his element, he was as clumsy as a newborn foal. Stealthiness didn't exactly develop overnight, but Vicente was somehow getting worse at it every minute that passed.

"You're sure we can't move any closer?" Vicente whispered. Iver preferred his voice like this, low and husky, over the booming arrogance it usually carried when he spoke.

"Positive. They'll notice us. And even *you* wouldn't be able to explain that away."

The farmers filled large burlap sacks to the brim with the harvest, and arranged them on a wagon standing unyoked, bereft of any draft animal.

Vicente stirred again. He folded his arms on the ground in front of himself and rested his chin against his wrist. "You know, if your gun had a scope, we could get a better look at what they're doing."

Iver had his rifle strapped to his back; they weren't expecting any confrontation, but he had brought it just in case. "There's nothing to see; they're just picking flowers. Besides, I don't use a scope because the glass lens would reflect in the sunlight and alert them of my presence. An iron sight is all I need, anyway."

Vicente said nothing, and Iver wondered what was going through his head. Was he impressed, caught by surprise? Iver wasn't stupid, irrespective of how Vicente and the others saw him. He had been dealt an unfair lot in life, was all.

Though Iver had been left orphaned when his parents enlisted and ultimately fell in battle, he had still received an education. A nice woman had taken it upon herself to gather the dirty and malnourished children in the Arkensaali slums, and she had taught them how to read and write. She did so free of charge, expecting nothing in return. She didn't have much, and those days were far from perfect. But when life got too rough, too painful, Iver revisited those memories, like he was making a nest out of broken things. Because of her, he knew there were people in the world who tried to help those in need. Had it not been for her, he would never have made it out of that miserable place.

Maybe that was why Iver had been so moved by Vicente's little rant last night.

Vicente put a hand on Iver's wrist and whispered, "here he comes."

Iver didn't look up immediately but kept his eyes on Vicente's hand. Vicente's skin was brown, like sun-lit bronze, and a stark contrast to his own. Unlike Iver, he was constructed entirely of warm and soft colors. His skin was warm, too. Iver had noticed Vicente liked to touch everyone he was being friendly with, and now Iver was apparently included in that group of people. He wasn't sure how he felt about that. Sometimes, he forgot other people were warm. Vicente was certainly warm.

Ottone arrived on horseback. He exchanged a few words with one of the farmers, then strapped the cart to his horse and slowly departed down the winding, rural path.

Iver and Vicente followed with some distance. They kept to the woods, enough to remain hidden by it but still able to see Ottone as he rode across the plains. Vicente made it clear he wanted to move closer, but he wasn't familiar with this sort of thing, and Iver was. If they were spotted, they would never get another chance.

They stalked through the forest. Vibrant hues of green provided a cool sanctuary that shielded them from the heat as they followed. The melodious calls of birds filled the air, and beneath the rustling leaves, a myriad of insects hummed and buzzed, all sounds of a thriving ecosystem that had survived the pinnacle of summer. A massive dragonfly, its wings spanning the width of Iver's outstretched arms, emerged from the trees. The creature's iridescent wings caught the sunlight, casting a lacework of colors onto the ground. The susurrus of wind in the trees was so peaceful he damn near could've laid down and taken a nap right then and there.

Something like melancholy ate away at him, and he felt it crawling out of his ribcage. Something like nostalgia. It wasn't a bad feeling necessarily; being in nature, he always felt like this. Going into the woods was akin to stepping into a different world, or even a different life. Yes, the memories rising unbidden from the depths of his mind were from another lifetime, where his current problems and his own achievements were insignificant. Nature was simultaneously eternal and fleeting, in a way that made him feel small. Mayflies here lived for a day, and oaks for three hundred years. From time to time, he appreciated feeling unimportant: because it meant his issues weren't important, either.

Ottone came to a halt in an open expanse. In this remote location, no buildings graced the horizon; only a canvas of untouched wilderness spread before them. Ottone unloaded his cargo, placing each burlap sack on the ground.

Iver was determined to find out the secret of Ottone's potions. They had to be connected to the deaths and the disappearance of the other children. The man had involved himself with the occult, Iver knew that much. Was he experimenting on the brats somehow? Maybe he was using them as test subjects, and they had died as a result.

No matter what was going on, Iver was going to stop it. There were people who had this idea that unclaimed kids were up for grabs, to be treated and hurt as they saw fit. People like that deserved punishment, and Iver had no qualms about delivering it himself.

While Ottone was distracted, Iver and Vicente moved a bit closer, still hidden in the woods. Iver listened as Ottone struck a match. He held his breath.

Then, Ottone set the cargo alight. Once a flame had taken its hold, it quickly devoured the entire harvest.

"He might use the ash," Vicente suggested, looking as bewildered as Iver felt.

Ottone stood by the fire and watched, hands in the pockets of his trousers. Before the fire finished burning out, he sat up on his horse and rode away.

"What in the Merciful's name is going on?" Vicente breathed.

Iver wasn't there to make sense of it all, just to make sure Vicente wasn't caught spying. "You're the academically gifted one. Is there some, like, chemical reason for burning the plants before using them?"

"Not to my knowledge." Then he offered nothing more. He looked at Iver like he was done speaking on the matter. It really irked him.

"You need to think a little harder than that, Vicente."

Vicente sighed, shaking his head. "But he just left it there. He didn't collect anything. It doesn't make sense."

"It looks like he got rid of it all."

"It does, doesn't it?" Vicente muttered. "But why?"

Vicente was easy to rile up, and Iver felt the urge to push his buttons again, his self-enforced indifference no match for it. Vicente's hold on his composure was fragile and Iver enjoyed probing it for weak spots, but now, he wished Vicente would just use that brain of his he took such pride in. "It looks like he's erasing evidence, Vicente."

"Still, this doesn't explain how he makes his potions." Vicente took two vials from his bag and handed him one. "Let's head back to Llyr, quickly before Ottone gets back."

Iver didn't want to, but he accepted the potion. After Vicente's explanation of how Stormwater and tunneling worked, he realized that going through one with him required a level of blind faith Iver considered himself unable to show. But Vicente had trusted him when he explained his powers. So Iver decided, begrudgingly, to give him some trust in return.

"I already told you," Iver said, "Ottone's quarters were locked with some electric shit, and I couldn't get it open. Besides, you shouldn't be opening tunnels."

"No one will notice."

They both drank their potions, and then Vicente took Iver's hands in his and they appeared in Vicente's room in the Sunfire Rest.

Iver shuddered. It was a peculiar feeling, disorientating and sobering, like waking up from a vivid dream. A shiver zipped down his spine and he thought he might vomit, but pressed his teeth against the nausea and let it pass. He didn't know what to say next—*was he supposed to thank Vicente for the ride?*—so he settled on, "holy Merciful's fucking shit."

Vicente smiled. *Always smiling.* "Yeah. Tunneling takes some getting used to."

"I'm not planning on doing that." Then Iver, bizarrely and out of nowhere, felt bad. When Vicente had shown him how to make Stormwater, he had been like a kid showing off a new drawing. He seemed happy Iver had taken an interest.

Wanting to kill him had been an easier feeling to accommodate.

Iver felt the warmth of Vicente's skin and realized with a horrible lurch that they were still holding hands, and quickly let go. "Could anyone learn?"

"Learn what?" Vicente looked to be a lot laxer than before. The anxiety had gone from his face. His wide shoulders drooped slightly, and his gaze softened, as if the usual edge in his expression had dulled. Even his hands, normally tense or restless, rested loosely at his sides. He must be relieved to be back in civilization, Iver thought.

"To open tunnels."

"Ah. Sadly, no. Only those born into certain lineages have the capability to learn. The potential to become a mystic is hereditary. Without that lineage, the person can't see the texts in the books teaching mysticism. Even with that, a mystic needs years of training with the quorum."

Vicente had simply been handed that position, then: born for greatness, plucked from the dirt and tutored by none other than the mystics of the god-damned Sensis Quorum. Through a lot of mental convincing, Iver rarely felt bitterness over his own situation, not anymore. He had accepted his role: he was meant for violence, not academia.

The two of them made their way to Ottone's apothecary. The sky was a brilliant, unblemished blue but despite the pressing heat, the townsfolk were out and about. Vicente was in his element again, surrounded by people he could charm. He was radiant when he smiled at others, when he greeted the people he had befriended and stopped to exchange a few pleasantries. His voice thundered when he spoke. It seemed innate to him. He was born with power and confidence, all the things needed to defend oneself—all the things Iver had to carve out of a world that didn't want to give him anything.

The queen's command to kill Vicente had been clear, but now, Iver was having second thoughts. He couldn't make up his mind. All because of Vicente's damn rant last night.

Iver had learned how Vicente's magic worked. Killing him wouldn't be hard, but he couldn't murder him with witnesses around: the queen couldn't pardon him if he did. He wouldn't be able to provide any evidence that the queen had ordered it, because that would make her look bad, and everyone with any sort of influence or status would deny it on her behalf.

Besides, there were other ways he could get his freedom: he could flee, and pray he was fast enough to not get run down like a dog. But unless he could steal his forged papers of identification, he would have to stay in hiding for the rest of his life. Not that this would be so different from how things had been before coming to Llyr.

Vicente took the lead inside the apothecary. Falco, Marcia's ex-fiancé, was working at the shop. Iver stood back and watched as Vicente, ever the charming wordsmith, spoke with Falco. It was impressive—as well as a little unnerving—how easily words flowed from Vicente's lips, almost like he could discern by the look of a person what they would like to talk about.

Falco kept talking, blissfully unaware that Vicente was fishing for information to use in future schemes. "When Lady Marcia left me heartbroken, Ottone reached out to me. Gave me a job here. To get my mind off it all, I assume."

Vicente put his palm down on the counter. "Oh, that reminds me: is Ottone in? I need to speak with him regarding a purchase I wanted to make."

"I'm not sure, but you are free to check." Falco nodded to the staircase. "He might be in his study."

Vicente and Iver went up the stairs and stopped in front of the closed door Iver had failed to open during his previous investigation.

Iver pulled out his lockpicking tools and tried it a second time. He heard a crisp snap from the latch as he triggered the electricity. Again, a shock travelled all the way up to his neck. "Believe me now? I'm not trying a third time."

Vicente crouched down to inspect the lock. "I can't see any wires. How in the world does he open it without getting a shock himself? Putting a metal key in there would trigger it in the same way."

Iver rolled his shoulder to shake off the numbness in his arm. He had his own suspicion, one he hoped was wrong: magic. It had to be something very different from Vicente's: a kind of mystic ability that allowed control over electricity and the temperature of a room. But that theory didn't align with the facts Vicente had presented—unless, somehow, the quorum had tutored Ottone without Vicente knowing.

"Fuck, it has to be—" Iver cut himself off. He did so reflexively, like a turtle shrinking into its shell. Wouldn't Vicente have been able to recognize magic if he came across it? Iver wanted to tell him about the coins, the dice made of bone, the freezing room in the basement.

But when Vicente had voiced his concerns about their safety in Llyr, Marcia had dismissed him, making him sound almost paranoid. In turn, Vicente would do the same to Iver—he was sure of it. If Iver told him about the weird shit Ottone was doing, he would ignore him or laugh at him. Vicente would ridicule him for jumping to conclusions and reading too much into details. They all believed Iver was stupid.

Vicente kept investigating the lock. "Has to be what?"

Iver decided against voicing his thoughts. There were probably logical explanations for it all, answers he hadn't found yet. "Could you open a tunnel through the door?"

Vicente stood and scratched his head. "I would need to have a receiver potion on the inside."

"Fuck this, maybe it's not even important." Although they had been invited up, being there still made Iver antsy. Ottone could return any second.

"He keeps his formulas, potions and ingredients in an unlocked laboratory, but the lock on his office is rigged. There's something in there he doesn't want anyone to find."

"Well, I know all the letters he receives are in there," Iver said with a shrug. "He was very adamant the brats bring all his messages to this room."

Vicente looked at him, eyes flashing with new ideas. Without offering an explanation, he agreed to give up getting the door open, and they left the apothecary. The street outside simmered, dust curling up from the cobbles in swirls beneath the rippling heat haze that made the whole world wobble at the edges.

Only a few feet from the door, Vicente stopped again.

A girl was walking down the road, with a raven perched on her outstretched arm. She held it at a distance, like she was afraid of it. The bird was almost half the size of her. It repulsed Iver that Ottone employed children to do his dirty work.

Vicente put a hand on his shoulder. "Follow my lead."

Iver stalked behind as Vicente confronted the girl with the raven: "My dear, you shouldn't be touching that."

The girl, who looked to be around eleven years old, stopped.

"I'm so sorry the information wasn't shared with you properly, my dear. Here, let me take that off your hands—which you should be washing, *immediately*." Vicente reached his arm towards the bird.

She sputtered a bit. "Sorry, but I am to deliver the raven to Lord Ottone's office—"

"You ought to wash your hands. We don't yet know if the illness can be transferred to humans."

Her eyes widened. All the Llyrians had been told the other messenger birds died from an acute sickness.

Vicente bore the convincing face of someone worried. "Are you feeling feverish, dear? Any soreness in the throat?"

She shook her head.

"That's wonderful. Now, I need to get that bird into quarantine."

She let the raven hop onto Vicente's elbow. "I should give the message to Lord Ottone."

The bird had a small roll of paper tied around its leg. Vicente untied and pocketed it, tutting at the bird as he was doing so. "I'll see to it that Lord Ottone is given the letter."

Iver saw that the message was sealed with wax; it would be a challenge to get it open without Ottone finding out they had read it.

But the girl was resolute. "Ambassador, I was told to deliver it myself. Please give it back."

Vicente said, "Of course, how ignorant of me. You are so responsible." He withdrew another small roll of paper from his pocket and handed it to her. "Now please, make sure you scrub yourself from head to toe."

The girl didn't seem to notice it wasn't the right letter. She gave a small nod and scampered off.

Iver clicked his tongue. "All that for something that might be unimportant." Though, he was a tad impressed. Where he committed his dirty biddings in the shadows, Vicente conducted his in plain sight.

Vicente looked proud of himself, holding his head a little higher, glowing like a nascent star. "No intel is insignificant."

They walked back towards the inn, the raven comfortably perched on the crook of Vicente's arm.

"You don't think you'll end up in trouble if Ottone finds out you stole from him?"

"You're dampening my dopamine, Iver. Now, let's figure out how Ottone makes his potions so that we can ruin it for him, trash his reputation, steal his land, and make the queen happy."

"Yeah, I guess if you can turn this into something valuable for the queen, she'll save your ass when you're caught for stealing."

"You mean *we* stole."

"I didn't do shit."

Vicente's smile didn't waver. "We're both lambs in the same pasture. Who knows, maybe if we grovel like servile little pawns, we'll convince the High Council of our usefulness—at least until betraying us becomes financially beneficial for them."

Iver decided then that he wouldn't kill Vicente. The people he murdered were all guilty, at least in the eye of someone. But Vicente's crime was that he was a threat to the establishment, which was not a fault in Iver's view. Sure, Queen Leandra had offered Iver freedom in return for this deed, but there was the glaring fact of the matter that Iver didn't quite trust her word. She had discarded him in the past, she could do it again. Even after he sacrificed his loyalty, his friends, his body, for the realm, she still abandoned him, and she didn't even remember him when they met again. *Fuck the establishment, anyway.*

He wouldn't kill Vicente.

CHAPTER 16

Vicente

The stolen raven perched on the backrest of Vicente's desk chair and cawed, beady eyes glinting in the light from the oil lamp.

"Why would he burn all the herbs?" Marcia repeated to herself. She absentmindedly licked her lips as she stared into the open flame of the candle on the table. Whenever she was deep in thought, she looked bordering on terrifying.

The potions were still a mystery. Spying on Ottone had raised more questions than it had answered. Rather than finding peace in the encroaching nightfall, Vicente's frustrations were only climbing. "I have no idea."

Iver held the rolled-up message above the flame.

"You've done this sort of thing before?" Daiyu asked.

"You really need to ask me that?" Iver said. "The trick is to soften the wax without melting it completely."

He gently slid a knife under the edge and lifted the seal off, leaving the imprint of the stamp intact. "We use it to close it again afterward."

Iver handed the letter Vicente had stolen from Ottone's raven back to him, and he read it out loud:

"*Moving five paces north-east.*" Vicente's tone was clipped now; the message wasn't providing them with anything useful.

"Well," Daiyu muttered. "That was pointless."

Iver jerked his chin towards the small paper pinched between Vicente's fingers. "Who's it from?"

Vicente had to read the name again. It hadn't stuck in his head. "Someone called 'the Resurrectionists.'" He looked up at Iver by chance, just in time to see the color drain from his face. Iver clenched his jaw, gritted his teeth. His shoulders tensed. Vicente waited for him to say something, but he remained still.

Vicente was so focused on him he didn't notice that Daiyu had the same reaction.

"Daiyu, what's wrong?" Marcia put her hands on Daiyu's shoulder and twisted her to face her. She blanched, too, and her eyelids peeled back in horror. She was blind, staring at nothing, all terror in her eyes.

She knew of them. "Who are they?" Vicente asked her.

Daiyu staggered backwards until her legs hit the bed and she sat down.

Marcia took Daiyu's chin in her hand and tilted her head. "These are the ones you were with?"

Daiyu pressed her lips together and her leg started bouncing with stress. She rarely spoke about her past, and Vicente never prodded: when someone who tends to overshare keeps something secret, it must be truly awful.

Vicente placed his hand on her shoulder, trying to comfort her. "Daiyu, this is a good thing; you have information about them. It doesn't matter what you did. We won't hold it against you."

Daiyu put her face in her hands, leaning her elbows on her knees. "Please don't make me."

"My love." Marcia wrapped an arm around her back, sitting down on the bed beside her. "It's a rare opportunity to be given the chance to make atonements for something horrible you did in the past. You cannot change what you did, but those events have awarded you a chance at helping us now. Please, my sweet thing."

Daiyu steadied her breathing, and her words came out hushed. "I just want to say, I never personally hurt anyone. It's not an excuse, there are none. I just… needed to say that."

Vicente nodded, though she wasn't looking at him. "Who are they?"

"It's an organization that's trying to break off from society. At least they were, when I worked for them. They were extremists, anti-government, that sort of stuff. That's how our paths crossed, but I swear I don't believe in that anymore." Daiyu looked up at Marcia and Vicente, a pleading look in her eyes.

Vicente was speechless. Questioning the order of the world was a natural part of growing up, but few ever acted on those doubts. The fact that Daiyu had joined them was nothing short of insanity.

Daiyu looked like she was close to tears as she started picking at her fingers. "I... I made chemical weapons for them. To use in their attacks on the military. I left of my own accord, and when I did, I burned all my work—"

"When was this?" Iver asked.

"I was young and dumb, maybe around eighteen—" Daiyu sputtered, and Iver interrupted her again.

"*You think I fucking know how old you are*—when was this?" Iver clenched his fist so hard that they were shaking. His knuckles turned white.

Daiyu's eyes overflowed with tears that streamed down her cheeks. "I left them six, seven years ago—"

"You're lucky." Iver yanked the door open and then slammed it shut behind him as he left.

Why was he reacting so strongly? Maybe he had been involved with them too. It wouldn't be unthinkable for Iver to have been part of such a violent group of insurgents.

"Vic, get him, please," Marcia asked, hugging her wife who was now openly sobbing.

Vicente hastened after Iver and saw the door to his room close. He made his way down the corridor and knocked gently on the door. Moments passed, and Vicente started to think Iver was going to ignore him, when finally, the door creaked open.

"What's going on?" Vicente asked.

"I got sick and tired of hearing you all talk and talk."

"Can I come in?"

Iver opened the door wider, and Vicente stepped inside. To reduce the risk of appearing confrontational, he sat down in the chair by the desk. Was Iver unhappy with Daiyu for having left the organization? Or was he perhaps distraught that Daiyu had been with them at all? "What's your history with the group?"

Iver buffed the hair falling across his forehead back with his wrist. "I don't have one."

"Then why are you upset?"

With a sigh, Iver dragged his hands down his face. "It's been a long day. Sorry for storming off. I'm just exhausted."

Vicente didn't believe him but decided not to press on. "Not sleeping enough? And please don't ask me why the fuck I care."

Iver's mouth snapped shut. There was a brief pause, before Iver said, "I'm getting predictable, aren't I?"

And then he smiled, a careworn smile, and it supplied Vicente with an unexpected warmth. "I would never describe you as 'predictable,' Iver."

Iver said nothing as he turned away, and Vicente's vision filled with the slight sway of his shoulders as he walked over and sat down on the bed. Vicente grasped at the threads of the conversation, eager not to lose Iver to his own wandering thoughts of Iver on top of him, of the velvet heat of his mouth. "I know you don't consider me an ally, Iver, but I do see you as one, and you can talk to me."

"About what?"

"About whatever is bothering you."

"Nothing is bothering me."

Vicente rose from his seat, slapping his knees just like his mother used to do, and he regretted doing so immediately. "Well, that's good. See you tomorrow at breakfast."

"I think Lord Ottone has something to do with the murder," Iver blurted out. "The murdered little girl. A bunch of kids have gone missing, too."

Vicente stopped. *Ottone?* "Why would you think that?"

"I could be wrong, I don't have any proof," Iver said. "But we're still going to figure out how he makes his potions, right?"

"That's the plan." The plan hadn't changed, and they had never discussed changing it either. Iver wasn't making any sense. It was like he was trying to get Vicente to stay, to rope him into conversation.

Iver looked down at his hands, resting in his lap. "It's odd Marcia's father won't let us leave Llyr, right?"

"Indeed, it is strange." Vicente had his hand on the door, but he hesitated to open it. There was something veiled in the topics Iver chose to bring up, something more potent, like a dare. Like a request. Something circuitous, a powerful thing, a controlling and infectious thing, centuries old.

Then it hit him like a stampede of horses: Iver was afraid.

Vicente returned to the chair by the desk, silently berating himself for taking so long to realize. Whatever Iver's history was with the Resurrectionists, it rendered him scared enough to want to stay with Vicente. Vicente had expected anger, not fear. He wasn't quite sure how to handle fear. "I wouldn't worry about it, though," he said, carefully. "They won't try to hurt us; they don't have reasons to even consider doing that. All of this, this is just… peacocking."

Iver lifted a leg to rest his arm on his bent knee. "Peacocking?"

"Peacocking. A dick-measuring contest, if you will."

"I know what it means." Despite still looking uncomfortable, Iver settled back further on top of his bed. Almost curling in on himself, with his back leaning against the wall. He ran both hands through his hair, then let them rest around his neck, almost like he was protecting it. "You think they're just trying to show who's boss?"

"That would be my educated guess, yes."

Iver opened his mouth and drew a shallow breath, but no words came. After a few seconds, he closed his mouth again. He frowned at himself. It was oddly charming.

Vicente snorted. "What, couldn't conjure a creative enough insult regarding my education?"

"Sorry to disappoint you. I'm tired."

"Then you should get some sleep: I'm not sure I can do my job properly anymore without your bratty comments spurring me."

"People don't kill diplomats on their missions, right?" Iver asked, now with that unmistakable edge of fear.

The look on his face was enough to give Vicente heart-pangs. "No, that is very uncommon. We have political immunity. And so do you, as long as this job is ongoing. Although, if you succeed in killing me, that deal would be voided."

"You're still stuck on that?" Iver muttered into the heel of his hand.

Vicente almost laughed. He had never spoken so casually about something so serious. It was dangerous and enticing, speaking about taking a life like that, like it wasn't something that could never be given back. "I've never had my life threatened before, of course I got quite hung up on that little incident."

Iver dug his teeth into his bottom lip, dragging it between them. Vicente watched as the blood momentarily drained from it, turning it white. "I'm not... going to kill you. I know you can't trust me on that, but I wanted to tell you anyway."

Vicente had a good intuition. He knew Iver was serious when he vowed to kill him, long before he even tried it. Now, his gut was telling him Iver was being honest. "I'm happy you changed your mind. A life behind bars or getting executed is not worth it, just to get your revenge."

"Revenge." Iver scoffed. "Queen Leandra promised me all my charges would be dropped if I kept you three safe."

Vicente had almost forgotten about that: the queen's lie. "That's right," he said to the ground, breaking away from the intensity of it all, staring at his own shoes. He prided himself on his ability to use his words to be all sugar-spun and kind, but now, he couldn't muster it.

"I don't believe her."

Being confronted with his own cognitive dissonance was the height of discomfort. Vicente didn't view himself as a liar. He was, though. "You can't know for certain she won't uphold her end of the agreement."

"But I can," Iver muttered, petulantly. "She's failed to do so in the past. This is what she does. This is what all of them do. No use in getting pissed about it." He lolled his head to the side to look at Vicente. "This is when you promise me you won't kill me either, by the way."

Vicente huffed a laugh. It sounded breathy and had a tiny hint of mockery he couldn't stop. "I'm surprised you haven't figured it out by now. You're a smart man."

Iver's eyebrows knitted together. "Figured what out?"

"You've seen how my powers work. I'm not actually dangerous. I can just move things around."

Iver looked Vicente up and down, taking stock of him. "Hm. I'd still call you a threat, though."

"Really?"

"It's a damn annoying talent, but you seem able to persuade anyone to do anything." Iver sucked his teeth. The look of disgust manifested out of nowhere. "Lying without issue, like it's the language your mother taught you. People like you make me sick to my stomach. People like you abuse other's good nature to get to their secrets."

The smile on Vicente's face turned forced. "I do what is necessary to get my job done." He heard the prim offense in his own tone and cringed at it, but why was Iver angry again? Was he hurt that Vicente had lied about his abilities?

Iver looked at Vicente like he had asked him a question with a ridiculously obvious answer. "Then you must be shit at your job."

Something ugly swelled in Vicente's chest, a rolling surge of anger that reverberated down his ribcage. "I would label you as manipulative too, you know. Popping open a few buttons on your shirt, pouting those pretty lips and getting any man on his knees seems like a talent of yours. Tell me, do men share their vulnerabilities with you more easily, once you've let them fuck you? Once you've let them have their way with you? Isn't it true secrets flow more freely from people's mouths in the afterglow of sex?"

Iver's face remained stone-cold and neutral as he received the tirade of insults. Vicente expected Iver to snap at him, but he didn't, he just glared at him with the same enthusiasm one would have when watching a coat of paint dry. "I wouldn't know." Vicente laughed, full of sadistic mirth. "Well, you're the expert."

"Not really."

"You're a bad listener as well?"

Iver shrugged and studied his own fingernails. "The fuck do you want me to say? I don't know what people do after fucking."

Distantly, Vicente felt his own face drop the smug smile. "What?" Ice skimmed over his skin as the realization dawned on him. *Was Iver a virgin?* That couldn't be possible. Given the way Iver spoke, his choice of words, Vicente never would've guessed it. Despite being unapproachable, the fact that Iver was attractive was undeniable. He was positively beautiful. He was also— supposedly—in his twenties. Could it be Vicente had been wrong about Iver's age, could it be he was even younger than he looked?

Vicente's anger burned out, leaving in its place the foul aftertaste of shame. "You've... never?"

"Nah. Not everyone grew up all safe and clean, you know." Iver peered out through the window at the night rolling in. "Some of us have had more pressing shit to deal with, other than getting off."

Vicente swallowed hard, mouth suddenly dry. That would explain why Iver had been so nervous when he came to his room. He should have realized then, when he noticed Iver's hands shaking. He should have realized then, when Iver kissed him like he didn't know how to—because he didn't. "Shit, Iver, I'm sorry."

"Don't be. It's so easy to get a rise out of you, I couldn't help myself." Iver's eyelids looked heavier now, as if provoking Vicente had provided him with the comfort he needed to relax. "Good night, Vicente."

CHAPTER 17

Marcia

Marcia watched as Iver skillfully re-sealed the message they had stolen from Ottone. He was being useful, which was a refreshing change of pace, but she still wanted to keep him at arm's length. He was an unpredictable criminal, and she always kept his identification documents with her so that he couldn't steal them and run away. He wouldn't be able to travel the realm without them. If she would ever give them to him—well, that would be up to the queen to decide.

"Me and Vicente should go," Marcia said, "I don't want to risk you two saying anything stupid."

There was little protest. Daiyu was exhausted. Last night, she had hurt herself a bit, and Marcia couldn't stop her. Marcia tried to talk to her, to reason with her and to comfort her, but she couldn't reach through the panic. Triggered by the mention of the Resurrectionists and Iver storming off, Daiyu had been inconsolable. It was always worse during the night, when the rest of the world was asleep. When morning came, it eased. Marcia was sure she would make it through this episode as well.

She and Vicente left the Sunfire Rest and started the walk to Ottone's apothecary. The sky was clouded, and both thunder and rain loomed over them. The halfhearted promise of rain did nothing to ease the temperatures, though. Marcia had always been a brisk walker, but it seemed she would have to take after the Llyrians while here. The locals didn't walk, they swam through the humid streets like fish through molasses, swatting away flies with the same absent reverence priests gave to incense.

"Ottone is going to be pissed you stole from him," Marcia said. The chance that Ottone would believe Vicente had swiped the message by accident was slim. She wouldn't have approved of this, had Vicente sought her council beforehand. He hadn't. She should be proud of him for showing initiative, but this recklessness wasn't anything she had ever taught him.

They found Ottone in the apothecary. Vicente bowed at the waist when he handed the small roll of paper to him. "My apologies, Lord Ottone. I didn't give your girl the right letter before."

Ottone accepted the letter and inspected the seal. "No worries at all, Ambassador. And thank you for returning it so quickly." He pocketed the message without reading it. "I gather Daiyu has taken her samples?"

The raven had been released that morning and had flown back to its perch on the rooftop of the apothecary. "She has. If this bird is ill as well, we will find out soon." PM Jadanza's lie that the ravens died from an unknown illness served them well in this regard.

Ottone's blond moustache covered most of his mouth as he smiled wide. "Would you mind joining me for a short conversation with Lord Eloy? I think you'll both find it interesting."

"It would be our pleasure," Marcia said.

The three of them small-talked on their way to the market. She wanted to keep up the appearances, but she was growing wary of Ottone. It appeared he was involved with the Resurrectionists, which was a violent group of people, as far as Marcia had gathered. Had she had all her usual tools at her disposal, she would've investigated their history, but alas.

Marcia noticed a young girl walking with them, albeit a few steps behind. Daiyu had mentioned that there were usually kids in the apothecary, running errands for Ottone. Was this a ploy of his, she wondered. Did Ottone help the children find work, surround himself with them and educate them to appear harmless and helpful?

Eloy was sitting by the fountain in the market square, waiting for Ottone. The fountain gurgled weakly beneath a marble statue of a woman with water streaming from her open palms, her gaze fixed somewhere far above the rooftops, as if she refused to acknowledge the town crumbling around her.

Eloy rose to his feet as they approached, brushing dust from his pants.

"Cattle-farm prince," Ottone said, "thank you for taking some time out of your busy day to meet with me."

Eloy only nodded at him. Unlike Ottone, he was dressed in simple clothes, made to be worn for manual labor. His fingernails carried a crescent of dirt underneath them.

Ottone clasped his hands behind his back, effectively puffing out his chest. "I won't waste more of your time than necessary; I know it was you who killed the courier birds." He said it so casually, it took Marcia a few seconds to register what he had said.

"Why would you think that?" Eloy asked, crossing his arms.

Marcia flipped through the possibilities: Why would Eloy have killed them? Did he, from the very beginning, believe she and Vicente would find proof the land belonged to the Cronin clan? Or was he involved in the murder?

Ottone beckoned for the girl to step forward. "You might have realized I employ some of the restless children of Llyr to keep an eye on things for me. Thus, I have far more eyes and ears than just my own, and they pick up on a thing or two. I know you killed the ravens, Lord Eloy, and I think I know why."

"Do tell, my Lord," Marcia asked. Her heart was beating hard, but she didn't let that show. She preferred to be stoic, a reliable and stable current in a stormy ocean.

"I think the ambassadors found something in the archives you didn't want known," Ottone said. "And so, you killed the birds before they could send word to the capital."

"Lord Eloy, is this true?" Marcia asked, thankful for the commencing blame-game, as she recognized the risk of her and

Vicente being caught in a lie: they had used the excuse of an illness to explain why they had taken one of Ottone's ravens. As long as they maintained ignorance and pointed fingers at Eloy, there was still a chance Ottone wouldn't think more about the theft and connect it to their true intentions.

Eloy uncrossed his arms, then crossed them again. "Look, you told me you found encrypted letters, I figured they were from the criminals that laid siege on the land, I didn't want Arkensaal to decrypt them for you—"

"Because you knew the land belonged to *my* clan," Ottone said, jabbing a finger into his own chest. "You have known all along. The elders of both our clans remember the tales of their ancestors, but you thought you could pull a fast one on me because your property borders on the land around Tal Llyrie."

"Do you have anything to say, Lord Eloy?" Marcia asked. This conflict was far more infected than the stakes should've rendered it to be. She wasn't sure who was the bigger idiot: Eloy, who tried something like that and hoped to get away with it, or Marcia, who hadn't figured it out. Eloy was making it really difficult for her to defend and side with him.

Eloy's cheeks were red. Perhaps he had begun to understand that his selfish act had made her and Vicente vulnerable without the guidance from Arkensaal. He said nothing, and couldn't look her in the eye.

Thankfully, Vicente kept his mouth shut. He had been acting strange lately, and she suspected that he had been opening tunnels. He always acted weird, almost drunk, after he did, and she was beginning to doubt Vicente had been ready for this job.

Ottone turned to Marcia. "See, Ambassador? The land belongs to my clan."

Deflect, make them grow frustrated and show their hand. Marcia wondered what Ottone was planning on using the land for: according to Vicente, the harvest from his plantation was all burned. The secret ingredient to his healing potions was still a mystery. "This is all word of mouth, my Lord. Same with any information found in the archives, it seems. Vicente and I still have some work to do before we can award the land to anyone. We will compile the data and get back to you with a decision."

"I respect that you are not yet done with your investigation, but I must insist you tell Arkensaal about this treachery immediately." Ottone's face was also growing redder as he spoke, though from anger rather than embarrassment. "They need to send a ruling clan leader here to punish him for what he has done."

"Indeed, our investigation remains inconclusive as of yet," Marcia said with a careful nod. Ottone was not privy to that they had been ordered by the queen to side with Eloy, and it had to stay that way. "We will absolutely inform the queen of this misdeed."

Eloy stormed off, making his way through the market and back north towards his clan's lands.

A roll of thunder rumbled from somewhere behind the Crooked Mountains. Overhead, the sky had sagged even lower with gray, swollen clouds. If only it would finally open, just crack wide and drown this entire meeting in rain, Marcia thought. Anything to bring it to an end.

Ottone shook his head in disbelief. "What nonsense. I'm so sorry this happened, Ambassador Marcia."

Marcia forced a smile, growing more and more agitated by their antics. "Nothing to worry about. May we send Daiyu to the capital with the information of Lord Eloy's offenses?"

Ottone looked uncomfortable, hooking a finger in his cravat and tugging at it. "Just like PM Jadanza told you, I'll allow Mister Iver to leave."

As Iver was the one to ensure their safety, pressing the matter was odd. Could it be that they wanted her crew to be even more vulnerable? But what for?

When Marcia said nothing, Ottone cleared his throat. "Or, you may use one of my personal ravens to send word to Arkensaal."

Relieved to see Ottone cooperating, she bowed her head. "Thank you, my Lord."

She took the lead back to the Sunfire Rest and Vicente followed. Finally, they had a way of contacting the queen for advice.

"What now?" Vicente asked.

"We'll split our tasks," Marcia said. "I'll handle the dispute and make sure Eloy is awarded the land. You, Daiyu and Iver need to focus on figuring out what's going on with Ottone's potions."

*

"Ambassador Vicente and I have found evidence that the land used to belong to Eloy Errani's clan."

Atli the blacksmith fanned the fire burning in the hearth. The heat in the smithy was unbearable, and Marcia dabbed sweat from her forehead. But Atli seemed unaffected by it.

"So, you'll give it to him?" Atli wiped his blistered hands on his soot-covered leather apron. He had his curly black hair tied in a knot on the crown of his head. Marcia couldn't discern any emotions from the stony expression on his face.

"I wanted to get your opinion, Mister Atli. I am here to support your community, not tear it asunder."

Atli continued working on a few horseshoes, hammering and bending them around the anvil to the desired shape. He shrugged. "As long as the two clans settle down with this nonsense."

"Very well. But I must ask you not to share this with anyone; it must be handled carefully by me and Vicente."

*

"We found no evidence regarding who the land used to belong to, thus, we will organize a vote that the entire Llyrian council is expected to partake in." Marcia leaned her elbow on the wooden counter dividing the apothecary, ignoring that Falco was wiping it down. Hundreds of bottles and glass containers were lined up on the multiple levels of shelves on the walls. Some jars contained brightly colored liquids, while others held powders of varying earthy hues.

Falco nodded. "I'm glad you came to that conclusion. That makes sense; it should be up to us."

"I wholeheartedly agree. And I came to ask you to act as a sort of broker on the day of the vote. It will be best if a Llyrian mediates, not me or Vicente."

Falco slung the towel over his shoulder to give the appearance of being casual but missed and it fell to the floor. "I can do that."

"Excellent. I must ask you to keep this to yourself. We're awaiting clearance from the capital."

"No problem."

*

"The land around the ruins of Tal Llyrie belonged to the Cronin clan, making Lord Ottone Cronin the rightful owner," Marcia told Sergeant Celia. "If there is a conflict due to this, can I count on you to keep the peace?"

The sunlight was fading, and Marcia was relieved that this was her final stop on her rounds. The sweat under her arms had stagnated and her feet ached from all the walking. Other than that, she was elated. She was in her element. After all her lies had been planted, she would sit back and wait to see what information came back to her, thus gauging everyone's loyalty.

"Thank you for the heads up, Ambassador," Celia said. "I can assure you, me and my soldiers won't let things get out of hand." On the field behind her, the warriors of the militia were target-practicing, feathering bales of hay with arrows.

She and Vicente would organize a vote—that part was true— and it was Marcia's job to sway them to vote for Eloy Errani. But before she could do that, she needed to know where their loyalties lay. It would be down to a council vote; thus, she had spoken to everyone in the council and all those who she knew were trying to get on the council. Sergeant Celia was one of them, and she was already an influential person in Llyr. "Wonderful. I must ask you not to share this information just yet. Me and Vicente will make an announcement once we get clearance from Arkensaal."

"I won't say a word. I look forward to seeing this dispute settled." Celia took a tentative step away. "Would you join me in my office? I have some letters you might want to take a look at."

"Gladly."

They walked towards the militia command post building, located on the other side of the training field. The sun was setting on another day, and Marcia couldn't wait to return to the inn.

Now that Daiyu had had time to collect herself, Marcia had questions for her regarding the Resurrectionists. According to her, they were a rebel group, and if the queen was unaware of them, Marcia had an obligation to inform her. But before she did, she wanted to know if that would put Daiyu in danger.

"It sounds like your time in Llyr is up," Celia said. "Heading for another mission after this?"

Marcia didn't know what her future would hold, and it bothered her. Normally, she would never have shared something so personal, but she felt a connection to Celia, a spark that could be fanned into a true friendship. "Daiyu wants us to settle down; no more jobs like this. She wants to have a baby."

Celia looked up at the cloudy sky, maybe wishing for rain. Her silky black hair fell from beneath her scarf and swept across her shoulder as she tilted her head back. "And you don't?"

"I do, I do. It's just… I have some apprehensions, and I don't think that makes me fit to care for one."

"What are you worried about?"

Marcia felt a drop land on her forehead and she wiped it off. "Us having a baby… we would have to jump through so many hoops: finding a donor if Daiyu is to carry it, the stigma and proving ourselves fit. There's a lot to it; it doesn't happen by accident for us. And in order to go through that… don't I need to be sure, one hundred percent? If I fail as a mother, or Merciful forbid, change my mind, I will have no one but myself to blame. Sometimes I wish it would just happen to us, so that I wouldn't have to make the decision."

They were approaching the end of their mission, and as soon as they got clearance from the queen, they would head back home. Then, Daiyu would continue to press the matter.

Celia pulled the scarf tighter around her head as the rain began to fall. "If you were to mess up as a parent, would you blame someone else for that?"

Marcia bristled. "Of course not." But it was a necessary question; what was she thinking? She sighed, like it was a relief and not a torment. "It is kind of selfish to not want to make the decision, isn't it?"

Celia took the lead inside. The office was tidy, which Marcia found commendable; her own office never looked like this.

Celia rummaged through her desk drawers. "People do become parents by accident all the time, and at least some of them turn out fine."

"I get lost in the thoughts of why I would even want one. Is it to immortalize myself? Is it to have that bond? I don't know."

"Do you need a reason, other than wanting it?"

There were a few rare moments when Marcia dreamed of having children, when she pictured herself making breakfast in a kitchen filled with young laughter. "Do you want children?"

Celia shrugged, still with a carefree expression. "I don't, and I don't have an explanation for why. I just don't. If you analyze everything like that, is there really a good enough reason for anything? Some have kids and some don't; it's just the way of life. Maybe Daiyu wanting a baby is reason enough?"

Droplets pattered on the glass of the windows. Marcia looked out through it, at the rain finally gracing the land. Celia was right. Perhaps she didn't need justifications.

Celia found was she was looking for, and brought Marcia a stack of papers. "A few years back, we raided a village the rebels occupied. These are all gibberish, but I heard you deciphered some."

Marcia took a quick look at them. "This is the same code." Her growing bond with Celia had resulted in something tangible and good. Their talks had paid off with this: Celia's trust. Marcia appreciated her more and more. This was what her job was all about, she thought. The connections between people.

"Do you think it's anything useful?" Celia asked.

"I think so. Thank you, I'll give these to Vicente to decrypt."
Celia smiled wide. "My pleasure."

CHAPTER 18

Vicente

Vicente read aloud as he wrote: "There has been a murder, and we need aid. Requesting ravens. Our decision is leaning in favor of Lord Ottone Cronin." Hopefully, that last sentence would be enough to communicate the urgency of a reply from Queen Leandra.

Outside, the cicadas hadn't shut up all day, and even now, with the sun setting behind the hills, they carried on like they were getting paid for it. The evening heat clung to the walls of his room in the Sunfire Rest, and condensation had begun to sweat from the stone, beading in slow trails.

Daiyu peeked over his shoulder. "You should sign it off with 'love, Vicente.'"

Vicente snorted. "She'd have me discharged for that."

"Or worse, she'd marry you."

"Yes, being king consort would be such a terrible fate." He sealed the message with wax and his stamp, the warm blob hissing slightly as it hit the parchment. The seal left its impression cleanly, despite the humidity. They'd been granted permission by Ottone to use one of his ravens to send word to Arkensaal, and soon, they'd be back in touch with the capital—assuming the bird didn't faint from the heat halfway there.

Daiyu's eyes narrowed with mischief, a smirk on her lips. "You couldn't continue sleeping around."

Marcia swatted her shoulder. "Excuse you, Daiyu Jadanza."

Daiyu turned to Iver, and he flinched away from her. "You're not a married man. You must have a few prospective partners waiting for you in the capital, don't ya?"

Iver glared. "Shut up or I'll jump out that window."

"Can I have your gun if you die?" she asked. In the right company, she could be quite the character.

Iver huffed out a laugh. "Sure."

That was the first time Vicente had heard him laugh, and his heart stuttered at the sound of it.

Daiyu took note of it too. "Did you just chortle? That was adorable."

Iver's smile mellowed. "Before you send that, there's something I need to tell you." He said it with such sincerity and weight that it made the three of them pause. He didn't say anything for a few seconds, and he stared at his feet, his jaw clenching. "The real reason I'm here, on this mission with you all, is because Queen Leandra ordered me to kill Vicente."

Vicente blinked. "What?" He knew Iver had wanted to murder him at one point, but he assumed it was for personal reasons.

Daiyu plopped down on the bed and looked between him and Iver. "Wait, what does this mean?"

"It means our queen, or perhaps the government, wants Vicente dead, dumbass," Iver said. "And before you ask, no, I don't know why. Not like she would offer me an explanation."

Marcia remained quiet.

"Why are you telling us this?" Vicente asked, voice neutral. Any emotions he might feel had yet to set in.

"Look, obviously I've changed my mind," Iver said, not sounding nearly apologetic enough, "but maybe writing to Arkensaal ain't the best idea."

Why would Queen Leandra want to have him assassinated? Vicente drew a blank. But now it made sense why she had insisted on sending Iver with them rather than dispatching part of her queen's guard. "Thank you, Iver. For telling us, and for changing your mind."

"Was Vicente the only one on your hit-list?" Marcia asked. "Not me or Daiyu?"

"Just Vicente."

That answer didn't exactly make the gears in Vicente's head move any more smoothly. "What are you thinking?" He tilted his head to the side to catch Marcia's eye, but she was looking blankly ahead, eyebrows pinched and chewing on the inside of her cheek. She had realized something, had connected some dots Vicente hadn't yet, and she didn't look happy.

"Could it have something to do with the fact that you're a mystic?" she suggested.

The reality of Iver's accusation started to set in, flickering into consciousness like the birth of a flame, young and confused, and Vicente's palms went sweaty. "I am the first to be trained as one, aside from the Sensis Quorum. Queen Leandra might see me as a liability. If I fail, it will paint the quorum in a bad light."

"I don't think that's it," Marcia said and stared at him, her gaze boring into his.

Vicente wanted to reassure her that no harm would come to him; at least he knew of the plan now, thanks to Iver. He had nowhere near the strength the sisters of the quorum had, but he was growing stronger every year. "But the quorum won't be able to bond to the Stag, only I can do that," Vicente continued. "Surely, the queen will understand that no matter how weak I am now, I'll bring unfathomable power to her once—"

"No, you'll bring power to the *quorum*," Marcia said, voice icy.

"Well yes, but that's the same thing."

"Is it?" Marcia said. "The quorum's biggest weakness is that they can't multiply, thus can't secure their own future; they depend on an alliance with the royal bloodline for that purpose. There are only six powerful mystics in the world, and that has been the case for generations. They are far too few to be a reliable source of power. But if they prove they can train more? Someone so successful that they can bond to another demigod? Suddenly, there is a future for mysticism, they can stand on their own legs.

Why would they need an alliance with the monarch? Why would our country need a monarchy at all?"

Vicente snapped his mouth shut. He sat down. She was right. For centuries, the six sisters had been alive and had whispered in the ears of every reigning monarch—never changing, never evolving. He recalled what Marcia had said about the monarchy before: even though it wasn't the sole deciding body in the realm, it was the glue holding the government together. The monarchy needed the quorum for their mystic powers and scrying abilities—for information. The quorum needed the monarch for stability, for influence. But if the quorum became influential, all on their own...

"Maybe," Marcia said slowly, like the words got caught behind her teeth and couldn't quite break free, "Queen Leandra wants you dead to stop you from finding the Stag. To prevent the quorum from getting more authority."

"No way," Vicente said with labored conviction, clinging to deniability just a little bit longer. "The mystics of the quorum are the most loyal servants to the crown—"

"They often act of their own accord: keep secrets, speak their minds and discredit Queen Leandra. They insult her every chance they get. They've done so for years now, since they were awarded more freedom." Marcia was holding her own hand in her lap. "Maybe, the queen has gotten sick of it."

There was a lot of truth to it. The quorum members didn't even address the queen properly half of the time and called her by her first name. They never explained their decisions; nor did they elaborate on their predictions. Maybe Marcia was right: maybe Queen Leandra had grown tired of them.

The dawning realization felt like a knife opening his chest, his stomach. He was being taught words he already knew: he had witnessed it first-hand, how the queen resented the quorum. It wasn't that he needed to prove his capabilities to the queen—she knew, and she didn't want it.

Vicente wanted to open a tunnel. The craving for Stormwater flared beyond his control. As soon as they were done here, he would go to his room and do it. It didn't matter that he didn't need to, because how could he handle learning that he was the most unwanted human alive on this planet? He had opened a few despite being told not to, but no one would ever find out, unless Iver decided to spill his secrets. Ever since he had opened that first tunnel in the archives, the mental blockade of doing it again had been lifted. He had already failed at abstaining from doing it whilst in Llyr: he might as well do it however many times he wanted to.

"Those are some bold claims," Daiyu said. "Can we even trust that she wants him dead? No offense, Iver."

"Why would I lie?" Iver asked.

"Let's just focus on the task at hand," Marcia said. "We'll address that message to the Sensis Quorum instead."

Vicente put his head in his hands. The quorum preached about putting an end to the war, but the rest of Arkensaal worshipped it. Many of the noble clans earned their riches from the war effort. And the realm worshipped Eldvittra, the god of war. He was sure of it now: the queen wanted the quorum to fail, she wanted to remove them from the queen's table. Had the quorum not had power, they would've been considered heretics. Vicente only then realized that was the light the queen saw them in, how she viewed them. The quorum had aided the monarchy for centuries and wasn't easy to get rid of. But a failure such as this, a failure such as *him*, could perhaps do that.

He couldn't go home until he bonded with the Stag. Once the queen found out Iver had abandoned his mission, she would send someone else to finish the job. But he had no idea how the bonding process worked, as the quorum kept it a secret. He would need to find a way to get them to tell him through messages sent by birds; suboptimal conditions, but it was the only way. When the Stag was bonded to him, it would fight to protect him, just as the Otter did for the members of the quorum.

"Marcia…" Iver said, and his voice sounded strange.

"Hm?"

Vicente noticed by Marcia's feet—he was staring at the ground, apparently—that she turned towards him.

"Hey, hey, Vic." She sat down next to him and wrapped an arm around his shoulders. "Let's not think about this now, yeah? You'll be safe, I'll make sure of that."

Vicente straightened his spine. He couldn't meet her eyes, but he tried for a smile. "I know."

He quickly excused himself and returned to his room. There, in privacy, he drank a bottle of Stormwater and opened a tunnel.

*

The morning after, Vicente and Marcia went to Ottone's apothecary. On one of the balconies, two courier ravens perched, awaiting their next mission. The bigger one had black, iridescent feathers, while the other had an almost blue tinge to its plumage. They both looked oily in this light, wholly black with just a kiss of rainbow colors, hues shimmering beyond the visible spectrum of human sight.

Vicente tried to get the small one, the one he had kidnapped, to step up on his arm; he wasn't sure if it still held a grudge.

Ottone stopped him. "Use the big one. That one doesn't fly to the capital."

Vicente found that strange. Was it trained to fly to a neighboring town? Or perhaps it flew to wherever the Resurrectionists camped. If they could figure that out, they could find them. Maybe they would clue them in on how Ottone's potions worked, if they were to receive adequate payment.

Marcia handed over the message addressed to the quorum, but instead of strapping it to the raven, Ottone opened it.

"Lord Ottone," Marcia warned, "the seal must be kept unbroken."

"You can seal it again, can you not?" After reading it, Ottone sighed. "I'm sorry, but I can't allow you to send this. You need to make it clearer to Arkensaal what Eloy Errani has done. This is in no way clear enough."

Vicente wanted to argue: who did he think he was, telling ambassadors of Arkensaal what they could or could not mail? But Marcia spoke first. "I assure you, once the reinforcements are here, we will let them know."

"Ambassador, I don't think you understand," Ottone said. "I mean no offence, but we do not want more agents of the crown to set foot in Llyr. Surely you must know of Llyr's turbulent past with the capital. We have accepted your entry, only because of the queen's insistence. We will not accept any more Arkensaalis to come here."

Ottone acted as though he was Llyr's prime minister already. Vicente knew Llyr's more prominent clans got upset whenever the capital meddled, but this was insane.

He was beginning to suspect that Ottone was the one who had killed the ravens. It sounded like he had enough reason to do so. Or did he reject their letter because it mentioned the murder of Natalina? Vicente remembered what Iver had said: he suspected Ottone had something to do with it.

Vicente would have to investigate. He was going to ask Eloy, in private, if he really had been the one who killed the courier birds.

Left with little choice, Marcia took the message back. "Of course, Lord Ottone. We will draft another one."

*

The next evening, Vicente went to Eloy's estate. It was already late when he arrived, but Eloy was still awake, tending to his fussing daughter. He carried her on his hip when he opened the door, and she wore a deep scowl.

They sat in armchairs opposite each other. "Are you sure the land belonged to Ottone's clan?" Eloy asked, skipping over the pleasantries.

So, Sergeant Celia was loyal to him. She would likely vote for him. "This is not over yet, my Lord. We, and Arkensaal, are on your side in this matter. The land is needed for growing crops, not herbs for science. We're considering a vote." He shifted in his seat. "We would've liked to check in with the capital first, but we have no way of contacting them."

Eloy's cheeks grew red. He placed the toddler on his knees, bouncing her gently. "You must understand, Ambassador, that I came into this role as head of my clan just a year ago. If I lose the land to Ottone, I will lose everything."

There it was, black on white, clear as day. He killed the ravens. *Fucking idiot.* "Were you aware the archives contained evidence pointing to Ottone's clan as the rightful owners?" Vicente asked, taking care to keep any hint of resentment from his tone. Eloy's childish actions, instead of addressing his concerns with the diplomats like an adult, had jeopardized the safety of four people. Did he even grasp the full extent of what he had done?

"I couldn't risk it," Eloy said. "Ottone is a pillar in this community. Every word he utters is accepted as law. If they could build him a throne, they would."

It was clear he harbored a tremendous amount of animosity and jealousy of Ottone. If Eloy had any dirt on him, he would've shared it already, without Vicente having to prompt him. This was a dead end, and so Vicente pivoted. "I have come across people like that before; those who think certain people ought to be praised for simply existing."

The girl fussed in Eloy's lap, so he let her grab hold of each of his index fingers. She looked a lot like him: the same black hair and the same eyes.

"Only a god should be held in such regard," Eloy said.

"And what god is that, if I may ask?"

As Eloy looked up at him, he frowned. "Eldvittra, of course. You're one of those people who doesn't believe Eldvittra exists?"

Eloy's daughter whined and he set her down to let her crawl around. She immediately went for the hound resting close to the fireplace. Its ears flicked when she grabbed its tail, but it didn't flee.

Vicente treaded cautiously with his words, weighing the risks against the benefits. Revealing parts of himself might result in

Eloy opening up. "I know Eldvittra exists, but I have chosen not to worship it."

"Why is that?" Eloy walked over to the table to refill his drink. The rug covering the floor from wall to wall softened the sound of his steps.

In the tone of his voice, Vicente heard only curiosity. Thus, he decided to take a risk: "Look around at the state of our realm, at the young soldiers dying by the thousands at our frontiers in a war that does not advance. Look at the way our society is being held back by the government funneling all funds to develop new weapons, at the cost of infrastructure, communication and education."

"Eldvittra is the god of war; it demands it."

"Indeed. Hence, I don't worship it. I believe Eldvittra does not deserve it."

Eloy sat down again, holding a new drink fragrant with thyme and orange peel. His cheeks were still red, and Vicente attributed that to the alcohol. "You're one of those philosophers?" Eloy asked.

Vicente let a disarming smile draw on his face. "I am no more than a diplomat in training, with a degree in history."

"Historian, eh? You ever met anyone in the Sensis Quorum?"

"A few times, yes." Perhaps that would've been considered a lie. Vicente had practically grown up with the sisters of the quorum. They were like family to him.

"Imagine being able to unite with a god, to be able to see the hidden truths of the world," Eloy said. "They say if you drink the blood of a mystic, you can gain their power." He swirled the whiskey in his glass, looking down at it as he did. Then he finished it all in one swig. "But that is not true. So many lies exist in this world, and I'm sick of it."

"How do you know it's not true?"

Eloy shook his head, his hair now loose. "Because I took your blood from the temple and drank it, and I'm still just me."

What?

"You…" Vicente stopped, voice halting. The snap of the fire in the hearth sounded like a gunshot. "You did what?"

Eloy let out a strangled sound, something halfway between a sigh and a groan. "At my daughter's blood drawing, I asked you about your family. Your reaction to that inquiry made me investigate you more. A holy brother—Fulvio was his name, I think—got together with your mother, and then he died mysteriously." Eloy spoke in a rough, cut-up voice, clearly clinging to logic. "Then, six women visited Llyr and took you to the capital. I have come to believe that those women were the sisters of the Sensis Quorum, and that you are a mystic. That is why you were allowed to move to the capital."

Vicente wanted to punch his teeth out. Had Eloy's daughter not been in the room, he might have done so. He barked out a laugh, but it sounded too unsure, too defensive. "Lord Eloy, this is absurd."

Eloy moved closer. The glare in his eyes was one of desperation. "You think you could escape this? You have history here. Your mother might have passed, but there are still people in Llyr who remember you. You were quite a disorderly child, Vicente. Beating your classmates, your old neighbors told me. Nightmares about beasts, pissing the bed until you were eight. I think you used your mystic abilities to kill Father Fulvio, and the quorum came to save you. So, tell me; why did I gain nothing from drinking your blood?"

Vicente was on his feet before the sound of Eloy's irate voice had stopped bouncing off the walls. The fear tightened around his torso, throat constricting. He figured Eloy must've been the one who broke into his room and stole a Stormwater potion, too. Vicente had read him wrong. Eloy wasn't a timid young man: he was a sneaky, power-hungry, selfish little man. "Good night," he bid, tone wavering from the deadly panic stirring in his chest.

Eloy leaned back into the couch, red-faced and not meeting his gaze. "Do you know how lucky you are to have been born with such a gift?"

Vicente walked out into the night and began the trek back to the inn. The summer heat still clung to the air like a second skin. He took a deep breath and tried to hold it, to ease his rushing heart. Beyond the town's edge, the Crooked Mountains loomed, their jagged silhouettes dark against the star-studded sky.

He couldn't shake the visceral panic. If people found out he had killed that man, they might ask him why. And he would never tell a soul about what Fulvio had done.

Halfway back, his vision still blurred. Eloy knew what Vicente had done. But he had no proof. This wouldn't haunt Vicente; he wouldn't allow it. He would deny, deny, deny, and then he would get the fuck out of Llyr. He should never have come here. *This was a bad idea.*

That old anger felt like a different world, buried in a different brain, but sometimes it would resurface. Self-restraint and logic trickled out of his hands, like sand slipping through his fingers. He had been through this chain of emotions so many times that he knew this dance by now, but as much as he was aware of it happening, he was equally unable to stop it.

The feeling of shame spread like smoke from a fire through a tavern where the air was already saturated with cigarette smoke; barely noticeable, simply uncomfortable. Nothing more than annoying. Until it graduated to indignation. How could father Fulvio have done that to him? What did Vicente do to make him feel like he could treat him like that?

Then the anger started to climb the ladder. When the pain peaked, all that remained in his mind were primal instincts. Pretending that anyone or anything else was important became difficult, pretending he gave a fuck about the rest of the world was impossible. Nothing mattered but the shame and how to rid himself of it. He would trade away everything he owned, would exchange all his current and future assets and riches, *do anything at all*, to make it stop. He would kill to make it stop.

Then the shame shifted. It became not about what had been done to him, but about what he himself had done. It was guilt. He had killed a man. Vicente imagined that Fulvio felt fear when he realized he was going to die. With a horrible, sinking feeling, he remembered that Fulvio had hopes and dreams and plans for the next day. He didn't know he was going to die that night. There had to be a few hours between his death and his elderly parents finding out, and during those hours, his family thought he was safe. They had no idea. They thought he was safe while he was already dead.

Vicente hated his own guilt, he resented it. He was angry with himself for carrying remorse he shouldn't have been burdened with in the first place, that he was bearing the weight of this thing forced upon him as a child. The anger grew.

The ladder never reached an end. Every time his fury reached for another rung, it shocked him. How far would it go? Was this the worst of it, or would it continue up? He didn't understand how he—one, singular mortal human person—could be aware of this level of pain. How was he awake for this, how was he still alive to feel this?

He became a beast walking on all fours. A beast of only teeth and claws and wrath and suffering. Reduced to an animal that couldn't be trusted and thus couldn't be blamed.

He found his room and slammed the door shut behind him. He had already chosen a sender and a receiver of Stormwater before he even realized it, driven by a primal need to feel safe again—to feel good again. As he drank the sending potion, the anticipation coursing through him was intoxicating, reminiscent of the restless excitement he'd felt as a child on the eve of his birthday. Back then, the joy of imagining the feast and gifts awaiting him had rivaled the thrill of the day itself. Tunneling was no different: the seconds leading up to the euphoria were as exquisite as the high. Vicente had indulged countless times, yet memory could never capture the experience. Like the deepest pain or the sharpest trauma, the pleasure refused to be confined to recollection. All that lingered was a hazy echo, a faded snapshot of ecstasy, a bliss demanding to be relived, again and again. When the high finally hit, it was a surprise each time.

He opened a tunnel and stepped through it.

CHAPTER 19

Vicente

It was still the same night when Vicente had carved enough space for his pain that he was allowed to finally reorient himself. His feet gradually returned to the ground. It didn't feel like amnesia, more like trying to recall a dream.

It was still dark outside, and the inn was utterly silent.

He was sitting at his desk. The letters given to him by Marcia had all been deciphered and translated. By himself, apparently.

In a haze, he made his way down to the empty kitchen and brewed some tea, then back to his room and began reading through the letters. He realized quickly that Marcia and Celia had gifted him a goldmine.

When searching through history, what he found valuable wasn't amongst what the scribes of the past had deemed important enough to document, but the correspondence between officials and merchants, travelers and civilians.

These old, brittle-edged letters were all written by Helio, the archer in the Bruvran Company, and Vicente thanked the Merciful that they had at least made some attempts to record their escapades:

The Bruvran Company slaughtered many beasts, but some still dwell in the mountain. There was the striped cat, bigger than a horse. There was the snake that could swallow a man whole, his feet still kicking. In a cave of black crystal, there was the one-antlered monster; thrice

*we tried to slay it, once we tried to reason with it. The
beast remains in the mountain.*

The Sensis Quorum had mentioned the Stag had *an* antler—
just the one. Perhaps this was the monster the text described. It
would make sense that it would be trapped in the mountains,
where few people ventured. Other than that, the mountains held
the largest deposits of schorl: a black crystal. Schorl, or black
tourmaline, was a potent mineral that warded off magic, even the
magic of the gods. Maybe there was enough of it in the cave to
keep the Stag imprisoned. Vicente would have to go there to find
out.

*

He recovered his consciousness again, now surrounded by a bunch
of children. He was reading to them. They sat in a circle, eager to
hear another story. Schools and history lessons were distant
dreams in Llyr, and most kids were apprenticed in the time-
honored crafts of their parents.

In Marcia's goldmine of letters, he had found a novel, a relic of
ancient stories harkening back to the birth of Tal Llyrie, the
precursor to Llyr. He hadn't finished reading it before, because he
wanted to share it with the world.

Story-time was a magical thing, as far as Vicente was
concerned. As he began to read, the young faces lit up, and
Vicente's heart swelled with contentment. He got his own joy
from the moment, as there was no greater pleasure than the art of
teaching these eager minds thirsting for the wisdom of their
ancestors.

*"The founder of Tal Llyrie was Prince Haoran the Vast,
of the esteemed Rhys clan. Prince Haoran chanced upon
a maiden named Elara. Her spirit, unbounded and free
as a zephyr, ensnared the prince's very essence. In an act
of unparalleled courage, he relinquished his princely
title and embraced the unknown. They ventured into the
untamed wilderness of the realm, discovering a hidden*

valley nestled amidst towering mountains and babbling rivers. Together, they breathed life into Tal Llyrie, and with that, they birthed the new Jadanza clan..."

Vicente stopped abruptly. He wrenched himself upright too fast, and the head rush nearly knocked him flat. *What?* If this was historically accurate, that meant the Jadanza clan were descendants of the royal clan, making them the ruling clan of the Llyrian prefecture. PM Jadanza and Marcia were part of a ruling clan. PM Jadanza didn't need Arkensaal's permission to settle the dispute about the land—he could do that.

Vicente looked around at the children before him, a few of them orphans of war. As a member of the ruling clan, Jadanza could stop the capital from drafting soldiers from Llyr. His decision about his people would overrule the queen's request. It would make their community stronger.

But still, Vicente couldn't tell him; he couldn't tell anyone. He and Marcia still needed to be in control over who got the land. *The queen always gets what she wants.*

Vicente finished up the story, leaving out any information on the Jadanza clan and even going so far as to make up a few details to hide what he had just learned.

*

Vicente's chambers had turned into their unofficial meeting spot. When Daiyu returned to the Sunfire Rest after her workday with Ottone, the four of them gathered in his room.

Vicente recounted what he had read. "We can't tell him, can we?"

"We don't know if he would make a decision Queen Leandra agrees with." Marcia didn't seem affected by the revelation. She was part of a noble ruling clan, a fact that could be proved to the historians of Arkensaal—she could earn a seat in the High Council.

"Couldn't Marcia decide?" Daiyu asked.

Marcia shook her head. "My father has the most authority; he would overrule me."

"We'll keep this to ourselves, then," Vicente said. He was bouncing his leg without meaning to. The euphoria was wearing off. It was always a tragedy when it did, but he had survived the initial shock of the news and Eloy's betrayal, and that was all that mattered.

Now though, he was stuck in a new reality: Eloy, and perhaps others, wanted to harm him. He would have to do something about that.

CHAPTER 20

Iver

The militia had finished their drills for the day, and Iver and Vicente had the entire training grounds to themselves. The field stretched out in baked patches of yellow grass and packed dirt, scarred with footprints under the white heat of late afternoon. Bales of hay stood at uneven intervals, bristling with arrows; some clustered in tight groups, others scattered wide like someone had been aiming with their eyes closed. Around the edges of the field, tall cypress trees loomed in orderly silence, their shadows long and sharp against the sun-bleached ground.

Iver rolled his shoulders a few times, eyeing Vicente as he warmed up his wrists. "If you're doing this because you're scared these assholes are going to try something, I'm sorry to tell you, it takes more than a couple of hours to learn how to fight."

Vicente had asked him to teach him, and Iver found the circumstances strange. Why now? But Iver had still agreed: he'd be lying if he said he didn't find it exciting to be able to fairly kick Vicente's ass. He also wanted to get his mind off the Resurrectionists and whatever they were doing together with Ottone. But as long as that organization didn't know Far Cry was in Llyr, he was safe.

Vicente wore his trademark puppy-dog smile. "I'm a fast learner. I'm pretty strong, too."

"Doesn't matter," Iver said. Vicente did look fit—for a scholar. "That's why fighting is considered a skill. Anyone can learn, if you practice hard enough."

Vicente raised his fists. "Do I need anything other than strength to fight?" He was still smiling, and Iver wanted nothing more than to rub his face in the sand.

"You tell me."

Iver charged head on, then sidestepped Vicente's line of attack and kicked at the side of his leg, purposefully avoiding his ankle and knee so he didn't inflict too much damage. Vicente's leg buckled and Iver spun around, dealing a backwards hammer punch to Vicente's jaw—a weak one, but still enough to stun him. Now by his other side, Iver wrapped an arm around his neck, twisting him and slamming him into the dirt.

"Fuck," Vicente choked. He tried to heave himself up, but Iver pressed his weight down on him, holding him in place.

"If you're done being a smart-ass, I'll teach you." Iver released him.

"Yes, sir." Vicente rose to his feet, like a monster emerging from the ocean. Despite his defeat, he stood tall.

It was clear Vicente was nervous about something, and Iver pondered whether he should be concerned as well—more than he already was. But if Vicente was truly worried about their situation, he would've announced the fact that he was a mystic and under the direct protection of the quorum. Although, Iver didn't know Vicente to be the person to make the smarter choice.

Iver showed him how to throw a punch without breaking the fine bones in his hands, as well as some grappling techniques. The sun and sky turned orange. Sweat ran down Iver's back and he couldn't wait to take a bath. He was a much more skilled fighter than Vicente, yes, but it had been a few months since he had practiced his hand-to-hand combat skills.

Only when Vicente looked lightheaded from exertion—he could barely keep his eyes focused, squinting, deep lines in his forehead and panting like a dog—did Iver end the lesson.

Vicente doubled over, braced his hands against the ground before rolling over his shoulder and laying down on his back, sprawling like a starfish. His chest heaved. "I'm going to throw up."

Iver clicked his tongue. "Oh, the drama."

Vicente took a breath, closed his eyes, and then—to Iver's dismay—started singing. It was an upbeat song Iver recognized, rhythm usually made up of hand drums and claves. Vicente's voice was rich and resonant despite his current condition.

He's a good singer. "What…?"

"Singing is good to not puke," Vicente explained, still humming through his words. He patted his hand on the ground to the beat of the song.

Iver's cheeks hurt and when he realized he was smiling, he spun around on his heel and walked away. Thankfully, Vicente had kept his eyes closed and hadn't seen it.

Alone, he left the training grounds and headed back. The neatly trampled field gave way to the rougher edges of Llyr: dust trails, dry grass and olive trees; those old, wiry bastards with silver-green leaves like dull coins and trunks that twisted up from the ground like they were trying to wring themselves free of it.

He took the less trafficked route back to the inn, a shortcut he had found, threading through the quiet backstreets. The evening cast its shadow, but the western horizon clung to the last of the daylight. Above the narrow alleyway, swallows filled the air, their forms darting across the darkening heavens.

He froze. Glassy eyes looked up at him and he staggered backwards. Tucked behind a few crates was the body of a young boy. His mouth was open in a silent cry. It was the same boy who had given him the die. Jairo. He had been disposed of, like trash. Iver had seen death before, made himself familiar with it, but this death was the tortured kind and laced with pleading, with surprise, the kind of dying that didn't register what was happening or why it was. The type of death Iver never dabbled in.

Despite the darkness, he could see the deep bruising around the tiny neck. It was the same culprit. A distant voice in the back of his mind called out for caution. He realized that if he was found here at the scene of the crime, it would only add fuel to the fire of the Llyrians' distrust. But he couldn't just leave Jairo like this, for some other poor soul to find.

He located Sergeant Celia, and she gathered the rest. As two holy sisters of Eldvittra wept over the body, Iver left. He felt empty. His own skin was too tight over his face. Adrenaline made him feel weightless. Paranoia crept black along the edges of his vision, something invisible and unspoken hunting him.

When he returned to the Sunfire Rest, word had already spread. Both Marcia and Vicente gave him space. Daiyu did not.

Iver sank slowly to the floor of his room and leaned his head against the wall. She put a mug stinking of wine between his feet and hunkered down next to him, nursing a mug of her own. They sat quietly for a while. Perhaps she wanted small-talk, pleasantries, so that they could pretend the world wasn't stewing in its own shit.

Then, Daiyu reached for something tucked into the waist of the back of her trousers. "I noticed yours went missing." She handed him a knife.

Iver could tell it was brand new. He was dumbfounded for a few seconds before accepting it. "I… thank you."

Daiyu looked at him oddly. It could be that she didn't expect politeness from him.

He used his thumbnail to carefully scrape across the sharp edge of the blade. After Vicente had stolen his, he couldn't catch more than an hour of sleep. He would feel safer now, and he wondered if Daiyu somehow knew that. He could try to convince himself he didn't need one, but there was something brewing beneath the picturesque atmosphere in Llyr. And Ottone was involved with the *fucking* Resurrectionists.

"I already spoke to Marcia and Vicente about this, but I think you should know, too," she said, taking a sip of her wine. "I shadowed Lord Ottone today, and he talked to me about the ambassadors finding proof the land belonged to Eloy Errani's clan."

"Atli the blacksmith was the one who told him." Iver was surprised to hear that; he thought Falco—the man working in Ottone's apothecary—would be the one most loyal to him and spill the curated lies Marcia had prepared for them.

Daiyu nodded. "Mister Atli is more treacherous than he lets on." She gave him a sideways glance and lifted her mug to her lips. "Another child dead, huh?" she said, voice low.

"Yeah."

"I'm sorry you had to see that."

"Me too. His name was Jairo, and he had a necklace with his name, too, like some fucking dog collar. But it wasn't around his neck."

"They said he was strangled, like the girl," Daiyu said. "Maybe it fell off during it?"

"It's just a hunch, but I think the killer is keeping them. Like trophies." He shot Daiyu a look. "I've been around a lot of murderers. And apparently, so have you." Iver still couldn't comprehend that Daiyu had once been part of the Resurrectionists, the organization working tirelessly to defy the laws of the realm and doing everything they could to break off from established society. She didn't look like the type, but then again, what type did he look like?

She nodded, slowly. "I have." She offered nothing more. He couldn't blame her for that.

They sat quietly, listening to the sound of the cicadas outside, while Daiyu finished her wine.

"You can have mine," Iver said and placed his mug in front of her. "I haven't touched it."

"You should have some; a bit of alcohol might help you catch some sleep." She looked at him, really looked at him. There was a different side to her then. Concern. "You look absolutely exhausted."

"I'll sleep better now that I have this," Iver said and held up the knife.

Daiyu didn't look convinced. "It's difficult sleeping alone, yeah? Without someone watching your back."

Iver said nothing. *Did she know what it was like?*

"Please don't punch me in the face, but if you want, I could stay for a few hours, let you catch some shuteye."

The thought of her staying soothed the rawness in his chest. "What would you be doing in the meantime?"

She grabbed his mug and shot him a smile. "I'll stare at the door, contemplate the meaning of life, and finish your drink. Now go to bed, young man. Don't you worry about me: all I need to be entertained is my mind!"

"I don't doubt that." Iver walked over to the bed and sat. He hesitated before laying down. "Why, Daiyu?"

"Why, what?"

"Why are you doing this for me?"

She sighed, slow and heavy. "Look. I don't know what they did to you... but if my actions in any way contributed to it... it's the least I could do. Plus, it's an experiment: I want to see if you're just as grumpy, even after a good night's rest." That singsong tone of hers that oh so annoyed him had returned.

Iver lay down on his side, hiding his relief beneath his reliable curtain of apathy.

But his fingers wrapped so tightly around the handle of the knife that they were going numb. The murderer would not stop. The culprit was most likely Ottone, and Iver had some evidence, however sparce. The chance of being believed, of being heard, was minimal. But he couldn't solve this by himself, and Jairo had died on his watch. Guilt eclipsed his fear of getting reduced to a laughingstock.

He would have to tell the rest of the crew about everything he knew.

CHAPTER 21

Vicente

"Ottone said that?" Iver asked after Marcia finished explaining what had happened when Ottone read and refused the message they were trying to send to the quorum. "He doesn't want you to contact Arkensaal, out of fear of them sending more agents?"

Vicente's room in the Sunfire Rest only came with one chair and one bed, and so they were all seated on the floor as they shared a bottle of wine. It reminded Vicente of his teenage years. Outside, the sounds of Llyr softened with the light. Evening pressed in against the windowpanes, turning the sky to bruised lavender and rust. The shouts of vendors had faded to the occasional murmur, and the clatter of carts had thinned to a lonely echo down the stone alleys. The air smelled of cooling stone and woodsmoke, tinged faintly with jasmine from the porch below.

"Yeah, he did." Marcia took a sip from her mug and drew her lips back in disgust. "He thinks the four of us are enough, if even too many."

"I've heard him say shit like that before," Iver said. The discovery of that dead child must have taken a toll on him, although he wasn't addressing it. But Vicente could tell by the far-away look in his eyes.

"When did you hear him say that?" Daiyu asked.

"I've been doing some investigating of my own," Iver said. "I listened in when he was speaking to your father, Marcia. They *really* don't want Arkensaali people to come here. I think they are going to try to pin the murders on us, to show the Llyrians that outsiders shouldn't be welcomed, that we only bring trouble. Those are the two reasons why he won't let you send a message like that: he doesn't want more Arkensaali people coming here, and he doesn't want the murder to be solved."

Marcia put a cigarette between her lips and struck a match. The light of the small flame painted her face a warm orange. "That's a bold accusation, Iver."

"Why wouldn't they want to find the killer?" Daiyu asked.

"Because Ottone is involved," Iver said. "I'm sure of it."

From what Vicente had heard, there were no new developments in PM Jadanza's investigation into the death, and now, they had a second one in their hands. The girl had been buried, not burned, an unusual practice in Llyr. There were still no leads, but surely, behind the scenes, they must've been working to piece it together. They had to be. "Do you have any proof of this?"

Iver took out his notebook and flipped through the pages. He showed them a rough sketch. It depicted the first murder scene. "The coins around the body had been staged, they weren't dropped. I saw Natalina's body in Ottone's mortuary, and she had coins under her eyelids. It looked ritualistic."

"Are you saying there are occult things afoot?" Daiyu asked, not at all alarmed. If anything, she sounded excited.

"You said magic comes from the gods," Iver said to Vicente.

"I did, yeah." *Magic.* Vicente wasn't surprised Iver drew such a connection, and Ottone's healing potions were the biggest clue: in the last decade, science had made mind-blowing progress, especially in medicine. But there were limitations to what they could accomplish. Was Vicente supposed to believe Ottone had pushed past those boundaries, all on his own, with no resources? He was suspecting something more sinister, but he didn't want to verbalize it. He didn't even want to think about it.

"Ottone has access to magic," Iver said. "I've seen it. I tried to break into his office and got a static shock. His mortuary is insanely cold, with no electricity."

Instinctively, Vicente knew Iver was right. What Ottone had done to his door had to be magic. The only other way was if

Ottone was as scientifically savvy as he claimed, which he had shown no evidence of. There was no other explanation for it.

"I'm sorry—you tried to break into Ottone's office?" Marcia asked.

"It's fine," Vicente said, "I told him to."

Iver took something from his pocket. It was a die, and he rolled it over to Daiyu. "Tell me what that is."

She picked it up with her index finger and thumb, pulled down her glasses further down her nose and peered at the die over the rim of them. "Ah. That is a human tarsal bone."

Marcia frowned. "A what?"

"Foot bone. From a human."

Vicente's stomach dropped. *A human bone.* What had Iver been up to? Given that he was throwing accusations at Ottone, he must've gotten it from him somehow.

"This is all pointing to something occult," Iver said. His gaze flickered between them all. He was checking to make sure they were hearing him out. "That would explain why Ottone burned his harvest. What we saw him do, it could've been an offering. A bunch of kids have gone missing. I think Ottone is killing them and using them as sacrifices. I can't figure out the rest of it, so…" Iver ground his jaw. "I'm asking you all for help."

Seconds of silence stretched into a minute, then two.

"That's insane," Marcia muttered.

"I believe you," Vicente said. "And I think he's using them for his healing potions." Vicente remembered reading about it; how could he not? Scholars had called it 'alchemy': a practice that could, in theory, make elixirs of immortality and be a way to cure any illness. Historically, many chemists and philosophers had embarked on the journey to make it a reality, and all of them had failed. All recorded efforts had one thing in common, though: they had all tried to harness the essence of life from other people. "Look, what Ottone is doing… I've read about past attempts at it. You can't just brew herbs to make an elixir that restores a person's health. There must be more to it. What if the dead children have something to do with it?"

"But Eldvittra doesn't require sacrifices," Iver said. "At least not... that."

"Could be for another god," Daiyu said.

"That would be very much illegal," Marcia said. "And what god would that be?"

Vicente couldn't understand why it had taken him so long to piece together that Ottone was using magic from a god. Perhaps because of the implications. Ottone had summoned a god and broken bread with it. The punishment for that was not a merciful execution: if the government found out, he would be kept alive to be tortured. Ottone's family, his entire bloodline, would be wiped out. And that was the least dramatic option. If Eldvittra learned of this, humanity would be doomed.

"You said the coins around the body were staged," Vicente said. "What were they staged to look like?"

Iver frowned. "'Look like'?"

"A circle? A star? What pattern were they?" From Iver's sketch, which looked more like a nervous doodle than anything else, Vicente couldn't make out what had tipped him off that the scene was staged. Whatever pattern Iver had seen among the coins, it escaped him entirely.

Iver pointed to his drawing again. "It tried to look random. But chaos cannot be faked."

"Randomness," Vicente echoed. "That would point to the Gambler." The die, the coins. His chest constricted. Had Ottone contacted one of the Usurper gods, a sworn enemy of Eldvittra?

"Who the fuck's the Gambler?" Iver asked.

Vicente put his head in his hands. It had to be the Gambler: only usurpers could grant magic to humans. The goddess of crops already had enough worshippers in the north, Themyr and Curiosity couldn't be bothered to speak to humans, and he refused to believe Ottone was insane enough to contact Rage the jackal. "The Gambler was a common name for one of the Usurper gods that fought Eldvittra in the war of the seven gods."

"Fuck me. What's it god of?"

"Fate, I think." Vicente was the one in the group with the most knowledge of history, but he couldn't recall a single time he had come across any detailed information about the Gambler. The Merciful Eldvittra was lord of the earth, and no other gods, aside from the horned god, would ever dare come close to it again after the war.

Iver nodded. "Yeah, Ottone spoke a bunch about fate. The whims of fate, he called it."

"That's the Gambler, alright." Vicente's heart was beating out of his chest. "Shit. *Shit.*"

Marcia dragged her hand down her face and put the cigarette out on the sole of her boot. "And you think all of this is the secret to his potions?"

"I don't think he's using them as sacrifices, I think he's stealing their life force." Vicente enjoyed reading about the dark magics of the past, where alchemists had tried to bottle the essence of life. But that was supposed to have been left in the past. The possibility that Ottone was either experimenting on the children or draining them made Vicente's stomach roil. If that was what Ottone was doing, they needed to know so they could stop him. "Daiyu, when you were with the Resurrectionists, did they ever mention a god?"

Daiyu accepted a cigarette from Marcia. "They... weren't worshipping the Gambler when I was with them, I swear."

Marcia took her wife's hand, stroking her thumb over her knuckles. "I think it's good if you continue spending time with Ottone," she said to Daiyu. "Try to figure out what the fuck is going on with his potions, and how the Gambler is connected to all this."

Vicente was convinced there were answers to be found in Ottone's office, but it was locked by arcane magic and had no windows to the outside. "If Daiyu can't find anything, could we summon the Gambler and speak to it?"

Marcia stood, her eyelids peeled back in a terrifying stare. She even pointed at him for good measure. "You will, under no circumstances, do such a thing. Do you hear me?"

Vicente swallowed. "Yes, ma'am."

"It's not like it would be dangerous," Daiyu said. "Would it?"

"It is illegal," Marcia snapped. "Do not argue with me on this."

"It would just be to talk to it," Daiyu continued. She must've been the only person on earth who dared to disagree with Marcia when she was like this. "There's no harm in that."

Marcia was having none of it. "If anyone were to find out, how would you prove your intent, hm? How would you prove you didn't intend to worship it?"

With that, they all stood to go back to their respective rooms. The lamps burned low, and the shadows were mellowed to a deep indigo as night had settled in.

Vicente stopped Iver before he could leave. "Iver... nicely done."

"Sorry?"

"You figured it out. Good job." Vicente wanted to say more, to tell him how bright he was, that they couldn't have gotten this far without him. Vicente still wanted to try. Iver's shape, the cut of his face, was so striking it demanded attention and any reasons to starve him of it had died. As Vicente tried to conjure and revive the feeling of hatred he once bore, he realized he couldn't summon even a ghost of that feeling now. But the words caught in his throat, blocked by a fear of overstepping, by sheer cravenness.

Iver swallowed, looked down, gritted his teeth. Then he gave Vicente a nod and left.

CHAPTER 22

Daiyu

When Daiyu awoke, she was frozen in place, arms stiff at her sides while the terror of the nightmare pulsated through her. Panic uncoiled in her chest, climbing up her throat like ivy. Why was it that she couldn't remember their faces, but the smell of burnt flesh and mustard gas still haunted her senses?

"Nightmare?" Marcia sat on the edge of the bed, her nightgown draping over her form. A vision of contrast, the pristine white fabric embraced her rich, dark skin, opposites entwined. Outside the windows, the shroud of night still prevailed, cloaking its inky veil around the world.

Daiyu sat up in bed, rubbing a hand over her face. Her glasses were on the nightstand, but she didn't reach for them.

"I wanted to ask you something," Marcia said, somewhat hesitantly. "Just tell me if you don't want to answer it. It's about your nightmares."

Daiyu knew what was coming, she had avoided it for years. In her vulnerability, it was as though her ribs were cracked and peeled back, exposing her heart. Yet, she felt completely safe as she looked into Marcia's eyes. "You can ask."

"When we found out about the Resurrectionists, you told us you never hurt anyone." Marcia squeezed her hands together. They were resting in her lap. It was something she would do when nervous or anxious; she would hold her own hand. "But you've told me some things about your dreams: that you can still smell it."

"Yeah." Marcia could see right through her lies. She knew—not what Daiyu had done, but that she had done something. "Is that why you hurt yourself?" Marcia's voice sounded small. "Because you feel guilty?"

They sat quietly for a moment while Daiyu tried to find her words. Her actions had resulted in emotions, and over time, those emotions had evolved into instincts. The bond between cause and effect had long been severed. "It gives me comfort," she said, remorse seeping into her tone. "I'll try to stop—"

"Please don't give me that again. I have empathy for you, you know I do. But maybe being honest is the way to rid yourself of those feelings?"

"Honest with who? I know what I did: I hurt people. I regret it every day. Telling the world about it won't change what I did."

Marcia watched her, a pleading look on her face. "Why? Why did you?" She looked so heartbroken that Daiyu had to look elsewhere.

Yes, why? How could Daiyu even begin to describe what life was like at twenty, when there was no place for her anywhere, when the very constructs of society made no sense to her, when she saw injustice in every detail but no one else seemed to notice? When everyone around her cheered for the amount of people lost in the war? "They promised me something different. They were the only ones who I've ever heard speak about ending the war instead of feeding into it."

"That's the reason you built chemical weapons for them? Tortured for them?"

*

"Then you add the water from the boiled lavender, like so," Ottone said as he dripped the liquid into the beaker. "Now it will need to steep for a few days."

Daiyu had yet to see a potion go directly from their workbench into the stomach of a patient. She had seen it work many times, but he always used the sealed bottles from the crate in the corner. Either he was keeping a secret ingredient from her, one that required the containers to be sealed, or he wasn't making the potions himself.

Ottone took off his lab coat and hung it on one of the hooks. He was dressed like her: button-down shirt tucked into linen trousers. Daiyu had not packed clothes for the rainy autumn looming in the distance, and she desperately wanted this mission to be over.

"You seem distracted today, Professor." Ottone started cleaning up their work area, indicating that it was the end of the day. "I consider you a friend. You can tell me."

Frankly, she was exhausted. She didn't know why Iver got so upset over her involvement with the Resurrectionists, but she suspected he had a history with them. Maybe that was where he learned to shoot; maybe he was once part of them as well. When she left them, she vowed never to speak of them again. But now, her past actions harmed Iver, and she had no idea how to fix it.

Daiyu asked, "When you were developing the formula, did you ever injure someone accidentally, before it was completed?"

Ottone sat down again, combing his fingers through his blond beard. "Yes. Yes, I did. There was my first patient. She didn't have long and agreed to try it out. The potion burned a hole in her stomach, and she passed away. Not a day goes by that I don't beat myself up over that. I felt powerless."

"Yeah, powerless. I feel that way too, sometimes."

She couldn't outright ask Ottone about his involvement with the Resurrectionists without him finding out that they had read one of his messages. She could bring up the topic by revealing that she once was with them, but she really didn't want to.

"And now you hurt yourself to make amends? That's why the saying goes, 'beat yourself up over,' doesn't it?" he said with a chuckle.

Daiyu pulled her sleeve over her bandaged arm. Clearly, she hadn't been doing a good enough job at covering it up. She had cut herself again, after Marcia had gone back to sleep. She couldn't help it. "I guess there's something to that."

"There's no way you can rectify your mistakes?"

"No, there's not." She was pushing Marcia away by keeping secrets—she understood that her silence was creating a divide, a chasm of unshared fears—but how could she even begin to tell a loved one about how she had done things most people would only read about in horror stories?

Ottone got up, walked over to one of the crates, and picked up a bottle. "At least try a healing potion to fix that injury on your arm, Daiyu."

She shouldn't. There could be, most likely *was*, something dark about his craft, something sinister.

But if she took it, she would heal in a second, and then she could cut herself again, in the same spot. It was her favorite spot; it hurt enough to get her mind off things, and it bled enough to jolt her, but not enough to require stitches. If she took the potion, she could get the same euphoria that night again, she wouldn't have to wait.

She shouldn't.

Ottone handed her an unsealed potion and she drank it. Minutes ticked past, but the wound never closed. Disappointment and shame bloomed in her chest.

"I'm sorry, I'm still not sure how they work," Ottone muttered. "Sometimes you need more than one dose. It's quite a mystery, even to me." He gently patted her on the shoulder. "All we can do is try our best. Would you mind taking another dose?"

CHAPTER 23

Vicente

Summoning a god that already had ties to the realm wasn't difficult, but it was very illegal. Because how could you prove that you were calling upon it for other reasons than to worship it?

Vicente was familiar with the practices—not by performing them but by reading about them in old scriptures and observing the quorum when they summoned the Otter.

Vicente drew the symbol with chalk on the floor of his room and placed his offering in the middle of it: Iver's die. Daiyu had yet to uncover any of Ottone's secrets and Vicente was growing restless from their lack of progress. He suspected they were all in danger, given that they weren't allowed to leave or contact Arkensaal, but as Marcia had pointed out, the crew hadn't been overtly threatened. Still, Vicente was getting anxious.

"How do you know this will summon the right god?" Iver asked. They were alone in Vicente's room; he knew Marcia and Daiyu would try to stop him.

"I don't. This is the crest the Usurper gods used, and I'm guessing they are still attached to it." Before their fallout, the humans worshipped all the gods. Traces of this era could still be found in many locations around the country, and Vicente had seen the symbol enough times to remember every detail of it.

"What, you saw a drawing in one of your history books and think that's enough to call on a whole-ass god?"

Vicente snorted. Sometimes Iver's anger felt forced, like a thin disguise for something else. Aside from that, it also allowed a short breath of amusement. "I have seen the members of the quorum summon the Otter many times. This is how it is done."

Vicente spoke the words, calling for the Gambler of the Usurper gods. His pulse pounded in his ears and his hands trembled as the floor began to shake. Iver moved to stand behind him, hand on the new knife strapped to his thigh.

A pair of paws materialized, emerging from the floorboards as if born from the very essence of the wood. With an uncanny grace, the god hauled itself up, its claws carving into the wooden surface as though it was supple butter yielding to its touch. A creature akin to a cat revealed itself, possessing an air of feline elegance, tail curving and forming an 'S.'

"What do you want?" the Gambler snapped, glaring at Vicente with emerald-green eyes that shone like the northern lights as they reflected the warm glow from the lanterns in the room.

"You are the Gambler, yes?" Vicente tried, once he found his voice.

The deity kneaded its paws on the floor, wooden planks splintering between its claws. "*You* called *me*, puny thing. You don't know who you called?"

"How do I know I'm speaking to the right one, the one I intended to call?" Vicente said.

The fur on its back stood on end and it bared its teeth at him. "I am the Gambler, god of chance and unpredictability."

Too late, Vicente realized he was faring through uncharted waters. Speaking with the Otter, a demigod, was something else entirely: he was unaware of the parameters of the Gambler's powers, how it wished to be addressed, how to respect it. Could it smite him in an instant?

"My apologies, Gambler, I seem to have angered you, and that was not my intention." Vicente bowed his head. "Forgive me, my kind has not documented your existence as well as you deserve. You must be powerful, more powerful than Eldvittra, to have come here undetected."

The Gambler barked a laugh. "Eldvittra has abandoned you humans; it is I and the other Usurper gods who rule in its stead to keep the horned god at bay."

Vicente felt unsteady on his feet, like a gust of wind could topple him over. He had spoken to the Otter—the keeper of all knowledge regarding the past—many times, and it had never mentioned that Eldvittra supposedly had abandoned humanity.

But it was still believable. Because no matter how hard humans prayed and how well they worshipped Eldvittra, it never showed up. It referred to itself as the lord of the earth, yet it never sat foot here. Meanwhile, the Gambler had—even though Vicente had called for it only once. Ottone, and maybe the Resurrectionists, had been involved with the Gambler for some time, and Eldvittra hadn't noticed. Perhaps the god of war had, in fact, deserted humanity.

When Vicente didn't speak, the Gambler seemed to grow even more agitated. "I move through the realms of many gods, and I push things over edges. I am the chaos, the chance of a coin toss. You shall respect me."

Vicente's mind was blank. He probably should have prepared some sort of speech, or at least some talking points. But he had readied himself for earthquakes and booming voices, not this. Not a cat. "Do you mean that you start conflicts? By driving people over the edge?"

"No," the Gambler seethed, all venom. "I wish to stand at the edge of the Milky Way and paw on things until they fall."

Vicente didn't know what to make of that. "May we ask you for some information regarding Lord Ottone and the Resurrectionists?"

"You may ask, but I shan't answer. You should make me an offer; then you might win."

Vicente looked to Iver, who had his arms crossed over his chest and one eyebrow arched as he regarded the god. He looked like he would prefer not to get roped into the conversation.

"What kind of offer would you be interested in?" Vicente asked the Gambler.

"You want secrets, you will provide secrets. Whoever loses shall share theirs." The Gambler licked at its paw. It didn't move its mouth when it spoke. "If you lose, it will be shared with the whole of Llyr; I'll make sure of that. If I lose, I will tell you everything I know about the Resurrectionists. About everything Ottone is doing to the children of Llyr. About his healing potions."

That confirmed it, then. Unless the Gambler was lying—which was a very real possibility—then Ottone was harming others. "I didn't know you to be bloodthirsty, Gambler."

"Blood is a payment which I accept," it answered. "I require compensation for my services, even from Ottone, and you cannot fault me for that. Now, it is your turn to offer payment."

What exactly Ottone was doing... they would have to win to find out. But Vicente didn't speak; did he even have any secrets?

Father Fulvio. Like a traitor, his mind immediately went to the most damning secret of all, the one he'd sworn he would never share, and now, he couldn't get it out of his thoughts. He wouldn't do it though, even if he had a chance of winning the Gambler's game. The risk was too great, he would never—

"I have one," Iver offered and stepped forward.

"Are you prepared to share it if you lose?" the god asked, but didn't seem to actually care.

Iver nodded once. "I am."

The god's back arched and it spit up a die. The die was ten-sided, and the polished edges glinted in the light from the lantern at Vicente's desk. "Even or odd?"

Would the winner be up to chance? Vicente wondered if that was fair, if the Gambler was the god of probability. He just hoped Iver hadn't picked too sensitive a secret.

"Odd," Iver said without hesitation.

The Gambler pawed on the die, and it rolled across the floor. It landed on a four. Vicente half expected the god to laugh maniacally, but it simply remained annoyed. "Now, you must tell me your secret."

Vicente doubted the Gambler could spill the information to everyone in Llyr. How would it accomplish that—would it run through the streets of Llyr and tell them, and risk being seen by Eldvittra, if it was watching? Maybe Eldvittra was still around, and the Gambler had slipped in unnoticed, quietly communing with Ottone.

Iver squeezed his eyes shut and sighed. "I am the Far Cry assassin."

"Now all of Llyr knows it." The Gambler stood, kneading its paws on the wooden floor for a moment. Then it slid into the floorboards again, like a seal diving into the ocean.

Vicente and Iver stayed silent for a few seconds, contemplating what had just transpired.

Then Iver sighed again, exasperated this time. "Well, that was a fucking waste of time."

How could the Gambler have informed the whole of Llyr of this already? And would the Llyrians even believe it? This wasn't making any sense at all.

He put his hand on Iver's shoulder. "Are you alright?" His hand was so close to his neck, that beautiful neck, that he could touch it with his thumb. He didn't.

Iver shrugged. "It's fine. Do you know how to win at something that is random?"

"How?"

"You make both possibilities work in your favor."

CHAPTER 24

Vicente

The next morning, Marcia came pounding on his door and insisted on gathering the four of them in Vicente's room.

In her hand was a sheet of paper. "Iver, what the fuck is this?" She held it up, and it was a drawing of Iver's face, as detailed as a photograph, with the text *Wanted dead or alive: Far Cry* printed underneath. "These are on every single fucking lamppost in town. From what I've heard, they've been up since last night." Her eyes were wide, her nostrils flaring, and Vicente searched for the best words to use to apologize.

"We fucked around with the Gambler," Iver said nonchalantly, like this hadn't put him in harm's way.

She crumpled the poster and threw it on the floor. "Why would you do that? I told you not to!"

Daiyu's chipper demeanor was gone. She pursed her lips and kept to the background. If even Daiyu feared her now, that meant Marcia was properly furious.

Marcia continued to unleash her anger. "Were you thinking straight? Be honest, Vicente, have you been using your powers? Opening tunnels? You get weird for a few hours when you do."

"I messed up and I'm sorry, but—"

"You don't think this fact will turn all of them against us, hm?" She snarled at him. "This is a delicate job, and you two have completely botched it. Iver is an assassin, and they will think he had something to do with those murdered children."

Vicente's patience had been running thin for a while, and he careened over the edge. "We are getting nowhere—it's time to act."

"Well, you've given us no choice." Marcia sat down on Vicente's bed. "We're intercepting one of Ottone's ravens. That might give us a fucking clue."

"How would we do that?"

"Iver is going to shoot it down."

"I don't think—" Iver started, but Marcia cut him off by snapping:

"Just do as I tell you, Iver."

*

Vicente and his crew remained inside his room in the inn for the entire day, out of fear of confrontation. When evening came, they finally headed out to Ottone's apothecary.

The sun was setting over the golden fields of wheat and oat. At that time of day, most of the Llyrians, aside from the shop owners, were maintaining their habit of gathering in the Harvest Heart. Thus, it was the perfect time to strike.

Sure enough, posters of Iver like the one Marcia had shown were plastered all around town. No one had come for him yet, but it was likely just a matter of time. Vicente hadn't realized the Gambler was capable of something like this, and now he felt like an absolute idiot.

"When we shoot this bird down, that will be our first attack to set off a war," Vicente said. "Are we ready to do that?"

"You've already made it inevitable, Vicente," Marcia said.

Iver looked up at the sky. "Here it comes. It's heading north." A bird flying to the capital would be travelling in a south-eastern direction. This one, the smaller one, was most likely on its way to the Resurrectionists.

Iver nocked and let an arrow loose in the span of a second. The raven made no sound as it was hit square in the chest and fell straight down. Iver picked up the dead bird and stole the message tied to its leg. Then he put the carcass in his bag.

"Don't hold on to evidence, Iver," Daiyu warned.

"I'm taking its feathers for arrows and then I'm burning it. The poor thing deserves a proper send-off. Besides, we're fucked anyway; they'll know it was us."

Vicente took the little roll of paper from his hand and read it.

"Anything helpful?" Daiyu queried.

"Not really: *To the farm: Requesting another batch, have ready in two weeks.* Could he be referring to the healing potions?" What was 'the farm'? Was this the place where the potions were actually being brewed, someplace far enough away from Llyr that the bottles had to be sealed to keep them from spilling on the long journey? A theory was forming in Vicente's mind, and even though he knew that premature judgement was the bane of finding out the truth, he saw no other possibilities: Ottone had taken the missing children to this farm, where he killed them and used their blood to make healing elixirs. He had left the two strangled children findable to serve as proof that Vicente and his crew were behind it all. Ottone planned on pinning the murders on them.

"Perhaps," Daiyu mused. "It all has to be connected somehow."

Marcia buried her face in her hands. "For the love of the Merciful, we're not getting anything of use."

Vicente moved closer, put a hand on her shoulder and squeezed. "Marcia, take a moment to collect—"

Marcia held up a finger to stop him and Vicente's teeth clicked shut. "This is all my fault," she said. "I should've known you weren't ready, Vicente. I should've asked to go alone. You are not fit for this, not yet, and Tal Miril will hear about this, *if* we're not killed trying to leave. I'm not sure you'll ever be fit for this job."

He had never heard her snap like that before, and he tried not to take offense. But maybe there was some truth to it: his strength resided in mysticism and history, not diplomacy.

Daiyu grabbed her arm gently. "Let's all calm down."

"No, I won't. Vicente and Iver need to go. You and I will sort this out."

Vicente had to bite his own lip to stop himself from arguing. Perhaps Marcia was right, maybe it would be best if she handled this alone. But Vicente would never consider leaving her here, at least not without Iver. Iver had made it clear he suspected Ottone killed the children and Vicente believed so too; they all did. But with no proof, they could do next to nothing. And if Ottone caught wind of their suspicions...

"They can't go back to the capital, remember?" Daiyu said. "The queen will have Vicente assassinated."

Marcia sighed. "Shit. We'll figure something out. But you can't stay here." She took the lead to the stables. "Go to Mariemoor, bring Iver's fake identification papers and show them your Arkensaali passport and they'll accept you. I don't care if anyone here gets pissed off if you leave."

Marcia wasn't thinking clearly; the prime minister wouldn't let them go, and he would take great offence if they went against his orders. Still, the crew followed her. A brisk walk and petting some horses might settle her down.

The light was fading all around them as the sun's golden fingers surrendered its hold on the horizon, but the buildings' terracotta roofs still radiated warmth as if the sun had only just left. Out on the outskirts of Llyr, the scent of sun-warmed clay and jasmine went unspoiled by the usual stench of a bustling town, and Vicente drew deep breaths of it before the inevitable reek of horses could reach him.

Iver was the first to enter the stables. He took two steps inside, then pivoted and walked back out again. "Don't look. Don't go in there." He put his hands out to stop them, but Marcia and Vicente pushed past.

The air stank of iron. Their horses were dead. The animals' necks had been cut, almost all the way through. They were semi-beheaded. Only their spines kept their heads attached. Blood pooled on the dirty floor.

Someone in Llyr was very keen on Vicente and his crew staying. "They think we killed the children," Vicente said, dazed.

"That's why they're doing this." How could the Llyrians think that they, Arkensaali ambassadors, were the culprits?

"If they think that, they're fucking idiots," Iver said over his shoulder. He hadn't come back into the stables with them; he was three feet outside the door and had his back turned to the dead horses. "Because a bunch of kids went missing long before we even got here."

Marcia spun around to glare at Iver. "And why didn't you think to tell us about that? For Merciful's sake Iver, I can't believe—"

"I did tell you," Iver yelled, still with his back turned. "I knew you weren't fucking listening."

Vicente kept looking at the horses, unblinking. "They're probably looking for us. We're getting arrested once they find us."

"Oh no, they won't get a chance," Marcia said. "We're ending this tonight. Vicente and Iver, see if you can find anything else on Ottone: we'll need all the dirt we can get. We're tearing him down, so that the people won't be too angry when we give the land to Eloy Errani. Daiyu and I will pack up all our things and set up a meeting with Eloy and PM Jadanza, then we're leaving. We have reason enough to appoint the land to Eloy; I don't care what anyone has to say about it. Quickly now."

CHAPTER 25

Vicente

It was the darkest hour of the night, when only animals prowled, when Vicente and Iver arrived. Their destination was the temple of Eldvittra, a sacred abode also housing the orphanage—they were going to try to talk to the children. The cries from the cicadas, sharp and ceaseless, were the only sounds to disturb the quiet night. The air smelled faintly of incense clinging to old stone, and as they crossed the courtyard, their footsteps sounded far too loud. "That's Ottone's horse," Iver pointed out. A brown horse stood in front of the gate. There was no mistaking it: Ottone was within the temple walls. Maybe that was a good thing. Maybe they could catch him in the act. Ottone must've figured out how to successfully drain the essence of life from a person. They only needed proof of it.

Vicente and Iver approached a side door, hidden from prying eyes, and pushed it open. The door protested their intrusion with a faint creak. They froze, hearts pounding, waiting for any sign that their presence had been detected. The temple stayed silent, as any inhabitants seemingly went undisturbed.

Once reassured, they slipped inside. Vicente's eyes adjusted to the dim illumination provided by flickering candle flames. They took cover behind a row of pillars and spotted Ottone sitting in one of the pews. He looked like he was praying, and he was alone.

But that changed within a few minutes, when the front entrance door opened. A young girl strode forward, closing the distance between her and Ottone, who remained seated. Vicente had met her before, but couldn't recall her name. She looked to be around eight or nine years old.

The two started a conversation, but the echo made it impossible to hear what they were saying. Vicente strained his ears, body pressing closer to the pillar. Iver shot Vicente a glance and he shook his head; he couldn't hear them, either.

Would this be a simple transfer of information between the two, or would Ottone do something to drain her life to use in his potions? Would he do that, right here, in the temple of Eldvittra? "I just need to see him do it," Vicente whispered to Iver. "That's all the proof I need."

Ottone put both hands on the shoulders of the child and spoke to her with a wide smile on his face. His voice sounded gentle, almost like he was reassuring her.

There was something else going on, Vicente felt it in his gut. His pulse roared in its conviction; the sweat on his palms was like glue, sticking him to that pillar. Would Ottone cast a circle around the girl, or would he puncture her veins and drain her? Would he strangle her with his bare hands, claim her dying breaths? More importantly, would Vicente and Iver be able to stop him before he completed it, and still gain enough evidence to prosecute him?

Ottone brought the girl to his lap, bouncing her like a toddler. Vicente noticed she had gone quiet, and he couldn't catch the look on her face. Ottone kept his smile. His words were soft, and Vicente cursed the echo in the temple. If they were to bring him to justice, they needed evidence.

And then they watched as Ottone began sexually assaulting the child.

The second it started, Vicente moved on instinct. He grabbed Iver before he could attack, one hand covering his mouth, and dragged him back the way they had come.

They finally had intel. Even though it pained Vicente, he couldn't let Ottone know that they knew.

Iver threw the door open and Vicente caught it before it could slam into the wall behind it and make a sound. In a haze, he quietly closed it. He sucked in the fresh air, but his stomach was in knots.

Iver staggered out onto the dark field of grass. Under the starry sky he doubled over and dry heaved. "I'll kill him. *I'll kill him.*" Vicente stroked circles on his back. "We need to tell Marcia, right now."

"Fuck your politics, let me kill him!"

"They'll execute you if you do. We can bring him to justice—and don't worry, we will. And if we don't succeed, then I'll help you kill him."

He tried not to think about what he had seen, but the moment it happened, he knew it would be etched into his mind forever. And he wanted nothing more than to rip every limb from Ottone's body, to tear his dick off and feed it to the wolves. He wanted to drive wooden spikes through his eyes, flay him alive. Rip every tooth from his disgusting mouth with pliers. The turning of his stomach became anger; an emotion much easier to identify. A hot, putrid rage boiled up his spine and settled nicely into his chest.

Iver spat on the ground. "Let me at least go in there and save her."

Calm down. Breathe. "He can't know that we know." *Grow more powerful.*

It made sense now. Why the children had been acting out. The walls surrounding the memories of his own childhood came crashing down. With clarity, he suddenly recognized his childhood self in the erratic behavior of the children. After it had happened to him, he had been acting the same. That was why his mother contacted the priestesses of Arkensaal.

He got the sudden urge to open a tunnel to forget it all. But that wouldn't have been wise. He instead, with practiced skill, rebuilt the walls around the memories, repeating his resolve to himself like a mantra. *Calm down. Breathe. Find the Stag. Grow more powerful.*

"Fine." Iver picked up a rock and threw it with precision through one of the stained-glass windows of the temple. "Let's go."

They crossed the courtyard again, gravel crunching underfoot as they hurried. Vicente still had no idea how Ottone made his god-damned healing potions. Perhaps their suspicions were way off. Or could it be that the Resurrectionists were more involved than they had first believed? That insurrectionist group was their only other clue.

Ottone must have killed those two kids after he felt he was done with them. Vicente had seen this sort of thing before: debauchery resulting in death. Or maybe Ottone killed the children to keep them from talking. *Breathe. Find the Stag. Grow more powerful.*

"He's not an alchemist, he's a fucking pedophile." Vicente could hear from Iver's voice that his teeth were chattering. "That's why he keeps all those brats around."

Maybe the deaths had nothing to do with the healing potions at all. It didn't matter: this was enough dirt on Ottone to tear him to shreds in the eyes of the townsfolk and justify giving the land to Eloy instead.

But why had Ottone left the dead bodies out to be found? It had to be because he wanted to raise Llyr's mistrust of the Arkensaali intruders, to prove bad things happen if they come. Ottone was really going to pin the murders on Vicente and his crew.

Vicente grabbed Iver's arm and pulled him closer. "We'll get him, I promise you that. Look at me. I promise you. When the time comes, I'll hand him over to you to handle at your discretion."

"You like making deals, don't you?" Iver sneered and ripped his arm away from Vicente's grasp. "You like making promises? Here's my promise to you: he defiled nature, and nature will handle him as it sees fit. I will tear into his jugular with my bare teeth and eat him raw. The 'right time' doesn't concern me."

They couldn't show their cards yet, not without solid proof. "We still need to figure out how he makes those potions."

"If I kill him, that won't be an issue."

He would not lose Iver to the law. Iver's brilliance would not rot away in a prison cell, Vicente wouldn't allow it. "There's something more sinister going on here, Iver. You can nip off the bud, but the roots will remain."

Even if their job with the land got completed today, they couldn't drop this. If Vicente could bond with the Stag, they would be able to return to Arkensaal and get back-up, and disassemble Ottone's entire operation. *Patience.*

"Fine." Iver stared up at him, threatening retribution. He was seething. "I'll trust your judgement."

CHAPTER 26

Vicente

At dawn, Vicente and Iver were called to Eloy's estate for the meeting. What would come after, he didn't know; he just knew he didn't want to spend another second in Llyr.

Surprisingly, Ottone was also there, standing by the fireplace. Everyone kept a great distance from each other, like they didn't want to breathe the same air. Marcia and Daiyu stood on the dais on the other side of the room together with PM Jadanza. Sergeant Celia was by the door, armed with both bow and sword.

"I have reasons to believe that the Arkensaalis murdered the two children," Ottone said. "They have a known killer with them."

Vicente scoffed. "That's ludicrous." Of course, that was to be expected. But without any substantial proof, they could do nothing to him and his crew. "And we have reason to believe Lord Ottone is the one who murdered the children."

"If we could focus on one issue at a time?" Marcia had her arms crossed over her chest. She wasn't taking the accusations seriously. "Vicente and I have done a thorough search of the archives and found no clear indication of which clan the land around Tal Llyrie belonged to. We were considering orchestrating a vote, but without clearance from Arkensaal, this will not be possible. Due to some recent events, we have decided to leave Llyr today." Marcia lifted her chin. "As we were assigned this mission by Her Majesty Queen Leandra, we were given explicit orders to award the land to Lord Eloy Errani—"

"What?" Ottone balked.

Marcia paid him no mind. "And during our time here, we have found that it would be in Llyr's and the realm's best interest if her wishes were fulfilled. The land around Tal Llyrie is needed to grow crops, not ingredients for 'healing potions' that you, frankly, are not brewing yourself. We have seen you burn your harvest, Lord Ottone. I will bring this evidence forth to Queen Leandra and by royal decree, the land belongs to Lord Eloy Errani. If Llyr has not yet gotten new ravens by the time we return to the capital, I'll make sure to send a rider with all the necessary paperwork to you. This issue is considered settled."

Vicente closed his eyes for a second. He was glad Marcia came with him to Llyr, as he would've never had the guts to do what she just did. In the future, they would probably look back at this time as one of the biggest failures in their careers. Ottone—and perhaps other Llyrians—would retaliate and put a strain on the capital's relationship with Llyr. At least, now that Marcia had given the queen what she wanted, she could keep her job as a diplomat.

There was no reaction from Eloy; he kept his gaze downcast.

"So be it," Ottone said, muttering between his teeth. "But there is still the issue of the murdered children."

"If you think we were involved, you need to bring forth evidence," Daiyu said.

"I have," Ottone said, raising a vial in the air. "This is poison, is it not, Ambassador Vicente? Poison you gave to Iver to kill the children?"

Vicente recognized it as his stolen vial of Stormwater. His pulse sped up, but he hid behind his practiced façade of insouciance. So, this was how Ottone was going to pin the murders on them. "Where did you get that?" Even though it was a ridiculous idea to him, he understood how someone might have believed that.

"Good question," Ottone said. "I stole it from you." He turned to PM Jadanza. "Vicente is not yet a graduated diplomat. The queen would've never sent him for this alleged purpose. You're accompanied by a chemist as well, and there are suspicions you might deal with chemical warfare. This is poison, correct?"

Vicente ticked his jaw. Both children had been strangled to death, but there was no police department here in Llyr, no officers to perform an actual investigation. "It is not. Those children were obviously strangled."

"Then, what is it?" Ottone said, ignoring his counter argument. "I couldn't figure it out. It's not medicine, that much is clear."

"That's none of your business."

"You'll need more than that to defend yourself. You are quite vague about what your specialty is, Vicente. The queen would never send a student on a mission as sensitive as this. You must've been trained by and graduated from Tal Miril, and they only deploy the very best. What are you the best of? Because I'm inclined to believe it is poison."

"I'm telling you, it's not," Vicente said. Ottone was just trying to point fingers to hide his own involvement, but if Vicente didn't dispute it, he would look even more suspicious.

"Vicente, maybe don't—" Daiyu started, but Sergeant Celia barked at her to shut up.

"Silence her," Ottone ordered Celia.

"You do not touch her, Sergeant," Marcia snapped.

Iver clutched the rifle strap that ran across his chest.

"Let me handle this, Daiyu." Vicente could feel the tension in the room escalating into a critical exigency, but he wasn't sure how to defuse it.

"Ambassador Vicente, prove me otherwise."

Ottone now bore a smug smile, and Vicente wanted nothing more than to show him how wrong he was, but he knew he wasn't allowed. "I won't be doing that."

"Vic, just do what he asks," Marcia said, defeated. "I'll vouch for you. I'll tell Queen Leandra you had no other choice. We're leaving Llyr today; you won't be putting yourself at risk."

Vicente trusted her. Perhaps this was their ticket out of Llyr: no one would want him to stay here once they found out what he was. Besides, he was itching to feel the euphoria from stepping through a tunnel. "Fine. Place the vial over there." Maybe this wouldn't make them less wary, but it would make them fear him, giving him back some control of the situation.

Ottone placed the vial on the ground.

Vicente took out the sender potion for the stolen receiver and drank it.

"Vicente, that potion looks weird, the color—" Iver said, but Vicente didn't listen.

He opened a tunnel.

And stepped through it.

He didn't end up next to Ottone. Instead, he ended up on the dais, next to PM Jadanza and Marcia. He looked at Iver as he went pale, his hands falling limp, his eyes locked on Vicente in silent horror. He looked at Marcia as she screamed, frantically clutching at her stomach as though she was clawing at it. Finally, he looked down on himself, and he was covered in blood. There was so much of it. Like a barrel of it had been dumped over him.

Marcia fell screaming to her knees.

Vicente whirled, slipping in the blood, to find Daiyu—but she was gone. He cried out when the realization set in. A few feet from where he stood, he saw a disconnected arm. Hers. A severed leg was on the floor next to him. *Had Daiyu drunk one of his receiver potions?* Vicente looked to where he had once stood, beside Iver, and there was a puddle, not a vial. The vial was still where Ottone had left it.

Ottone walked up onto the platform and squatted in front of him. "How did you move so fast? Did you transport to her? I don't understand."

"It doesn't work like that!" Vicente shouted. "It doesn't—" he screamed, wordlessly.

Adrenaline, as familiar as cigarette smoke, spread through his body while he tried to force his mouth open to breathe, despite the blood clinging to his skin. His chest constricted. He was suffocating himself.

Iver raised his rifle, aiming it at Ottone. "Come to me!" Iver barked, and Vicente complied, stumbling down the short stairs as he staggered to his side. "Marcia, come here!" Iver yelled, but Marcia remained on the ground, wailing, rocking back and forth.

"Should I get her?" Vicente asked, doing his best to wipe the blood off his face.

"Nobody moves!" Iver was trembling. "I'm killing that scum."

Vicente spat up blood. It looked like vomit after drinking red wine. His temples throbbed. His head was a pulse. Just like that, Daiyu was gone. He had torn her asunder from the inside. She was gone, just like that. Like she hadn't mattered. Death should not happen that fast, not without warning, not without the possibility of undoing it—it had happened five seconds ago, five seconds was nothing, why couldn't he go back?

Ottone raised his hands in the air, but there was that perfect concern in his expression, so utterly convincing. "Now, let's all calm down. I understand you're upset you killed Daiyu—"

"You did that!" Vicente clutched at his own abdomen, desperate for something to hold onto. Ottone must've tricked Daiyu into drinking the Stormwater he stole from him.

"Lower your gun, Far Cry," Sergeant Celia warned from behind them.

"Get fucked." Iver pulled the bolt handle of his rifle back, chambering one of the loaded bullets.

If Vicente didn't act quickly, Iver would start a war. He couldn't rely on Marcia when she was in such a state. The dizziness turned his stomach, but he managed to force the sick back. His sanity was slipping like sand through his fingers, but he needed to do his job.

Sergeant Celia notched an arrow to her bowstring and pulled it back, aiming at Iver.

"Iver, do as they say." Blood had been shed; they were in danger. It didn't matter how good of a shot Iver was, they were outnumbered. "Trust me."

Iver lowered his rifle.

"I'm getting my daughter out of here," PM Jadanza announced. He grabbed Marcia by the hand and guided her out of the room.

"Vicente, he's taking her," Iver warned. He gripped his rifle so hard his fingers were turning white.

Vicente spoke low to him. "We need to act calm. Iver, please."

"We have to get the fuck out of here, right now."

"Not without Marcia." Vicente's voice was shaking. "They won't hurt us, I promise you. Ottone tricked me into doing it, because he knew he'd never get away with it. He won't hurt us."

Ottone walked past them, towards the exit. "Get cleaned up, Ambassador. Then we'll talk this through."

Vicente listened as the door closed behind Ottone as he went outside.

"I'll grab our stuff," Iver whispered.

"Don't let anyone see you."

*

The sun was at its zenith when Vicente was called to the town hall for a cabinet meeting. He had changed his clothes and washed himself of the blood. After this, he was going to retrieve Daiyu's remains and get the fuck out of Llyr with Marcia and Iver. He was still numb and high, but the grief of losing Daiyu would set in soon and disable him. He needed to act before then.

His head still felt woolen. He gritted his teeth as he stepped up to the table where all the council members were seated, as well as Sergeant Celia, Atli the blacksmith and Ottone. But Marcia was missing.

"Is this the best time, Ottone?" PM Jadanza said. He was leaning back in his chair, hands resting on his bloated belly.

"I have given you what you wanted," Ottone said. "The election is to be held today."

"What's going on?" Vicente's mind was still clouded from opening the tunnel.

PM Jadanza cleared his throat. "Ambassador, I'm stepping down as prime minister and you are needed to be part of the council to elect someone else."

Why was he resigning at a time like this? "We're doing this now? We should give Marcia some time to collect herself." He was so tired. The ropes holding his composure together were frayed and close to snapping.

"She won't be coming," PM Jadanza said. "She's currently being held in my house."

Being held? Wouldn't he let her leave? "You can't do that."

"Her partner is dead, her marriage is nulled, and I am her father."

Vicente's blood ran cold. This was all part of their plan. Jadanza still wanted to marry her off so she could continue their family line. Vicente felt sick. Killing Daiyu was their intent all along. Jadanza and Ottone had been conspiring right under their noses.

Vicente took a seat next to Eloy. He had no other choice: as a member of the Llyrian council, his participation was mandatory. But there was still hope. He needed to do everything in his power to stop Ottone from getting more authority. Marcia's work in figuring out everyone's loyalties had not been in vain; instead, they were voting for a new prime minister rather than who would get the land. But with Marcia gone, would they still have a majority in the vote against Ottone?

"I knew you were a mystic," Eloy whispered to him. His eyes were alight with awe. "What happened back there, did Ottone interfere with your powers in some way?"

"I am, yes," Vicente said, choosing not to dignify his question with a response. Soon enough, all those who witnessed Daiyu's death would likely spread the news about Vicente's mysticism. He needed them all to think he was dangerous.

Atli took on the mantle as moderator, effectively forfeiting his vote, and opened the meeting. "Lord Renato is stepping down as prime minister. Before the vote, we need to fill the two positions in the council left behind by Marcia and Lord Renato."

Ottone volunteered and the members approved him.

Celia too. Vicente was part of voting her in. Now they were again nineteen in the council, and with Celia, they still had a majority against Ottone. In addition, Celia had seen what Ottone had done to Daiyu and Marcia.

"It's time to elect a new prime minister," Atli said. "I know you, Lord Ottone Cronin, step up. Anyone else?"

The floor rocked underneath Vicente's feet and his face was numb. Should he suggest Eloy? He had no idea if he would accept the role. Eloy was a farmer fighting for land, not a politician. Vicente hadn't prepared for this, and his thoughts were moving at a snail's pace.

Vicente raised his hand. "I volunteer myself for the position as prime minister." It would make sense for a diplomat to take on the burden; he knew the intricacies of guiding a community. Besides, he wanted to personally sign the order of Ottone's execution.

"Very well, Vicente," Atli said. "Let's cast our votes."

They went around the table, and it played out as he suspected: half voted for Ottone, the rest for Vicente.

It came down to Sergeant Celia. She didn't meet his eyes when she said: "I vote for Lord Ottone Cronin."

The world disappeared underneath Vicente's feet. He had thought he had it in the bag: she had seen what Ottone had done. Bile rose in his throat.

"Then it is settled," Atli said. "A round of applause for our new prime minster, Ottone Cronin."

Vicente remained seated while the others stood and congratulated Ottone. His grip on the seat of his chair had his fingers going numb. He shouldn't have volunteered himself. He should have remembered that he was too cocky in the aftermath of opening tunnels. In a matter of minutes, he had failed.

They all took their seats again, and Ottone spoke: "With the ambassadors' decision to grant the land to Lord Eloy based on nothing, Ambassador Marcia and Ambassador Vicente have displayed an immense disregard of Llyr's wellbeing. This is not their fault: they are acting on behalf of Her Majesty Queen Leandra. But they have shown us that Llyr is a simple pawn in the monarchy's war. Due to this, I propose a complete embargo on all trade between Llyr and the capital, as well as with any region hosting her soldiers."

"I agree with you," Lord Renato said. "But we cannot afford an embargo."

"Yes, we can," Ottone said. "I didn't need the land for my potions; I *wanted* it because it is mine. But nevertheless, production of the potions will continue. With them, we can afford it."

"Let's not discuss this in the presence of an Arkensaali ambassador," Lord Renato said.

Atli nodded. "Meeting adjourned."

Everyone left quickly, but Vicente couldn't move.

Celia was still sitting opposite Vicente, a concerned look on her face.

"What's the meaning of this, Celia?" he asked. "You saw what he did. He killed Daiyu."

She clenched her jaw. "I heard you say that right after it happened. But it was you who suddenly was covered in her blood."

"You don't understand, he tricked me into—"

"I didn't see Ottone do anything to her," she said. "Putting aside whatever transpired this morning... I cannot in good faith vote for someone who won't ever live here. The other prefectures have prime ministers from the capital; that is not our way here in Llyr. I won't have it."

"Ottone is now the leader of the militia, Celia." *A murderer at the helm of Llyr's warriors.* The aching was persistent and difficult to assuage. He wanted to scream in her face, but that went against everything he had made himself into. That would break down the mask he wore so necessarily.

"I have cast my vote. I'm sorry, Vicente." She leaned across the table and placed her hand on his wrist. "Look, I don't think you killed her on purpose. It was an accident; I believe that with my whole heart. People will find out, and I'll tell them what I know: this was an accident. But people will find out you're a mystic, and I'll do my very best to protect you."

Vicente couldn't feel his own feet when he stepped out of the town hall. His eyes found Iver immediately, standing underneath one of the tall aqueduct arches speaking to a rider. Before Vicente reached them, the rider spurred his horse and disappeared down the street. "Who was that?"

Iver clutched the sling attached to his rifle. "A brother of Ottone's. Apparently, the Cronin clan has ravens of their own, and word about me got to the Resurrectionists last night." Iver looked at him, eyebrows furrowed. "My plan worked. They have requested that Far Cry meet with them. He gave me their location."

This was their out, then. That was good. He didn't know what to do next; he needed some time to think. They were getting the fuck out of there. "You made a smart move. We should leave Llyr, right now." If Ottone's suggestion with the trades embargo was accepted, they would have an even bigger problem on their hands. They would have to find Ottone's farm and destroy it.

"What about Marcia?" Iver asked.

"We can't do anything to help her right now, we need to let tensions ease here. We're going to the Resurrectionists."

CHAPTER 27

Vicente

Darkness rapidly descended on them, the wake of the setting sun spreading purple from one tree line to the other, and the temperatures were dropping with it.

"They revealed their location willingly," Iver said. "They'll be waiting for me."

A couple of squirrels were roasting above the flames, which burned in a firepit in front of the single tent they had managed to bring with them. For five days they had ventured northwest, seeking sanctuary in the woods.

Vicente wanted to ask Iver to teach him how to shoot with a bow, but his voice had been unused for a few days, and he didn't know how it would sound. He knew Iver was uncomfortable with having to be the one to do all the talking, but Vicente couldn't muster it.

"This one is done," Iver said and pointed to one of the cooked rodents. "Take it."

Vicente grabbed the skewer. He wanted to say 'thank you,' but instead he just nodded. The chirps of the cicadas were deafening in the face of his silence.

He wished he had brought two tents with him so that he could cry alone. Not that he felt like crying. The numbness and the incomprehension of it all still had a stronghold in his mind. He still couldn't believe Daiyu was gone. He needed to speak with her. She would've known the right thing to say, and then she would've said something light-hearted to make him laugh.

Iver moved from his seat across the fire from him and sat down by his side. "About Daiyu. That wasn't your fault."

Vicente propped his elbows on his knees and put his face in his hands. "I should've taken a second to think before I acted." His voice sounded hoarse and broken.

Why did he not think? Why did he not listen? Iver had warned him the potion looked off, Daiyu told him not to do it. Had she known? Had she been aware of what was coming? Ottone must've tricked her into drinking his Stormwater, most likely under the guise of it being a healing potion. Why did she drink it? Was it the scientist in her that overrode her common sense? He wanted to reprimand her for it, wanted to scream at her and cry with her and laugh with her. Every minute passing was like a new spell of amnesia: his heart kept forgetting she was gone forever, and the fucking tidal wave of realization left him paralyzed every time it hit.

Iver leaned in closer to his side and he could feel the warmth radiating from him. Maybe that was his way of giving a hug. "There was no way you could have known that fucker would do such a thing."

"What do the Resurrectionists want with you?" Vicente asked, changing the subject. His mind had built a wall around the worst of the feelings, and he didn't want to tear it down. The craving to tunnel was already strong and anxiety crept in, snaring Vicente's chest. When would he find an excuse to use Stormwater again? If he didn't encounter a reason soon, then he'd make one.

Iver leaned away from him again. "Kill me."

The Crooked Mountains were to the east. Iver claimed to know the precise location of the Resurrectionists, but for some reason, he wasn't bringing Vicente in that direction.

"Why would they think you'd come?" Vicente plucked the flesh off the charred squirrel. The food they had brought with them had run out on the second day.

"Because they're on my hit list, and they know it."

Vicente hadn't had time to talk to Marcia after it had happened, and he wondered now if she blamed him. It was selfish to worry about such a thing, he knew that. Even if she resented him, it wouldn't be more than he deserved. "When this is over, we need to save Marcia."

"I don't think we can save her from being married off."

"We're going to have to try."

Iver picked apart his rifle, wiping down all the metal parts with a piece of cloth. The sound of it was soothing, almost hypnotic. "You think Celia and the militia are on our trail?"

"I don't think so. They all got what they wanted. Ottone got his new role, Eloy got his land. And Renato got his daughter." Vicente should have foreseen the gathering storm. The peril that had loomed over Marcia and Daiyu had been present all along, hidden in the shadows of the careful pressure exerted by Marcia's father.

Iver inspected each bit of metal before assembling his weapon again. "Sorry to break it to you, but you'll need to fight as well."

"I'm not actually dangerous."

"No, but you had me convinced. Go for the same approach with the Resurrectionists and they'll swallow it whole."

"Not sure I'll get the opportunity; they might shoot me on sight."

"Yeah, maybe," Iver said levelly. "We'll stay in hiding for a few months, and I'll train you as best I can."

"A few months?" Did Marcia have that long? Her spirit was in danger, even if her life wasn't. There was also the fact that Vicente would run out of Stormwater and components to make it if they stayed in the woods for that long. He was unsure he could cope with that.

In addition, summer was dying all around them; he could tell by the muted green of the leaves, right before they turn brown. 'A few months' meant the return of harsh winter winds. He was uncertain he could cope with that, too.

*

The space was burning hot. He had never stepped through a tunnel into something so small before. It was so tight. The walls around him pressed his arms to his chest. But it only lasted for a millisecond. It felt like bursting out of a cocoon. He was soaking wet with blood and clumps of flesh were—

Vicente forced his eyes open. His whole body was tense, like he was constricting. He let out a wheezing breath.

Iver was sitting up next to him, hair tousled. It was dark inside the tent, but Vicente could make out from his silhouette that he was facing him. "You okay?" he asked, the words disarmingly tender.

Vicente tried to steady his breathing. "Just a nightmare." Pain bloomed against his ribs, an aching swelling and shrinking, like bruises he couldn't see.

Iver turned his face away and stayed quiet for a moment. "Is there anything I can do?"

Vicente wondered, was Iver familiar with this terror? Did he know what it was like? He must've been, because he didn't assure him the dream wasn't real, didn't try to feed him lies, didn't ask any questions, aside from a useful one.

Vicente knew what he wanted. He wanted Iver in his arms, to feel his skin against his lips and hands. He needed to be engulfed in his presence, feel his warmth around him to forget everything else. But he wouldn't ask that, not when Iver's desire was to comfort him. Iver was not to be used as a distraction.

Vicente rolled over to face the other way. "I'm fine."

CHAPTER 28

Iver

Iver awoke to the soft cooing of a mourning dove. He could tell through the thin fabric of the tent that daylight had already come, but their small sanctuary was still cast in sleepy washes of gray. He and Vicente were tangled in bed. It happened from time to time, there was nothing strange about it, especially when the nights grew particularly cold. Vicente's hand was resting on Iver's chest. He felt bad for Vicente: he had no one else to grope, and he would die from touch-starvation if Iver didn't indulge him in this.

Iver ran a tight schedule. If they were to bring down the Resurrectionists, Vicente needed to become a fighter. They had discussed it a few times, whether they should go after the Resurrectionists first, or even at all. Iver had a personal stake in that game, but still, bringing them down was objectively the best thing to do. Iver was convinced there were dead people in Ottone's potions, and Iver would make him pay for that. The piece of shit had a lot of things to be held accountable for. It didn't matter that he was working together with a god: he had raped kids. Iver vowed to make Ottone pay for his crimes in all ways possible. He would crush Ottone's dreams and ambitions under the sole of his shoe, like crushing an ant, with the same indifference he'd had when killing Daiyu.

Iver had other motivations for spending a few months training Vicente, too. Vicente was still grieving the death of his dear friend, and Iver couldn't trust him until he recovered.

"Keep both eyes open," Iver reminded.

The golden-hued forest was calm, basking in the warmth of the sun. The azure sky stretched far and wide, adorned with wispy clouds moving with the breeze.

Vicente, drawing the bow string taught, opened his other eye. "How do I know where to aim? What do I align the arrowhead with?"

Iver took up archery before the age of thirteen. He had just assumed he would be able to teach it to anyone, but apparently, he wasn't quite that clever. "That's why we're practicing. You'll just... figure it out."

Vicente let loose an arrow, and it landed several feet from its target at the end of the forest clearing. He wasn't exerting his full strength; a child could shoot that distance.

"Pull with your back, not your arm. And raise your drawing elbow up." Iver circled him, inspecting his form, ever so slightly distracted by his shirtless torso. "And when you release, pull your hand back, don't keep it in place. You need to follow through with the movement."

Vicente nocked another arrow and drew, holding the pose as he forced his body to store the memory. Even though he was a bookworm, his back held the telltale signs of strength, but not the kind born of hardship or necessity. His was a cultivated strength, the result of deliberate, controlled effort. It wasn't rugged or hardened by survival; it was refined, sculpted, and sheltered, sought out for appearance rather than utility. A strength that, paradoxically, seemed fragile in its perfection. Weak.

Iver felt the familiar taste of metal. He had chewed the corner of his chapped bottom lip to the point of bleeding.

The bowstring snapped against Vicente's forearm and he hissed. "Shit, that hurt."

"That means you're doing it correctly."

"A fair warning would've been nice."

"Look, I'm not good at teaching. To me, it just comes naturally. If you put on a fucking shirt, it might soften the blow."

Vicente scoffed but kept his smile. "Have I displeased you?"

"Affirmative." Iver snatched the bow from him along with a few arrows from the quiver hanging from Vicente's belt. "This is how skilled I need you to be." He held three arrows in his draw hand and nocked each of them, one after the other, firing rapidly and hitting the target every time.

"Now you're just showing off."

Iver handed the bow back. "Isn't that how teaching is usually done?"

Vicente's gaze slid down Iver's form, coming to a stop by his hips. "Teach me how to use your rifle."

"You fidget way too much to be a sniper, Vic."

Vicente let out a sharp breath through his nose. "*Vic*. Daiyu was the one who coined that nickname, said 'Vicente' was too pretentious." The grief crept in like the morning mist, clouding over his eyes. He laughed lightly, smiling at the memories from a lifetime ago.

Iver, not sure what to do with himself, walked over to the target to collect the arrows. "She's right about that. Makes you sound like a lord or something."

When he returned, Vicente was absentmindedly scraping his thumbnail over the wooden arc of the bow. His smile trickled off.

Iver had faced death and loss before, and in his case, there had rarely been any time to ponder it. But one thing he wished for—still, all these years later—was to have someone to talk to about his loved ones. "How long did you know her?"

"About seven years. She came looking for me when she got hired as a professor at Tal Miril. She grabbed my hand, asked me if I was 'the mystic,' and when I said yes, asked if she could get a blood sample." Vicente's smile returned, appearing as slowly and softly as the first light in the morning. "I introduced her to Marcia, and to this day, I consider that to be my best accomplishment."

Iver wanted to assure him her death wasn't on him, but words couldn't fix such a thing, not if Vicente believed it. All he could do was hope Vicente didn't truly believe that.

Later that evening, Iver got lucky on his hunt, shooting and killing a fallow deer. When he returned to their camp, Vicente had already started a fire. Days had slipped by, forming a comforting routine. This was all Iver could gift him: routine. Routine was the remedy for all things mentally painful, at least according to his own simple knowledge of the way the world worked.

Iver cleaned and bandaged up the blisters on Vicente's draw-hand. He was twitching and squirming as usual. Vicente, the fidgety extrovert who loved skin-on-skin, was the complete opposite of Iver, and not someone he'd ever consider befriending. But it had happened anyway.

Iver had to grab his wrist to stop him from pulling back. "You act like you've never gotten hurt before."

Vicente tossed his head back, like a child throwing a tantrum, but kept his wounded hand still. "Maybe I haven't."

"That's sad. Get your mind off it, think of something else."

Vicente spoke in a low murmur, the same voice he'd use to charm a Llyrian into giving up all their secrets. "Got any ideas as to what would distract me?" He said it lightly, without a shred of shame.

Iver never thought of fucking him—not beyond passing curiosity, at least—but he did have another idea. "What do you call a dog with no legs?"

Vicente slowly turned his head to look at him. His face was bare and unguarded in surprise and maybe even disbelief. "What?"

"It doesn't matter what you call it, because it's not coming."

Vicente's mouth fell open. He looked so shocked. Then he laughed and Iver's pulse galloped unevenly.

Vicente's laughter shook his whole body. "I really like you, Iver," he said, shaking his head like it didn't mean something.

Perhaps Iver was reading into it too much. Not that Vicente's intentions would make any difference: the Resurrectionists had almost killed Iver two years ago, and so he didn't know if he'd make it out of this impending confrontation alive. "You'll get over it."

After eating, they both went to bed.

In his sleep, Vicente wrapped an arm around Iver's waist and pulled him closer. He could've blamed it on the cold. But Vicente still hadn't given up on flirting with Iver every time he got the chance. Most of the time it was in a joking manner, but sometimes there was something more potent underneath. Iver was fairly certain Vicente wanted him. Iver wasn't sure he wanted him back, though, not when he had spent all his life *not wanting*. Not wanting anyone... he hadn't done that on purpose. It just happened.

Before he joined the army, he'd been too focused on survival to care. Growing up, he would often team up with older, stronger kids to survive, and if they wanted sex in return, he would simply find someone else. Everyone was dirty and starving, there was no room for any feelings.

It wasn't like he'd never had the opportunity. Even in military training and in active duty, there were plenty of opportunities. He just didn't want to. Because by the time he was finally safe enough to explore, he'd also been around on earth for long enough to know how people viewed him: he looked younger than he was, and he was short and small. He attracted the type of men he despised, the type of men that belonged dead in a ditch.

He was also pretty, not handsome. Men wanted him because they thought they could force him down, make him submit, and fuck him. So, Iver played up the tough-guy act, he behaved as grossly and offensively as humanly possible, and that usually drove people away. If someone wanted him, they would have to deal with the fact that he was stronger and angrier than they were.

What he fantasized about though, was something vastly different. He wanted to be grabbed, picked up in strong arms, and by the Merciful, did he want to be fucked. He wanted to be pampered and taken care of. He wanted the man to think Iver was the most beautiful person he'd ever seen. He wanted the other guy to be so madly in love with him that he could look past Iver's bullshit and love him anyway. So, he was stuck in an impossible situation, where he didn't want the things he actually wanted. His whole deal with relationships was oxymoronic, like he was acting unapproachable on purpose so that his potential partner could prove their commitment to him by approaching him anyway, which was a very counterproductive thing to do, and he knew that. Still, he wasn't sure if Vicente wanted him for his looks, or because of proximity and a lack of better options, or because he really liked Iver. He couldn't tell. If he wanted to have sex with Vicente in return all hinged on this distinction, and he didn't know how to make it.

CHAPTER 29

Vicente

Vicente was the first to wake up. The air was sharp and clear, the temperature dropping lower with every passing day, it seemed. His muscles weren't sore anymore, as he had gotten accustomed to the rigorous training schedule Iver subjected him to everyday. Iver made these content little grumbles in the back of his throat when he nuzzled into the balled-up jacket he used as a pillow. Vicente found the most pleasure in him when he was like this, early in the morning, soft and pliant to the touch from sleep. Iver would moan or sigh when he stretched awake. Vicente stole touches whenever he could, and the skin on Iver's hips, waist and over his ribs was so warm and smooth it had his head spinning.

He would never try anything with Iver, though. Intimacy was easy to Vicente. Sex was a fun, simple activity, to be shared with whomever piqued his interest. It seemed different to Iver. He was the kind of person to whom sex meant something. He seemed like the type of person who would only sleep with someone he was in love with. Vicente wouldn't ruin that for him, because he wasn't in love with Iver, he only wanted to sleep with him.

"Mornin'," Iver said as he noticed Vicente looking at him. Then he groaned as he stretched his arms, and Vicente filed that sound away for later.

Their muddied shoes were waiting for them outside the tent, ready for another day of trekking. They were moving in a direction that Vicente guessed was towards the Resurrectionists. They needed to find the Farm and destroy it. If he and Marcia returned to the capital, now with a complete trades embargo between Llyr and Arkensaal, they would have their heads on spikes.

"Llyr won't be able to afford an embargo," Iver said as Vicente told him this.

"With Ottone's potions, they will. That's why we need to make sure he can't ever rebuild his farm."

Speaking of the future was the only way to fill the silence as they travelled through the woods. Despite their isolation and proximity, Iver still refused to disclose anything about his past.

Vicente felt oddly at peace there, as if the world had forgotten them entirely; and in forgetting, had chosen to leave them untouched. The forest wrapped around them, quiet and golden beneath the thinning veil of morning mist. Autumn had set the leaves ablaze in yellow, red, orange, and brown, their colors bleeding through the fog. When the sun climbed high enough to warm the treetops, a chorus of birds stirred, breaking the stillness with tentative song. He and Iver walked for hours, speaking only a few words to each other.

That same afternoon, they found a decrepit building, sitting in the middle of the woods. A chain-link fence, bending under years of neglect, marked the boundary of the overgrown clearing. The barbed wire that once coiled atop the fence now sagged beneath the weight of ivy and wisteria vines, nature reclaiming what had been left to crumble.

Iver scrutinized it over the iron sight of his rifle. "Looks abandoned."

"What is it?" The building was a squat, rectangular construction of weathered concrete. Moss clung to its walls, spreading like veins through the cracks. The windows were boarded from the inside, the edges splintered and warped.

"Solar panels on the roof, looks to be intact," Iver said. "The setup's old but solid."

Vicente tried again. "Iver, what is that building?" Iver rarely explained what he was thinking, he simply barked orders at

Vicente, and he was forced to listen with his head down. Vicente was getting tired of it.

Iver chewed on his bottom lip. "I think it used to be a field outpost. Military. Fuck, look at that: the cistern on the roof, I think it's intact too."

Iver spoke as though Vicente ought to know what he meant, or as though he was too stupid to see its value. "Are you saying we can find ammunition inside?" Vicente asked. "Food?"

Iver scoffed. "No way, they would never leave shit like that behind."

Vicente stifled a sigh. "So, what are you saying?"

Iver let the rifle drop to his side, caught by the sling over his shoulder, as he turned to face Vicente. There was a spark in his eyes Vicente hadn't ever seen before. "I'm saying, I think there's water."

Vicente had his canteen in his bag, Iver had one too. No matter where in the forest they ended up, they always found fresh water. "We have water."

"Hot water, Vic." Iver's voice was reverent. "A shower."

Vicente had nearly forgotten what a proper shower felt like. Weeks of grime layered beneath the forest dust on his skin, sweat and dirt trapped in the seams of his clothing. A shower would be worth the risk of entering the building.

Iver stepped closer to the fence, testing its strength with his boot. The gate had been locked with a chain, and there was no way to get it open.

He watched as Iver scaled the sagging fence with ease and plopped down on the other side. Vicente followed his lead, taking care not to get his clothes stuck on the barbs.

With his rifle aimed, Iver approached cautiously, his boots crunching on the overgrown path.

Unsurprisingly, the door was locked as well, but Iver had his lockpicks with him and got it open in seconds. Vicente didn't have a better explanation for the building, but there was no way it used to be military: they would've had higher security.

The air inside was musty with the sour tang of decay. Their boots crunched on splintered wood and shattered glass as they moved through the first room, a wide space littered with debris: broken chairs, rusted metal scraps, and a few long-forgotten ration cans, empty and chewed through by scavengers. Sunlight filtered through cracks in the boarded windows, illuminating the green streaks of moss creeping along the walls.

Iver led the way, his rifle raised. The deeper they went, the cooler the air grew, until they arrived at a door marked with the faint outline of a painted symbol: a droplet of water.

Inside was a modern bathroom, the same kind Vicente had been used to in the capital: a toilet, a sink… and a shower.

"Please, Merciful," Iver muttered under his breath. He reached his hand inside the stall and turned the knob.

The pipes groaned, shuddering to life with a hiss, and then a cascade of water spilled from the showerhead. The sound filled the room, echoing off the walls, and for a moment, neither of them moved.

Vicente could see the excitement in Iver's eyes, but even with this, he didn't smile.

Iver put his rifle and backpack down on the ground. "I found it, I'm going first."

Vicente smiled. "We could shower together."

Iver shot him a scathing look. "Stop being fucking nasty. Stand guard, in case this dump isn't as abandoned as it looks."

"Don't use all the hot water," Vicente called over his shoulder as he exited the bathroom. "And shave your face while you're at it."

Vicente wandered back into the main hall, letting Iver revel in his discovery. The rest of the building yielded nothing of value. There was no food, no weapons, and no tools left behind, and the fabrics of the furniture, bed linens, and towels were all chewed to ruin and back by moths.

By the time Iver emerged, water beading in his black locks and eyelashes all stuck together, he looked civilized again. "Still hot," he said, slinging his jacket over one shoulder.

Vicente didn't wait for further invitation. He felt disgusting under his clothes, stale sweat sticking to his skin. He stepped into the stall, relishing the spray of warmth. The grime of weeks in the wild melted away. For a fleeting moment, it was almost possible to forget where they were.

*

While Iver tended to the fire he'd decided to make in the middle of the main hall, Vicente continued to explore. He passed a rusted locker toppled against the wall, its door yawning open to reveal nothing. The air was heavy with mildew, and the faint drip of water echoed from somewhere.

Their routine had been helpful to Vicente the first month: walk for hours, train archery, watch as Iver hunted, find water and set up shelter, repeat. There was little space for wallowing. Now though, Vicente was growing restless. Had Marcia been married off yet, or was there still a chance of saving her? Did she think he and Iver had abandoned her, and would never return?

Vicente felt strong enough to face the Resurrectionists and whatever was happening on Ottone's 'farm.' He pictured advanced machines and secret ingredients. He and Iver would destroy it all, and without Ottone's potions, Llyr couldn't afford to enforce the proposed trading embargo with the capital. And if the ingredient to the healing potions was something sinister, they would weaponize that to discredit Ottone and strip him of his role as prime minister. If it was disturbing enough, they could use it as a legal reason for killing Ottone. Vicente still didn't know how the Gambler was involved in all of this, but they would find out eventually—if Iver would only bring him to the Farm, which he wasn't doing, and he refused to tell Vicente why.

Vicente stepped into another room, the door hanging crookedly from one hinge. A shaft of light from a crack in the boarded window lit the space, revealing a cluster of objects arranged on a table.

They were cylindrical and metallic, like oversized canteens but with wires protruding awkwardly. Some were marked by peeling text Vicente couldn't decipher. His curiosity burned as he leaned closer, his fingers brushing the cold surface of one of the devices.

"What the fuck are you doing?"

Vicente whirled around to see Iver standing in the doorway. The dim light barely illuminated his face, but the tension in his posture was unmistakable.

"Exploring," Vicente replied. "What does it look like?"

"Like you're looking with your hands again," Iver said, stepping into the room. His gaze darted to the table, locking on the metallic objects with an intensity that made Vicente's stomach churn.

Iver's black hair stood in stark contrast to his fair skin, and he had a deadly look in his eyes. Vicente was unfamiliar with the feelings he held for Iver—not separately, but the odd mixture of them created a color he'd never seen before. It was a confusing amalgamation of emotions. He admired him, feared him, felt for him. Curiosity, weariness, adoration, resentment.

Iver's voice lowered. "Step away from the table. Slowly. Don't touch anything."

"Why? You don't know what this is either." Vicente was getting sick of Iver's secrecy. He had them walk all day, every day, in an undisclosed direction. Whenever Iver found reason for them to stop for the day, they were on the brink of too tired to hunt or gather food. Then Iver had him practice his archery until his fingers bled. He would've been fine with all of this, if he could be sure Iver was taking them to the Farm and the Resurrectionists. Iver had been so scared of them, maybe he wasn't taking Vicente there at all.

"Vicente," Iver said, "I'm serious. Back off."

Vicente hesitated, his eyes flicking between Iver and the strange objects on the table. "You don't get to bark orders at me without explanation," he said, his pride outweighing his unease. "What would you know about this kind of stuff?"

Iver's jaw tightened, his hands clenching into fists. "Just listen. Do not—"

But Vicente's hand was already moving. His fingers grazed one of the cylindrical devices, tilting it slightly on its base. He was sure it wouldn't cause anything to happen, but he was wrong.

Iver lunged forward as a click sounded out. A sharp, high-pitched whine followed, building in volume every passing millisecond.

"Run!" Iver shouted, shoving Vicente toward the door with enough strength to knock the breath out of him.

They bolted, Vicente stumbling over the uneven floor as the wail became a piercing scream. The room erupted in a flash of light. The explosion hit with a concussive force that sent them sprawling to the ground outside the room, debris raining down.

Vicente coughed, his ears ringing, his vision blearing. He rolled onto his side and saw Iver, already on his feet. Dust and ash clung to his hair and jacket.

Vicente heard the snap of fire behind them.

"Get up!" Iver yelled.

Vicente scrambled to his feet. The smoke was rapidly filling the space.

Iver took both their equipment, and Vicente was at his heels. "How did you know?"

Once outside in the clean, fresh air, Iver began pacing in tight, furious circles. "You idiot," he spat, voice shaking with rage. "Military-grade explosives. Fuck, Vic, you could've killed us."

Vicente wiped soot from his eyes. Iver had recognized those devices instantly. "How did you know what they were?"

Iver didn't answer. He threaded his arms through the straps of his backpack and started walking away.

Vicente clenched his fists, his pride stinging more than the bruises blooming across his body. "Maybe you should explain instead of pretending you're some kind of authority."

Iver didn't look back. "Next time, don't touch shit you don't understand."

Vicente picked up his own pack. Only then did he register the sharp pain in his shoulder.

CHAPTER 30

Iver

It didn't matter that Vicente blew up the building. They couldn't have stayed there long anyway; Iver wouldn't have trusted it. It didn't matter that Vicente blew up the first hot water they'd had access to for weeks. It didn't matter that Vicente almost killed them both; because then they wouldn't have had any more problems, as far as Iver was concerned.

What mattered was the shard of metal sticking out of Vicente's shoulder.

The bastard was still upright, though leaning against a tree. His hand hovered near the injury, like he was afraid to touch it. Dark blood soaked through his shirt.

Iver rummaged through his pack for bandages. "Let me see."

"I'm fine." Vicente tried to push off the trunk, but his legs buckled, forcing him to catch himself.

Iver grabbed Vicente by the good arm and eased him down to sit. "Let me see the damn wound."

Vicente grimaced as Iver swatted his hand away. Iver tore the fabric of his shirt, revealing the shard lodged below the shoulder blade. The sight made his stomach tighten. The metal wasn't embedded too deep—at least not as bad as it could have been—but it was jagged and dirty.

Iver poured water from his canteen over the cut. Vicente hissed in pain, his fingers curling into fists.

Iver gripped the shard with a piece of cloth to avoid cutting himself. "Hold still. This is gonna hurt."

He yanked the metal free in one swift motion. Vicente's breath came in shallow bursts. Blood welled up, but it wasn't gushing.

"We can't stay here." Iver grabbed a clean shirt from his pack, pressed it against the wound, and tied it in place. "The smoke might attract people we don't want to meet."

"There's that paranoia again," Vicente said with some humor, but the pain was seeping into his voice. "It might also alert people who could help us."

"It's too risky." For weeks they hadn't met a single soul, but it wouldn't be unthinkable that others occupied the woods. If they were to run into people, it was more likely they would try to take Vicente's and Iver's supplies and tools, rather than help them.

"Right."

Iver stood. "We're moving." His anger hadn't faded, but it wasn't directed at Vicente anymore. It was aimed at himself. He should've stopped Vicente sooner, should've recognized the signs of his reckless curiosity.

Vicente groaned as he got to his feet. "I can walk."

The fading light threaded gold and red through the canopy of autumn leaves. Iver chose an elevated location for their next campsite, where the undergrowth grew densely and offered them a natural windbreak. While Vicente, whose face was drawn and pale, leaned against a tree, Iver rushed to get a fire started before the sun went down completely.

Iver gestured to the spot upwind from the fire. "Sit."

Vicente didn't argue this time. He sunk to the ground, clutching his injured shoulder. A groan trembled between his clenched teeth.

The tent went up in minutes. He tossed a blanket to Vicente, then knelt beside him, inspecting the makeshift bandage. Blood had soaked through.

"We need to stop this from getting worse," Iver muttered, more to himself than to Vicente.

"That makes me feel better, thank you."

"Shut up." Iver stood, grabbing his knife and slipping it into his belt. "Stay put."

Iver disappeared into the trees, eyes scanning the ground and the low branches for what he needed. The forest offered more than most people realized, and Iver knew what to look for. Near a fallen snag, he spotted a patch of a familiar plant, its small white flowers still clinging despite the season. He cut a handful of stems of yarrow, good for stopping bleeding and preventing infection; a field remedy he'd relied on before.

The forest was thick with pine trees. On a couple of them, he found enough crystals of hardened resin to last Vicente through the healing process. The sap from pine was an antiseptic, and even though it was speckled with dirt and trapped insects, it would have to do.

When he returned, Vicente was still upright, but he looked even more haggard under the flickering light of the fire.

Iver dropped some of the resin crystals into his metal canteen and tossed it into the fire to melt. With the remaining water, Iver cleaned the cut again. For once, Vicente stayed still, and Iver wondered if he was about to faint. When the wound was as close to clean as Iver would ever get it, he got the melted resin onto a cloth and glued the edges of Vicente's skin back together, sealing the injury against infection. Vicente didn't make a sound. He was a fighter, Iver would give him that.

He placed the yarrow on top, then bound it all in place. "This'll hold for now. Don't move too much, or you'll make it worse."

Vicente loudly let go of his breath. He turned around to face Iver, looking at him so fondly it made Iver's chest do a funny little swoop, and said, "didn't think you'd know so much about plants. You're full of surprises."

"Gotta keep you on your toes." Iver leaned back on his heels, wiping his hands on his trousers. Once the danger passed, he suddenly remembered to be angry again.

He huffed, grabbed his rifle and settled himself on the other side of the fire, scanning the dark forest beyond.

Vicente closed his eyes, exhaustion overtaking him.

They sat like that for a while, listening to the snap of the fire and the wind moving through the treetops. Iver turned his face to the fire, letting the warmth comfort him, before turning his gaze back to the trees, but saw nothing but the ghost of the fire in blue.

What would he do if Vicente died? The force of that thought, the effect it had on him, had him shaking his head trying to dislodge the dread. Iver was the only one who could keep Vicente safe, as he didn't have the necessary experience to do that himself. Vicente could not die. Iver wouldn't let this idiot die out here. Not after everything. Not on his watch.

Once the hooting of owls started up, Vicente slowly but steadily got up and moved to the tent. "I'm going to bed. You should rest too. No one's coming to hurt us."

Iver squinted into the dark. "I'm not done being pissed off."

Vicente retreated into the tent.

Iver sat vigil, rifle in hand, listening to the night for any sign of trouble. The air around him smelled of cold water and wet bark, and it was so clean. He tried to feel safe, but it was hard to get out of a pit that felt more like a burrow or a nest. Operating under panic, making do with few tools, and the threat of death hanging above his head felt like putting on an old coat and finding—with grief and disbelief—that despite it all, it still fit.

*

"I can't breathe… I can't breathe, I can't—"

Vicente's hands moved urgently, pressing against Iver's chest, brushing over his neck, cupping his cheeks, dragging through his hair. His movements were frantic, trembling, his voice tight with fear. "Iver, wake up!"

Iver woke with the sickening lurch of a fall, limbs jerking in desperation to catch himself, and he grabbed Vicente's forearms hard, vicelike. His own breaths were ragged, he choked on the frigid air, drawing gulps of it. They were both sitting up. He didn't know why.

The wild thrum of Iver's heart gradually eased. Vicente's hands stayed steady, holding the sides of Iver's face, his thumbs brushing against his cheekbones as if to ground him. Iver couldn't see Vicente clearly in the pitch-dark tent, but he could feel him. His breath came in warm puffs over Iver's face. "There you go," Vicente murmured, "you're safe. Big breaths. There you go."

Iver figured he must've had a nightmare. "I must've had a nightmare." He couldn't remember what it was about. "I'm sorry." His voice was hoarse.

Vicente huffed a small laugh. "Don't apologize, Iver." His hands slipped from Iver's face, resting briefly on his shoulders before pulling back. "I thought an animal or something... big breaths. Are you in any pain?"

"No." Iver rubbed his hands over his face, the cool air biting at his skin.

"Good," Vicente said. "Do you want to talk about it?"

Iver didn't reply right away. He stared into the dark, his jaw tight. For a moment, he thought about telling Vicente the truth, about the memories that nightmares like this dragged back to the surface, but the words stuck in his throat. "No."

They both laid back down, but Iver's eyes stayed open, fixed on the faint outline of the tent ceiling. He listened to the welcoming, steady sound of Vicente's breathing as they rested side by side, not touching, just sharing space.

*

About three weeks later, once Vicente had healed enough, they started their journey again. Iver was taking them in the direction of the Resurrectionists, but he had reasons to stall. Iver couldn't take them down himself, and he needed Vicente to become a fighter. At this pace, he was unsure if it would ever happen. Vicente getting injured had disrupted Iver's plans, and now, autumn had progressed far, bordering on the beginning of winter. Iver's control of their situation was slipping through his fingers.

They heard the river long before they laid their eyes on it, and Iver could smell the rushing water in the air. It roared like a living creature, the churning water white and frothing as it surged over the rocks.

"We need to cross," Iver said.

Vicente stood a few paces behind. His injured arm was in a sling, but he could move it, and the wound had healed. Pain was the only thing stopping him. "We could try downstream, see if it calms down."

Iver didn't want to. He was exhausted. The chill of the water sprayed against his face as he studied the route ahead.

The rocks jutted out like jagged teeth, slick with algae. Some looked dry, others half-submerged, shifting under the push of the river. It wasn't a path anyone would take lightly, but it was the only way across.

If either of them could make the throw, they could tunnel to the other side. But Vicente had a limited amount of Stormwater and ingredients, and Iver didn't even want to broach the subject; he had no idea if Vicente was willing to do it again, after what had happened to Daiyu.

"I'm going first," Iver said. "If it's not safe, I'll find another way."

Vicente's voice rose above the rush of water. "You're weak. You haven't eaten properly in days, neither of us have. You'll—"

"I'll be fine," Iver cut him off. "Just stay put."

Iver's body ached from weeks of pushing too hard with too little rest, but before Vicente could protest further, he moved forward.

The first stone wobbled under his weight, and he steadied himself, one foot finding purchase while his arms balanced. The second step was easier, the rock broader and more stable. He kept his focus ahead for each precarious leap from one slick surface to the next.

The deafening roar of the river filled his ears. His breath came in sharp bursts, and the exertion sent an ache through his entire body, but this was still better than walking miles downstream in search of a safer crossing that might not exist.

Halfway across, he paused on a boulder to catch his breath. His legs trembled, threatening to give out, but he pushed the weakness aside. He glanced back, catching sight of Vicente on the bank, his face tense with worry.

"It's fine!" Iver shouted over the roar, though his voice didn't carry the confidence he intended. He straightened, shifting his weight to step onto the next rock.

His boot slipped.

The world tilted sharply as his foot skidded off the slick surface, and his balance evaporated in an instant. His body hit the stone hard, a sharp pain shooting through his ribs as he slid into the rushing water.

The cold was immediate, a shocking, biting force that stole the breath from his lungs. The current grabbed him, yanking him under.

Iver's fingers scraped against something solid and he clawed at it, forcing himself upward. His head broke the surface, and he managed to latch onto the rock with both hands. The churning water battered him, trying to tear him away, but he held on with every ounce of energy he had left.

"Hold on!" Vicente's voice was closer, and through the spray, Iver saw him on the same path as he had been just seconds ago.

Iver would lose his grip any second now. His arms burned. He would have to be swept downstream, to somewhere the current calmed, and pull himself up there. *It would be fine.* Vicente was clever enough to find him.

Iver's hands lost their hold, he slipped beneath the surface and resigned to the force of the water.

Then, something clamped around Iver's wrist with a grip so fierce he expected his bones to snap. Air exploded back into his lungs as he was wrenched upward. Vicente was in front of him, on the rocks, Iver's wrist in one hand. Iver didn't have time to comprehend what was happening before Vicente *fucking hauled* him out of the water with a strength that didn't make sense. He wrapped his other arm around Iver's waist and carried him across, feet barely touching the ground. It was so fast it felt like they were flying.

They both collapsed onto the muddy shore, gasping. Iver coughed, puking up water as he rolled over on his stomach.

"You're an idiot," Vicente said, words punctuated by gulps of air. "Unbelievable. You are the dumbest idiot I have ever met."

Iver closed his eyes. His entire body was heavy, like the river had soaked through to his soul. He was freezing so badly he didn't even have the energy to shiver. "What the fuck."

"Yeah, wet rocks are slippery," Vicente said. "Who would've thought."

Iver turned his head toward him, the world still spinning. "How did you do that? How the fuck did you...?" He trailed off, his mind still grappling with the memory of Vicente pulling him out like the current meant nothing. *I couldn't even get myself out.* But Vicente had done it with one hand.

Vicente didn't look at him. "Let's get you in front of a fire."

They didn't speak much as Vicente helped him stumble to a clearing beyond the riverbank. Iver's legs were weak, trembling with the aftershock of adrenaline and the cold sinking its claws deep into his body. His hands wouldn't stop shaking, and his teeth chattered so violently it felt like they might crack.

Vicente lowered him to sit against a tree. He crouched beside Iver, tugging at the straps of his drenched backpack. Iver tried to help, but his fingers wouldn't cooperate, fumbling uselessly at the buckles.

"Stop moving," Vicente said. "You're not doing yourself any favors."

Vicente wrenched the bag free. The contents spilled out— everything soaked through, including the change of clothes Iver had been counting on to stave off hypothermia.

"Shit," Vicente muttered as he sifted through the wet fabric. He dragged his own bag closer. "All right, don't fight me on this."

Iver barely registered Vicente peeling his jacket off. Vicente quickly stripped him of all his clothes, and Iver wanted to scream when the cold air hit his skin, but Vicente was already pulling his own dry, spare shirt over his head. It smelled faintly of pine and sweat, and the fabric was soft from wear. It was big on him, it reached halfway down his thighs, but Iver didn't have enough cognitive wherewithal to be embarrassed about that.

He tried to speak, but his teeth wouldn't stop chattering, his words coming out garbled and broken. *Acute injuries. Shelter. Fire. Lesser injuries. Water. Food.* These were their needs ordered by priority. But Iver couldn't get it out.

Vicente got to work on a fire. Iver wanted to help him, tell him what to do, but he couldn't. It didn't matter though; Vicente knew what to do. He got the fire started.

Iver sat as close to the fire as he dared, maybe even too close. Sparks leapt from the fire, landing on his bare legs, but to his dismay, he couldn't feel them. His body was numb, his hands trembling violently in his lap. But at least he was shaking now, which was a good sign.

He couldn't wrap his head around it. How had Vicente managed to free him from the currents? The image of Vicente hauling him out, carrying him over the rocks like it was nothing, played on an endless loop in his mind. Was it his magic? Did his abilities go beyond what Iver understood: did they make him superhumanly strong?

"That was a nasty fall," Vicente said as he set up the tent. "Are you injured?"

"No." It sounded like denial. But Iver wasn't injured. He wouldn't have accepted that. He couldn't afford to be, not when their survival depended solely on him.

"I don't believe that." Vicente grabbed his own blanket and wrapped it around Iver. "I'm checking you over once we've gotten some food in your stomach."

Shit. Food. Iver's chest tightened as he remembered they had run out. Hunting was on Iver's agenda today. That's why he didn't want to walk some extra miles just to cross the damn river.

He tried to stand. His knees shook uncontrollably. "Probably pheasants in the area—"

Vicente planted his hands on Iver's shoulders and pushed him down to sit. "I've got it."

Vicente grabbed the bow and disappeared into the trees, leaving Iver sitting by the fire.

But Vicente couldn't hunt on his own, he didn't know how to. They could manage a few days without food. And Iver wasn't injured. He just needed a second to warm up.

Worry made Iver attempt to get up again, but the cold bound him to the ground. His uncooperative body manacled him to the fire. He was so cold he felt blue. His teeth chattered relentlessly, his jaw aching with the effort of keeping it still. He huddled closer to the fire, its steady heat the only thing keeping the numbness at bay. He focused on his breath, forcing it to slow. Gradually, warmth returned to his arms and legs, prickling uncomfortably at first. Sensation returned to his fingers. He had been in that river for no more than five seconds, but he was sore all over. If Vicente hadn't been there, would the river have killed him?

*

"I'm back."

Iver hadn't noticed the sky blackening, hadn't noticed the hooting of owls. Vicente had been away for a while. "You did your best; we'll try again tomorrow—"

Vicente stepped into the light of the fire, with two dead pheasants in hand.

"Oh." Iver cleared his throat. "You did it."

Vicente smiled, although it didn't reach his eyes. "Don't sound so surprised. I've seen you do it a hundred times by now."

He knelt by the fire as he plucked the feathers from the birds and prepared them for cooking, like Iver had done for him many times. The smell of roasting meat soon filled the air.

When the birds were cooked, he set them down in front of Iver and then sat beside him, his legs crossed. "Eat."

Iver pulled his knees up to his chest. He was hungry, but it was more important that Vicente ate first. He didn't know how to starve, but Iver did. "You first."

"No, don't start." Vicente's voice didn't contain any of the humor it used to. *Oh, he was pissed.*

Then, he hooked his arms under Iver's knees and *spun him around* on his ass to face him. "I'm having no more of your noble, self-righteous bullshit. This is exactly why you couldn't make it across the river: you've been too busy making sure I eat, like a dumb idiot, and that nearly got you killed. I'm sick of it. Eat, and I'll patch you up."

Iver didn't know what to say. "Vic, calm down."

"Does it hurt anywhere?"

"No."

Vicente's maddened eyes fixed on him. "God damnit, Iver. I don't believe you." He surveyed Iver, analyzing him from top to bottom.

He wasn't going to drop this. Reluctantly, Iver held out his hands, palms up. The skin was raw and bleeding from gripping the rocks. Displaying his injuries went against Iver's nature. Seeing Vicente's jaw tighten at the sight of the blood hurt more than the lacerations did.

Vicente drew a handful of yarrow from his pocket. It looked fresh; he must have picked it on his hunt.

When Vicente poured water on Iver's hands to clean the cuts, he hissed in pain. "Oh, fuck me, that stings."

Vicente pressed the yarrow to the wounds. "You're acting like you've never gotten hurt." He mocked Iver in a tone void of any emotions, but clearly hiding something beneath the surface. A shark swimming through calm waters. Normally, he wore his feelings on his sleeve. Iver had never seen him like this before.

When Vicente finished wrapping up his hands, Iver inspected his work. "Damn near looks halfway decent." It was difficult to admit, but he couldn't have done a better job himself.

"Thank you, Iver. That's the nicest thing you've said to me in a while. Maybe even ever."

Iver had been giving Vicente a hard time, hadn't he? But they weren't in civilization anymore, it was survival of the fittest out here. Though, it seemed that Vicente had learned.

As Vicente combed his fingers through Iver's hair scanning for injuries to his head, Iver ate in silence, like a petulant child in time-out. But being taken care of was uncomfortable. His old reality was familiar, at least. Feelings of safety and affection were new, therefore treacherous and untrustworthy.

Once Vicente was satisfied, he took his knife and started shaving slivers of wood from sticks to feed the fire. Iver felt himself relaxing, the warmth of the fire finally cutting through the lingering cold in his bones. But something still gnawed at him. "How did you do it?"

Vicente raised an eyebrow, not looking up. "Do what?"

"Pull me out of the river. You're not…" He hesitated, searching for the right words. *You're not a soldier.* "You must've gotten an adrenaline rush. Life-or-death situations make people stronger, you know."

Vicente sighed and tossed the stick into the flames. He stood. "Can you get up?"

Iver grimaced. "I don't want to."

Vicente's lips quirked into a smile, but his eyes held something else. "Get up," he said. "I need to show you something."

Iver rolled his eyes, but he slowly shifted up and onto his feet, his legs still unsteady. He turned to face Vicente—all six fucking foot of him—who was standing far too close. "What?"

Before he could react, Vicente's hands were on his waist. Iver's eyes widened as Vicente lifted him clean off the ground. Iver automatically grabbed Vicente's shoulders to secure himself, his fingers digging into the fabric of his shirt. Vicente wrapped his healthy arm around Iver—under his ass—and then held him like that, pressed close together, with *one* fucking arm.

"What the fuck?" Iver snapped in disbelief.

Vicente held Iver aloft as if he weighed nothing. "I know you think of me as some pampered, useless city-boy," he said evenly. "But even before learning to shoot a bow, I was quite strong."

Iver's mouth opened, then closed again. He wasn't sure how to respond, his mind still grappling with the sheer absurdity of being held in the air.

"For weeks now," Vicente continued, "I've been by your side as you hunt and scavenge for supplies. And I have learned. I might not be as skilled as you, but I'm not incompetent. I'll let you take the lead in our survival because you know best, but when you stumble, I'll be there for you. You can count on me to protect you, too."

Vicente was pressing him so, so close. He was looking up at Iver, resting his chin against Iver's chest. Iver's mind was blank, he only noticed the muscular arms and shoulders he was sure he'd dream about later.

"I pulled you out of that river because I'm strong," Vicente finished.

"I get it," Iver said. "Put me down now."

Vicente's smile grew into something more mischievous. "You're not enjoying your view from up there?"

Iver's stomach did a strange little wiggle. "Vicente."

Vicente lowered him until his feet hit the ground. As soon as he was standing, Iver swatted Vicente's shoulder, his scowl doing little to mask the blush creeping into his cheeks.

"You could've just said that," Iver muttered, adjusting his shirt as if the indignity could be shaken off. He was still half-naked, for fuck's sake.

"Would you have believed me?" Vicente finally sat down to eat.

In the light of the fire, Iver picked apart his rifle to clean it, trying not to look at Vicente every few seconds.

Everything was different now. Their first meeting felt so distant, like it had happened to two different people. Iver hadn't just tired of hating Vicente; over the last two months, Iver had grown to like him and enjoy his company. The resentment died so slowly he hadn't noticed it.

He respected Vicente now. Respect didn't flicker in and out of existence. Once it was established, it was solid. It was a reliable feeling, based on history that proved its worth. It came to him so rarely he always trusted it when it did.

"We'll stay here for a few days, yeah?" Vicente asked.

Iver nodded. An unspoken subject lingered: where to next? A question Vicente gave up asking weeks ago. Iver was finally ready to give him the answer. "Ships End."

"Sorry?"

"It's an old, abandoned military fortress, near river Zinat. That's where the Resurrectionists are. We're heading there next." There was another reason Iver had been stalling. He wasn't ready to die yet. But it couldn't be helped. "I think we're ready to face them."

CHAPTER 31

Vicente

Winter had the land in its cold grip by the time Iver decided they were ready to make their first attack.

Iver leapt from the tree to the ground, which was carpeted with fallen leaves that crunched beneath each footfall. "A fire, two clicks from here." The air held a crisp chill, a threat of the icy days yet to come.

Only two miles? Today was the day. They had been travelling east for some time now, always hot on the Resurrectionists' trail. "You sure it's them?"

Iver made it clear he intended to kill all the Resurrectionists. It seemed personal. Iver's nightmares were getting more frequent, every other night he awoke in a panic, eyes frantic and unseeing, voice reedy with terror. But he always ignored Vicente's questions.

"Positive. Let's move." Iver took the lead with his rifle aimed ahead.

Because of Iver's rigorous schedule, Vicente had grown skilled with the bow. The quiver hung from his belt, and Iver had given him a few knives as well. When things had gone awry in Llyr, and while everyone was distracted at the council meeting electing a new prime minister, Iver had stolen as many hunting knives as he could find.

"Are you prepared to get blood on your hands, Vic?"

Vicente avoided the question, like he hadn't been covered in Daiyu's blood two months ago. "I'd kill for a whiskey."

"Doubt they have any with them. But fuck me, let's hope they do. And some meat other than game. If you manage to get your first kill, I'll cook you up a nice dinner."

Vicente sucked his teeth. "Sounds romantic. I wouldn't dare try my luck with you."

"No? Word has it I put out on the first date."

They pressed onwards. Sparse rays of sunlight filtered through the lacework of barren branches, casting pools of light on the forest floor. The air smelled perpetually of pine needles and rain.

Iver tapped the side of his arm and they crouched down. "A lookout ahead. One man. This one's yours, Vic. You've got a visual?"

"Negative. I need to get closer."

"I've got your six. Lead the way." Authority imbued Iver's tone, and Vicente was swept up by the obedience it commanded.

Vicente stalked forward. Before him, the man on watch stood guard, peering out into the shadows, blissfully unaware of the impending danger creeping in.

If things went south, Vicente had a fallback plan. Using all his available ingredients, he had prepared sending and receiving potions of Stormwater. Despite his grief and agony, he had managed to stop himself from opening tunnels when he didn't need to.

Vicente inched closer. As he neared the sentry, his fingers wrapped around an arrow.

The man, distracted by the distant sound of a bird's call, remained vulnerable.

With a deep breath, Vicente steadied his stance, his muscles coiled like springs ready to release. He drew back his bowstring, and the tension pulled against his fingers with a satisfying resistance.

He let the arrow fly. It soared through the air, soundless in its trajectory, until it found its mark in the man's back, right below his ribs. He stiffened. A muted gasp escaped his lips before he crumpled, and Vicente dashed forward. The man was making too much noise. Vicente slit his throat without hesitation.

He remained quiet for a few moments, listening. All he could hear was the sounds of the forest.

Iver emerged from his hiding spot and stood next to him. "Good boy, Vic."

"Not as good of a shot as you would've made," Vicente reflected as he pulled the arrow from his victim's back. "It didn't kill him. You would've gone for a throat-shot, right? You'll need to work with me on my precision. If I'm going to get as good as you, I can't always aim for the biggest target."

"Shit, you've got me kicking my feet like a schoolgirl. It was good enough; you got the job done."

They ate up the distance between them and the campsite. The sentry he had killed was stationed about eight hundred yards from it.

The fact that the group had decided to make camp revealed that they were still far from the Resurrectionists' main stronghold. Being far away was a good thing. Iver said the rebels had more advanced weapons: they had anti-personnel explosives buried in the ground, and stepping on them would be fatal. Vicente didn't know how Iver knew all this, but he had his suspicions.

"You nervous?" Iver whispered, shooting him a glance.

"Please don't," Vicente begged.

Iver proceeded anyway. "What do you call a police officer with only one hand?"

Vicente quietly groaned but complied. "What do you call him?"

"By his fucking name."

Vicente snorted, not because the joke was funny—they never were—but at how deadpan Iver was when he told it. Iver never laughed at his own jokes, but Vicente knew Iver found himself hilarious.

The camp came into view. Five men were sitting around a fire in a small clearing. They didn't appear to have their guards up; they were feasting on something that was grilling over the fire.

"I'll take the lead, you back me up," Iver whispered. "I'll go for the ones at eleven and twelve, you keep your eyes on the other two."

"Affirmative," Vicente replied.

Iver took aim, taking his time. Silently, he pulled the bolt handle back and then downwards. He fired. The loud bang caused the birds in the trees to take flight. Iver loaded another shot and fired in quick succession.

The unharmed men got to their feet and started to run. Iver shot a third man as he ran for cover. "Where?"

"One behind the oak at ten, one behind the cart."

Iver shot the fourth man through the cart, and then he needed to reload. The fifth man noticed, drew his knife and dashed for them.

"Go!" Iver barked at Vicente.

Vicente's heart raced. The moment demanded action, but his lack of practice in shooting a moving target plagued him.

Vicente notched an arrow to the string, trying to steady his aim as best he could. He watched as the man moved among the sunlit trees. Each step eluded Vicente's attempts to aim. He released the arrow, but it flew wide of its intended mark, embedding itself harmlessly into the soft earth.

Iver had reloaded by then. Yet, instead of raising his rifle, he chose to relinquish it and stood. The man charged forth, lunging at Iver. Iver blocked the initial onslaught, retaliating with a punch to the man's stomach. The force of the blow caused the man to recoil, and he staggered back a few paces. But Iver withheld further aggression. *What is he doing?*

The man, finding his footing, straightened himself. He kicked, striking Iver's ribs with a brutal impact. Though momentarily winded, Iver maintained his balance and refused to falter. He drew one of his knives and in one sweeping motion, slashed the man's throat. He waited until the man fell to the ground before he collapsed to his knees.

Vicente did a quick scan of the perimeter to make sure no one was left. He didn't trust himself to not snap at Iver. Why had he decided to fight the man hand-to-hand? Iver was a damn sniper: he could've ended it clean, without theatrics.

Iver groaned, clearly affected by the kick to his side. "Vic, take a look at the cargo."

A dog on a leash was tied to a post of the cart. It was whining but still wagged its tail. Smaller than a wolf, the dog still bore the patterns and colors of one, and its eyes were an icy blue. Vicente had never seen a dog like that before.

When he approached it, it didn't snarl or chomp at him; instead, it greeted him. Perhaps it wasn't loyal to its deceased owners.

He pulled the tarp off the cart. As suspected, it was loaded with boxes containing Ottone's sealed healing potions. The Resurrectionists were involved in manufacturing them. They were getting closer to figuring out the mystery, and closer to halting their production of them.

Vicente pocketed five bottles—the rest of them had broken and spilled when Iver shot through the cart—before returning to Iver, who got on his feet on his own, refusing Vicente's outstretched hand.

Vicente brought the dog with them, and it followed willingly. They moved back four clicks, back into safe territory. Even though he was hurt, Iver insisted on it so that they could sleep well during the night.

By the time they reached their old campsite, Iver was barely able to walk. It had started raining, and when his foot slipped in the mud, he yelped from the pain.

"Sit down. I'll take care of this." Vicente unpacked the tent and pitched it where it had stood last night. There were still scorch marks on the stone from their campfire.

"I'll start a fire," Ivers said, limping past.

Vicente's rage hit him like a train. He was getting sick of Iver's reckless antics. During their two months together, they had grown accustomed to each other's parameters and bonded by unforgiving circumstances, yet Vicente had no idea why Iver had fought the man with his fists instead of just shooting him. "Iver!" Vicente didn't want to ask the questions again, but they threatened to spill out of his mouth anyway.

Iver's face fell when he saw the fury in his eyes. "Vic, I—"

"Sit. Down."

Iver eased himself down to the ground.

Vicente tried to calm his emotions as he went through the routine of setting up a campsite, but he couldn't. Fighting the man hand-to-hand had been idiotic.

Vicente's fingers were shaking as he crouched in front of Iver. His pulse was frantic. Jittery. "You were way too reckless back there. I thought I would lose you. Tell me. What's your history with the Resurrectionists? Were you part of them?"

Iver couldn't look him in the eye, his gaze kept darting between his own hands, his feet, over the tree line behind Vicente. "It doesn't matter—"

"You're not just risking your life by being this unpredictable," Vicente snapped, "you're risking mine as well. I deserve to know why you want to kill them all, so that I can decide whether it'll be worth it or not."

Due to the pain in his side, Iver moved slowly as he rubbed a hand over his face, through his hair and down the back of his neck. "Fine." He took a shallow, unstable breath. "I didn't run with them, like Daiyu did. I fought them. I was in the army. And I... I deserted my post."

CHAPTER 32

Iver

Two years ago

"Hey, Far Cry!" Lieutenant Siege called from the peak of the hill. "Come take a look."

Iver sprinted up the hillside. The rucksack was so heavy that the straps dug into his shoulders, but being beckoned specifically lifted his spirits. Iver had graduated at the top of his class, but now, as part of the Tactics and Assault Operations Team, he was the weakest link.

Iver hunkered down next to Siege and Broker, looking out onto the open, golden field of tall grass. They were miles away from the closest settlement.

"What do you think of that, Far Cry?" Siege asked.

Iver raised his rifle and looked at the deserted campsite through his scope. "I would guess—"

"Don't guess—*think*," Siege interrupted.

Iver took in the sight before him, analyzing the traces left behind by the rebel group. "They wouldn't risk lighting a fire if we were near their safehouse. Judging by the smoke, they departed less than two hours ago. They can't be more than five, six clicks from here."

"Six clicks, eh? Means we're a bit too close. Let's give them a chance to increase the distance, so they don't pick up on our scent." Siege slammed his hand down on Iver's shoulder, squeezing hard. "Good man."

Broker shot Siege a look. "Don't let the small fry decide what we do or don't do."

"He needs to learn," Siege said, winking at Iver. "Besides, I think he's right."

Siege turned around to the rest of the team, laying behind them. With their beige uniforms, they were camouflaged in the tall grass. He gave them the signal that they would be making camp there.

They went under the common name of 'rangers,' as they were all about nicknames. Lieutenant Siege was the one who had held Arkensaal ground in the uprising of the northern clans, and Broker had negotiated the agreement that had brought the Vale of Rayon Vostok into the fold. Iver had earned his name on his first day with them: they already knew he was the best sniper to ever go through military training.

The name stuck, and they had referred to him by nothing else during his eight months with them. Iver had joined the rangers the day he finished boot camp. While his comrades got shipped off to the frontiers, Iver had been given a unique offer.

The rangers were everything the realm needed them to be: an extension of the queen's guard, a special operations team for the police, or crowd control when the civilians rioted against the army taking their pick of the litter. No one else was like them, and they knew it. They were the élite. They hadn't taken on a new member in ten years, yet they had welcomed Iver with open arms.

All tents were pitched by nightfall. They trusted that Iver's estimation of the rebels' whereabouts was correct and risked lighting a fire. Their jackets, distinct only by the different patches they had all earned, were hanging on a line to dry.

Siege grabbed Iver's arm and pulled him down to the empty spot next to him around the fire. "Merciful, lad, you've got to eat a fuck-load more than that if you're to gain muscle," Siege said, nodding at Iver's plate.

"Get us something else than dried, wrinkly meat every day and I might," Iver retorted.

Broker jostled him by the shoulder. "Calories is not how you gain muscle; you need to train harder. I'll be so kind as to let you carry my backpack from here on out."

Iver laughed with them. These nineteen men had become like brothers to him within months.

Siege draped an arm around Iver's shoulders. "If you suffer a blow like that again, Broker, Far Cry might have to carry *you* out of active battle."

Broker grumbled at first, but then smiled, sharing the laugh with his comrades.

"Don't worry, Broker," Iver said. "I've got your six, always. I'll shoot down any bastard that comes near you. Pick them off like a hawk picking white rabbits."

Siege laughed loudly and squeezed him harder again. The strength of his embrace was something Iver had never even known he sought.

Siege stood. "Now, some business, lads," he said, and the men groaned. "Tomorrow, we will launch the attack on those fucking Resurrectionists. I'll have the battle plans ready before reveille. I need you well-fed and rested—that's an order."

"Yes, sir!" they shouted in unison, but there was a playful, mocking tinge to it. They worked like well-oiled machinery, and that wasn't because of some enforced military hierarchy: they were a squad. Family.

"What about those god-damned thugs of the Bruvran Company?" Broker said to Last Wing, the man sitting by his other side. "They still hunting cats in the mountains?"

Last Wing shoveled food into his mouth. "They won't be a problem. But if they interfere, I'll personally chase those fuckers up a mountain cliff."

Iver didn't doubt he could. Last Wing was the fastest soldier ever recorded, and he completed any obstacle course with such ease, he was practically flying.

"I can't wait to shoot them straight through the eyes," Iver said.

"Easy now, don't get all riled up," Last Wing said. "You've got a full mast going on under there? Damned kids, like dogs in heat at the prospect of adding another mark to their tally score."

"At least my junk is still working," Iver said with a smile. The men laughed.

"Far Cry, may I have a word?" Siege was standing in the opening of his tent, holding the flap open.

Iver joined him inside, lacing off his boots at the entrance. "Yes, sir?"

Siege waved his hand at him. "I know those fuckers at the boot camp hammered that shit into your head, but I will have none of it. Now sit. That's an order." He winked at him.

Iver sat while Siege pulled the stopper off a bottle. The acid smell of the liquid inside filled the tent within seconds.

"Am I in trouble?"

"Nah. I want to get to know you better. Firstly: how do you like your liquor?"

Iver had never had any: the legal drinking age in the capital was twenty-five, and Iver was a month into his eighteenth year. But he couldn't let his command know he'd never gotten drunk; he would tease the living shit out of him. "Neat," he said, like he had heard Broker say once.

Siege poured them both mugs. "Atta boy!" he cheered, but then he cringed. "I shouldn't call you 'boy,' should I? We're a good gang, but respect means everything." He sat down across from Iver and handed him one of the mugs. "And you're the smallest and youngest of us. Lots to prove. But still, you're one of us. I won't call you that again." He raised his mug. "Cheers."

Iver took the entire drink in one swig and promptly coughed. It tasted just as foul as it smelled.

But Siege reached over and smacked his palm on the back of his neck, like he did with all comrades. "Good man!"

Siege followed Iver's lead, and even he grimaced. He raked his hand through his blond hair. The tendons showed in his strong neck as he sucked his teeth. He wore a simple, black t-shirt, and the short sleeves barely contained his biceps.

Iver tore his eyes from his commanding officer, swallowing down the saliva pooling in his mouth from the liquor.

"Now tell me: how are things? Do you feel like you've found your place in the squad?"

"I think so, yeah." Iver knew Siege wanted a more developed reply from him, but his veins were starting to tingle, and the warmth that had started in his belly rapidly spread to the rest of his body.

"You tell me if there's anything you need, you hear me? It's my job to guide you all."

They talked well into the night as the others went to sleep in their own tents. It began as an interview to see how Iver was doing, but turned into Siege sharing battle stories and Iver telling him about his childhood.

Iver was laughing so hard his eyes teared up and his sides ached, and he initially didn't notice that Siege had moved to sit next to him to show him a scar on his ankle.

His head swam, and he guessed he was properly drunk at that point. Siege reached an arm around Iver, like he had done many times before, but this time it seemed different. Now there was something intimate about how Siege spoke into Iver's ear, sending earth-shattering shivers through him. The soft murmurs of his voice made desire pool in Iver's stomach. He felt safe and strange and tender.

Siege looked too fucking good in that shirt, the way it stretched over his wide chest. It fit him like a second skin. Iver's similar but smaller shirt was loose around his upper arms, and when he leaned back into Siege's arm, it draped across his chest.

"You should let me take the left flank tomorrow," Iver said boldly.

Siege laughed but tried to keep his voice low so as not to wake the others. "You've seen battle, yes, but tomorrow will be different. The Resurrectionists will be in their stronghold, and it will be heavily fortified. You'll be positioned near the rear and the last to take your position, once we've cleared a perimeter. I'm rather protective of you, Iver. But don't you worry, I'll give you your chance to properly shine." Siege was looking down at him. He was smiling, and his breath bloomed across Iver's face when he exhaled through his nose.

Iver put a hand on Siege's chest and clashed their mouths together. He wasn't good at this, but he needed to feel Siege's lips with his. Siege's breath was burning hot against his tongue.

Siege gently pushed him off, and he looked at him, eyebrows furrowed. "Far Cry, I'm sorry, but you've got the wrong idea, I—"

Iver recoiled. "Oh, fuck." Embarrassment, agonizing and putrid, leaked into his bloodstream.

Siege still held his upper arm with a firm grip. "Listen, you're a very beautiful man, but I—"

"Fuck, I am so sorry. *Shit.*"

"I'm not... that way. Besides, within the squad, sexual relationships are never okay."

"I'm so sorry, I thought you were—"

"You thought I was making a move on you? Far Cry, if an officer in command ever tries to put his hands on you, you grab his balls and you rip, you hear me?"

Iver scrambled to his feet as he realized he was only worsening the situation. "I didn't think you were—it was me, I fucked up."

Siege grabbed his wrist before he could leave. "Don't run off embarrassed. I've trained you better than that. Face me, and let's resolve this right now."

Iver tried to tear his arm out of his grip, but Siege held him there. He had no other choice but to try and explain himself. "Look, I'm drunk, I've never had alcohol before, and I just... admire you a lot. I like you, a lot."

Siege's smile was gentle and comforting. "I shouldn't have done that, should I? No more alcohol for you. And admiration is a good thing, I respect that. As for the *like* thing... you'll get over it. It happens." Siege dipped his head to catch Iver's eyes. "Now, this is settled, right? No embarrassment, no shame. I'll see you at reveille. Get some sleep."

Iver could only nod in agreement. He respected Siege even more after that night.

*

They were all awoken at dawn. Iver laced up his boots and was determined not to let his nerves get the best of him. He put on his uniform jacket, strapped his utility belt on, and checked over his weapons and ammunition. Then he put on his helmet and pulled up the scarf to cover his mouth and nose to protect himself from all the sand the wind was kicking up.

"Good morning, Far Cry." Siege placed his hand on Iver's shoulder like he normally would, and Iver was relieved nothing had changed between them.

"Why did you remove your scope?" Iver asked.

Siege, already dressed in his full uniform, was inspecting his firearm. "It's a bright and sunny day; the sun might reflect in the lens and alert them."

They all stood at attention as Siege briefed them on the situation and the plan. Iver had his sniper rifle propped against the crook of his arm, barrel pointed skywards, as he listened.

Siege's voice boomed as the briefing drew to a close. "We show no mercy to those who threaten the realm!"

They all slammed their chests with their fists and cheered.

"Rangers, lead the way!" Siege roared.

*

The rangers walked straight into anti-personnel weapons littered over a field one and a half clicks from the Resurrectionists' safe house. Three of them died on impact, five more maimed, and all survivors were taken as hostages inside the damp caves.

The days lasted for years. Iver felt revolting, stewing in his own sweat. He had been engulfed in the stench of mold since they dragged him in, but he still couldn't get used to it. Despite being locked up in the same room for the whole time, he was still disoriented.

"Tell me again what they looked like," Siege prompted. Iver knew he would've put his hand on his shoulder if he could've reached him, but they were all chained up along the cave walls.

"Metal." Iver tried to keep his voice from shaking. He wasn't brave, but for the sake of his comrades, he could at least try to pretend to be. "Circular. There were wires running from the tab on the top. It was partly covered by dirt, and it triggered when we stepped on it."

"Good man." Siege dropped his head against the wall with a thud.

Siege had them all recite this and other information, so that the ones who made it out would be able to give the intel to the government. These anti-personnel weapons had been unheard of, until now.

Last Wing was the one being tortured and interrogated that day. They had yet to drag Iver into that separate room—the room from which they could clearly hear each other's screams. Some held out for hours without making a sound, but eventually, they all ended up screaming. No one had given the Resurrectionists any intel. The rangers had been trained for scenarios like these. But, by then, days had passed, and no one was coming to their rescue.

The door flew open and Iver shook. Five men dragged Last Wing's unconscious body to his chains and fettered him again. Iver wanted to call out to him, but that would be giving out classified information, so he kept his lips pressed together.

"You do realize what will happen if you don't start talking, right?" one of the Resurrectionists said. "You're prepared to die to keep the queen's secrets?"

None of them said anything.

Iver stole a glance to check if Last Wing was still breathing. His chest heaved, but he didn't stir.

"I know one of you is in command." The leader squatted to look them all in the eye, one by one. "Let me take the first step to establish some trust: my name is Ulrich. I was once an army man myself. I know not all of you have clearance for the information

I'm after, so there's no need for me to hurt every single one of you."

Iver's stomach dropped. They were after Lieutenant Siege.

"Now, one of you tell me, who of you is in charge?"

No one replied. It didn't matter if they peeled the skin from his flesh; Iver would never sell Siege out, nor anyone else in his squad.

"I'll rip the fingernails off all your fingers until you tell me," Ulrich said.

No one said anything.

"We're only after your lieutenant or sergeant—we'll let the rest of you go. I don't give a flying fuck about the rest of you."

No one said anything.

Ulrich's gaze landed on Iver and he held eye contact, staring back in defiance. There was nothing they could do to make them talk. They were brothers.

"Get me the small one," Ulrich said to his men.

Fear bit into Iver and the dizziness hit, but he remained resolute.

The other rebels unshackled him and started dragging him towards the door. He didn't fight it. It was his turn to suffer what his brothers had suffered.

"No, no, I'll have him right here," Ulrich said and pointed to the dirty floor. "Hold him down."

Terror made his breath ragged, but he breathed through gritted teeth. Was Ulrich going to try to invoke sympathy from his squad by torturing him in front of them? Too bad—they had seen worse.

They pinned Iver face down, but no weapons of torture were brought out. Instead, Ulrich unbuckled his belt. "Listen here, boy, this is what's happening: I'm going to rape you in front of your team. See him, over there?" He pointed to one of the men guarding the door. "When I'm done, he will have a go. And then he will. Then him, and him. I will pass you around to all my men to have a go at you. And when we've all gotten our fill, I'll force your own brothers to take turns fucking you."

Iver said nothing. Fear tightened his chest like a vice, so hard he was going to vomit. At that point, he did start to struggle, but they held him down. He kept his mouth sewn shut as Ulrich tore his clothes off him. He squeezed his eyes shut.

"I'm their lieutenant," Siege said.

The scream bubbled out from Iver's throat before he could stop himself. No. *No. Siege.*

"That's more like it." Ulrich buttoned his pants back up. Iver was tethered to the wall again. "No, don't! He's lying!" He wanted to call his name but couldn't. "He's not our lieutenant!" *Why would he tell them?* Now they knew he had the information they sought, and they would torture him until he either spoke or died.

The rebels paid him no mind as they lifted Siege by the arms. He looked at Iver, his brows weighing down his face. "I'm sorry, Far Cry, I couldn't." Then they dragged him out of the room and slammed the door shut.

Broker let out a guttural moan. "Fuck!" His face contorted as he screamed wordlessly, yanking on his chains so hard dust flew from the rock where they were anchored.

"Broker, I'm sorry! I'm so sorry! Broker, *look at me*, I could've handled it, he shouldn't have—"

"This is your fault!" he yelled, "he knew you were too weak. We all knew it!"

"Broker, stop it," another ranger barked.

Siege never returned. By the forty-first day, only Iver, Broker and Last Wing remained alive. The rebels all knew their nicknames by then, and they used them to mock them as they were beaten. Siege had never told them anything, and so they took out their frustrations on them.

Iver was burning hot yet shivering. A fever, then. He stared up at the ever-glowing light dangling above their heads, blinking stinging eyes. The Resurrectionists did everything they could to stop them from sleeping, another torture technique.

"It's dark in here, right?" Last Wing said, his voice faltering.

"Yeah, they keep the lights off to scare us," Iver said. "Try to get some rest; you'll need it." Iver lolled his head to the side to face him. The blood around his empty eye sockets had turned brown, and his face was white and waxen.

"Fuck, my face hurts," Last Wing mumbled.

"They beat you up pretty bad. A week in the infirmary and your ugly face will be as good as new."

Last Wing let out a tired laugh. "I'll tell Siege you said that." Despite the pressing heat in the cave, he was shivering. He must've had an infection, too. "How long has Siege been gone, anyway?"

"A few hours or so. He'll be back before you know it."

Last Wing didn't respond. He had stopped moving. Iver turned his face away.

"You'll have to answer to our general for this," Broker said. "You made Siege sell himself out and they still didn't let us go."

Iver didn't have the energy to raise his voice. "I didn't make him do anything."

"You did," Broker said. "By being weak. And making yourself precious to him. I'll never forgive you for that."

Then Iver drifted off into darkness.

When he awoke again, his feet were dangling off the ground. He was suspended from the ceiling by his arms. He was hung like a pig for slaughter. It was hard to breathe like that, and the rough texture of the bindings chafed at his skin. The air was cool and damp, carrying with it an earthy scent that permeated the cave.

He looked around the room to get his bearings. He was alone, and he was tied to a pipe that ran along the ceiling. They must've thought he was already dead.

The adrenaline from being someplace new made him act. He curled up, brought his feet up and kicked against the rock above the pipe. The pipe broke and he crashed to the floor, slamming his head hard. Black stars appeared behind his eyelids. Afraid that they had heard it, he quickly got to his feet and undid the rope around his wrists. The sound of dripping water echoed, punctuating the silence.

The rangers' uniforms were in a pile by the door, their guns lined up against the wall. Straining his ears to pick up on any sounds of movement or voices, he got dressed. He took Siege's sniper rifle. It still didn't have a scope attached.

The subterranean labyrinth was empty; only faint, distant echoes reverberated through the cave system. Every so often, a gust of air would sweep through, telling him he was heading in the right direction.

He heard gunfire in the distance. On shaky legs, he arrived outside, squinting in the sunshine. Only a click away, there was a battle. Flags bearing the queen's crest stood proud in the army's midst. The queen's guard had come, as well as part of the military. The Resurrectionists were retreating, leaving their stronghold behind. His allies would find Broker alive inside and they would question them both about what had happened. They would learn about how Siege had sacrificed himself for him.

So, Iver ran.

CHAPTER 33

Vicente

The first snow arrived. Small snowflakes, the size of grains of sand, fell over the frostbitten landscape. The trees were now barren, save for a few evergreens scattered amongst them, but the woods still gave Vicente and Iver adequate cover from prying eyes.

Vicente loaded his quiver with arrows of varied origins. Some were haphazardly fashioned by Iver from materials scavenged in the wild. Others were the result of skilled craftsmen, carefully manufactured to achieve lethal accuracy. "What's their ambition?" His breath mingled visibly with the frigid air as he spoke.

They had located the Resurrectionists' hide-out, where the river Zinat cut through the Crooked Mountain range. There, they were holding up in Ships End, an abandoned military fortress. When the army still dispatched soldiers by boat, this was the farthest they could travel.

Iver pulled the bolt handle of his rifle back to inspect the chamber before feeding it ammunition. "They were trying to break off from society, essentially. They laid claims to land, made their own laws and formed another government. I bet they're still on that same track. Lieutenant Siege never mentioned the Gambler being involved, though."

Vicente could understand why following the Gambler would be enticing, if they truly believed what the Gambler said about Eldvittra giving up on humanity. Many felt abandoned by the gods they worshipped, and Vicente had always marked that down as something to be expected in faith. He saw no moral issues with other's revering a different god—but these people were aiding Ottone, and they needed to be killed for that.

"The dog would've been fine back at camp," Iver said.

Vicente patted the dog on the head. It was a yapping mess, stomping its front feet. "You said they had explosives in the ground around their previous keep. If they've decided to go with the same approach here, I've brought a good girl that knows a safe way across."

"Good point," Iver said. "Although I have no idea if they still have access to that sort of technology: they lost a lot of people when the queen's guard attacked, I assume. To be honest, I thought they were all dead. The queen obviously failed."

Vicente had finally grasped the full extent of Iver's mistrust of the queen. Iver had never believed her when she'd said he'd be pardoned for his crimes, because he already knew what she was like. Before Iver told him, it had never clicked for Vicente, and now he felt stupid: of course Iver had been a soldier. But soldiers didn't leave the military. At least, that was what Vicente used to believe. The constructions of the realm's government were all lies, he knew now.

Vicente scratched the dog's ear as they walked. He carried the bow on his back, leaving his hands free. If things went according to plan, he wouldn't have to use the weapon at all.

They followed in the tracks of the dog as it scampered off towards the keep. Ships End still stood, after almost a century. A marvel of architectural ingenuity, taking advantage of the natural rock formations to serve as the foundation and support for its walls. The rugged terrain made it difficult for enemies to breach its defenses. But hopefully, they would be invited inside.

"Their leader is called Ulrich, ask for him by name," Iver said. "And don't tell them how you found them."

Vicente agreed. If he mentioned that he had their dangerous former captive with him, they would surely have their guard up from the get-go.

Ulrich was the one who had sent that message to Iver, inviting him to Ships End, all those weeks ago, and Vicente still couldn't understand why they wanted to meet Iver, Far Cry, again. Was it really to kill him?

About one click from the fortress, they started walking low, crouching occasionally, hidden by the tall grass. By the time the entrance came into view, the dog had run off.

Two men were standing outside, smoking, far enough away that Vicente couldn't make out their facial features. They had rifles, leaning against the wall.

Vicente and Iver reached the final hill before Ships End. Iver got down on his stomach and aimed his rifle at the men. "Ready?"

"Yeah." Though not an experienced diplomat, Vicente still had a few dealings with sensitive meetings under his belt.

Vicente moved slowly between the trees, inching his way closer until he was within throwing distance.

He threw a potion of Stormwater and opened a tunnel to it, right in front of the two Resurrectionists. As he appeared, he raised his hands and tried not to make any sudden movements.

The men stared at him. If any of them were to move towards their weapons, Iver would take them down.

Right away, Vicente was fighting off the euphoria from having stepped through a tunnel. It had been so long since he last tunneled. He'd had to be frugal with his potions, and he had yearned for this moment for months. "I'm here to speak with Ulrich. My name is Vicente Lamor, mystic in the Order of Tal Miril and personally trained by the Sensis Quorum."

"That's a lot of fancy words, Vicente," one man said. "I'm Ulrich. How did you find us?"

Vicente slowly lowered his hands. "I have my sources."

"Do you, now?" Ulrich, a white man of sharp features and an air of casual confidence, took the cigarette from his lips and threw it to the ground. "What do you want, Vicente Lamor of Tal Miril?"

"I've heard about the potions that Lord Ottone of Llyr brews," Vicente said. "I want to know how they are made."

Ulrich furrowed his blond brows. "I'm not so sure Lord Ottone would appreciate it if I told you. He pays me well, Vicente. I don't really feel like losing that."

"I can offer you my magic in return. I have potions of my own; ones that give me the ability to travel long distances in the blink of an eye. I'm offering to teach you how to make them."

"Or we could just take them from you," Ulrich said.

Euphoria clouded Vicente's thoughts. He blinked hard. Why couldn't he think of anything to say? He had a plan that considered all the possible scenarios and how to get out of them, but he couldn't remember any of it. His mind was blank. He wasn't even afraid; he was simply high as a kite.

When Vicente said nothing, the other man went for his rifle. *Damnit.* Vicente had messed up again. He could tunnel out of the situation, but he needed to speak to Ulrich before Iver killed him.

A loud bang rang out. Resting magpies flew from their perches with such hurry it made the naked tree branches tremor and rattle from the force of their departure. Ulrich's comrade went limp, collapsing at first to his knees and then faceplanting in the dirt.

Ulrich didn't run. Aghast for a mere second—as he glared at his dead comrade, who had an exit wound right between the eyes—his composure returned quickly and when he met Vicente's eyes again, a smile was creeping over his face. "You have Far Cry, don't you?" he asked. "That's how you found us. Well, guess what? Now I'm up for a bargain. No fire, just bring him with you."

Vicente tried to rally something like fear, perhaps *caution*, as he considered the consequences of doing what Ulrich had told him to do. He didn't lack foresight, not in the slightest, but every fiber in his body screamed at him to finish this now. They had waited long enough.

Plan B, then. "Come, Iver!" Vicente shouted and held up one arm to signal him. Even though he realized it was a trap, he also trusted that he could get himself and Iver out of there instantly, if shit hit the fan. Two receiver potions were safely tucked away at their camp, and Iver had already drunk his. All they had to do was to always stay within touching distance of each other. They could both get to safety in seconds, without issue. Besides, this had to end, they had no other choice but to end this now.

Vicente held his breath as he waited for Iver. Ulrich, who for his part looked altogether too placid given his dead friend on the ground, said nothing. He simply smiled politely at Vicente. Meanwhile, any inclination to observe caution morphed into hard-drug adrenaline in Vicente's bloodstream.

A few minutes later, Iver appeared between the trees. Vicente hadn't heard him approach. It had to be that, despite heading straight into danger, Iver still kept his steps light. In this regard, he was still a soldier.

Ulrich's face lit up. "There you are. How I've missed you."

Iver scanned the area—another military affectation—before stepping into the clearing. He gave Vicente a long look, requesting any type of reassurance, an instinctual hunger for a foothold. Vicente held his gaze. He was Iver's anchor to safety, and he would staunchly refuse anything less than the two of them succeeding and making it out alive and whole.

The worry line in Iver's forehead eased. He dipped his head down before facing Ulrich again. "Ulrich."

"Please, join me inside for a chat. Both of you." Ulrich's attention dropped to the rifle in Iver's hands. "I won't ask you to leave your weapons at the door; we outnumber you by quite a lot. If you decide to spoil this little reunion, you being armed won't change anything."

"No fire," Iver said, sniffed, "let's talk."

They followed Ulrich through the main gateway. The air inside stank of gunpowder, a sort of metal acidity that burned through all Vicente's senses. He tasted it in the back of his throat, felt it stinging in his eyes. Still, the smell was welcome: if the Resurrectionists had resorted to using gunpowder, perhaps that meant they no longer had access to more advanced technology to manufacture and power their weapons. At least the counterinsurgency operation Iver had been part of hadn't been fruitless.

The corridor yawned into a massive hall with a vaulted ceiling. The space had been carved into the belly of the mountain, which was evident in the bare, oily rock of the cave walls. Before becoming the Resurrectionists' compound, Ships End was a military base, and before that, it served as a fortress. It was a relic from a time preceding the monarchy, when noble houses had ruled the realm, and it was, by the looks of it, impenetrable.

Vicente heard the hum of electricity and looked up. Glass bulbs dangled from their cords and offered lackluster light.

He nearly jumped out of his skin as a figure shuffled past him. Once his eyes adjusted to the muted illumination, Vicente noticed that they were not alone, despite the silence. It was a strange quiet; not empty, but efficient.

Rows of desks were tucked into one of the vast hall's many corners, and people were seated there. They looked like regular people, and they appeared to be working: shuffling papers, scribbling notes and speaking in hushed voices. Steam engulfed another section, where people were doing laundry. Ulrich led them through the area, and they zigzagged past sheets hanging wraithlike from the laundry lines.

"All hail," said Ulrich to one of the workers as they passed.

The man didn't look up, he kept his attention on the vat of steaming water where he was washing clothes. "All hail the fateful Gambler."

Vicente spotted women amongst the workers. He hadn't expected this. He had expected to face a group of armed soldiers, not a community.

"I'll take you to my office," Ulrich said over his shoulder, "it's a bit more private."

As they moved through the hall, Vicente noticed a place tucked away from the bustling activity. Metal bars stretching from floor to ceiling formed a cage large enough to hold over a hundred people. Vicente couldn't tell how many prisoners were in there, as the prisoners within were mostly obscured by the shadows. Was this what they were farming? Were the Resurrectionists using these prisoners when making Ottone's healing potions? If that was the case, Vicente and Iver would have to free them.

They entered another hallway, and Vicente was quickly becoming disoriented. Not that it mattered, as they surely wouldn't be leaving the same way they came.

Ulrich stopped in front of one of the doors and knocked. The people that exited were more in line with what Vicente had anticipated: the men were all armed, blades and firearms glinting in the muted light. They silently filed into the narrow hallway, eyeing Vicente and Iver as they did, before trailing behind their leader. Vicente kept his chin high.

They reached a staircase that connected to a loft, or something akin to a second floor. Series of banners hung from the railings, with iconography of their god, the Gambler's likeness embroidered onto the fabric. Tucked against the lowest baluster was a narrow shrine, holding a curved single-edged sword surrounded by unlit candles and a handful of dice crafted from bone.

Ulrich grabbed the sword and ascended the stairs. His men followed him, and Vicente counted them as they passed: thirty-two. Not an army, but still, he and Iver wouldn't stand a chance in a battle. After they had gathered the necessary information, they would have to tunnel out of there and return to destroy the farm either in secret, or with reinforcements.

"Hey," Iver whispered to him.

"Hm?"

"I don't trust stairs; they're always up to something."

Despite the gravity of their situation, a snort escaped Vicente. The fact that Iver found the audacity to crack a joke amidst their dangerous surroundings bolstered Vicente's own resolve. He nudged him with his elbow and then they began to climb the worn steps.

The walls of the hall on the next floor were covered in black rock, like brickwork but with uneven and smaller pieces than customary. The surfaces were iridescent in the light. A cluster of couches was nestled in one distant corner, and wooden boxes were scattered across the expanse. A bar counter stood along another edge. The vast chamber was dimly lit, its walls adorned with all kinds of mirrors; some hung on the walls whilst others leaned against them. It looked almost like a hall for theatre.

"As you can see," Ulrich said, "We're in the business of moving cargo around." He picked up a wrapped package from one of the crates and threw it on one of the mirrors, making it swivel on its hinges. The bundle ruptured and the dust and scent of saffron filled the air.

Vicente tried to hide his burgeoning unease as they walked deeper into the room. Dead people, or some kind of rare spice? The secret to Ottone's healing potions would be revealed here. And with that information, Vicente would tear Ottone to shreds.

Ulrich took a seat on one of the threadbare couches, draping one arm along the backrest and crossing his legs. His men remained standing, and so did Vicente and Iver.

The Resurrectionists clearly didn't need funds to go through with their plan of breaking off from society, but they might need the manpower. Vicente had to take advantage of this. But his mind was still muddled, he couldn't think straight. If they could find or bring with them some proof of what Ottone was doing, and that he was involved with a usurper god, they could turn him in. He needed to be punished for what he had done to those children. There was no death penalty for child abuse, but there was for heresy.

"I don't want to kill you, Far Cry," Ulrich said. "I want you to join us. I've kept tabs on you: you didn't return to the rangers. Rumor has it they want you dead. Join us. You're already a criminal."

Iver glared back at him with a look of profound hatred. "No thank you."

"You're still holding a grudge?"

"We're here to learn about the potions," Vicente said. "Then we can get further into what we have to offer."

Ulrich placed the sword across his lap. "I've heard that those potions can perform miracles. Lord Ottone pays us well to transport his precious cargo—"

"Enough with the shit-talk," Vicente snapped. "I brought you Far Cry, the best sniper in this country. One that survived and escaped you once already, who has been terrorizing the capital to the point where they had to hire a mystic just to bring him in. Tell us how the potions work, or we walk." Vicente hoped Iver wouldn't beat him up later for pretending to sell him out. But through the miasma of his cloudy, soupy euphoria, the realization of what he wanted emerged with rabid desperation and glass-pellucid clarity: he wanted to make a difference in the world. He needed to make a positive change. He would do, he *will* do, anything and everything to achieve that.

The mirth trickled from Ulrich's face, slowly at first, but then dropping completely. "Fine." He sighed hard. "Lord Ottone's potions don't work. The prisoners downstairs? They are sacrifices. The Gambler is given two 'sacrifices': one of our captives, and whichever patient Ottone feeds his potions to. Then, the Gambler casts its die; even for one of ours, odd for one of Ottone's. If the die lands on an odd number, the ailment of the patient is passed over to a sacrifice. His healing potions are just smoke and mirrors," Ulrich said, opening his palms. "It's all just a gamble. There. Happy?"

The world rocked under Vicente's feet. There was no secret ingredient, no alchemy. There was nothing, nothing at all, to Ottone's healing potions. It was a façade. The power of 'healing' came solely from a god: not in the form of a granted tool, but as divine intervention. It didn't matter if they destroyed this farm, it didn't matter if they destroyed a hundred more like it, because Ottone's source of power would never run dry. Unless they found a way to stop the Gambler, Ottone would continue.

Another failure. They would have to go back to Llyr and kill Ottone to succeed. At least that meant they didn't have to wage a war with the Resurrectionists. He and Iver could leave Ships End unharmed. Iver wouldn't like it, but that was their only choice. They didn't stand a chance against these people.

But Vicente didn't like how easily Ulrich forfeited the information. Did he think Vicente and Iver wouldn't be able to get out of there? "What does the Gambler get out of this?"

"The Gambler requires payment and worship for its miracles," Ulrich said. "And we gladly give it. Eldvittra abandoned humanity long ago, and even in its absence, look at what it has us do: endless war, for nothing. We helped set up Ottone's relationship with the Gambler in exchange for the money, and we don't condone what he's doing, but the end justifies the means. Far Cry, you have seen the sullied underbelly of the queen's reign, the result of her unwavering devotion to a god of war. Help us stop it."

"And the money is enough reason for you to aid in what Ottone is doing?" Vicente tried to maintain an air of authority despite the unsettling atmosphere.

Ulrich leaned forward, elbows propped atop his knees. "Ottone and his cult of Llyrians despises the queen, just like we do. They pay us a fortune to guide them on building an empire of their own. An empire of the Gambler, not of Eldvittra."

Cult of Llyrians? Were there more people in Llyr who knew of Ottone's scheme? The Llyrians hated the capital, but this? They wanted an empire of their own. Would it end there, or would they wage war on Arkensaal given the chance? "Why are you telling us all this?"

"I thought that was obvious." Ulrich looked at Iver. "I want Far Cry to join us." He stretched his arms out. "We are rich enough to employ many mercenaries, and soon we will have an army of our own. I'll make you the general of that army. If that's what you want; else, name your price."

Vicente suspected Iver would've at least considered it, before joining the military. As an orphan of the war, he had been given reason enough to loathe the crown. But Ulrich had tortured him and killed his comrades. He knew where Iver stood in the matter. Under other circumstances, it was possible Vicente would've joined them as well. He finally had some clarity into why Daiyu had.

"You're loyal to this god?" Vicente asked. "The god of chaos and random acts?" Did they truly believe Eldvittra had abandoned them? Vicente couldn't understand how they felt, as he himself didn't believe gods deserved worshipping. They were only beasts with too much power.

"The Gambler proved to be... intense," Ulrich said. "Hence, we surround ourselves in this mineral, called schorl, to keep the Gambler out when we don't need it. Perhaps you have heard of it? If you're a mystic and your powers come from the Stag or the Bird, it would null your powers as well. We know more about your dark magic than you think, *Ambassador* Vicente. And we also know that drinking the blood of a mystic—not your potions—gives you their connection to their entity."

Vicente scanned the room again. The bricklike walls around them were made of schorl, the mineral that diminished his mystic abilities. He was encased in it. The realization washed over him: he couldn't get them out of there. The skin on the back of his neck prickled as blood drained from his head and the world went quiet for a moment.

"We were getting powerful enough to kill the Stag beast in the mountains."

To Vicente, Ulrich's voice sounded like they were both underwater. With his nails, he pinched the webbing between his fingers, using the sharp pain to clear his head.

"We have tried a few times," Ulrich continued, "but the beast does not go down easily. Which is probably why the quorum is searching for it. Having it fall into the hands of the quorum would be unfortunate for us. You understand."

They knew where the Stag was. They wanted to kill it, which meant they knew how to get back to it—they might even have recorded the location. No matter what, Vicente needed to get his hands on all their documentation.

The rest of the Resurrectionists were all gathered behind Ulrich. Only a couple of them had rifles and bows; the others were armed with swords. Vicente still didn't think they stood a chance, but damnit, they didn't have a choice.

"Then we thought, why not take the beast, make it fight for us?" Ulrich said. "A few of us have tried to bond with it, but they were either simply rejected or killed instantly. That is a mission of yours, as a mystic: bringing the three entities back together? You are going to tell us how the bonding is done."

"I don't have that information," Vicente said. "The quorum has not yet clued me in on the process, as they feared I would find myself in a compromising position and share the information."

Ulrich tilted his head to the side, frowning. "How convenient for you."

"Really isn't."

"Why does it need to bond to be able to travel?" Ulrich probed. "Who trapped it in the mountains, and why?"

"Very curious, Ulrich. You ask a lot of questions; perhaps you ought to apply to get the mystic training from the sisters."

"I'm asking you."

"I don't know," Vicente said truthfully. The Otter needed to be bonded, and Vicente didn't know why. He just knew the Otter insisted on it.

The sword still rested across Ulrich's lap, a clear threat. He grabbed the hilt of it. "We have figured out one thing: to accept a bond, the Stag needs something. Isn't that right, Ambassador? It wants a gift of some sorts. It has told us many times, but it refuses to tell us what that is. A special gift, I assume."

Vicente's heartbeat kicked up. This was news to him. What could it mean? Did it want riches, sacrifices? Evidence of strength and power? Perhaps it wanted proof that the person trying to bond with it was a mystic.

Ulrich continued to press. "What is it that the Stag wants?"

"I do not know."

"Fine. Now..." Ulrich slapped his free hand on his knee. "You have gotten what you paid for."

Vicente hoped Iver understood the situation they were in. Ulrich was right: Vicente's powers were null. "Paid?" He felt his fingers tremble and clasped his hands behind his back to hide it. "I will be taking your blood, Vicente," Ulrich said. "If you decide to leave, Far Cry, you'll do so alone."

Vicente couldn't open a tunnel to get them out of there. He would have to think of something better to offer to them as payment. But his mind was moving too slowly. If Ulrich took his powers from him, Vicente would be left with nothing. He was nothing without them. Everything he had ever accomplished in life was because of them. No feeling could ever compare to the one he got when he stepped through a tunnel. And if he were to lose that, he'd die.

Ulrich smiled and stood, sword in one hand. "You probably wonder why—"

A loud bang rang out as Iver fired. He shot from the hip, not even bothering to lift the rifle properly to aim. The bullet hit one of the Resurrectionists right in the head, and he dropped dead.

Vicente and Iver darted behind the wooden bar counter and took cover as arrows flew their way.

The rest of the Resurrectionists took cover too. A few wayward bullets whistled through the air. The mirror above the bar counter shattered and shards of glass rained over them.

Vicente brushed the glass from his hair. "My potions don't work in here; I can't get us out. Could you shoot through the crates?" He couldn't understand why Iver hadn't shot Ulrich first. Perhaps he wanted to fight him, hand-to-hand. *Idiot.*

"Probably, but I don't have much ammunition left—I don't want to waste it." Iver pressed his back against the counter. "Come out here and face me, Ulrich," he shouted.

"No thank you, Far Cry," Ulrich responded. Someone from their side took a few shots, hitting the wooden bar, but it didn't go all the way through.

"I have an idea," Iver said, his voice barely audible over the sound of the rebels' shouting.

The shattered mirror above them was high enough to allow them to see the rest of the room. Iver couldn't risk peering over the counter to assess the situation. Instead, he stuck out the barrel of the rifle. Resting it on the countertop and looking behind himself, he used the mirror to take aim.

Iver pulled the trigger. A sharp crack echoed through the room as the bullet shattered one of the mirrors. The glass fragments scattered. Iver adjusted his aim and fired at another mirror, and then another—hitting mirrors behind the group.

Vicente understood what he was doing. Iver needed to know where their enemies were positioned to mount a successful counterattack. The mirrors on the walls were designed to add grandeur to the room, but now they could become a tool. The mirrors turned enough to offer a glimpse of the rebels' positions behind the crates.

As the mirrors shifted, Iver relayed the information to Vicente in hushed tones. "Two at eleven, four or five at twelve. Two behind the couch…"

Vicente's heart pounded with adrenaline as he took the bow off his back and drew an arrow from the quiver. But he couldn't peek out over the bar.

"It's still not too late, Far Cry," Ulrich cried out. "You and Vicente won't make it out of here. Please don't make us kill you. Are you prepared to die here, like this? After all you've survived, you'll die here protecting the blood of your captor?"

"Yeah, probably." Iver shot one of them, straight through the crate he was hiding behind. Iver pulled the bolt handle of his rifle and an empty cartridge popped out and clattered to the floor. In quick succession he fired again, shooting through their cover, and another rebel fell. Then another, and another. The room erupted into chaos once they realized Iver wasn't firing blindly. The Resurrectionists struggled to adapt to the shifting battlefield, and Iver's tactical advantage thwarted their attempts at retaliation. The Resurrectionists were firing back as well, but no shots made it through the wooden counter.

Iver pulled the bolt handle back and down to load, pushing the rounds into the chamber. Shells clattered to the floor on either side of the room.

Bullets were hard to come by. Everyone ran out after a few minutes, reducing the battlefield to hand-to-hand combat and archery, and Vicente was finally in the game. But that left Iver with no long-range weapon.

Vicente stood, scanning their surroundings. The only exit he spotted was the stairs they had used to get there: on the other side of the hall. They would have to fight their way out. "Iver, you take the bow."

The remaining Resurrectionists took to the floor; fifteen men still standing. Ulrich spun his sword once and charged. *We won't make it.*

"Keep it." Iver, with a murderous look in his eye, drew his knife.

"Iver, don't—"

But Iver had already started running towards Ulrich. Iver wanted to fight him as closely as possible, he wanted his sweet revenge, but he couldn't possibly fight with a knife against a sword. Vicente was going to lose him.

Staying behind the counter, Vicente drew an arrow and nocked it onto the bowstring. All he could do was clear the path for Iver. All he could do was try to keep the others away from him.

Iver was faster than Ulrich, much faster. He used his knife to deflect each slash of the sword and his agility to get out of Ulrich's line of attack. But the sword was longer and Iver couldn't get close enough to Ulrich to hurt him. He would have to tire him out. He circled Ulrich like a rabid wolf. When Vicente caught a glimpse of Iver's face, he saw the whole world burn in his eyes.

True aim was sacrificed for speed as Vicente fired rapidly, trying to drive them back and overwhelm the other rebels. It held them back momentarily, until they realized it was smarter to split up. Now with some room to breathe, they fired back. Vicente evaded their counterattacks, and with every dodge, they took turns to move in closer. If he managed to clear a path to the stairs, would Iver run away with him, or would Vicente be forced to flee alone?

Ulrich's sword slashed across Iver's upper arm. Blood spilled from the injury at a terrifying rate. If Vicente had been able to aim at Ulrich, he would've killed him right then. No one from either side dared to shoot at them, afraid of hurting the wrong person. Meanwhile, Vicente tried to hold the others off. He shot and killed a rebel and Ulrich roared furiously when he noticed. *He's getting tired.*

Iver deflected another slash and brought the blade of Ulrich's sword down. He managed to hook the tip of the sword with his knife, and with a stomp to the center of it, snap it in half. But as he held the knife low, Ulrich kicked it out of his hand. The hilt and the halved blade remained in Ulrich's hands.

Iver backed up, panting heavily. He had mere minutes left before the blood loss would render him unconscious.

Ulrich threw the broken sword, and Iver raised his arms in defense. The sword lodged in his forearm, right between the two bones. Iver gripped the hilt of it. For a second, he looked at it, eyes tearing up from the pain. With a roar through gritted teeth, and charging towards Ulrich, Iver ripped the sword back out, and slashed Ulrich across the throat.

The force of the slice sent Ulrich spinning sideways and he was already limp when he hit the floor.

The volley of arrows ceased as their leader bled out on the floor.

Iver was still standing, though crumpled and gasping through exhausted, rattling breaths. He pressed his arm against his chest to quell the bleeding. His face was pale. He was losing a lot of blood.

With the last of Vicente's adrenaline spent, time snapped back into motion—what once dragged like minutes now flashed by in fragments.

A rebel drew another arrow, but didn't aim it at either of them. He pointed it at the ceiling and let it loose.

The arrow pierced through a pot hanging from the rafters, and in union with the ceramic shards, black powder rained down between him and Iver.

It smelled like sulfur. Vicente didn't even have time to shout at Iver to get back.

The rebel ignited a lighter and hurled it into the dust. The explosions were blindingly bright, small and everywhere all at once. Sharp cracks split the air, louder than thunder and twice as fast.

Unseeing, Vicente stumbled backwards and managed to slam into the wall. He didn't feel any pain. His ears rang. Once the light gave way to a normal amount of shadow and contrast, he looked down at himself. He was whole, he was unhurt.

His hearing returned next. The rebels had all run and were thundering down the stairs.

Iver hadn't been hurt by the gunpowder either. He was farther from Vicente than he had been moments before, but he was still on his feet. His eyes were wild, whites glaring through the red and black coating his face. The explosion, Vicente realized, wasn't an attack: it was an alarm.

Iver and Vicente had won. The rebels were escaping the compound and telling the other cultists to do the same.

"We won," Vicente said, and he felt himself shaking now, like his body had finally been given permission to express the fear.

The last few months, he had spent oscillating continually between elation and worry; fighting for his life, constantly in danger of losing Iver to his own recklessness, but simultaneously delighted to be with Iver, to have been living a life with him. Vicente wanted to yell at him, wanted to scold him for putting himself in danger instead of trying to escape. They had failed their mission anyway. And if he lost Iver now…

Iver was going to need stitches. Vicente dropped the bow and stepped towards Iver to tend to his injuries, and as he did, something vulnerable bled into him, something cagey and fearful. Then it dawned on him with full force: losing Iver would be the worst thing to ever happen to him. Everything about Iver held him captive. His skill, his body, his face, his powers and his weaknesses had all woven around Vicente's heart like vines.

For months, he had been clinging to invented logic and flimsy justifications: that he needed Iver for protection, that Iver was a means to an end, that he stayed with Iver to achieve his goals. Vicente couldn't recall when it had happened, because he couldn't form coherent thoughts in Iver's presence. How long had Vicente's mind been on the back foot due to the signals from his heart, signals of a desire that fed its own frustration? He conceded defeat. Not that his mind needed persuading in the first place: he was in love with Iver. So very desperately, in fact.

"Iver, come here."

But to Vicente's horror, Iver broke into a sprint after the fleeing rebels.

CHAPTER 34

Iver

Kill them all.

Iver barreled down the stairs after them.

The scene downstairs was panicked, but not disorganized. They all ran in the same direction: towards another piece of shit narrow hallway.

The non-militia cultists screamed as they fled, but Iver could barely hear them through his own, over-loud pulse beating in his ears.

One rebel paused, turned and fired an arrow, to give the others time to run. Iver easily stepped out of the target line, but had to momentarily halt his pursuit. He felt like a tiger trapped in a circus, waiting for the cage to open.

"Iver!" cried Vicente behind him. "Stop!"

Iver didn't want to stop.

Once the rebel started running again, Iver followed. Through the hallway, down the stairs, into a tunnel. Screams echoed from up ahead. He ran so fast he bounced off the walls as the passageway curved. He hardly remembered he had a body anymore, fueled by anger so filling he needed nothing else to sustain himself.

The Resurrectionists had broken him. Constant nightmares weren't even the worst of it. He was a different person because of what they did. The memory of it, of becoming who he was now, had been lying dormant; but when Vicente had arrested him, it had stirred. Now it had resurfaced.

Though physically miles away from the location it had taken place, he was back there again. He remembered how he had spent his days vacillating between escape plans and questioning why he hadn't resisted harder during his capture. Being arrested by Vicente had triggered the same thoughts, the same uncertainty. Doubt. Could he have acted differently, changed the outcome? Could he have saved Siege? Daiyu? *Was it my fault?*

Those were broken thoughts—and it was the Resurrectionists' fault that they plagued him. Every single one of them was to blame. They were the architects of his misery.

Kill them all. There was no fear in him now.

Iver cleared another bend in the claustrophobic tunnel and came face to face with a straggling rebel. The man panted so hard his shoulders heaved. He stood there like a lost child. He was waiting.

"Let us go," said the man. He held a torch in his hand.

Iver's vision pulsed black. The underground tunnel smelled like stagnant water and any sensory impression was a warning that he was calming down and so he suppressed it: he couldn't slow down now, because if he did, he wouldn't be able to restart. This was it. He felt himself coming undone at the seams, like he was an engine threatening to shake itself apart. He couldn't focus on the dim light from the bare lightbulbs lining the walls because that meant he would also feel the nausea that preluded fainting. His body was a mere instrument for the accomplishments of his will. It obeyed his command without complaint, and if it did complain, he ignored it.

"No." Iver lurched forward.

The man dropped the torch and ran.

Iver tried to follow, to force his body to move, but the loss of momentum was detrimental to his pursuit. Something inside him rolled over and gave up.

Kill them all.

He had to kill them all because they had killed hundreds of innocent people, killed his comrades, killed Siege, because they had broken him. They should all die because they *broke him.*

The ground sizzled and popped where the flames touched it. But was he really broken, still? For how long could he use his trauma as an excuse to treat himself with such recklessness? To act like shit? Perhaps that excuse had expired a long time ago. He was so hurt. He was so damaged. He didn't want to be this anymore. He didn't want to be angry anymore, didn't want to be the beast they'd made him into. He didn't want to drag his past with him everywhere he went, like dragging a bloated corpse behind him that spread its foul odor no matter how far away he ran. Because he had entered new places, and he hadn't even noticed. He had made a new life, he had made new friends. *Vicente.* He had moved on, in a way. But the corpse he adamantly dragged with him spoiled everything. And worst of all; he hadn't even realized that he was holding onto it. He was holding on; it was all *him.* He could let it go. *I could decide to do that.*

The air smelled like scorched metal and spent matches. He was already halfway down that section of the tunnel before he saw the numerous pots of gunpowder on the floor.

The pressure from the explosion slammed him against the wall.

CHAPTER 35

Vicente

When Vicente found Iver in the tunnel, he didn't allow himself to feel the pain of seeing him like that; pale and bloody, covered in lacerations from pottery and metal fragments, blinking rapidly and fighting so desperately to stay conscious. No, he wrapped the worst of Iver's injuries and carried him back up to Ships End. He freed the prisoners. More than one of them had medical training, and before midnight, Iver was stitched and bandaged up, and propped full of antibiotics.

For the first time in months, they had real beds. But Vicente dragged a mattress to Iver's room to lie next to him. During the night, Vicente felt Iver's pulse on his wrist, where the blood beat blue against the skin. He put his hand on his chest, feeling the rise and fall of it. That first night, Iver made these ripped-raw noises, that welled past his lips. For days, he continued to sleep.

Most of the prisoners decided to stay at Ships End, recounting how the Resurrectionists had burned their homes and that there was nothing for them to return to. The compound was stocked with plenty of food and medicine, and safe from any potential attacks. The men that were well enough took to arms to guard the fortress, and the rest cleaned out the place of bodies.

A few days in, winter came in full force. Vicente stared out the window at the snowfall and the snow-covered plains outside. It looked like death.

Iver's sleep was unnatural. He wasn't moving at all. Vicente couldn't shake off the worry. Iver's injuries had resulted in a fever, and he wasn't getting well fast enough. He had lost a lot of blood, and no amount of force-fed liquid could replace it fast enough. The color of his lips was dull. He whimpered in his sleep. He was unconscious from the fever, his breaths shallow.

A woman, a doctor, came into the room. She checked Iver's blood pressure and temperature. Vicente tried to stay quiet as she listened to his heartbeat. Then she sighed.

"Is he going to make it?"

"That is still uncertain," she said. "He's stable, but if he's gotten an infection... Keep giving him fluids and come get me right away if anything changes."

She left again. She had quite a few patients to tend to. Many of the previous prisoners suffered from ailments given to them by Ottone's patients, because the rebels had offered them as sacrifices to the god.

Vicente couldn't take it anymore. He couldn't take this uncertainty.

In his bag, he found the five healing potions he had taken from the cart. Now he knew how they worked: if he gave one to Iver, and the Gambler's dice landed on an odd number, then Iver's wounds would transfer to someone else, to one of the prisoners Vicente had been sharing meals with the last few days. If Iver was going to succumb to his injuries, then that person would die instead.

Vicente sat down behind him, propping him up against his chest, and poured one of the potions down his throat, carefully so he wouldn't choke. He waited half an hour, but nothing happened.

He fed Iver another one.

The desperation for solace forced the embarrassment out of him. He looped his arm around Iver's shoulders and held him tightly.

Thirty minutes later, his fever was letting up. Vicente undid the bandage wrapped around Iver's forearm and saw that the sticky wound had closed over the stitches.

Vicente's relief was a physical thing, and it flooded his entire body. His shoulders slumped as he released his breath. He let his head fall back, hitting the wall, panting, like he had been running all night. Still hugging Iver's torso, he drew a new breath, and the scent of Iver's hair filled his lungs. "You're going to be okay." It sounded small and scared, like he was talking himself down after a nightmare. His hand was on Iver's waist, over his chest, cupping his face, in the curve of his neck. "You're okay."

Vicente grappled for his composure. It felt wrong to hold Iver so intimately when he was unconscious, and he tucked him back into bed.

A woman staying at Ships End suddenly fell ill, with the same symptoms Iver had. Cuts opened on her forearms, sticky and black. Three nights later, the fever took her life.

*

Once they had secured the perimeter and made sure no Resurrectionists remained, Vicente started sifting through their documentation. He found maps marked with possible locations of the Stag. They knew about the effect schorl had on gods, and Vicente wondered if his suspicions were correct: the Stag was trapped in a cave of the same mineral. It didn't eliminate its power, but it diminished enough of it to keep it subdued.

The Resurrectionists proved to be meticulous with keeping logs. Among the records were detailed reports on their numerous attempts to slaughter the Stag, and Vicente wasn't surprised by their failure. The Stag wasn't mortal in the common sense: it didn't starve or bleed or burn. Just like any other god, peculiar steps were required to kill it.

Once Iver was all healed, they would need to return to Llyr. They had failed to destroy Ottone's production. They had destroyed this farm, but as soon as Ottone learned of this, he could just make a new one, together with the Gambler. There was no way of stopping it.

If they were to end this, they needed Ottone dead, or for the people of Llyr to know what he was doing. But Ulrich had said that there was a cult in Llyr. Maybe all of them were in on it.

But there was no way they condoned what Ottone had done to the children. There was no way Llyr was in on this—that had to be Ottone's personal, secret depravity.

*

The winter wind found its way through a few cracks in the wooden window frame. River Zinat had not yet frozen, and Vicente watched the men and women as they fetched freshwater from it.

The group that had chosen to stay at Ships End had made it a home, and the hallways filled with the scent of garlic and saffron. There had been one attack from two straggling Resurrectionists that returned, but that was it.

"This sucks ass," Iver said. "It hurts, and I'm so fucking bored." He was lying on the bed staring up at the ceiling, as he had for almost a week.

"I would give you opium if I had any," Vicente said. Many of the prisoners were badly hurt after being offered up as sacrifices for the Gambler, and any medicine had run out after a couple of days.

The healing potion had saved Iver from death, but he was still unwell and weak. In Vicente's opinion, he deserved the pain: he had been so reckless in the fight. He would've died if Vicente hadn't cheated, all to get his revenge.

"You're right, I need some euphoria to distract myself." Iver looked him dead in the eyes and completely straight-faced said: "Mind stepping outside so I can jerk off?"

Vicente snorted. "You don't want an audience?"

"I guess I thought you'd rather not, but given that you've had to keep me up as I've taken a piss all week, maybe we'll both feel lonely if you leave. Could you wink those pretty eyelashes at me? I'll finish faster if you do."

Vicente doubted Iver could manage it: his arms were still so badly hurt he couldn't close his fists. "I'll do you one better: I'll help you." The words tasted tempting on his tongue. It felt like letting go of the reins.

Iver groaned as he sat up, propped his pillow against the wall and sagged back into it. "I mean, if you're offering."

Vicente wanted. Desperately, fiercely he wanted.

Before he was even aware of deciding to do so, Vicente was sitting next to Iver on the bed. He put his hand on the curve of Iver's neck, thumb brushing over his jaw. Iver's breath shook against his mouth. His own exhale was a shuddery, trembling thing too.

Iver's chest heaved. His gaze flickered down to Vicente's lips, then back up again. "Vic… I was just joking," he whispered.

What Vicente felt was unexpected, but he also recognized it immediately: fear. He had never been scared in situations like these before. He didn't know what to do or what to say. Being rejected wasn't something he took issue with. So then, what was this?

He swallowed around the tight lump forming in his throat. He forced his face into a smile, fleeting and pained. "Of course. So was I."

He stood back up, feeling the sudden urge to escape. Like a coward, he walked towards the door.

"Vic, wait a second."

Vicente hoped he hadn't shattered their relationship. "Don't worry about it; get some rest." He opened the door to leave. He didn't want to talk, fearing he would mess up even further. Their regular banter now felt too inappropriate, too real. "I need to run an errand. I'll be back in a few days."

He heard Iver move off the bed, heard his bare feet striking the cold stone floor as he stood. "You're leaving?"

Vicente stepped outside and shut the door.

He rode into the village of Naka-Toda, cursing loudly to himself the entire way there. He had to restock his potion ingredients, having used the last of them while preparing for the escape from Ships End.

He felt ill. Anxiety twisted his chest and the sensation of thousands of crawling ants plagued his arms and legs, a haunting that wouldn't stop. He knew what it was. He needed to open a tunnel, and it didn't matter if there was no practical reason for doing so.

On the road back to Ships End, he stopped. He prepared new potions, entangling them to each other. He could've entangled any two objects and opened a tunnel between them, but that never gave him the same rush as stepping through one himself.

Vial in hand, he allowed himself to feel his feelings, knowing escape was within reach.

Iver had rejected him countless times before. Why had he expected this time to be any different?

There was a conflict between his own desires. Something circuitous, something paradoxical. He wished for Iver to have everything he ever wanted, for him to be safe and happy and loved. He loved Iver so much he would annihilate himself and the world to make that happen. He wanted to express his love in all ways, including sex. But if Iver didn't want him, then Vicente would oblige. If Iver didn't want to see him ever again when he found out more about Vicente, then Vicente would leave. And knowing this, realizing this outcome could very well be possible, ripped him apart.

Vicente threw a receiver vial as far into the woods as he could. Then he downed the entangled Stormwater, opened a tunnel and stepped through it. He had just wasted a potion, but the guilt faded once the bliss swept him away. It felt like drinking a whole bottle of wine, but without the weight of the liquid settling in his stomach.

CHAPTER 36

Iver

Iver paced around the room. Exhaustion and ache settled into every muscle and bone in his body, but he couldn't sit still. He had never been so anxious in his life. Other bad feelings had a purpose: fear kept him alive, anger defended him, sadness made him seek aid. Anxiety, however, was useless. He didn't want to accommodate a feeling like this, didn't want to keep space for it. He had no opportunity to remedy anything, because Vicente wasn't here.

Was Vicente pissed at him? Did he misunderstand Iver's shyness as rejection? It had started off as a joke, and then suddenly, Vicente had been preparing to kiss him.

Iver hadn't been ready to affirm, and he hadn't been ready to refuse. Vicente was stubbornly flirtatious, and Iver always shot him down, and Vicente always bounced back. But this time, Vicente had run out of the room like his ass was on fire. Iver was getting angrier the more he thought about it.

Footsteps passed outside the door, and he heard chatter and laughter before the sounds faded again. The previous prisoners, most of them not having homes left to return to, decided to make Ships End their new home. Iver refused to leave his room. He didn't want to talk to anyone. He wanted Vicente to come back so they could fix this.

Iver's legs trembled. He sat down on the bed again and began unwrapping the bandages around his arms, both at the same time in frustration. Vicente had been doing this for him, but now he wasn't here. All his life, Iver had taken care of himself, he didn't rely on anybody else, and he wouldn't let Vicente undo all that for him.

Iver expected to see dried blood and raw edges of flesh. Instead, he found that the cuts had already healed into pink scars. This was impossible. The blade had gone through his forearm, between the two bones and poking out the other side. But this, it looked like his injuries were six months into the healing process— Vicente had given him a 'healing' potion.

Iver slumped forward. "Fuck." His vision blurred. It shouldn't have appalled him, but it did. Even though Vicente knew that someone else would get Iver's wounds, he had administered a potion anyway.

Iver had murdered hundreds of people in his life. That didn't change the fact that he viewed himself as a good person: they had all deserved to die. There was that cognitive dissonance again, he reckoned. But if anyone was callous enough to steal life, it should've been him. And he would've never even considered doing that to somebody.

Yet Vicente had been the one to pour a life-stealing potion down Iver's throat. Vicente had killed only a handful of people— armed and violent people, at that—yet he did this. He killed an innocent person, just to save Iver.

Fighting against his own reluctance, Iver went down to the main hall. He talked to the people there. Sure enough, a few days ago, a woman had died of injuries appearing out of nowhere. No one suspected Iver and Vicente, though. Dozens of times, they had all seen prisoners meet a similar fate. They believed the wounds and ailments came from Llyr, where Ottone still used his remaining potions.

All the previous prisoners spoke of the same thing: they would have this guillotine blade hanging over their necks until their deaths. They had been offered up as sacrifices to the Gambler already, and there was no escape.

Iver returned to his room where he promptly threw up.

*

The next morning, Iver was sitting on the bed, staring out the window, when the door to his room opened. Vicente stepped inside and Iver shot to his feet.

"You're looking spry. How are you feeling?" Vicente smiled at him. Like nothing had happened between them.

"Fine." Iver shifted under the weight of his attention. "I know what you did. I figured it out."

Vicente's brows pinched. "What did I do?"

"You killed someone, Vic," he said. "She died of her—of my—injuries."

Vicente stared at him for a moment, then gave a whispered *shit* and closed the door behind him. He looked down, swallowed, ticked his jaw, scowled, before holding his head high again and looking Iver in the eye. "Yeah... I knew. I know she died."

Iver recognized what he was trying to hide: guilt. At least he was warring with himself, at least he had some apprehensions. "You okay with that?" He didn't know what he wanted Vicente to do. This, was this Iver testing him, like he tested everyone he cared about? Was he doing this because he wanted to see what Vicente would choose?

Vicente chose anger. "You're not? I mean, that's pretty rich coming from you, given your past."

Iver scoffed, grinding his teeth together. He dragged his gaze from Vicente to the window. "Fuck you."

"You wouldn't have done the same? Don't lie to me."

Iver wanted to say no, because that would've been the truth before. But when Vicente was looking at him, that changed. Just being around Vicente altered him. To save Vicente's life, he would have done the same. "It's different."

Vicente was still staring at him. "How?"

Iver had murdered unarmed people in the past. He knew what that did to a person. No matter how he twisted the truth, he knew he was a bad person, and he desperately didn't want Vicente to be one, too. "I have killed civilians before; I know what it means to—"

"Oh, cut the crap, Iver," Vicente snapped, rolling his head back for dramatics. "Don't tell me this is some heroic bullshit again, about saving my conscience? You don't want me to be consumed by guilt for the rest of my life, is that it? But it's too late for you, right?"

"I'm just hoping you thought real hard about it before you did it." Was he that transparent to Vicente now? Iver was getting flustered. The words spilled out of his mouth before he could stop them: "Look at the state of you after Daiyu's death."

Fuck. Why did he say that?

Vicente drew a deep breath. "Oh, I remember. And do you want to know why I was so torn up about that? It wasn't because it may or may not have been my fault." His voice grew louder. "It didn't wreck me because I killed someone. It was because my best friend *fucking died*, Iver."

Iver felt Vicente's voice rattle his bones.

"Not because a person died, but because a person I loved died, and I care more about my loved ones than I do the rest of humanity. It's not a secret, it's not special, and I sure as shit won't feel bad about it. Everyone is like this, and if that makes us terrible people, then so be it. That's the reason I gave you the potion at the cost of that woman's life. I don't know her, I don't care about her, and I don't love her. No one can make me feel bad about that."

He stormed towards the door.

Fuck it. Iver didn't need to know why Vicente wanted to sleep with him, it didn't matter why, what mattered was the fact that he did. The only other thing that mattered was that Iver wanted to sleep with him, too.

Iver was going to do it, reasons be damned. He was going to have sex with Vicente. "Thank you."

Vicente stopped. "What?"

"For saving my life."

"You're welcome," Vicente said, in the same angry tone, hand on the door handle.

"I'm sorry I tried to give you shit for it. That was kind of fucked up." Iver was being awkward, and he knew that, but he didn't normally do stuff like this. He didn't apologize. It was unnatural, revealing, like there was something in the words that exposed him.

"It's fine." Vicente blinked, anger mellowing, still sounding confused. He removed his hand from the door. "I know you meant well. I think."

"I did." Iver promised himself to do better. Vicente was worth it. "I don't—" *want you to leave. Don't go.* "Please stay." As soon as he said it, he flushed from embarrassment. He blushed so deeply he felt it on the back of his neck. *I missed you.* "Wanna tell me about your trip?"

"I got some supplies, is all. It was fine. Went well." Vicente said it in a way that made it seem like he didn't find it either fine or well.

Iver was fidgeting. He felt inside out. He wanted to ask Vicente to kiss him, but he didn't know how to. "…That's good."

The silence that followed swelled in Iver's ears.

Vicente stared down at his own feet. His hands clenched and unclenched at his sides. He cleared his throat. "I… I killed a man when I was seven years old."

Iver said nothing. He bit down on the inside of his lip hard enough to draw blood. He didn't know what to say. He figured something awful happened to Vicente before he had left Llyr as a child. But he hadn't expected this.

Vicente wasn't looking at him. His gaze turned inwards. "He… One day I snapped. Shot him with his own pistol. He deserved it. He was—" Vicente began, but his voice cracked and so he stopped.

"Shit, Vic…" Iver stepped closer to him. The information felt like a punch to the chest. All his strength evaporated from his body, making him small and defenseless. "I'm sorry."

He reached his hands out. Tentatively. Vicente didn't move. He kept his eyes glued to the floor.

Iver put his hands on the sides of Vicente's face, stroking his thumbs over his cheekbones.

Vicente looked at him, blinked. His eyes finally cleared. "I don't feel bad about it."

"You shouldn't. You should never feel bad about protecting yourself." Iver knew that he himself was broken, and he had thought he had a complete grasp of the world around him. Turned out other people could be carrying heavy baggage, too.

"Thank you." Vicente's voice still sounded distant. "I have to get back to work. You still need to rest, Iver."

Vicente had just said he considered Iver to be a loved one. He had killed someone for him. Iver was sure. His life had been shrouded in uncertainty, but when the final piece of the puzzle was placed, his entire vision cleared. He wanted Vicente.

Iver was on his toes. He looped his arms around Vicente's neck, and he pulled him down for a hug. Vicente hugged him back, stiffly wrapping his arms around Iver's torso. Then he sighed and relaxed, melting into Iver's embrace and clutching him even closer.

"You could stay," Iver said against his neck. *Please stay.*

"I need to go through the cult's documents. They know where the Stag is, and we've got to prepare before we return to Llyr." Vicente broke the hug and stepped away from him. It looked like he was withdrawing into himself again. "Get some rest."

Vicente opened the door to leave, gutting Iver in one, swift motion. Was this a 'no'? Or had Iver picked the wrong moment? This was probably a terrible time; he shouldn't have tried this now. Or had Vicente seen him vulnerable and decided then that he didn't want Iver after all? Or had Iver read everything incorrectly, had Vicente's flirtations been a joke all along? Had Vicente never actually wanted him?

Oh. It was fitting, Iver thought, that there was doubt in this moment too.

Petrified, Iver felt the onset of tears burning behind his eyelids. He squeezed his eyes shut against the barrage of emotions. For months, Vicente had made it clear what he wanted from Iver.

Now, Iver didn't know if he actually had. Once Iver had finally gathered his courage, the world turned on him again.

Vicente closed the door behind himself.

CHAPTER 37

Marcia

Marcia was sitting by the fire, staring into the flames. Her months had been filled with preparations for the marriage ceremony. Falco's family arrived last week. Thankfully, she hadn't been forced to spend much time with him. Rather, her company had come in the form of two groups: maidens who had been following her around like servants, and married women who had been charged with preparing her for her new life. She had been taught how to 'properly' cook and clean, and how to care for a baby. All she felt was resentment, and she was so disconnected she didn't speak for hours at a time. It was all so backwards; she couldn't believe this was her life.

She would go through with the ceremony, and after a few months, when the heat was off, she would make her escape. She had an active correspondence with Sergeant Celia, who had promised to help her when the time was right. She just needed to be patient. Not that she wanted to do anything, anyway.

She had been allowed to collect Daiyu's remains and burn her body. Daiyu had lived all her life in the capital and deserved a burial that reflected her culture. Daiyu's only crime had been that of trusting, and perhaps seeking solace from a life of pain, and Marcia wished death to be kinder to her than life had ever been. Marcia built a nest in her bed, with all of Daiyu's belongings. Her clothes still bore the scent of her skin.

Her heart lay shrouded in mourning, the ache of her loss casting a shadow that stretched endlessly. When Daiyu slipped beyond the veil of life, it left Marcia to grapple with a solitude that felt insurmountable. How terrible it was to have loved something that death could take. She longed for one more meaningless conversation. Grief was her companion now, and the journey through its depths was a solitary path she had no choice but to tread. She was left behind, trying to figure out life without her. And Marcia was nothing if not Daiyu's wife.

There was a knock at her door, and one of the maidens peeked her head in. "Lady Marcia, you have two visitors. They're waiting for you downstairs."

Marcia's heart raced as she quickly got dressed. *Could it be them?* Months had passed. The last she had heard, Vicente and Iver had fled Llyr. There was never any doubt in her mind that Vicente would come back for her; the question was only 'when.'

She hurried downstairs, her bare feet hitting the carpeted stairs with soft thuds. In front of the glass-door entrance stood Vicente and Iver, shoulders and hoods covered in melting snow.

Marcia ran up to Vicente and threw herself around his neck. He wrapped his arms around her waist, picking her up, and hugged her tightly. Instantly, she wanted to cry, to beg him to carry her out of there, back to the place he and Iver had been hiding for months.

When Vicente put her down again, she was shaking with relief. Their eyes met in a wordless exchange and the pain flickered out of existence, for just a moment. Vicente blinked at her heavily, mournfully. There was emotion there she wasn't sure she had ever seen before. Not directed at her, at least. She never thought she would find herself at the other end of a look like that.

Vicente cupped her cheek. "I am so sorry."

She knew he was.

The maiden had followed her partially down the stairs and was leaning her hip on the staircase banister, taking in the scene.

"Bring my guests some dry clothes," Marcia told her. "We would like to speak in private, in my chambers."

"Certainly, my Lady."

Marcia took the lead up the stairs, Vicente and Iver at her heels. Behind closed doors, she stole another hug from Vicente, ignoring the melting snow on his cloak wetting her sleeves.

"I'm sorry we didn't come for you sooner," Vicente said.

"Please don't worry about that. I can handle myself." Marcia took in the sight of him. His hair had grown, and the curls were less defined, more tousled, but nothing a good bath couldn't fix. His usually styled beard now covered his cheeks and she guessed they had been someplace where razors were not at their disposal. "I gather you've made yourselves useful?"

Vicente shot Iver a look. "We have."

Marcia noticed the difference in their relationship then. A subtle change in the way they interacted. In the way Vicente's eyes found Iver's, immediate and familiar, like flowers seeking the sun. In the way Iver's gaze lingered on Vicente even as he turned to face Marcia and said, "We located the Resurrectionists, killed them all. They won't be a problem."

There was something tender between them, and if Vicente had chosen to trust Iver, Marcia would have to do the same. "Have you figured it out? How are the potions made?"

Vicente put his hands on Marcia's shoulders, thumbs stroking the bare skin above her gown. "We have, but let's not discuss this now. We need to get you out of this mess. Has it been done?"

Marcia sighed hard through her nose. She had already fought that battle and lost. "The ceremony is tomorrow. There's nothing you can do."

Vicente began to pace the room. "There must be something. This isn't right."

"Out here in Llyr, you'd have to convince either the groom or the father of the bride. If you can do that, you'll save me."

Falco would never concede. He had waited for her for seventeen years, and apparently never once considered another bride. His clan was small and not revered, thus he would take on her family name and climb the social ladder. The only daughter of the Jadanza clan leader was worth waiting for, and he would never give up without a fight.

"Then I'll do just that," Vicente said. "Let me speak to your father."

Marcia gently grabbed Vicente's elbow, trying to calm him down. "I will arrange something. In the meantime, make yourselves at home. You'll be guests at the wedding. My father will allow me this."

*

"You ought to know Ottone suspects you two had something to do with the murders, and if he finds out you have returned, you'll be detained," her father told Vicente before taking a sip from his wine glass.

The three of them were seated in the main dining hall, sharing a dinner that Marcia couldn't stomach. She felt both flighty and exhausted. Hope needed close to nothing to nourish it. It was still there: despite having lost so much, she still clung to the hope of keeping what she had left.

"I understand, Lord Renato," Vicente said. "After Marcia's ceremony, me and Iver will return to Llyr and face our judgement."

The passing of Daiyu remained an unspoken specter, a heavy veil draping the conversations of those around her. The words, so loud in their absence, gnawed at Marcia's soul. It was as though the world had forgotten the tragedy that had shattered her heart. But Marcia understood that this moment was not ripe for the vengeance that was whispered for in the recesses of her mind. The day of reckoning would come, a promise she held close, a pact she had forged within. She knew the orchestrator of these machinations, her own father, had wielded Vicente as a pawn in his elaborate design.

"You know Marcia objects to this union with Falco," Vicente said.

The soft glow of candlelight danced on the fine porcelain plates and crystal glasses. Marcia's father set down his fork and knife, his expression tranquil as he savored every bite. He was able to feast without a care in the world. "It does not matter; a deal has been struck."

"I come to you with a better proposal," Vicente said. "*I* want to ask you for Marcia's hand in marriage."

Silence settled as her father leaned back in his chair, a contemplative glint in his eyes. Seconds ticked by.

Vicente spoke again. "She would not object to this. We are dear to each other. Unlike Falco, I have status and an education in diplomacy and history. I offer to move here to Llyr, to bring my learnings with me, offering more prospects to the children of Llyr."

Her father pulled the napkin from his collar, folded it and placed it on the table. "You are an outsider."

"I was born here."

"And you are under investigation for murder. I will not have my only daughter marry a criminal."

"The trial has not yet been performed, and until then, I am to be considered innocent," Vicente said. "But I understand your concern. I'll extend my proposal until after the trial, after I have cleared my name and all suspicions have been dropped." Vicente's back was straight, upholding the charade he had been meticulously schooled in by Marcia. When they first met, he displayed his emotions and his words were unfiltered. But she had sculpted him, etching him with practiced cordiality and a veneer of unyielding dignity. Gone was the boy who wore his heart unabashedly on his sleeve. Now, he carried feigned sincerity and an unbreakable pride that had been carefully cultivated. "If I am convicted, you can marry Marcia to Falco. All I'm asking is for you to wait."

Her father reclined in his seat, a contemplative air enveloping him as he leaned back, his fingers idly toying with the tendrils of his moustache, lost in thought.

Marcia held her own hand, hidden beneath the tabletop. Her palms were sweaty. *Please, gods, do not intervene with Vicente's plan.*

Her father sighed. "My answer is no. Falco's clan have all dropped their duties to come here; it would be an embarrassment to keep them waiting."

"This is a life-long commitment," Marcia chimed in. Not that her father would listen to her. To him, she was simply a beast of burden, of childbearing; a mere chattel. "It can wait a few weeks. Please, consider it." She never thought she'd find herself in the position of pleading with her father, but this could be her only chance.

"Ambassador Vicente," he said, "I understand you cannot control the circumstances of your own heritage, but I can control the fate of my legacy. I do not wish you ill, but I will not have tainted, mystic blood coursing through the veins of my grandchildren." He rose from his seat. "My decision is final."

*

All the maidens and married women of her clan gathered in her chamber. Her family tree was drawn with black ink on her back, the first of their name written above her tailbone and then branching out all over her skin. Her father's name was penned at the base of her skull, her cousins' names on the backs of her arms. Drawings of branches connected them all.

She was dressed in a bright yellow tunic, the color of saffron and sunshine. The color of Daiyu's soul. Her hair was braided, her make-up done and a veil placed over her head. A ceremonial silver dagger dangled from the belt around her hips.

The main dining hall was clad in vibrant fabrics, with silk drapes hanging from the ceiling and tapestries showing every memorable event in her clan on one side of the room, Falco's on the other. On the wall behind the altar hung a newly woven tapestry, depicting her and Falco's union in marriage. It was beautiful. She wanted to burn it all.

The guests were seated on cushions scattered all over the room. Her gaze found Vicente's and she held it. Then, she stepped up to the altar.

Standing there, her father was holding a string of silk. Using the silver dagger, she cut the string in half, just like her mother had done, and her mother before her.

Falco did the same thing with his parents.

She and Falco faced her paternal grandfather and Falco's paternal grandfather. Another string of silk was brought to them, one end wrapped around her ring finger and the other around Falco's.

After the ceremony, the feast began. Marcia couldn't stomach any of it.

She drank some wine just to have something in her hands. Guests were handing her gifts, and after she pretended to admire them, they were placed on a table for everyone to ogle at with envy.

The maidens still tended to her, serving her like slaves, but this would stop tonight, once the marriage had been consummated. She wouldn't be a virgin in the eyes of the clans anymore; that she had had sex with women didn't matter to them.

After speaking with Falco's parents, she sought Vicente and Iver. They had been given traditional Llyrian suits, and she wanted to comment on how this was the first time she'd ever seen them in such fine clothing, but she couldn't muster humor—couldn't muster anything in the face of it all.

Vicente gave her a healing potion as a wedding present. "This is one of Lord Ottone's potions. At least take this. It would make me feel better if you had it."

She nodded and accepted it.

"I have a gift for you as well," Iver said.

"Oh?" She had not expected that, not when they had both been given only a day's notice.

Iver tilted his head to the closed balcony doors. "I need to give it to you in private. Could we step outside?"

She was hesitant, but she followed him into the cold winter evening. The darkness had a texture, it was that absolute.

He looked her over, and she wondered if he was admiring the dress. "You've got one of those bands on your thigh?"

"Excuse me?"

"To hide this." Iver offered her one of his knives. It was the one Daiyu had made for him. "It's of no use if anyone sees you with it."

She snatched it from his hands, unkindly. "I'll hide it wherever I see fit."

He looked at her, his expression contrite. And just like that, Marcia saw her fourteen-year-old self in him, a child that had struggled through that pantomime of living until there was nothing left of her but anger. It could be that he too tried his best, but carried with him some scars that had him act the way he did; displaying defensiveness that read as vulgarity.

Vicente had chosen to trust this man, and despite it all, she trusted his judgement. "Thank you, Iver."

Iver's nose had already gone red from the cold, and he wrapped his arms around his upper body. He shrugged. "Kill him, problem solved."

"There will be repercussions if I do that."

"Worse than this?"

"I'm still debating it." The truth was that getting rid of Falco wouldn't matter. If it wasn't him, then it would be some other man. The world was full of men waiting their turn.

Falco's parents gifted her cured opium and an ornate glass waterpipe with which to smoke it. She celebrated with them on the balcony, treating everyone in the group to some. Then she invited Vicente to smoke with her. When they were done, she invited her father. Then Iver. Then one of her cousins.

By the end of the festivities, her body was comfortably numb, but her throat watered from the nausea. When midnight struck, she and Falco were led to their new bedroom. It was time to consummate the marriage. He was drunk; she could tell by the way he slurred his words. All her gifts were brought to her, placed in the room by all the guests as was custom.

Two maidens took her scarves and tunic off her, leaving her in her slip. Then they left, closing the door gently behind them.

Falco was lying on the bed, naked. Despite the heat in the room, he was shivering. Perhaps it was nerves. "Take off your clothes and come here, my sweet wife."

Marcia pulled her thin undergarment over her head and dropped it to the floor.

Falco's brows furrowed. "What's that on your leg?"

Marcia drew Iver's knife from the garter on her thigh. The blade was long, almost the length of her hand.

Falco sat up, pressing his back against the bed's headboard. "Marcia, please. Don't do this. Forget I called you that, it was stupid and I'm sorry. Please. We're a team; I can help you."

She tried to consider a good life with him.

Tried.

It would be worse than death. Being tied to him and a child whom she would be forced to love for the rest of her life. Giving her body away to someone to leach off, like a parasite she would eventually grow to adore. She did not fear the baby—she feared her soon-to-be husband, she feared pregnancy and the acts that would lead to it. Her body would not be hers; it would belong to so many others. They would take her flesh, the only thing she could claim as hers, the body that suffered and endured so much, that carried her through all of life's pain. The body that survived beatings and abuse and assault. They would take it from her. The body that nature crafted just for her, placing birthmarks and moles on her skin like the twirls and swirls of the letters in a teenager's first love poem. Everything, from the lightning stretchmarks that had formed, as rings on a tree do, when she grew too fast, to her toes prone to ingrown nails, to her breasts, which were only for her and Daiyu. They would take it all. They would lay claim to her body, and she feared they would do the same to her heart, but not her mind, leaving her aware and in agony over the broken person she would become.

Her free hand was resting low on her belly. She could barely feel it because of all the opium. The women had told her where her uterus was. Right behind her bladder, it rested like a monster waiting to be unleashed.

She turned the blade towards herself and plunged it inside.

She looked up before the sight of her blood would cause her to faint. It hurt, despite the drug. She pulled the knife to the side, slicing through her skin, and black dots appeared in front of her eyes.

Falco was screaming for help. It sounded like they were underwater.

She had no idea if she had managed to do it, but she could do no more, as her field of vision shrank and her legs shook.

Still with the blade in her, she staggered over to the table of gifts and took Vicente's healing potion. She downed it all. The floor vibrated as people flooded inside.

Close to her ear, she heard the purring of a cat. She must have been hallucinating, she thought, as she collapsed.

CHAPTER 38

Vicente

"Mister Falco has withdrawn his proposal, and seeing as the marriage was never consummated, we will uphold his wishes," Renato slurred, the signs of inebriation evident as he sagged into the contours of the couch, his demeanor far from composed.

Vicente and Iver flanked Marcia's sides. She had recovered quickly: it was still nighttime, but dawn would break within two or three hours. Guilt plagued Vicente's mind: had they come to Marcia's rescue sooner, perhaps she wouldn't have had to resort to such a drastic act. Her father would still have refused his proposal, but it would've given Vicente more time to figure out another course of action. Nevertheless, Marcia had made her choice, and in some odd way, he was happy for her.

He sat by her side, feeling the warmth coming off her. She appeared exhausted, but otherwise fine. Dark circles lined her eyes. Vicente had no idea if the healing potion had restored her body to its original state, or if it had simply closed up her wounds but leaving her uterus split. Iver still had scars on his arms, even after drinking those potions.

Vicente took Marcia's hand in his. Her fingers were cold. "You need not search for another man, Lord Renato; my proposal still stands."

"It doesn't fucking matter anymore: she's barren!" he spat, gesturing to his daughter. "I want you all gone and facing justice in Llyr."

"Will Marcia be coming with us?" Vicente asked, polite, calm, offering no argument.

"She can do whatever she pleases. I will give you all a week for her to recover, then I want you out of my home."

"Thank you, Lord Renato." Vicente stood and helped Marcia to her feet. "You have Lord Ottone to thank for her life."

"What life is that?" Renato raked a hand through his hair. "And who gave her the knife? Was that you, Far Cry?" He spoke about her like she wasn't in the room with them.

Iver wore his usual stone-cut, unreadable expression. "Maybe."

With that, the three of them went out into the hallway, where a few maidens were waiting. They all looked disheveled and dog-tired, glassy-eyed and yawning.

Vicente held Marcia's shoulders in a firm grip. "How are you feeling?"

"Weak, but fine. Exhausted."

"I hate to ask, but... what do you think the potion did?" Vicente was curious by nature, and though it felt wrong to ask, he couldn't help himself.

"I have a scar on my stomach now," she said. "It's not like it undid my impromptu procedure. It just... healed it."

Somewhere out there, a former prisoner of the Resurrectionists had a fatal wound splitting open their stomach. They had most likely died within the hour. At some point, he would have to tell Marcia how Ottone's potions worked, but not tonight. "There are amazing surgeons in the capital."

Iver had been mostly quiet the whole time, silently observing with a look on his face Vicente couldn't place. His features were soft but both eyebrows raised. Maybe that was what caught Vicente off-guard: that his face was readable for once, showing a mixture of surprise and awe as he watched Marcia.

Marcia's voice was thin and stretched. "If this didn't do it, I hope I caused enough damage to require a hysterectomy. I'll just have to wait for my monthly bleed to see. And I do hope my bladder is fine."

Vicente hugged her closely, cupping the back of her head as he gently rocked her. "You are raw power, Marcia. Now please, get some rest."

"There she is!" someone called out. Falco and his family were loitering farther down the hall, bags at their feet, looking ready to depart.

Falco stormed up to them. "How could you do that to me?"

The maidens formed a tight circle, standing shoulder to shoulder around Marcia. They all held their heads high, chins up.

"Marcia, how could you?" Falco tried to stare her down, but the women were in the way. When he put his hands on one woman's neck to shove her out of the way, Iver attacked.

It wasn't much of a fight. Iver kicked his knee and then tackled him to the ground. Falco didn't stand a chance, he just screamed.

Iver pinned him face down and grabbed his wrists, pulling them painfully far up behind his back. "You left- or right-handed?"

"What?" Falco sputtered.

"Which hand do you hold your dick with when you piss, moron? I'm giving you the courtesy of breaking your non-dominant hand."

"Let him go, Iver," Marcia said. "This man will never speak to me ever again."

Iver let him go.

The maidens all laughed as Falco stumbled up to his feet and hurried back to his family. As soon as they were gone, the women helped Marcia back to her chambers.

It must've been three or four o'clock in the morning, but Vicente was too riled up to catch any sleep. "Would you join me for a nightcap?"

Iver gave a quick nod and turned on his heel, like he expected Vicente's invitation. He closed the door to Vicente's room behind them, then let out a breath. "Fuck me. I can't believe she really did that."

Vicente noticed Iver said 'fuck me' a lot, and every time he did, Vicente imagined doing just that. "She's insane," Vicente said fondly.

His room was so fancy it could've been found in the Arkensaali palace. A bed overcrowded with profusions of pillows stood against one wall, and a marble bathtub stood opposite side of it. Above the tub, a shelf held a treasure trove of scented and unscented oils and soaps. The day they had arrived, Vicente had soaked in that tub for a good thirty minutes.

Vicente opened one of the windows and the cold air felt wonderful on his burning skin. A small bar cart of brass was parked next to a potted palm tree, holding a plethora of alcoholic drinks and various shapes of tobacco. He lit a cigarette and looked over to Iver. "Want one?"

Iver had his arms crossed over his chest and glared at him with one eyebrow cocked, but then he resigned with a sigh. "Fine."

Vicente was transfixed by the movement of Iver's hips as he walked towards him with determination. Iver accepted a cigarette and lit it. Drawing his first breath, he didn't choke or cough, but instead snarled. "Fuck, this is awful."

Vicente could tell by the look on his face when his head started to swim. His face was often unreadable, but his eyes were not, and Vicente had fallen in love with the way they held all of his emotions.

"So, what's next?" Iver asked, breathing out the smoke through the open window. "After I've killed the fucking pedophile, what do we do?"

Vicente leaned his hip against the deep windowsill. Frost had grown on the window glass, creating delicate, beautiful swirls. "I don't think any of us can return to the capital; the queen wants me dead, and last I heard, she wanted to send you to the front lines. But if I can bond the Stag, that would put me in a more favorable position."

"You're still going on about that monster?"

Vicente snorted. "It's not a monster; it's a weapon." He would never give up on this dream. Pure motivation to reach that goal had brought him out of even the darkest of places. "What about you? What will you do after you kill Ottone?"

Iver threw his cigarette out the window. He lolled his head back, audibly cracking his neck. "I think I'll just go with you."

"You will?"

"Of course. I always got your six." Iver's gaze wandered over Vicente's face, then down to his lips and back up again. For a second, his eyelids fluttered but never closed, due to the buzzing caused by the nicotine.

"Don't look at me like that, Iver," Vicente chided playfully. His stomach rolled and rolled.

"Like what?" Iver didn't stop regarding him thoughtfully, instead tilting his head sideways, absentmindedly, and his black hair fell across his brows.

Vicente chuckled. "You're driving me insane, you know."

"How?"

Vicente lowered his voice to a murmur. "You look at me like you want me to do something to you."

Iver watched him for a long, careful moment before replying. "So, what if I fucking do?" Red was spreading over his cheekbones.

Vicente felt his own smile drop off. He had never loved anyone as much as he loved Iver. He had never told anyone about his past, and when he had told Iver and seen the sorrow and pain on his face, he had been hit with an undeniable truth: he was terrified. Vicente's past could not only hurt him, but it could hurt Iver as well. The last thing he ever wanted to do, he realized, was to hurt Iver.

Iver's hazel eyes searched his. "Vic?"

"You and I are quite different," Vicente said, taking another drag of his cigarette. "I understand that you don't want to sleep with just anyone, you need a deep connection."

Iver nodded. "I need to know they love me if I'm going to let them in."

A fond but crooked smile twisted Vicente's lips. "I know, I figured that out before we left Llyr. I'm not the same, but I respect it."

Iver swallowed hard, and Vicente could see his throat bob with it. "And still? You knew that, and you still tried to…?"

Vicente allowed his mask to melt off his face, all pretense of confidence abandoned. He was a man of fragile pride. He didn't want to be that anymore. So, he stripped himself of the fake charm, of his preferred joviality, of the mannerisms he mimicked from people in his past, and he tore down the walls. What was left was just him. Raw and open. He looked at Iver, and showed a level of honesty and vulnerability he had previously deemed himself unable to. "Yeah."

Iver drew a sharp breath. "Oh."

Love like this was terrifying. How insane it was that people sought this, that people embraced this. "I'm in love with you, Iver. I love you so much it scares me."

Iver pressed his lips into a thin line and looked away for a moment, blinking. When he looked back at Vicente he spoke, and the words were just a whisper: "kiss me, then."

Emotion flooded Vicente's chest. He threw his cigarette out the window and cupped Iver's jaw, fingers touching the warm pulse of his throat. Iver was suddenly taller, and Vicente looked down at their feet. Iver was on his tippy-toes.

"Wipe that goofy smile off your face," Iver said as he looped his arms around Vicente's neck.

Iver's hot breath poured into his mouth and Vicente caught his parted lips in a kiss, fist curling in his soft hair. Without words, his mouth spoke his adoration for him and Iver voraciously replied. He wished to use his whole body to convey it all, to fill Iver with this sensation of desire and admiration that was so new to him.

He curled over Iver, kissing the pale curve of his neck, but Iver wrenched him back, meeting him open-mouthed and desperate. Iver sighed, gasping between kisses, kissing him like he thought Vicente might push him away.

With fumbling fingers, he got Iver's shirt open, managing to rip only a few of the buttons. His hands raced over Iver's chest and down his ribs until they found his waist and pulled him even closer.

Iver undid the buttons on Vicente's shirt, reverently stroking the skin he uncovered. His own skin was hot with want and his eyes had glazed over. "Vic, I want you to fuck me."

Vicente nearly died on the spot. The words raised the hair at the back of his neck. He wanted to, of-fucking-course he did, but he was not going to mess this up. "Are you sure?"

"Yeah, I'm sure."

"You sure you want anal for your first time? You don't have to; we could do other things."

Iver pitched forward, burying his face against Vicente's neck. "Vic, I'm not... I've used my fingers before; I know I like it, alright?"

Lovely images of Iver in that position flooded Vicente's brain before it shut down completely.

Vicente backed Iver up towards the bed, where he sat down and started pulling on Vicente's belt. "Not sure I can take your huge-ass dick, though."

Vicente raked his hand through Iver's silky black hair, admiring the view of him at this level. "Have you been checking me out?"

Iver looked up through his lashes. "It's kind of hard not to notice."

Vicente laughed and pushed Iver down onto his back. He climbed on top of him and captured his mouth with his again. His heart trilled with every beat.

He got Iver undressed and ran his hands over his naked body, fingers skirting over his ribs, tracing the grooves of his abdominal muscles, taking his time tracing every detail. Vicente's eyes drank the sight of him as he pushed on his thighs to spread his legs. "You are so unbelievably beautiful, Iver."

"Shut the fuck up," Iver said on an exhale.

Vicente grabbed a bottle of unscented oil from the shelf above the bathtub and used it to work his fingers inside Iver. Iver gasped at the touch and shuddered, full-bodied. His breathy 'ah' made Vicente feel hysterical. He stroked his thumb over the sensitive skin of Iver's inner thigh to soothe. Iver swallowed every sound and draped an arm over his face, moans muffled by his own flesh.

"None of that. I want to see your face, Iver. Put your hands above your head."

Iver complied. As he stretched out, the muscles of his abdomen rippled. His hips lifted to Vicente's touch, eyelids fluttering before closing. Vicente allowed time to truly behold the sight of Iver's body, the strength in his torso, his flushed skin, savoring this long-awaited moment, the culmination of months spent yearning.

Iver stayed on his back and Vicente settled above him, with Iver's thighs bracketing his hips. The air around them was sharp and crisp and tasted like smoke, and the difference in temperature between it and the searing heat of Iver's body had Vicente's skin erupting into goosebumps.

He took one of Iver's legs over the crook of his arm and slowly pushed inside.

Iver's brows knitted together.

Vicente stopped. "Does it hurt?" he said and noticed that his own voice was shaking from anticipation and arousal.

"Yeah," Iver breathed. "Keep going."

Vicente found a rhythm Iver enjoyed, the pace that made his back arch and toes curl. He was sensitive and perfect all over. Vicente's lips were drawn to Iver's neck, and he groaned against his skin in between peppering it with kisses, feeling Iver's pulse where Vicente's own skin was the thinnest.

Iver was still quiet, biting his lower lip so hard Vicente thought it might bleed.

"Let me hear you, sweetheart," Vicente begged, grabbing Iver's chin and prying open his mouth.

To Vicente's delight, Iver moaned to every beat of their skin clashing. He rolled his hips up to meet Vicente's, letting go, unravelling. He clutched the sheets, his voice was so high he was practically mewling, breath catching melodically in his throat. Vicente found the comfort he so desperately needed in Iver's expression, in his bliss, in his voice, his hooded eyes.

"You're close, are you?" Vicente said. "Go on, sweetheart. Be loud for me."

He made sure Iver came first, reveling in the sensation of Iver's body constricting around him as he did. He pressed his mouth against Iver's bare sternum, tasting his frantic heartbeat.

After they cleaned up, Vicente sat back in bed and watched Iver's chest heave. He looked completely languorous, his lips parted, damp hair sticking to his forehead.

"Don't give me those puppy-dog eyes, bastard," Iver said, slurring his words a little. But he remained stretched out on the bed, legs open and lax. "How do I look, anyway?"

"With your eyes," Vicente said without a second thought.

Iver snorted. And then he started laughing. A holding-his-stomach kind of laugh. It sounded like singing, and affection welled up inside Vicente with such force it felt as though he would burst from it.

CHAPTER 39

Vicente

"What's he going to do; kill me? He can't do shit to me." Iver was still sitting in bed, watching Vicente as he worked.

A few days had passed since Marcia's impromptu surgery and she was still resting, getting stronger each day. They couldn't leave until she was well enough for the impending fight, but her father had made it clear that they, especially Iver, had overstayed their welcome. "There are other ways to hurt someone. And he knows you were the one who gave Marcia the knife."

Vicente shredded the paper and put it in a bowl of water, stirring until it transformed into a thick sludge. Then he poured in the ingredients he used for his Stormwater—calcium, phosphorus, potassium, sulfur, salt and magnesium—using way more than he would use for one potion, as he was uncertain how this would play out. He pressed the pulp into one average-sized parchment paper. He would have to cut it into four to be able to send it with a raven.

"What *are* you doing?" Iver asked.

"I have this incredible, moronic idea, and I won't tell you about it until I'm at least five percent certain it will work."

"You're either certain or you're not." Iver donned that familiar expression again: that look Vicente had once misinterpreted as a veneer of resentment or even disdain. But he knew him better now; that was Iver's manifestation of puzzlement. Iver was a bright man, and confusion was a feeling he abhorred with passion.

"I'll tell you later."

Vicente prepared a whole jug of sending potions and then began the entanglement process, placing the liquid and the paper into a superposition on a microscopical level. If he could find a way to send the paper, he would be able to teleport something. He still poured the Stormwater into individual vials, in case some were stolen or he lost some.

Then he returned to bed, wrapped his arms around Iver and clutched him close. His body was smaller than his and somehow felt fragile against his own. He was warm and pliable and touchable, smelling of sleep and soap. Vicente wanted him to stay like that forever; warm and safe, naked and tucked into bed. Safe.

*

"With all that has happened, Ottone won't let us send anything to the capital." Marcia leaned with her shoulder against the wall. "At least not without having read it first." The color had returned to her cheeks, and while her posture remained stiff, she no longer trembled with every step. She insisted she wasn't in pain anymore, though Vicente noticed the occasional wince betraying her discomfort. Still, he was hopeful; if her recovery continued at this pace, she would be strong enough to reach Llyr within a day.

"I think you're right, Ottone will certainly try to read it again," Vicente said. "If we are to send a message to Arkensaal, we'll need to encrypt it."

Vicente, Marcia and Iver sat by the fireplace in her chambers, feeding off the heat from the flames and each nursing a cup of tea. It was snowing heavily outside. Vicente would rather have waited for kinder weather before undertaking the short trek to Llyr, but they were wearing out Renato's welcome.

"The fuckers will notice the message being scrambled," Iver pointed out. "They won't let us send a letter they can't read first."

Vicente knew he was right about that. "What if we hide a message in plain text?"

"That will be a lot trickier than you think," Marcia said. "Besides, how do we convey that to Tal Miril, that they ought to look for a hidden message? They have no clue what's going on up here. They have no reason to suspect things aren't going according to the plan."

They needed to come up with something quick. It had been about seven weeks since they slaughtered all the Resurrectionists, and Ottone had most likely realized something was amiss. Vicente couldn't predict how Ottone would lash out. Everyone in Llyr now knew Vicente was a mystic, and Vicente hoped this would work in his favor, rendering them too frightened to try to harm him or his crew. Then there was another problem with returning to Llyr: the murder of the children. He didn't think that there would be serious grounds for suspicion, but they would still have to prepare for that risk. Ottone had accused him and Iver, after all.

"I do have another suggestion." Vicente hesitated. The plan hinged entirely on luck, but with no better alternatives, it seemed their only option. "I have put the components for several receiving potions into a paper. I have entangled it with a whole jug of my potion. We could communicate that way."

Marcia's eyes lit up. "We could send one inconspicuous letter, and once it arrives at Tal Miril, we substitute it for one calling for help."

Relief washed over Vicente, he exhaled and leaned back against the velvet cushions of the lounge chair. He had messed up before, but he did have some faith in this plan. "We could send anything, really. We also need to request for a ruling clan leader to come to Llyr, if we want Ottone sentenced and punished."

"Why?" Iver asked.

"To act as a judge," Vicente said, swirling the last of his tea in its porcelain cup. "With crimes as serious as this—"

"Marcia could do it," Iver cut in, his gaze flicking briefly toward her. "Right?"

"Right." Vicente blinked, then sat up a little straighter. He'd forgotten about that: the Jadanza clan were descendants from Queen Leandra's line. Marcia could do it, and no one would dare contest it.

But Marcia shook her head. "We can't tell anyone about that just yet. My father would be the de facto judge, as he is the oldest.

We need reliable evidence pointing to Ottone before we even breathe a word of the Jadanza heritage. Send a message to Naka-Toda and ask the Sassanov leader there to come here and do it; that'll give us some weeks to prepare for any investigation."

*

Renato didn't bid them farewell when they left. As they approached Llyr, the towering aqueducts came into view, festooned with the same snowy mantle that graced the land. Vicente needed to keep his guard up every second while in Llyr. The Resurrectionists leader had said there was a cult in Llyr. It was possible everyone was in on it.

A crowd formed in the town square. Prime Minister Ottone stepped forward, greeting Marcia by bowing his head.

In the lake of faces, Vicente couldn't spot Sergeant Celia anywhere. "I expected the militia to be waiting for us." Were he and Iver no longer suspects in the murders? Vicente doubted it. Ottone was scheming—of that, he was certain. Still, Vicente wasn't concerned. Without concrete evidence to prove their guilt, accusations would fall flat.

"They have more pressing matters to tend to," Ottone said with a forced smile. "There has been an attack at one of my plantations, and they are investigating."

Vicente wondered how much of that was because of what he and Iver had done to the Resurrectionists. They had left no survivors and many questions unanswered for Ottone.

The tip of Ottone's nose was red from the cold. "I'm glad you could come to your senses, Ambassador Vicente. We really did miss you. And I'm sorry to hear your marriage didn't work out, Ambassador Marcia."

She nodded.

Vicente returned Ottone's false smile. "I gather you have new ravens? Me and Marcia must send a message to Arkensaal." If Ottone was this calm, it meant he was confident Vicente and Iver would take the fall for the murders—suggesting he had a strategy or fabricated evidence. However, he couldn't carry out a trial without approval from Arkensaal or a ruling clan member. That gave Vicente plenty of time to disrupt his plans. If Vicente wanted to kill Ottone without ending up in jail, he would have to bring forth Ottone's misdeeds into the public eye.

"You may give it to me." Ottone held out his hand. "I'll read it and send it as soon as possible."

Piece of shit. Vicente handed over the letter. It detailed how Ottone was now the new prime minister and that they needed someone from Arkensaal to act as a judge. There was nothing in there that Ottone would object to. It was also made of the paper Vicente had entangled, and it showed no evidence of mysticism.

Ottone cleared his throat and looked between him and Marcia. "The winter solstice is upon us, and there will be a celebration at my brother's manor tomorrow. All three of you are, of course, expected to join us: I see no reason to keep you from celebrating another year passing since Eldvittra defeated the horned god of darkness. It is important we honor the god who protects this country."

Vicente almost laughed. So, Ottone was going to deny his faith and act like he didn't know Vicente knew. "Thank you, my Lord. We will be there."

He didn't necessarily disapprove of Ottone's faith, but he needed to be punished for the suffering he had caused, and if the only way to make that happen was for Vicente to reveal his cult to the capital, then he would do just that.

They left Ottone and started walking towards the inn, footsteps crunching in the snow. Despite the cold, the town bustled with activity. Children raced past, dragging sleds behind them. Smoke curled up from chimneys and the scent of burning wood filled the streets.

There was little Ottone could do to hurt two diplomats from Tal Miril. And as for Iver—he would never get the chance to even try. "You've got to bring the militia back here," he told Marcia. "When we confront Ottone, we need Sergeant Celia on our side."

"You think she would disobey Ottone's command?" Marcia looked utterly wrung out.

"I don't know, but she's loyal to the Jadanza clan. If things go sour, I do trust her." Celia's heart was in the right place. He did remember that she hadn't voted for him in the election for prime minister, but that was because he had messed up—he wouldn't make the same mistake again.

Marcia nodded. "So do I. I'll ride tomorrow."

Vicente's eyes landed on the blacksmith's shop. Atli was bent over a crate, his arms straining as he hoisted it onto the wooden bed of a cart. His breath came in visible puffs, and beads of sweat clung to his brow despite the frigid air.

"Still at it, I see," Vicente called out.

Atli's shoulders heaved as he caught his breath. He wiped his hands on his apron before turning to face them. A grin broke across his face. "Well, look who decided to show up."

"Nice to see you again," Vicente said. "Business is going well, I take it."

Atli groaned as he lifted the last crate onto the cart. "It is. But this is not my business; I'm helping Ottone. Fortune for him means fortune for all of Llyr, after all."

Vicente turned his face away, hiding the need to close his eyes for a second. "Is that so?"

"He's expanded trade of his potions to Naka-Toda," Atli said. He sounded proud. "They have ordered fifteen crates already. These potions are becoming one of our biggest sources of income; almost as much as all our farms combined. They make up about ten percent of Llyr's economy now. It would've been more had it not been for one of Ottone's plantations burning up."

"That's amazing." Vicente nearly threw up. The crates were full of healing potions. Ottone had already compensated for the loss of his farm, the one Iver almost died destroying. If Llyr could have potions dominate their trade—maybe even a third of all income—then an embargo with the capital wouldn't cripple them.

They got their old rooms in the Sunfire Rest. It felt like a lifetime ago that they had conspired there. And Daiyu was gone. During his months on the run, he had distracted himself with training and the danger they were in, but now, the memories came flooding back. He felt ill. Chills skimmed over his skin and his muscles ached. The restlessness from wanting to open a tunnel had him twitching.

Marcia bid them goodnight and retired to her own room.

Iver stayed with him. "We need a plan, Vic."

Vicente unpacked his bag and set the vials of entangled Stormwater on his desk. "Could you get me a bottle of wine from the inn's kitchen?" He was done with Ottone's game of chess.

"You're sure you want to be drinking now?" Iver asked.

"I'm putting some Stormwater in it," Vicente said. "The Stormwater that's entangled to the message we gave to Ottone." The plan was to open a tunnel and substitute the letter Ottone had sent on their behalf as soon as it reached Tal Miril. But Vicente had no way of knowing when, or even if, it would reach Tal Miril. They were in dire need of back-up plans, a network of fail-safes. "I'm having Ottone drink the Stormwater-wine tomorrow at the festival."

"If you open a tunnel while the raven is in the air," Iver said, "and send Ottone through it, he will fall to his death."

Too quick on the uptake, that one. "If we're lucky, yes."

Iver nodded, his gaze turning inwards as he ran with Vicente's idea. "I'll help you forge a new label, make it look like some fancy Arkensaali wine. Maybe that'll make it easier to trick him into drinking it."

CHAPTER 40

Vicente

Iver had snow in his hair, small flakes of white against pitch black that refused to melt. Vicente had to curl his hands into fists to stop himself from brushing them out for him. "I need to get a read on the Llyrians, their current state," Vicente said. "It looks like the embargo proposition is close to being finalized."

Marcia had just departed, in search of the militia and Sergeant Celia. He trusted that Celia would do everything within her power to uphold the law. What that law was—well, that was yet to be determined.

Iver wrapped his arms around his torso. Cold crept into him faster than it should have, even though the walk to Cronin's estate was short and they were walking briskly. "They won't give an Arkensaali ambassador the details, you know."

Vicente had opened a tunnel last night, and his head was still buzzing. He hadn't slept, but he didn't need to. He was in control. "I'll find out, no matter what."

They both joined a few guests gathered outside Cronin's manse, engaging in small talk as they walked through the manor's entrance. Vicente's eyes darted from guest to guest, taking note of who was there and what titles they went by. The odds were stacked against him and Marcia, but he *would* rectify their mistakes here. He had no other choice.

The great hall lay beyond. Silk banners hung from the rafters, swaying with the draft, each one a tribute to the battles between Eldvittra and the horned god.

Vicente's heart pounded as he and Iver split up. The hum of chatter and laughter filled the hall, blending with the melodies of flutes and strings played by musicians on the dais. Servants moved through the crowd, offering trays with delicacies.

Ottone, dressed in traditional Llyrian fashion, stood at the center of the festivities with his family, welcoming all his guests with a smile.

Vicente adjusted his jacket and joined a group of guests engaged in conversation. As the night wore on, he mingled among the others. Some were hesitant, as they most likely had heard about his mystic abilities. But he guided the conversations from awkward to casual and warm.

If Vicente was going to make Ottone trust him enough to drink his Stormwater-wine, he would need to convince him it wasn't poison. He would do so by offering it to others.

"Could I interest you in some Arkensaali wine?" he asked Atli and his wife after steering the conversation in that direction. Their eyes lit up and he poured three glasses for them. After raising a toast to Llyr, Atli took a sip. He and his wife would be safe, as long as they didn't go near the tunnel.

"Exquisite," Atli said about the wine. "PM Ottone would be honored if you shared some with him, I'm certain."

Phase two. Vicente thanked him for the suggestion, grabbed two clean glasses, and searched for Ottone.

He stood on the periphery of the celebration, speaking with Iver. Vicente noticed that Ottone was standing far too close to him, his fingers digging into the fabric of Iver's sleeve.

"Isn't he a bit too old to fit your taste, Lord Ottone?" Vicente said. It slipped right off his tongue.

Ottone's mouth opened in shock.

Iver's brows furrowed. "Ambassador?"

"Ambassador Vicente, how are you finding the solstice celebrations?" Renato said as he emerged from the crowd.

Vicente's heart hammered against his ribs. He hadn't anticipated seeing Marcia's father again so soon. "My Lord, I wasn't expecting you here. What a pleasure."

Renato stood beside Ottone, his gaze distant as he watched the dancers twirl across the floor. "I was in town, visiting the archives. I must say, I regret not spending more time there; we have a fascinating history here in Llyr."

"Indeed," Vicente said.

Renato looked at him, and his smug smile made Vicente's stomach sink. "Ottone's little spies told me a story you read to them, and I investigated it further," he said. "It seems my clan, the Jadanza clan, is descended from the ruling Rhys clan."

Vicente's temperature reached a fever pitch in a millisecond, putting his senses on alert. His surroundings faded into the background, as though the world ceased to exist beyond the conversation. He had been high when he read that story to the children. It happened months ago, and he had forgotten all about it.

"That would make us the ruling clan of Llyr, isn't that correct?" Renato said.

Vicente could only nod, struggling to find the right words, but his mind was only filled with one thing: panic stirred in his chest, and he wanted to open a tunnel to rid himself of the feeling. If he could only open another tunnel, then he would be able to think.

Ottone clinked a knife against his glass, catching everyone's attention. "Now that we have a member of a ruling clan here, let Far Cry's trial begin."

Shocked whispers rippled through the crowd as the music stopped. People stepped closer to the walls; the majority didn't seem privy to this scheme. Even Atli looked confused. Vicente turned his eyes to Iver, whose expression mirrored his disbelief.

"We have to wait for the response from Arkensaal," Vicente said. His jaw hurt, he realized he was gritting his teeth and so he tried to relax his face. Was he no longer a suspect in their eyes? Either that or they didn't dare touch him due to him being a mystic.

Ottone scoffed. "There will be no response. I never sent your letter, Ambassador. You think I'd risk that? It will never be sent— unless a raven can find it on my very cluttered desk. You could've written it in a code I don't know about. You will not leave Llyr until I say so."

Around them, the sounds of the celebration dwindled to a hush. The sea of faces morphed into an indistinct blur. Vicente's stomach twisted and contracted like a rabbit thrashing in a trap.

"We believe Far Cry strangled the children during his stay," Renato said loudly for everyone to hear. "I call the first witness: Prime Minister Ottone."

Iver stayed by Vicente's side, still as carved stone. He said nothing to defend himself, simply listened to the accusation with a neutral expression.

Ottone stepped up on the dais, where the musicians remained seated. "Iver, also known as Far Cry, is an infamous assassin in the capital. Only days after they showed up, little Natalina was found dead. Weeks later, Jairo was killed." Ottone flung an arm in Iver's direction. "He carries weapons with him wherever he goes, concealed knives and a rifle are strapped to him at all times. Let me remind you that there hasn't been a murder here for generations. Then, the Arkensaalis showed up."

"Very well," Renato said, too quickly. "I hereby sentence Iver Russo to a lifetime in Llyr's jail."

People started to whisper.

Vicente had to tread carefully. With Marcia gone, he was alone, and Celia wasn't there to keep the peace. "Will you pass your judgement without hearing everyone with a stake in this matter?"

Renato sighed hard through his nose. "State your case then, Ambassador."

In his pockets, Vicente curled his hands into fists, digging his fingernails into his palms. "I have personally witnessed Lord Ottone sexually assault a child in the Holy Temple of Eldvittra."

Around them, the crowd's murmurs grew louder, a cacophony of shock. This was not how he wanted to break the news, but he was left with no other option.

"I believe that Lord Ottone killed Natalina and Jairo to keep them from talking," Vicente continued. "He has abused other children too."

Renato, too, looked shocked. "Do you have proof of this?"

Pressure rose in Vicente's blood, making his ears ring. "Is my statement not enough for you?"

"As you are an ambassador of the crown, I am inclined to believe you," Renato said. "But, as Far Cry is a part of your crew, you have reason to lie to protect him."

"I do not." Vicente's mouth tasted bad just saying it. "We were sent here by Queen Leandra, and Iver was assigned to our party to safeguard us. Neither I nor Marcia had any say in whether he should come or not. As a matter of fact, I was the one who arrested him. Far Cry hates me for this, and I don't like him very much, either." Vicente broke his own heart as he spoke. But love like this, love so strong that it felt like pain, was dangerous, and he would sooner cut off his own leg than let anyone harm Iver. He would rather beat Iver himself to a pulp if it proved something, if it meant keeping him alive and free.

"But you do have a reason to lie." Renato glowered at him for a moment before saying, "I have seen and *heard* the lust you two have for each other. Thus, I will disregard your statement, Ambassador. My sentence stands. Seize him."

Renato was angry with Iver for providing Marcia with the knife she had used to ensure his bloodline would die. He had paid Ottone with his influential position just to get his daughter back, and Vicente and Iver had taken that from him. No words of reason could convince him to acquit Iver. Vicente needed tangible proof and the rest of the town on his side.

"*Wait.*" Vicente's voice cut through the echoes of shock. "There is something else." His gaze swept across the room. There was no turning back now. He had to act swiftly.

He walked up to Atli, who was still holding his wife's hand.

Before Atli could speak a word, Vicente grabbed their wrists.

He felt a familiar pull, deep within. The world warped and bent around them, reality distorting as he opened a tunnel, and it drew the three of them in. Vicente's grip on their linked hands tightened as they hurtled through.

The bliss was instant, shapeshifting into whatever he needed. Pain vanished, anxiety dissolved, and he was whole—fully himself, fully in control. Stormwater was freedom, calm, and stability in a bottle, consuming his mind and molding him into what he had always longed to be. What he was meant to be.

The world swirled before settling into a new reality. Vicente's senses reorientated themselves. They were now in Ottone's chambers. Ottone had told the truth: he never sent the letter. Instead, he had kept it locked away in his office.

Atli and his wife looked around in shock.

"What is this?" Atli balked, eyes wide.

"Using mysticism, I have brought you to Ottone's chambers," Vicente said. "Please, Atli. If you hold justice in any regard, help me look for anything that belonged to the two children." He remembered Daiyu's words, the insight Iver had shared with her about murderers and their trophies. It was a leap of faith, a gamble that the evidence they sought was hidden within these walls. "You will face no repercussions; I'll take the blame for this intrusion."

Perhaps it was the gravity of the situation, or the realization that they were united by a common goal, but Atli and his wife set aside their fears and began to rummage through the belongings in the room. The silence broke only by the rustling of papers and the shuffling of boxes.

Vicente moved to the desk, pulling open drawers and sifting through the contents. Distantly, he recognized that he should've been anxious about what he was doing. But the bliss swallowed all the bad feelings. That was a dangerous state to be in, but he needed his abilities to do a good job, and no one was going to take that away from him.

An open book containing a sketch caught his attention. Or rather, it was the words written on the top of the page piquing his interest: *Tal Llyrie*—the disputed land. He picked the book up from the desk and studied it. The sketch looked very much like a blueprint for a temple. According to this plan, multiple statues of

362 ◦ ISABELLE TÖRNQVIST

the Gambler were to be placed around it. So, that was Ottone's real plan for the land: to build a temple for the Gambler. He never needed it to grow herbs that he wasn't using anyway.

Vicente flipped through the pages, revealing more plans: factories, invasions, a prison. That was why Ottone wanted control over the militia: the large-scale production of potions from human sacrifices, with the help of the Gambler.

Vicente pocketed the notebook. He could use it as evidence of the cult when reinforcements came from the capital.

As they combed through the room, every second without finding evidence felt like a wasted hour.

"Vicente," Atli said. From one of the boxes, he picked up a silver object: a thin chain with a pendant dangling from it. "Natalina's name is engraved on it."

It was just like Iver had predicted: Ottone, that sick bastard, kept the necklaces of the children he murdered.

Vicente couldn't keep the pleading out of his voice. "Please believe me. Iver had nothing to do with this. It was all Ottone: I saw him assaulting an orphaned girl. You can ask her if you don't believe me."

In the same box, Atli found the other necklace, the one that had belonged to the boy, Jairo. "Can you point this girl out for me? We need to question her."

The door to Ottone's quarters was easily unlocked from the inside, and they made their way back to Ottone's brother's estate on foot. When they returned, they were met with a scene of chaos, the aftermath of their sudden disappearance evident in the disarray. It was expected, given that the three of them had vanished into thin air, leaving only a small piece of paper on the floor where they had stood.

Vicente's euphoria started to slip away. He looked at the clock on the wall. It had only been half an hour. Going through one tunnel usually lasted him thrice as long.

Iver was backed into a corner, but the people surrounding him all stayed at least an arm's length away from him. They were locked in a stalemate: the blade of a knife glinted in Iver's hand.

"Let Iver go," Atli called out. "He wasn't the one who did it."

CHAPTER 41

Vicente

The truth had been exposed, and the very next morning, it was time for justice to be served. Vicente watched as Atli and the others took charge.

"It was an accident," Ottone said. "I didn't mean to kill them." Ottone resisted, still desperately clinging to his own innocence, but the noose of deceit was tightening around him.

Vicente wondered if he was telling the truth: it had been an accident. Nevertheless, the assault of the little girl in the temple proved he didn't care about young lives.

Atli and a few other Llyrians escorted Ottone to the holding cell in the town hall. He protested loudly, a last attempt to avoid the consequences of his actions.

"Arkensaal has already be notified of your crimes, Ottone," Vicente announced.

Vicente had not caught a wink of sleep; neither had Atli or the other members of the council. The night had been spent compiling evidence from Ottone's office and interviewing the holy sisters of Eldvittra in charge of the orphanage. At the first light of dawn, Vicente sent a proper message both to Arkensaal and Tal Miril, detailing Ottone's crimes. Within the next few days, reinforcements would arrive from the capital.

Vicente was still worried, though. He had taken a leap of faith, and it had paid off—but if Ottone hadn't been so depraved as to keep evidence, it would've been Iver facing arrest. It all came down to luck, and Vicente felt wholly out of control.

The Llyrians flooded the hallways of the town hall, watching as the holding cell's door closed behind Ottone. The revelations shocked them, but it was a necessary upheaval, a means to cleanse the wounds festering beneath the surface.

Then they filed into the pews in the main chamber. The council was in shambles, and everyone agreed that it was time for a democratic election for the new prime minister.

Vicente sat at the table on the dais. He would make the right decision this time. The game was not yet over.

Atli announced to the council, "We need volunteers for the position as prime minister."

The members of the council were to make their proposals, and then it would be up to the people to vote. All the members of the council volunteered themselves.

Then they got to Vicente. "I propose Marcia Jadanza," he said. "She is a member of the ruling clan of Llyr, she was born here and spent her adolescence here. Now, she is showing her devotion to this town by joining Sergeant Celia and the militia on their search for answers about what happened to Lord Ottone's plantation."

Vicente remembered that Ulrich had said there were other worshippers of the Gambler in Llyr. Suggesting that Marcia was aiding the militia should appeal to them. Vicente continued, "and while she is away, I propose that Mister Atli rule in her stead."

The time came for everyone to cast their votes. Vicente watched as the community stepped forward, one by one, voicing their choices. As the last vote was cast, Atli announced the new prime minister: Marcia.

The Llyrians poured out of the town hall, but the cabinet members remained. Iver approached, joining them on the dais. Vicente hadn't seen him all night, but he looked like he hadn't slept, either. The skin beneath his eyes was purple from exhaustion.

Atli stood and shook Vicente's hand. "I am grateful for your support. When do you expect Marcia to return?"

"That is uncertain," Vicente said. He wished there was a way of contacting her. "It all depends on when she will be able to locate the militia. In the meantime, I trust you to take care of things."

Atli smiled reassuringly. "Of course."

Then, Vicente excused himself and returned to his room, promising Iver that he would meet him for dinner.

Iver had nearly been jailed because of Vicente. Vicente had arrested him, brought him to Llyr, made him fall in love with him, and given the potion to Marcia. There were so many dangers to Vicente. His past, his future. The queen wanting to kill him, the quorum wanting to use him. All these dangers would now apply to Iver as well. Risking his own life was one thing. But putting Iver at risk?

He shouldn't have told Iver about how he had killed Father Fulvio. The more entangled they became, the more potential harm Iver faced. Vicente shouldn't have ensnared him and put him in a position that if he was harmed, they could get to Vicente. Now Iver was at risk. If Vicente and Iver continued their relationship, Iver would be at even more risk. Because he knew Iver would never sell him out, not after what happened to his lieutenant in the rangers.

Vicente wasn't ready for these thoughts to return yet. He wasn't ready to deal with it yet. Alone in his room, he opened a tunnel just to feel the euphoria again.

CHAPTER 42

Iver

As Iver lay on his stomach on the snowy hill, he watched Renato and his five bodyguards over the iron sight of his rifle. The chilling winter wind brushed against his face as he took measured breaths to steady his aim and positioned himself for the perfect shot.

Waiting for the right moment, Iver tracked the movements of the guards, anticipating their patterns. As the opportunity presented itself, he rolled his shoulders back, squeezed the trigger and eliminated all five bodyguards, one after the other. He would hide the bodies later, and no one would find them until spring. By then, he, Vicente and Marcia would be long gone.

With the guards taken care of, Iver's focus shifted to the main target, Renato. This was a personal vendetta that must be settled honorably.

There was nowhere for Renato to take cover. He hunkered down in place, surrounded by bodies now coloring the snow red. His breath was coming out in puffs, visible in the cold air.

When he saw Iver, he stood, hands raised in the air.

Iver stepped over one of the bodies. "You understand why I'm here?"

"Of course we suspected you were the killer," Renato spat. "You're a mercenary! It was the logical conclusion—"

"That's not the reason I'm here." Iver placed his rifle on the ground. From one of the sheaths strapped to his thigh, he drew a knife that he tossed at Renato's feet. "You murdered Daiyu, and you hurt Marcia. Badly."

"I was not the one who killed that woman!"

That woman. Iver unsheathed his other knives and placed them on the ground, all except one. The one Daiyu had gifted him, the one Marcia had used to slit open her stomach. "Not with your own hands, no."

Renato trembled. "Let Marcia settle this with me; this is none of your concern!"

"She's not a killer. Pick up the knife."

Renato kept his hands in the air, as though showing his belly like a dog would affect Iver's intentions. "I'm not a fighter! You wish to humiliate me before robbing me of my life?"

"Yes. Pick it up. Or don't. It won't change the outcome."

Renato picked it up and planted his feet in the snow. Iver watched with hunger as the fear in him metabolized into adrenaline to defend himself, to fight for his life.

Iver lunged, using his surroundings to his advantage. The winter terrain that might have slowed others down became an asset for Iver, who adapted his fighting style to the slippery conditions. A punch, then retreat. Another one, then a move out of his reach. *Kill him slowly.* But it was impossible. There could never be enough time to relish it, enough time to strain the sweetness from the violence.

Renato swiped the knife through the air and Iver moved out of the way with ease. He was slow.

Iver wanted to prolong the fight, but his craving for revenge usurped control. This could never have been a fair fight. He pounced one last time, planting the knife low in Renato's generous belly—right where Marcia had stabbed herself. Then he slashed his throat, and Renato went legless all at once. Iver watched as the light in his eyes died.

Fulfilled revenge always bore a tinge of emptiness. Nothing could bring Daiyu back or undo what had happened to Marcia. But these were the laws of the land that had ruled since inception: water flowed downstream, trees reached for the sky, death took the sick and the elderly. And those who hurt their pups would be turned into a feast for the pack. These were the laws of nature, and Iver needed only to uphold his end of this intrinsic agreement.

*

Iver looped his arms around Vicente's neck. "You told me I'd be the one to kill Ottone."

"That time will come." Vicente kissed him, touching his tongue to his. "I have sent word to Arkensaal for back-up, and there will be a trial for Ottone. He will be sentenced to death for heresy, and I promise you, that honor will be yours."

"Good." Iver kissed his lips, his chin, along his jaw. "I want to be the one to do it."

"You will."

Vicente grabbed the back of Iver's thighs and picked him up, pushing him up against the wall.

Iver wrapped his legs around Vicente's waist. "You've been acting weirdly the last couple of days. You've done some dumb stuff, and you forget things. It's like you're not thinking. It's not like you."

Vicente pulled down his collar and sucked a mark into the skin. "Really? You call me some version of 'idiot' more often than you say my actual name."

"I'm just worried—" Iver began, but was interrupted when Vicente kissed him deeply.

Vicente rushed, hardly containing his excitement, and Iver found his eagerness endearing. He loved this, too, coming together like this and becoming one. He shouldn't have been surprised by his own carnality, but he was. He had never known pleasure like this, hadn't known that his body was capable of anything remotely close to it.

Iver sat on the bed while Vicente kneeled before him and sucked his dick. Iver raked his fingers through his curly, dark brown hair and Vicente looked up at him through his eyelashes. Vicente on his knees was a beautiful sight. He blew him clumsily, with increasing desire and fading commitment to his own composure.

There was something in him that called for Vicente, a thing that yearned, a thing that begged. He was distantly aware that he was making embarrassing sounds from deep in his throat. When he finished, Iver flopped down on the bed. Vicente's lips brushed over Iver's collarbone. "So beautiful," he said against his skin, more like a hum than actual speech. Iver's hands found his shoulders, his neck, his back, hot and slick with sweat. Vicente was the one who was beautiful. Brown skin, dark hair, a healthy and strong body. The veins on the back of his hands and on his forearms protruded like roots under the skin, the hair on his chest curled, and Iver could stare at him for hours.

Iver let him push into his body, relishing in the sensation as his body stretched to accommodate him. He held Vicente's face, sighing into his kiss. Their breaths came in little pants, sticking to each other's open mouths. He could feel the sweat collecting in the gorge of his own throat.

They moved against each other. Touching Vicente ignited something dormant in Iver, he went half mad at the contact, it compelled him to press his face into the juncture of Vicente's neck, to put his hands on as much of his skin as possible. His own skin was singing.

His second orgasm ripped through him like a lightning strike. He had to shove his face into Vicente's shoulder to smother the cry that escaped him.

Vicente continued. He was being rough with him. He pinned Iver's hands above his head. "You take it so good," he breathed, gulping for breath.

Overstimulation set in quickly. Iver was exhausted. He was still sore from the sex they'd had mere hours ago, before he had killed Renato Jadanza. His moans became sounds of agony as Vicente continued, unrelenting, ostensibly unaware that Iver's voice lacked any expression of pleasure. His other hand gripped Iver's waist so hard it hurt.

Before Vicente had finished, Iver had had enough. "Vic, give me a second."

He didn't stop.

Iver started wriggling under his grip. *Can't move, I can't move, I can't*—"Vicente, stop!"

Vicente stopped. "What?"

"You're hurting me, let go!"

Vicente let go of his wrists and pulled out but stayed hovering over him. Iver rolled out from under him, gasping for breath. "If I tell you to stop, you stop right away."

The air in the room was freezing, and Iver considered getting dressed again. When he stood, the floor swayed beneath his feet. He staggered over to the chair by the desk and sat down, grappling against the darkness creeping in at the edges of his field of vision.

"I'm sorry, I didn't hear you." Vicente was stuttering. He looked genuinely shaken. "I'm so, so sorry, Iver, I didn't realize. I was so swept up—shit, I am so sorry."

Iver believed him, his anxiety dissipating a little. Vicente had made a mistake. He hadn't meant to hurt Iver, he would never hurt him on purpose. He tried to smile, and looked up at him. "Fuck, don't worry, I—"

Vicente's eyes were alight. He was confident and relaxed, slack almost. So safe, not a care in the world. And all of a sudden, Iver saw right through it. The realization hit him hard, the illusion of it all shattered. Vicente bore stunted, false confidence. Something sickly. The adoration in his eyes was sticky-sweet and rotten, something cloying and decayed, barely holding itself together.

He was high.

Iver wrapped his arms around himself and crossed his legs, embarrassed and uncomfortable with being naked before a person he didn't recognize. He felt gutted, ripped open, completely wrecked against the rocks. "Have you just opened another tunnel?" What was this? Had Vicente somehow gotten addicted to opening tunnels, to using his Stormwater? Wasn't he aware of how stupid he became after he had done it?

"Not just now—"

"Recently, dumbass!" Iver snapped. "Have you opened a tunnel *recently*?"

Vicente had the gall to look ashamed. "Yeah."

Iver's entire torso ached so suddenly and violently that he thought he had somehow cracked a rib. His legs shook underneath him as an unwelcome emotion rose and swelled unfettered. His chest caved in around the emptiness. "What for?"

Vicente shrugged hesitantly, awkwardly, like his body was uncomfortable and foreign, like it wasn't his own, like he was a puppet getting its strings pulled. "No real reason."

CHAPTER 43

Vicente

Vicente stood by the statue of Eldvittra in front of the town hall, eagerly awaiting the arrival of the reinforcements sent by Tal Miril. Iver was by his side, and he wanted to hold his hand, but he couldn't.

Vicente had hurt him last night, and Iver had kicked him out of his room. He couldn't sleep, so he had opened a tunnel to get his mind off it. He shouldn't have done that.

Marcia was now the prime minister of Llyr, and she didn't even know it yet. They had no way of contacting each other; he could only hope she had already found the militia and was on her way back with them.

Their job was technically done: the land had been given to Eloy, just like the queen had requested. But they still needed to execute Ottone, and to do that, Vicente had to prove Ottone was worshipping another god.

The sound of hooves against the ground broke through the silence, the rhythmic beat growing louder as riders approached. A group of men rode through the street, quickly approaching.

"That man…" Iver said. His eyes were wide.

Vicente recognized him too; in the forefront was Sergeant Broker of the Tactics and Assault Operations Team, also known as the rangers. He had been there when he had arrested Iver. He was the one Iver had left behind when he had deserted the rangers.

"Don't worry, sweetheart," Vicente said, "I've got your six."

Iver whipped his head around to glare at him with fear before scanning their surroundings to check if anyone was within hearing distance. "Shut the fuck up, Vicente," he hissed. There was no tinge of humor in his voice, and somewhere deep inside Vicente's mind, he suspected he had messed up again. He probably shouldn't be saying such things in public.

The squad of twelve rangers stopped in front of the town hall. They all wore the same uniform Iver did: beige cargo pants with an abundance of pockets, as well as military uniform jackets, though theirs were adorned with different patches and insignias signifying their affiliation with the rangers. Iver had stripped his jacket of those. Slung across their backs were standard-issue rifles.

Sergeant Broker dismounted his horse. "Hello, Far Cry."

Iver gave a small nod. "Broker."

*

The town hall's doors swung open, and the group stepped inside. Vicente and Iver walked side by side, their gazes forward. He took a deep breath, heart pounding. This was the culmination of their efforts, the final step towards justice. He had been nervous that morning, but using Stormwater had gotten his mind off it, and now he was riding the high.

Chairs were arranged in a semicircle facing the center of the room, where a table had been set up. As he took a seat next to Atli, the hall filled with others who had played pivotal roles in the conflict. The witnesses were there to provide their accounts. The rangers oversaw the investigation, and Vicente had no idea why Falco had been called as a witness.

As the room settled into a collective focus, Vicente tried to catch Iver's eye, but he wouldn't look at him.

With a nod from one of the rangers, the proceedings began.

Vicente started. "We have discovered that Ottone Cronin, now confined to a holding cell, was worshipping one of the usurper gods, the Gambler. We want him convicted and executed of the crime of heresy. We believe there are more people in Llyr who follow the same faith."

Sergeant Broker, who was seated at the table, jotted down notes. "I understand Ambassador Vicente is saying some people in Llyr are worshipping another deity. Is this correct, Mister Atli?"

The chair creaked as Atli shifted in his seat. "That is incorrect. Anyone who would express loyalty to another god would be reported to Arkensaal, I assure you of that."

The words squeeze the air from Vicente's lungs, but he forced himself to breathe. He should've suspected it: Atli was part of the cult. *The entire town is steeped in corruption.*

"What about you, Mister Falco?" Broker asked.

Falco shot Vicente a quick glance, although it seemed involuntary. "I have never heard the name 'the Gambler' before today, Sergeant."

Vicente's thoughts were moving so, so slowly. This interrogation was his chance, but his mind came up with nothing. He couldn't think of a single thing to say. Every opportunity to speak slipped right past him, and before he knew it, he hadn't spoken for over an hour. *Perhaps I should excuse myself for a second, step outside and open another tunnel?*

Everyone the rangers asked denied the existence of the cult. No one had heard or seen anything suspicious, no one knew anything. Vicente didn't ask a single question or offer any explanations. He just sat there. He felt his heart like a distant drum. He and Iver were in danger, but danger was a negative feeling, and the afterglow of opening a tunnel didn't allow for those. The rush of adrenaline to fight for his life was blocked. He couldn't access even a drop of it.

"And Ottone murdered two children," Vicente blurted out when he noticed Broker wrapping things up. "We found proof." He came across like he was grasping at straws.

Broker was dismissive; he didn't look at him when he spoke. "Is that true?" he asked Atli. "Even though that is not a crime for the rangers to investigate, we would still like to interrogate him, if that's the case."

"No." Atli sighed hard. "Those children died of exposure. We had a remarkably hot summer."

Why was he lying? Atli knew Ottone had done it; he was the one who found the evidence. Nausea welled up in Vicente's throat. It was the withdrawal coming in way too soon—he needed to open another tunnel.

Broker closed his notebook. "I understand that your mission in Llyr is completed, Ambassador. You have given the land to its rightful owner?"

"That is correct," Vicente said, swallowing the saliva that pooled in his mouth.

"Good." He shot his fellow rangers a look and they stood. "Now, the queen has given us custody of Far Cry, and he will finally be reprimanded for deserting the rangers."

What?

Three soldiers grabbed Iver.

Iver struggled, but he was a head shorter, unarmed and powerless in the other men's grips.

Vicente stood, but the world rocked and one of his knees hit the ground. "Don't touch him!" But he was too messed up to do anything, and he could only watch as they dragged Iver out of there.

CHAPTER 44

Iver

They had him strung up by his arms, and he was barely able to stand on the tip of his toes. The window in the small holding cell had been covered. An oil lamp on the floor did its best to illuminate the room.

"We've heard a lot about you," one of the new rangers said to him. "You were the greatest marksman in a century. And you only lasted nine months with the squad."

The punch to his stomach came out of nowhere. Darkness encircled Iver's vision. He couldn't even curl up. White-hot nausea welled up inside, alongside the searing pain, making his head go blank. Pain pinched his skull. When his ears started ringing, he knew he would either pass out or vomit, and he would rather die than do the latter.

Vicente wouldn't be coming for his rescue; he was probably inebriated to the point where he no longer functioned. Iver wanted to smash every last one of Vicente's god-damned fucking Stormwater.

The door opened and Broker stepped inside. "Leave him to me," he barked, and the two other rangers left quickly.

Broker looked older, even though only two years had passed. Sun had worn the skin on his face. Some strands of his black-pepper hair had turned to the color of salt.

He pulled up a chair and sat down in front of Iver. "You left me to die."

Iver spat the saliva gathering in his mouth due to the nausea. "I was going to get help. When I went outside, I saw the queen had already sent her troops. They were already there."

Broker moved slowly as he got a pack of cigarettes from a pocket in his jacket. He lit one and took a deep drag of it, all while pinning Iver with his stare. "Then why did you run?"

Iver pulled on the ropes tying his wrists, but that made them constrict even more. "You told me Siege died because of me, and I fucking believed you. For the longest time, I fucking believed you. You hold that against me still?"

The room filled with tobacco smoke and made it even harder to breathe. If he could just get one full breath, he'd be able to think of something.

Broker sighed. "It doesn't matter what I feel, really. The laws of the rangers' demand that you be held accountable for deserting."

"What will my punishment be?"

"A good beating and some humiliation, Far Cry. Some of the boys want you dead, too. I'll send word back to Queen Leandra and she'll deliver her verdict. But the good news is that you won't have to wait long." Broker leaned his elbows on his knees. "You have missed so much. All the technological advancements only the military has access to. We no longer need birds to talk; the Department of Defense invented something they call a 'radio'—it sends waves in the air that allow us to hear each other's voices, even though we are miles apart."

Iver wanted to hear more about it, wanted Broker to keep that tone in his voice that he remembered so fondly. The new technology sounded like magic. Nostalgia hit him like a shot in the chest when he recalled why he had chosen to enlist in the first place, the power and comradery they'd had as part of the rangers.

But that time was long gone. "Will I be executed?"

"The queen has been made aware that you failed in your mission of killing the mystic. Now she wants both of you dead."

What?

"She wants him dead before he can set foot back in Arkensaal," Broker continued. "And since you failed, it has fallen on the rangers to pick up your slack. 'Make it look like an accident or a robbery,' she said. Other than that, she's given us free range."

Iver pulled on the ropes. *No, no, no.* He couldn't let them hurt Vicente. "Don't do this, Broker. We are the last of the true rangers. You and me."

Broker put out the cigarette on the sole of his boot. "That we are, indeed. And you left."

The skin underneath the fiber of his shackles broke as he pulled. "Vicente had nothing to do with that. You can't hurt him. Please, Broker, let him live." Iver felt so incredibly small. Insignificant. He didn't feel like that very often, not anymore.

Broker quietly regarded him as his panic rose. They had been family once. Of course Broker could see it. Of course he knew what this meant—how Iver felt about Vicente. But Iver didn't bother hiding it. Let him see. Let the whole fucking world see. It didn't matter anymore.

"I am begging you, please don't hurt him." He needed to warn Vicente; he might still have time to run. What if Vicente got so high he wouldn't see the danger coming, and would be unable to escape?

"Like I said, it's not up to me. You remember what these things are like. Men like us simply follow orders."

Iver choked on his panic, on the pleading that leached into his voice. He blinked rapidly to hold back the onset of tears, but his vision still blurred. "I'll do whatever you ask, anything at all. Please, leave him out of this." Begging left Iver's throat scraped raw, like he had swallowed broken glass. He was good at suffering. He was good at taking it, as well as giving it. But he could not suffer this.

He loved Vicente, he could no longer deny it. It had all happened so fast and out of order. Their first kiss happened before Iver even liked him, even trusted him. The months spent hiding resulted in him trusting Vicente with his life, an unfathomable feat. The bastard had crashed through Iver's carefully built walls without so much as a backwards glance. And Iver had submitted to it, just like that. He never thought he would.

Broker stood. "You know, Far Cry, we all have our weaknesses. And you found yours in a man, and I think that makes you the worst kind there is. Because Lieutenant Siege's weakness was you, and that was the death of him."

CHAPTER 45

Vicente

Vicente watched as Ottone left the town hall, now a free man. When he spotted Vicente, he had the audacity to give him a casual wave. Vicente promised Iver the honor of killing Ottone was his, and he wasn't ready to fail him in that.

His blood had been in his ears ever since they took Iver away. As he sobered up, his right mind returned to him. Why had Arkensaal even sent the rangers in the first place, when he requested a member of a ruling clan? He should have been on high alert the moment he saw the rangers, but he had been high out of his mind.

The heat in the smithy almost felt like summer. "Why?" Vicente was so filled with rage he could barely see.

Atli hammered away at a piece of metal wrapped around the anvil. "You wish for us to be persecuted for our faith?"

"He killed two children and abused many more!"

"If they bring Ottone in for interrogation, he might reveal things that ought not to be a crime." Atli put the unfinished horseshoe down on the anvil. "The Gambler brings fortune to Llyr. It revealed to us that Eldvittra gave up on humanity long ago, and Llyr will build a temple in honor of the Gambler to protect us from the horned god. I don't expect you to understand, but you should know that any attempt to sway us is futile."

If Eldvittra truly had abandoned humanity, then what were the divine risks of worshipping another god? Still, "Once Queen

Leandra finds out about this, you will all either be imprisoned or executed."

"Then we will make sure she doesn't." A drop of sweat ran from Atli's sideburn and down his jaw. "Lord Eloy told me you wished for peace; is that not blasphemy too?"

"I guess it is." Within the confines of the realm's ruling religion, striving for peace wasn't an option. "You'll let Ottone go unpunished?"

"I did not say that. He sealed his fate when he decided to murder *five* Llyrian children." Atli threw his hammer to the floor. "And abuse many others. Look, I am sorry about Iver—"

"Do not speak his name. You have not made yourself worthy of that." Vicente stormed off, returning to his room at the Sunfire Rest. *What were they doing to Iver, right now?* The thought of their hands on him made him want to scream.

He had to stay calm. Perhaps he could open a tunnel in his room? He shook his head as though to get rid of the thought. He couldn't do that; he needed his head to be clear. When trying to remember the past, his mind felt mushy, and he couldn't remember the first time he opened a tunnel just for the pleasure of it, and it scared him.

He went downstairs again and plated some food, but his stomach was so tightly ensnared he couldn't force a single bite. No one else was going to save Iver. He needed to be strong. He required the energy, but the food turned to gore in his mouth.

Sergeant Broker was suddenly standing next to Vicente. "Ambassador, you need to come with us to the town hall."

Vicente glared at him. "Is this about Iver?"

"No, this is about you. Don't fight me on this."

With a nod, Vicente surrendered to Broker's command. His steps were heavy as he followed him outside. As they traversed the twisted cobblestone streets, anxiety clawed at his chest. What was this about? Were they going to try to use his words to hurt Iver? Vicente swallowed hard. His throat grew parched in his apprehension.

Broker took him to the town hall, which had been turned into a base for them to temporarily operate out of. They passed by the door to the holding cell, and it took every ounce of strength from him not to go inside to check on Iver.

Walking down the hall, they passed another door that opened suddenly. "Sergeant, we were not able to contact Lady Darius," said the ranger standing in the doorway. Then, the ranger spotted Vicente with Broker, and looked caught off guard.

Broker muttered, "Try again in two hours."

"Yes, sir."

Vicente recognized the name Darius; she was the secretary of the Department of Defense. But what did he mean by 'not able to contact'? Vicente recalled hearing about a new communication device only the military had access to: a radio. Had they brought one with them to Llyr?

Broker ushered Vicente into a room, where maps were spread across a table and strategically placed candles fought against the encroaching shadows. "We have orders to arrest you, Ambassador."

Vicente took a seat in one of the chairs. "For what?"

Broker also sat down. He didn't meet his gaze; it was like he was ashamed. "The murders of two children."

Five children. Vicente almost rolled his eyes. That accusation would never stand. "And who issued the order, if I may ask?"

"Arkensaal."

They must have brought radios with them, then, if they were able to communicate with Queen Leandra so fast. "We are in the territory of the ruling clan of Jadanza. The crown has no jurisdiction here regarding murder."

"There is no ruling clan of Llyr."

Vicente huffed. "Do your homework before you waste my time. The proof is in the Llyrian archives. This matter will be settled by Marcia Jadanza upon her return." Vicente leaned his elbows on the cluttered table. He was seething with rage. "Now, you know I can just leave by ways your small mind cannot comprehend, but I'd rather not depart with bad blood between us. Am I free to go?"

Broker looked even more unsure of himself. "Let me check."

He left Vicente alone in the room. Vicente could leave whenever he wanted, but he needed to see Iver first. He waited as the minutes ticked by, turning to an hour, then two.

He had spent so many years of his life carefully working and navigating within the framework built by the crown, the quorum and the noble clans in the High Council. For what? For his own safety, that was no longer a guarantee, and perhaps never was? Now, this framework was going to do everything it could to punish him and Iver. It was all rotten to its core. Maybe it all needed to come down.

Vicente stepped out into the hallway. A ranger was posted in front of the door to the holding cell. He looked over at Vicente. "Do not leave the interrogation room, Ambassador."

"Sergeant Broker has been gone for two hours and will likely be away for a few more. Do you suggest I relieve myself in there?"

The ranger's mouth turned into a thin line. "Be quick."

Vicente turned the corner and quietly walked down the hallway, listening intently. He heard a voice engaged in conversation. Just one voice.

The door was ajar. The speaking ranger sat at the desk with his back to Vicente. He spoke to a machine the size of a brick, which he held to his ear. This was the portable two-way radio transceiver Vicente had heard about. "Lady Darius, how do we proceed?"

The voice emerging from the machine was crackling. "A squad of recruits is heading from Mariemoor to Fallowfort. Have Iver Vasiliev join up with them."

They were going to have Iver join the army at the frontiers. Then, he would surely never return—no one ever did.

The conversation ended.

Vicente retraced his steps and then walked up to the door again, this time letting his footsteps resonate throughout the corridor. A knock on the door announced his presence.

The ranger turned, his eyes meeting Vicente's. Before he could speak, Vicente's said, "Pardon me, but would you happen to know where Sergeant Broker—oh, this is a radio, correct? I've heard a great deal about them. Mind if I have a look?"

The ranger narrowed his eyes. "Sure. Just be careful." He handed it over to Vicente.

Vicente inspected it. He turned one of the knobs and suddenly heard Broker's voice. They were speaking on different frequencies. He turned the knob back, taking note of which one connected to the capital.

"We got them about a year ago," the ranger said, "there's a radio tower at Fallowfort and one at Mariemoor that forwards the signal. The Department of Defense is building towers all along the frontiers…"

Still holding the radio in his hand, Vicente placed his other hand on one of the buttons of his coat. Then he focused.

The entanglement process was silent and undetectable. All he needed was to touch two objects and have a few moments at his disposal.

"Are you listening, Ambassador?" the ranger asked.

"My apologies; my mind wandered." Vicente handed the radio back and left. He returned to the interrogation room, and within forty minutes, Broker came back as well.

"We have checked, and you are correct. Lady Marcia will be handling this matter," Broker said as he stood in the doorway. "You are free to leave."

Vicente groaned as he stood, like he had been seated for the entirety of the hours he had been left there. "I will speak to Iver on my way out."

"And I'll be supervising you."

Broker dismissed the guard posted outside the door to the holding cell and knocked. "I'm opening the door, Far Cry. Don't try anything."

Iver was sitting on the bed, hunched forward, clasped hands hanging loosely between his knees. When he saw Vicente, he shot to his feet. "Vic."

Forcing the worry back down his throat, Vicente asked, "Are you hurt?"

Iver was still in his usual clothes, but his sleeves were rolled up. Bruises had bloomed over his forearms. Vicente could have killed Broker right at that moment.

"I'm fine." Iver glanced at Broker where he stood next to Vicente in the doorway. "Vic. Why do you never see pigs hiding in trees?"

This confused Vicente. Iver was obviously telling one of his bad jokes, but at a time like this? "Why?"

"Because they can't climb trees." He delivered the punchline with caution as he pinned Vicente with his stare. He looked at Broker for a split second before looking back at him.

Iver always told his jokes when Vicente was nervous, right before danger. He understood. Vicente was in danger.

Vicente gave him a small nod and faked a smile. "Always the comedian. I'll see you at your trial."

CHAPTER 46

Vicente

Eyelids drooping, Vicente struggled against the ropes of sleep. He had been busy for hours, mixing the ingredients and pouring his magic into vials of Stormwater. He had placed them in hidden alcoves throughout the town: behind potted plants in the temple, behind the counter at the Harvest Heart, and in the nooks of the stable, as well as in every empty room at the inn. Sergeant Broker knew about his powers, and he needed to outwit him. He played the game in his mind's eye a hundred times over. *Where is the best place to hide? Well, the place where they have already looked.*

The anticipation tasted like panic. As Llyr's old clock tower chimed the final notes of another day, Vicente opened a tunnel and substituted his button for the radio. The device was heavy in his hand. The radio crackled to life, the speakers emitting static and distant murmurs. It was as if the very ether was alive with the whispers carried on invisible waves.

The moon hung low when the rangers came for him. He listened in on them talking to each other. They had apparently split up in their search for him, and Broker was heading towards his room in the inn. The weight of being hunted felt familiar, like Vicente's body had grown around it.

"Target is a flight-risk; he can travel through the air in an instant. Be on high alert and stay quiet," Broker said. They believed they were closing in on him.

They would check Vicente's own room first, but he didn't know where the other rangers were and didn't dare leave the inn yet. So, he opened a tunnel to the vial he had placed in Iver's room. In an instant, reality bent and twisted, and Vicente found himself standing within its confines. They would look for him there next.

"The clerk told me he hasn't left the inn," a voice said.

Vicente turned the radio's volume down, his attention split between the barely audible hum of it and the sounds beyond the closed door. The wooden floorboards in the hallway outside groaned. As the seconds ticked away, Vicente imagined the rangers, rifles raised, sweeping through the inn's hallways in search of him.

And then, Broker's voice broke through the crackling of the radio. "One-five, how copy?"

The radio sizzled. "Target is not with the blacksmith. Clearing out."

Vicente's heart pounded as he listened. He caught the creaking of a door nearby, hinges protesting movement.

"Target is not in his room. Checking Far Cry's."

Two sets of footsteps echoed down the hallway, a rhythm Vicente could feel in his chest. He had to move. There was no way of knowing if the other locations were clear yet, but he had to risk it.

He downed the sending potion to the smithy and opened the tunnel there. In the span of a heartbeat, he found himself in Atli's workshop, the air filled with the scent of metal and the dim light of the moon filtering through the windows.

Vicente stood amidst the darkness. He was alone. *Thank you, Merciful.*

"Fuck, where is he? He is not in the inn."

Conversation turned tense as the rangers came up short. Vicente absorbed every fragment of it to decipher their next move.

"Tavern is clear."

"Stables are clear."

"The entire inn is fucking empty."

The sound of footsteps reached his ears, a familiar rhythm: Atli was coming.

Vicente grabbed the vial he prepared for this very scenario. He uncorked it and drank it.

Then he was in the stables. The earthy scent of hay and the musk of horses was suffocating, but the only sound he heard was of horses stirring in their sleep.

Vicente dared to take a step forward. The stable doors were ajar, offering a glimpse of the world outside. He peered through the opening, eyes narrowing as he surveyed the scene.

In the square in front of the town hall stood two rangers, their figures silhouetted against the backdrop of the moonlit night.

The radio transmissions continued. "Searching the streets next; keep an eye on the inn," Broker directed.

"Yes, sir."

Broker's voice called out again, "Base, how do you copy?"

The silence that followed spoke volumes. They must've been calling for the radio Vicente had stolen.

"I can't get a response from the base."

Another voice joined the conversation. "One-three, anything?"

The response was a swift, "Negative."

"No response from base," Broker said. "Consider one of our devices to be compromised. Radio silence, all units."

Vicente had disrupted their plans, unveiling the vulnerability of their communication channels. The exhilaration of his victory left a taste of triumph that fueled him.

The final acknowledgment carried out, "copy."

The temptation to press the call button and answer 'copy' was almost overpowering, but Vicente decided against it. Now, time was of the essence. The rangers were regrouping, recalibrating their tactics. And so, Vicente took a risk and changed the frequency, aligning the radio's signal to reach the Department of Defense in the capital. He had no idea if the rangers suspected that he might try to reach the capital, but if they heard him, then so be it.

"Ambassador Vicente Lamor, seeking Secretary Darius, how copy?"

A few moments of static noise. Then, a familiar voice came through. "Excuse me?" Her voice sounded like she had just woken up.

"Good evening, Secretary Darius."

"How did you get access to this device, Ambassador?"

"Sergeant Broker was so kind as to let me borrow it. I have an urgent message for Indra of the Sensis Quorum. Mind fetching her for me?"

Secretary Darius clicked her tongue. "This is not how these devices should be used—"

"I must remind you of my status as an ambassador for the crown," Vicente said. "The quorum will not be pleased if they find out you've kept this from them."

A tense pause followed. Secretary Darius's concession came reluctantly. "I'll fetch her."

Thirty minutes stretched, but every minute felt like an hour. Vicente's senses remained on high alert, eyes scanning the surroundings for any signs of movement.

The radio crackled once again. "This is Indra speaking."

Vicente relaxed at the sound. "Indra, how are you?"

"I'm alone. You are free to speak your mind, Vicente."

He needed to be to-the-point and concise, as the rangers could interrupt his transmission at any moment. "The Stag has been located. Asking for permission to proceed."

"Have you made contact?" she asked.

"Negative." He knew she would ask him to return to the capital before bonding with it, but he couldn't go there before he had better stakes in the game. "Indra, the queen has a bounty on my head; I suspect the quorum is in danger. You need to tell me how to bond it, right now."

The quorum was always secretive. Even the queen herself wasn't allowed to know the details of their dealings. Vicente was no exception, but that had to end tonight.

"Are you alone?"

Vicente looked around the stables again. "For now."

Indra's voice came out hushed. "The Stag will ask you for something that is yours. A gift. And it will not mean a belonging of yours. You'll get one chance to offer it a part of your body: blood, hair, a finger, anything. Anything else that you were not born with, it will reject and it will kill you. You will get *one* chance. Do you understand?"

Was that really all there was to it? "I do. Thank you. I most likely won't get access to this device again. Stay safe."

"You too."

As the night wore on, the rangers' pursuit eventually waned. The hours ticked away, and by the time the clock struck three in the morning, the streets of Llyr had quieted. In the deepest dead of the night, Vicente returned to the inn, leaving the radio in the stables.

He went to Iver's room, a place that had been combed through by the rangers. Vicente surveyed the room, taking in the details: the overturned furniture, the ransacked drawers, the disarray. He didn't know what else they had been looking for.

Vicente settled onto the bed. The realization of his past actions bore down on him, a burden he could no longer ignore. The pain of hurting someone he cared for cut deep. His heart ached with regret. He couldn't believe he had hurt Iver like that. Would he ever forgive him?

Withdrawal symptoms manifested as the euphoria ebbed. His body felt drained and sluggish. The bliss of the night's maneuvers gave way to a dull ache spreading through his muscles and bones, limbs heavy and unresponsive, sapped of vitality. Nausea coiled in the pit of his stomach. A tremor wandered through his fingers.

The darkness around him closed in, suffocating him with its weight. His breath came in shallow gasps, each inhalation a struggle that left him raw and exposed.

It had been two hours since he had opened his last tunnel. Vicente sought solace. He opened another tunnel, a place where the familiar sensations of pleasure awaited. It whispered in his ear, asking him to let it in, and then every problem in the world would fade away.

Pleasure trickled into his senses as he stepped through it, a balm for the torment. But this time, it was different. The rush he had once experienced, the intoxicating wave of euphoria, was muted, diluted. It lacked the intensity he had known, the feeling of pure escape that had once washed over him.

His frustration swelled, threatening to consume him. In desperation, he opened another tunnel. He stepped through again, but the result wasn't what he had hoped for. The high, when it came, wasn't complete. It was fractured, a fleeting glimmer, a shadow of what it had once been.

He opened another one.

CHAPTER 47

Vicente

Vicente woke the next morning with a dry mouth and skin-skimming chills. A dull ache stretched awake in his neck. As his eyes fluttered open, he was met with the harsh reality of daylight streaming through the window. He had fallen asleep on Iver's bed, exhaustion catching up to him. But now, the sun was already up. He had overslept. Vicente's stomach dropped. What if they had already left with Iver?

As he rushed to the town square, his gaze fell on a scene, freezing him in his tracks. A crowd had formed, a gathering of curious onlookers. His chest clenched as he saw Iver, his hands bound and secured to a post that had been driven into the ground.

The world slowed. The rangers stood around Iver. Iver was kneeling and shirtless in the cold, and his skin bore the marks of whiplashes. His back was bloodied from being whipped and beaten. Red clouded Vicente's vision. He was going to kill them all.

There was a fluttering panic at the back of Vicente's chest, near his heart. He had been absent during a crucial moment. His thoughts blurred and fragmented, disjointed. He needed to act, to navigate this new situation with the same determination that had guided him through the night.

A detachment of about fifty soldiers waited on the outskirts of the square. They had come for Iver. The soldiers stood in formation. The glint of their swords caught the sunlight.

Vicente steeled himself, course set on the scene before him. The crowd seemed to part as he moved. The rangers, with so many witnesses present, wouldn't risk taking extreme measures against him. They wouldn't try to kill Vicente here.

Sergeant Broker eyed him as he approached. "Ambassador, we thought you left Llyr."

Vicente worked his tongue around his mouth, tasting the leftover adrenaline, coppery like blood. "I have come to argue for Iver's freedom." His saliva tasted like acid. He spat.

"This is a case for the rangers," Broker said. "You have no say in it."

Vicente's mouth opened to speak, but the words that emerged were jumbled, a nonsensical string of syllables holding no meaning. His focus wavered as he struggled to maintain his grasp on the situation. Everything clashed with his weak state. His ability to form coherent arguments was gone. His mind was a puzzle with pieces refusing to fit together.

Broker's eyes narrowed in confusion as he registered Vicente's struggle. "Step aside, Ambassador."

The ground began to tilt beneath Vicente. As he swayed slightly on his feet, he did as he was told. He stood amidst the crowd, grappling with the remnants of his composure.

Broker interrupted the awkward silence. "This man, Iver Vasiliev, deserted the military, a crime punishable by death."

Vicente's gaze drifted to Iver. The sight of the dried blood marring Iver's back ignited a surge of anger. The anger quickly died, to be replaced with nothing.

"Due to his skill as a marksman, his life will be spared," Broker said. "By Queen Leandra's decree: Iver Vasiliev, you will now be conscripted." His reprieve from death would be brief: no matter his skill, he would die in the war.

Vicente began formulating a strategy to navigate the new circumstances. Rescuing Iver under the watchful eyes of the rangers would be a near-impossible feat. He needed a plan that would allow him to gather information and find a way to intervene at a time when the odds were more favorable. He needed to follow the troop on their way to the frontiers and identify the best opportunity to free Iver.

Broker untied Iver's hands.

On trembling legs, Iver stood. "Vic…" His voice sounded so small, so desperate.

The unit's lieutenant spoke to Broker before ushering Iver towards the other soldiers. The reality of Iver's conscription was a bitter pill to swallow. Vicente had no choice but to watch as Iver was led away.

His gaze remained fixed on Iver's retreating figure. They would not take Iver from him. The troop began to march, probably for Fallowfort, and there, they would continue their journey to the frontlines on horseback. He needed to get to Iver before then.

As the soldiers and Iver disappeared over the horizon, the sun descended. But the night held opportunities that the day had denied him.

"Now, as for you, Ambassador," Broker said.

Vicente was immediately alarmed. "What?"

"Your activities last night made us suspect you have been opening tunnels, which the queen strictly forbade you from doing. That was part of the agreement, and you broke it."

Vicente's actions hadn't gone unnoticed by them. "That's a load of horseshit—"

"We also learned about an incident where you spiked wine and involved two other Llyrians in your antics. You are now under arrest, and you'll come back with us to Arkensaal tomorrow morning."

"What?"

The rangers moved in to apprehend him. Vicente's defiance of the queen's orders, the use of his Stormwater and the risks he had taken had all led to this moment. The consequences of his actions were now inescapable. He had come face to face with his own recklessness.

A shift occurred in the distance. A group of figures emerged over the western horizon, the same one the soldiers had disappeared behind. The sight caught the attention of everyone present, drawing their gazes away from Vicente and the rangers.

Vicente tried to make out the figures in the distance. And then, he saw her: Marcia was leading the group. Beside her was Sergeant Celia. The realization that the militia was accompanying them made hope flutter its wings in his chest.

Marcia and her group approached, and they had Iver in their midst. Someone had put a jacket over his shoulders, and he was barely upright.

As Broker confronted Marcia, his voice was tight. "This is ridiculous. Bring Iver back to the soldiers, right now."

Marcia smiled politely at him. "Oh, you've got the wrong Iver. This is Iver Russo." From her bag, she produced a document: Iver's forged identification papers, made on the queen's orders to let him travel outside the capital. His fake identity, his freedom.

"This man is not Iver Vasiliev, and here are the documents that prove it." Marcia handed it over and pointed to the page. "See that crest there? This was issued by Arkensaal officials. This man is a citizen of Llyr, and his family name is not Vasiliev."

Broker's face reddened. "You're joking, right? I know it's him—*I fucking know him!*"

Marcia scoffed. "I'm sure you do, Sergeant. But here in Llyr, he no longer has that identity. He is a Llyrian citizen. Thus, he is not eligible for conscription, as per my decree as the head of a ruling clan."

Broker couldn't do anything to overrule her. Not even the queen could.

"You will have to fight for him." Broker pointed his rifle at Marcia.

Marcia's response was instant. "Take up arms!" The militia stood in formation, weapons raised, bows drawn, arrows aimed at the rangers.

The standoff stretched for seconds. The rangers and the militia of Llyr were locked on one another. No one dared to let the first arrow fly or be the first to pull the trigger. In a battle, the rangers would win by a landslide. But war would be declared with Llyr by the capital, and everyone knew the rangers would be disbanded if that were to happen.

Broker grumbled, "fuck this," and acquiesced.

The rangers' stance faltered as they lowered their firearms.

"We're heading back," Broker said to his comrades, before turning to Vicente. "When you return to Arkensaal, Ambassador, you'll be held accountable for your misdeeds."

As the rangers left, the tension in the square dissipated.

Vicente's expression transformed into a smile as he walked up to Marcia. "Brilliant." His words held genuine admiration. The situation had been navigated with finesse.

Marcia stared at him. "You should have thought of that, Vicente. You have a copy of Iver's papers. Were you just going to stand here and let them take him? Are you okay?" She drew a sharp breath. "You are completely strung out on Stormwater, aren't you?"

Vicente's smile faded. He didn't know what to say.

"Take Iver to the infirmary and get him patched up," Marcia directed Sergeant Celia, who was helping a staggering Iver.

Vicente took a step towards Iver to follow, but Marcia stopped him with a hand on his chest. "Go sober up, Vicente. For fuck's sake, get a grip."

He could only nod.

*

It took four hours for Vicente to feel steady on his feet again. As soon as the world no longer rocked when he turned his head too fast, he went to the infirmary in the temple.

The infirmary was modest. A row of beds lined one side of the room, each adorned with clean linen.

Vicente's eyes settled on Iver, who lay on his stomach on one of the beds, back patched up and wounds dressed. Vicente didn't know what to say to him. He had failed him.

"Vic!" Iver sprang to his feet and threw his arms around his neck.

Vicente let out his breath, felt his chest collapse into the space left behind. He grabbed Iver's waist, afraid to touch his back and cause further injury. His skin was soft and warm and *alive*, and Vicente wanted to be engulfed by it, encased by it, wishing he could crawl into the cage of his chest and rest there. Iver smelled of sterile bandages and rubbing alcohol, but his hair still carried his scent. Vicente drew deep breaths of it.

"I love you, Iver," he said with a tearless sob, unable to contain the feelings of love and guilt but equally inept at expressing them in words. "I'm so sorry I hurt you. I'm so sorry I failed you."

Vicente fitted their lips together and Iver surged up to meet him. He tasted warm. Alive. Vicente didn't match Iver's hunger, instead kissing him slowly.

"Vicente," Iver crooned, not entirely lucid, as he grabbed Vicente's face. "I love you too, you bastard."

CHAPTER 48

Atli

For a few agonizing days, Ottone moved through the town square, his steps light and his posture exuding a sense of carefree confidence. Freed by the rangers, he relished his liberation. Though this was none of the Arkensaalis' concern, the rangers had insisted that Ottone be released right then and there, fearing he was behind bars only because of Ambassador Vicente's mistakes. Atli could only smile and comply at the time.

Ottone's interactions were unburdened by the tension of the past few days. He engaged with those around him, his words playful and his demeanor obnoxious—he acted in the way that only someone who was truly free could. Atli watched him like a hawk, unable to do anything as he poisoned the ground he walked on.

Then, the rangers finally left.

As the break of dawn painted the sky with soft hues of pink and gold, Atli summoned those he felt safe enough to ask. Beside him, twenty individuals from Llyr had gathered, each chosen for their willingness to partake. Atli had said nothing to the diplomats; the two of them were outsiders, and this was none of their concern. A holy sister of Eldvittra stood among the group, her commitment to the cause evident in the unwavering rage in her eyes. For days they had let it brew.

The lie Atli had told the rangers was necessary; he wanted to kill Ottone himself. Ottone had assaulted children of Llyr, and he would be killed at the hands of Llyrians.

As the small group arrived at the door of Ottone's house, Atli raised his hand and knocked. The sound echoed in the stillness of the morning. Each member of the group held sticks, canes or metal pipes.

The hushed atmosphere amplified the sound of their movements: the knock on the door, the shifting of feet, the rustling of clothing.

The door swung open. Ottone's eyes fell on Atli, the figure at the forefront of the group, and his confusion was plain. "Mister Atli, what…" However, as his gaze shifted and took in the rest of the gathered individuals, his bewilderment deepened. "What is going on?" He looked from face to face, eyes narrowing slightly as he tried to piece together the purpose behind this assembly.

Atli said nothing; this man was not worth speaking to. He had killed and assaulted children. When the holy sisters had asked the children, many of them had recounted what he had done to them. Their stories had pained Atli so deeply he couldn't sleep. He was unsure he could ever sleep again.

Atli wielded the cane and smashed one of Ottone's windows. The sound of shattering glass cut through the quiet. The others stood still, watching. Brimming with rage.

"Merciful, what're you doing!" Ottone stepped outside in an attempt to stop Atli, but he didn't stop. The shards of broken glass glinted in the sunlight as he smashed one window after another. He had hoped that, maybe, this act of violence would quench his thirst. Instead, the casualness of the destruction fueled him.

When Ottone grabbed his arm, Atli shoved him to the ground. He loomed over him, searching for words to offer an explanation to him as he trembled in fear. But Ottone ought to have known; he knew what he had done and that it was unforgivable. Atli could offer no words to this man.

They all surrounded him. The holy sister of Eldvittra was the first to strike. Ottone screamed out in pain as the cane snapped in half over his head. Utter carnage. It broke the curse binding the others to passiveness. They took turns hitting him. It turned to a rhythm that sounded too much like a pulse. They continued beating him until he lost consciousness. They beat him until his skull cracked.

CHAPTER 49

Vicente

Iver had taught Vicente how to read the map he had stolen from the Resurrectionists, and using the scale on the back of it, he tried to determine the distance he'd have to travel and the altitude he'd have to climb to reach the Stag.

The sound of the door closing startled Vicente—he hadn't even heard the door open. "They got your stitches out?"

Iver rolled his shoulder once, testing it out. "It was an absolute fucking bitch; hurt worse than getting whipped."

Vicente chuckled. He found Iver's foul mouth amusing. Charming, even. "They didn't offer you any more opium?"

"That shit's addictive—can't have it more than a few days in a row."

Vicente stood from his desk, leaving behind the map. His time in Llyr was limited. If he could just bond the Stag, he could return to the capital and the queen wouldn't be able to touch him.

Vicente dipped his head and kissed Iver. "Sounds like you're all healed up, then."

"Why, what are you thinking?" Iver asked, voice low.

"Fucking you into the mattress. I prefer it to bending you over my desk." He smeared kisses down the length of Iver's throat.

"Well, aren't you back to your normal self."

The warmth of Iver's skin sank into his bones. Vicente hadn't opened a tunnel in a few days. He felt sluggish and slow but ultimately happy about his decision. He needed to prove that he was acting responsibly. The fact that the rangers wanted to arrest him and that the queen was aware he had gone against her orders was a rude awakening and a stark reminder that he had strayed from the path. He couldn't be giving them more ammunition than they already had. Besides, the true withdrawal, the powerful need to open another tunnel, hadn't set in fully yet. He was going to find the Stag before then, and then he would get his high again.

Vicente pressed his thigh between Iver's legs, drawing a sharp hiss from him.

Iver gripped Vicente's upper arms to steady himself and rested his forehead on his chest. His voice was low and smoky. "I won't stop you."

Vicente didn't like the sound of that. After what he had done to Iver, he would accept nothing less than enthusiastic consent. He wanted to hear Iver beg for it. With a finger under his chin, he tilted his head up. "On second thought, maybe we should wait. You shouldn't be laying on your back so soon."

Iver's pupils were blown wide with lust, his cheeks flushed. "You're such a fucking tease."

He had canted forward, Vicente noticed. He steadied him with a hand on his shoulder. "And you are so beautiful like this."

"Say that again and I'll rip your tongue out of your head."

Vicente's lips found his chin, his jaw, his neck, nosing against it. He traced kisses over his throat with parted lips, touching his teeth to his skin. His arm snaked around the small of Iver's back and he held him closer, gripping his hard cock through the fabric of his pants.

Iver moaned high in his throat, and Vicente blushed at the noise.

Iver had a dreamy look in his eyes. Seeing this side of him, this vulnerability in him, was a privilege Iver had given to Vicente only. He wanted Iver to be like this forever, because it meant that he felt safe enough to show it.

"Vicente... please." Iver's fingernails dug into his shoulders. "Please fuck me. Please."

"Damnit, Iver... That's more like it."

*

Vicente tacked up the second horse. The saddles were practically threadbare, but he couldn't complain: Atli had lent these two horses to him and Iver, free of charge. The journey to the mountains would take about five days one way, and they couldn't ride the whole way due to the steep terrain. The horses would probably not return.

Marcia leaned against one of the stalls, eyes fixed on Vicente as he adjusted the girths of the saddles. "Will you be coming back here after?"

"Are you planning to join us on our return to the capital?" Vicente asked. Her newfound role as prime minister might tie her to Llyr. She was doing an amazing job settling everyone down after the intense drama that had unfolded.

Marcia's expression mirrored his contemplation. "I haven't decided yet. There are still a few matters I need to tend to here."

Vicente squeezed her shoulder. "We'll come back to Llyr afterwards, then."

Under the embrace of the sun, Llyr's charm was painted in brighter hues. The snow sparkled in the sunlight. Vicente and Marcia walked along the path leading away from the stables, the air crisp around them.

"Did you clear out Ottone's apothecary?" Vicente asked.

The sunlight caught the strands of Marcia's hair in a delicate halo. She had a new glow about her. "Lord Eloy helped me. We purged the remnants, burning everything."

"Any word from your father?"

"Nothing. He's just vanished."

Marcia didn't seem too upset about her father being gone, but Vicente always found her hard to read. He wondered if Iver had had anything to do with Renato's disappearance.

"As for the Resurrectionists," Marcia continued, "I have asked around a bit, and not a single person claims to have heard about them before."

"They don't know about the human sacrifices, then?" Vicente considered that they could all have been lying, but it didn't matter anymore.

"I don't think they do."

Atli and Marcia summoned all the Llyrians to the town hall. The townsfolk gathered, seeking shelter from the chill in the heat from the multiple hearths in the room.

Iver was there too, with two rucksacks at his feet containing all their belongings. As soon as this was done, Vicente and Iver were going to find the Stag.

People gave Vicente a wide berth as he walked through the hall and stepped up on the dais to join Marcia and Atli. Despite finding concrete evidence of Ottone's crimes, people disapproved of Vicente bringing Atli and his wife through the tunnel. Had he been in his right mind, he wouldn't have brought them with him, and he wouldn't have made such a public spectacle of it.

That night, Vicente had stolen Ottone's book detailing his plans to build a temple for the Gambler, but because he had been high, Vicente had completely forgotten about it, until now. He knew he had lost his mind, but he couldn't remember when. He would lay off the Stormwater until he was back to normal.

"As you know, Lord Ottone Cronin has been executed," Marcia said to the crowd. "The reason for this is that he had assaulted many orphaned children. He was also the one who killed Natalina, Jairo, Gabriel, Ettore and Olive." Marcia spoke clearly and to the point, leaving no room for confusion.

Gasps and murmurs of unease rippled through the room.

Marcia let them settle down before continuing, "Ambassador Vicente has also brought forth convincing and reliable evidence showing that Ottone Cronin sacrificed human beings to the Gambler god to produce his healing potions."

A collective shock surged through the crowd, a wave of surprise and disbelief that swept through the assembly. Wide-eyed stares were exchanged as people began to yell. "*What?*" someone shouted. "What does this mean?"

It appeared that the Llyrians believed her, and Vicente was relieved. Without Ottone's potions, Llyr couldn't afford to halt all their trade with the capital. The queen and the High Council would be happy with Marcia, and if she wished to, she would be safe to return to Arkensaal. Even if Vicente didn't, Marcia still had a career there.

Again, Marcia stayed quiet until every voice had died down. "I want all of you to know that this issue is settled. The citizens of Llyr will not be subjected to any more investigations by the capital. Whatever faith some of you hold close to your heart, will not be punished. Thank you for your time."

CHAPTER 50

Vicente

Steeling themselves against the frigid winter winds, Vicente and
Iver left the horses behind and trudged up the mountain.
Everything around them was cloaked in a blanket of snow; the
only sounds were the crunch of their boots and the occasional
distant howl of wind. The sky above was gray and low, heavy with
the threat of impending snowfall.

Vicente held the map in his gloved hand. The parchment's
edges were worn and frayed, the ink lines blurred by moisture and
time. But it was their only guide through the wilderness, a
crumpled lifeline leading them over jagged rocks and through
thickets of snow-laden trees to the heart of the mountain where the
Resurrectionists had found the Stag.

The snow grew deeper, forcing them to struggle against its
weight with each step. Vicente's legs protested and he cast a
weary glance at Iver. There was determination etched across his
face. He wasn't ready to take a break yet, and Vicente couldn't
take the hit to his pride if he suggested that they would, so he kept
his mouth shut.

As the hours ticked by, the wind became more insistent,
carrying with it a biting cold that seeped through their clothing.
Vicente's fingers were numb around the map, but he dared not
relinquish it. Iver's teeth chattered. His face was tinged with a
rosy hue from the cold, yet he pressed on.

The terrain shifted, forcing them to navigate a narrow ledge
carved into the mountainside. Below them, a sheer drop fell away

into a white abyss. The wind howled with renewed ferocity, threatening to tear them from the path. Vicente's heart pounded in his chest, eyes fixed on the rock in front of him, shutting out the dizzying expanse below. Iver followed suit.

As the light around them faded, they stumbled upon a clearing. At its center stood an entrance to a cave, its yawning mouth hidden beneath a layer of ice and snow.

Vicente's chest swelled with relief as he looked at the map one final time. "I think this is it."

Iver drew back his hood and looked up at the cliff before them. "Looks fucking inconspicuous."

With trembling fingers, Iver struck a match and lit two of the torches they had brought with them. As they stepped into the cave, Vicente was immediately taken by its beauty. The walls, ceiling and floor were composed entirely of the mineral schorl. Its deep, glossy black surface gleamed in the glow of the torches.

The cave was vast, and the walls were studded with schorl crystals of various sizes, forming patterns and formations like works of art. Stalactites and stalagmites of schorl hung from the ceiling and rose from the ground. Their presence gave the chamber an almost cathedral-like look.

The cave was also hot—so unbearably hot—and the air carried a suffocating musky scent, so pungent Vicente tasted it in the back of his throat. As they walked deeper into the chamber, the ground beneath their boots crunched. Peering down at his feet, Vicente realized the cave floor was covered in a layer of small schorl fragments.

As they moved forward, the cave opened into a larger chamber, and the light from the torches swept over a colossal form resting at the heart of the cavern. The sight stole the breath from Vicente's lungs and rooted them both to the spot. Before them lay the Stag, of mythical proportions, its magnificent form stretched out in slumber. The creature's scales shimmered in shades of iridescent blue and green, and its serpentine body curled in graceful arcs. But it was the singular antler rising from the center of its head that captured Vicente's attention. The antler resembled the regal crown of a fallow deer, its ivory hue contrasted against the Stag's vibrant scales.

"Fuck me," Iver breathed.

Its huge eyes snapped open. Vicente saw entire civilizations arise and crumble in those eyes. The pupils of the beast dilated, like a cat's when it spots its prey. Fear made Vicente's breath stutter.

When the Stag lifted its head, Vicente got a good look at its deer-like face. "Took you long enough, Vicente Lamor," it said.

It had always been a nebulous thing, far away. But now, he was finally standing in front of it. "You know my name?"

"I am the Stag. I am the future."

The ground vibrated as the Stag stood, its antler striking the cave ceiling with a loud pang, like the ice on a frozen lake cracking. Four cloven hooves supported its weight. It was compressed, trapped, stifled underground. "I am the sun. I am the merciful. I am the future. I am the river Zinat and I am the rain, I am the Crooked Mountains, I am the field of battle. I am the circlet of the brave Ōekenese girl, Svala. I am the voice of the realm." Its guttural growl made the very air tremble. "Puny humans. Worship me. Long may I reign!"

In all of Vicente's studies of history, he had never come across the name *Svala*. Perhaps she was from the future. "Then you know why I have come, and I offer you—"

"Kneel before me, human," the Stag roared. "Worship me."

Vicente wanted to, but he was frozen in place, like he had lost control of his arms and legs.

Iver was standing close behind him. "Vic, maybe—"

"Stop speaking," the Stag interrupted. "This is between me and the descendant of those who trapped me."

Was that the reason Vicente's mystic powers were in his blood? Because it was his ancestors who wielded the Stag last? Why would they have given that up, and trapped it here?

Iver pushed on his shoulders. Bowing his head, Vicente knelt before it, shards of schorl digging through the fabric of his trousers into his knees. Nothing would stop him from getting it out of there.

The Stag glanced down at him, standing more than thirty feet tall. "I am the future. I will be united with the past and the present—the Otter and the Bird. Take me to them."

Vicente's heart was racing, pounding in his chest. "I have come to bond with you, Stag. I will offer you a gift."

The Resurrectionists had said that the Stag had killed the men who tried to bond it because they had offered it an insufficient gift. But Vicente knew what the Stag wanted: it wanted a part of his body.

Using a knife, Vicente cut off a lock of his hair. "This is a gift from my body."

The Stag regarded it. Then it laughed, a thunderous laugh that shook the walls of the cave. "I don't want that."

Vicente didn't understand. This is what Indra of the Sensis Quorum had told him. They themselves must have offered blood or hair to the Otter in order for Indra to even have suggested it.

The Stag shook its head, and broken pieces of schorl rained down and collected at its cloven hooves as its antler raked over the ceiling. "In order to free me, human, you must give me something that you value over all else."

This was not what the quorum had said. But Vicente wasn't in a position to argue. It must have been that the Stag and the Otter were vastly different to each other, more so than the quorum could have ever predicted. Instead of wanting a part of his body, the Stag required this. Something worth more to Vicente than anything else.

Vicente looked over at Iver in horror.

But the Stag shook its head again, pushing around the sweltering air and filling the cavern with the intense smell of musk. "Not him. There is something you value more: give me your ability to open tunnels."

Vicente didn't understand. Without his powers, how could the Stag ever consider him to be strong, or powerful? "Why would I do such a thing?" He had dedicated his life to studying the path of the Stag. The Otter enhanced the quorum's mystic abilities; the Stag was the source of his own—and now it wanted him to give them away?

"*Tch*," the Stag spat in frustration. "I know why you seek me: to raise more mystics for your realm. You don't need my power any longer, and it consumes you." The Stag's voice was so loud it rattled Vicente's bones. "You have gone too deep, and not even I can save you now. If I were tied to you, it would leave me vulnerable. You may not forge a bond with me unless you forfeit your powers."

"Stag, I have not failed you yet, I promise you," Vicente begged, still on his knees. "Let me prove to you just how powerful I am."

"The apprentices of the Otter all share its powers," the Stag bellowed. "But you have taken all of mine for yourself. That is where you failed. That is why it consumes you. You have already failed."

Vicente clasped his hands. "Please, Stag, I am strong—"

"Trash!" It shouted. "Do not question me; I am the future. I cannot exist on earth unbound, and if you die, which you will, then I will die. Give up your powers, and bring me to the Otter. Give me your blood, Vicente."

Without his powers, Vicente couldn't accomplish anything. His powers were a part of who he was and everything he wanted to be. Without them, his future was hollow and empty, void of anything of value. He couldn't do it. He could not.

He could not do it.

"I can't."

The Stag rumbled. "*What?*"

Vicente rose to his feet on trembling legs. "I'm sorry… I can't do that." He turned and walked past Iver, who tried in vain to stop him, and back the way they had come.

Iver followed him out into the freezing cold. He yelled, "Vicente, think about this! When you're no longer a mystic, you won't be a threat to the queen. You can return safely; you won't have to hide in some shitty part of the capital."

Vicente continued to walk but slipped in the snow. He was too tired to stand. His legs were too heavy. Even when he removed his rucksack from his back, he was too tired. Drained. He needed to open a tunnel to feel like himself again.

Iver caught up to him and helped him up. He cupped his jaw, trying to catch Vicente's gaze with his. "Vic! All this time, you've been searching for this fucking thing. And now we're here, you're just going to walk away?"

Vicente couldn't look him in the eye. "I can't do it."

"Yes, you can!"

Vicente broke free from his grasp. "You don't understand. Opening a tunnel... I have never been happier. I have amazing things in my life. I have been happy, and I have experienced wonderful things—but nothing will ever compare to going through a tunnel. If you've never felt it, you wouldn't understand. I am nothing without it. Nothing matters if I can't do it."

He tried to picture it: a life without the euphoria. It would be a life without happiness. Everything he did revolved around his mysticism; he organized his life around when he could open another tunnel. It was everything he was meant to be. Giving it up would be the same as killing himself. He had no future without it.

The wind howled all around them. Falling snow whipped across their faces.

Iver stared at him. "What the fuck do you mean when you say that? You don't need your fucking Stormwater—why would you say that?"

"It makes me confident—"

"No, it makes you reckless. Have you been paying attention at all? How you act after going through a tunnel? You fuck up, time and time again, because you're high!"

Iver yanked his rucksack from the ground and rummaged through it. He grabbed Vicente's satchel of Stormwater vials, and before he could stop him, Iver threw it on the ground and stomped on it. Despite the whistling wind, Vicente could hear the glass shattering.

There was fury in Iver's eyes, unlike anything Vicente had ever seen before. It was a fury without civility. He had never looked more dangerous. "What about everything you fucking said," Iver shouted, "about bringing peace to the realm? How the Stag will bring more power to the Sensis Quorum, how it will bring prospects to us? Was that all bullshit?"

Iver searched through the pockets of his own jacket. When he found what he was looking for, he held it up for Vicente to see, and his stomach dropped.

In his hand, Iver had the vial of Vicente's blood from the temple. "If I drink this, I take your powers from you, right?"

No. *No, no, no, no*—Vicente lurched forward. "Iver, don't."

Iver took a step back. "You won't be able to do it anymore, right? I would take your powers." His hand was shaking.

Vicente realized that Iver was panicking. *Hone in on his weakness.* "Iver, please, listen to me. You don't understand how terrifying it is. Nothing compares. The high is like nothing you have ever experienced before, and I want you to understand how horrifying that is, how awful that is. Nothing you will ever do will ever compare: food, liquor, friendships, sex, love. If you drink that, you'll ruin everything else for yourself."

Iver stared at him, open-mouthed. Then he jammed a fist into his own mouth to stop the sound of the sob that ripped through him.

And all at once, grief flooded Vicente's body. He would do unspeakable things to never hear that sound again.

Iver tossed the vial of blood at Vicente's feet.

Vicente picked it up.

Iver swabbed his eyes with the back of his hand. "I'm not going to ruin myself, annihilate myself, for you, Vic. I can't bear this burden for you. Everything you said... *Fuck*, Vicente, you gave me hope. I have given more of myself to you than I thought I would ever give. Everything I've been through... and you were the first person who's ever even begun to try and fix all that shit. You care more about your powers, about getting high, than bringing the Stag to the quorum?"

Vicente swallowed hard. He looked away, blinking against the sting in his eyes. "Yes."

Iver threw Vicente's backpack on the ground. His jaw trembled. "More than the future of the realm?"

"Yes."

"More than me?"

Silence.

Vicente took too long to say no. He didn't lie when he finally said it—the answer was no. Of course it was. He loved Iver more than anything. But he took too long to say it.

Iver turned and left.

CHAPTER 51

Vicente

Vicente was sober for a few days. Iver had smashed his potions, after all.

At one point, he had gone after Iver, but couldn't find him anywhere, and he soon got lost in the mountains and thick woods. He couldn't find his way back to the cave without the map, which he didn't even remember misplacing. Thus, he pitched the tent in a clearing and then braced for the withdrawals.

He was in pain from Iver leaving him, but he had no energy to go back to Llyr, not now that he had failed his mission. And if anyone tried to attack him to steal his blood, he had no way of defending himself. And so, he had no choice but to stay put and try to stomach the enormity of what he had lost.

The echoing fear of bears and wolves was faint as he lay on his back in the tent, staring up at the fabric ceiling for what felt like days. The dark thoughts were replaced by dead ones.

He stayed in the tent, drinking melted snow whenever he could muster it. He didn't feel hungry. His body was so heavy, he couldn't move. Pain made his world very small, and before long, everything outside his tent ceased to exist. He was twitching, sweating. He could feel his own bones. His bones hurt. He knew it didn't make sense, bones couldn't hurt, could they? But his did, it felt like they were covered in bruises. He couldn't sleep, he couldn't turn off his brain, he couldn't even sit still. But it also hurt to move.

He dreamt of tar. Of sinking into it.

416 ∘ ISABELLE TÖRNQVIST

Grief turned to anger when he questioned how Iver could have left him when he was at his lowest. Did Iver not love him? Yes, he had hurt Iver, hadn't stopped fucking him when he had asked, but everyone makes mistakes. Iver was a murderer: he too wasn't perfect.

Vicente shivered like he was cold but was still sweating. He was yawning, again and again and again. He yawned until he threw up.

When the pangs of hunger became too intense, he went to look for something—anything—to eat. He found a dead deer that had been shot with an arrow. It had probably escaped the hunter and died from the injury in the mountains. He ate pieces from it. Then he returned to the tent to putrefy.

He started crying, and then he cried for days. He was inconsolable. It didn't stop. He missed Iver so badly that it turned his stomach. He missed Marcia and Daiyu and Indra. He began missing his mother. Missing the way she hugged him, laughed with him. She had died all alone. He had never missed his mom before. With snot and tears dripping down his chin, he called out for her. He pleaded with her to come and save him.

The waves of emotion crashed down on him, persistent. Nostalgia. Regret. The grief was disabling. He cried and screamed until his voice broke. Then came the guilt. *What have I done? What have I done?*

He regressed into an animal. Not a wild one, not a free one, but a slave to humanity. A beast of burden that paid for a human's goals with its body, bearing the weight of their ambitions on its back. Every step he took was not his own but dictated by the invisible leash of purpose imposed upon him, dragging him farther from his own essence. He bore the scars of servitude, etched deep into his flesh and soul.

Days blurred, turning into one consecutive nightmare.

It was in one of those nightmares that he realized something, when he finally came face to face with what he had done.

Opening tunnels incurred a debt. He hadn't realized it before, that the euphoria and the good emotions he was stealing, wasn't an act of theft at all. He was borrowing them, and he was borrowing them from himself. From his future self. And now, he needed to pay it all back.

CHAPTER 52

Marcia

The sun was on its way up and only caught the tops of the trees, leaving the ground in warm shadow. Marcia watched as a few Llyrians raised a bronze statue of the Gambler. The sacred sculpture now occupied the very spot where the grand likeness of Eldvittra had once graced the land. Early spring had brought kinder temperatures, and she turned her face to the warm sun as she contemplated her decision. Most people in Llyr now worshipped the Gambler, and who was she to rob them of their faith? The rise of the cult was proof enough that they wouldn't yield to the laws of the realm, laws she didn't necessarily agree with in the first place. Thus, she had allowed them this, to revere their god in the open. Besides, the people of Llyr would most likely never leave this town, and they were all determined to keep it a secret from the outside world.

A large, gray cat emerged from behind the statue, and the people bowed their heads to it. Soundlessly, it approached Marcia and sat by her feet to admire its likeness. It wasn't the first time the Gambler had decided to pay Llyr a visit.

"Ottone Cronin promised me a temple, near old Tal Llyrie," the Gambler said. "But I saw you all are using that land to grow crops instead."

"Since Arkensaal decided to expand the army and draft even more soldiers, we're going to need the food," Marcia said. With Ottone gone, the proposal for the embargo had been dropped, and

Llyr economy had flourished under her rule. The queen was happy, the High Council was happy. The quorum was less so.

Right on cue, a distant rumble resonated through the air, heralding the imminent arrival of a zeppelin. Its silhouette emerged as a dark speck against the eastern sky, a colossal creation of engineering prowess. It headed westward towards one of the frontiers. Its propellers span with a rhythmic cadence, driving the vessel forward. As it drew nearer, its details came into focus, revealing a complex network of glistening metal and reinforced fabric. Onboard were about a hundred soldiers, ready to face their first battle.

"I'll promise you a temple, if you can convince Eldvittra to descend to earth and tell Arkensaal to stop this madness," Marcia said.

The Gambler licked at one of its paws. "I told you already: the Merciful Eldvittra is nowhere to be found; it has left you all to rot. It is I and the rest of the pantheon that protects the earth from the horned god."

Marcia didn't quite believe it; how could a god just disappear? The Gambler had every reason to lie about it, as it held a deep desire to gain more followers. If it could convince everyone that Eldvittra was gone, it would take its place as the ruler of the earth. "Then tell the rest of the Usurper gods to protect us from this."

"We cannot protect you from yourselves," the Gambler said simply.

As the zeppelin glided overhead, the town square was engulfed in its shadow, but Marcia was no longer curious enough to look up at the airship: this was the fifth zeppelin that had passed by in the span of two weeks. She had seen enough of them.

She headed back to her office in the town hall. A few months ago, she had been facing the dilemma of whether to return to Arkensaal or stay in Llyr and shoulder the burden of being prime minister. The decision had been made for her: she had been fired from her job as diplomat. Only a few diplomats had kept their jobs as the order of Tal Miril scaled back on its operations. In the wake of Vicente's failure to bring forth the Stag, the members of the quorum had been promptly demoted to simple advisors. They no longer had a say in how the realm should be ruled, and when they lost their power, the queen gained more. With the support of the noble clans of Arkensaal, the funding was pulled from the quorum and Tal Miril and funneled into the war effort.

Around her, the last of the snow was melting, and the naked branches of the cherry trees bore pink buds, soon to burst open. Day by day, it was getting easier to breathe, though her recovery was slow. A month after Vicente and Iver had set off on their mission, Iver had returned alone. He told her that Vicente had failed, and she never heard from Vicente again. Iver stayed a day and then left. She had given him his papers, his new identity, and hadn't asked where he was going.

The hope of seeing Vicente alive faded slightly each passing day. Eventually, she had been forced to break the news to Arkensaal, and the queen had promptly exerted her power over the quorum to break them down. The quorum would never be allowed to train another mystic again. In addition, they had been relegated to the shadows. The government could never function without the knowledge from the Sensis Quorum, but they now needed to hide in the shadows until called upon.

*

"Another riot?" Celia asked over the loud buzz in the Harvest Heart.

Marcia handed her the newspaper—she had them delivered from the capital—and continued eating her dinner. "They've sent the rangers to deal with them all. There's going to be a death toll on the cover of the next issue, I'm sure of it."

Celia read the article, the frown on her face deepening as she did. "I would've never guessed so many people cared about the fate of the Sensis Quorum."

"It's just a few hundred protestors," Marcia said. "Not that many know or care about what the quorum does for the realm. Either that, or they don't dare to take to the streets."

Celia put the newspaper down on the empty chair beside them, took Marcia's hand in hers and fondly kissed her knuckles. "I'm really glad you're not there. I'm glad you decided to stay here."

Marcia smiled at her. "Me too."

The two of them had made it official a few weeks ago, and it felt good to be able to display their affection in public.

Marcia's world was a little grayer than it used to be. The vibrant colors had died with Daiyu, like the world only knew color because of her. Though she missed the vibrancy, her love for Celia didn't need it. It was one of structure and routine, and it didn't need color to thrive. And the grief Marcia carried within allowed her to love with a fierceness she had not had before, now that she knew what was at stake and how easily it could be torn away. Now that she knew what it cost, she knew the value of it.

Still, it was hard to revisit the memories, knowing that their main focal point would never star in them again. Her heart still sank when something reminded her of Daiyu's humor. But the only way to heal was to forget, and that was the last thing she wanted to do. So, she revisited as much as she needed, cried when she had to, made the memories a home and the grief a member of her family. She knew grief would last forever, because love did.

CHAPTER 53

Vicente

When the last snow of the winter melted, Vicente left the mountains. He had no real destination in mind; he just needed to speak to a human. It had been months since he last had. The isolation made him feel weak. Hollow. He felt like a stranger in his own life, in his own skin.

A small cottage sat on the top of a hill, in the shade of a willow tree. Sheep were grazing in the fields around it. A gravel path snaked its way from it to a small stone bridge arching over a creek. This structure on the outskirts of Llyr was the first he had seen in months, and he wanted to approach it, but his legs shook, and his chest was tight with exhaustion.

To catch his breath, he sat down on the low wall that surrounded the pasture and watched as the sheep crossed the bridge. There was rain in the air, and winter was giving way to spring. The weather might have seemed poor to some, colder than it ought to be and darker than the day before, but all of a sudden it felt so real: he was here. The sky was overcast and the stone beneath him was dirty and damp, but he was alive. He could dig his fingers into the earth or smell the budding lilacs by the road— when did he forget it was all real? When did he forget the world? Being high out of his mind, strung out on Stormwater, he forgot it all; reality was substituted with this beautiful dream, and it was sweet until it wasn't, until the power it gave left him drained and he had forgotten the smell of soil, of sweat. Until he had forgotten the feeling of hunger.

There was a balance in him again. When he had been high, it was only good. When he was going through withdrawal, everything was awful. Now, he could feel both. He needed the bad too, because the suffering was his, it made him, he didn't need Stormwater to shoulder it, because it was *his*. It was raw and it hurt, but it made him human.

He looked at the dirt under his nails and couldn't recall when he forgot what it felt like, couldn't recall exactly when the numbness had set in. His chest was heaving; he was gasping for breath. *Oh god, when did it get that bad?* He could feel the soft caress of the wind for the first time since he had first let the Stormwater devour him, and he sobbed. The sky above was a gentle gray—and it was infinite, it existed despite him. The pitter-patter of the sheep reminded him of what he had gambled away; the sweetness and embrace of the world, found in the small, ordinary details. The world no longer held him, and he was ashamed of what he had done.

He had bestowed upon his potions the name of Stormwater, as it replenished the spring in his core, as it refilled the wellspring within him, replenished his vitality. But when there was nowhere for stormwater to drain, it could become infected; it could fester, bearing contagions capable of toppling even the mightiest citadels. Surface runoff, a consequence of torrential squalls, bore the capacity to erode both roads and bridges. He could only hope he could rebuild the bridges to his loved ones.

*

The pain in his knuckles sent a jolt through his arm as he knocked on the door. It was like his nerves were on top of his skin, and had been for months.

The door opened, and Vicente had to battle away his embarrassment to look Eloy in the eye.

"Vicente?" Eloy's eyes were wide in shock. "I thought you were dead."

Vicente tried to rally some humor. "Feels like I am."

Eloy opened the door wider. "Merciful, you are emaciated. Come inside. Where have you been?" Eloy's wife prepared something for him to eat and he gratefully accepted a bath and some new clothes. The food was comforting, gifting him the internal warmth only a hot meal could give, like fuel for a furnace. Eloy sat with him as he ate, looking at him like he was a puzzle or a ghost.

Eloy's daughter was playing with the large hound. She had grown since he had last seen her, both in size and in vocabulary.

"Marcia told me you were gone, and she sent word to Arkensaal about it," Eloy said as they watched the child play with the dog. "Apparently, the Sensis Quorum have been shunned for your failure."

Vicente wasn't surprised to hear that. The sisters of the quorum had fought for centuries for acceptance from society, and their reputation rode on Vicente's success. He had failed them, as well as the realm and all its mystics in hiding, but he didn't care. Power such as this should not be held by anyone.

"Remember when you took my vial of blood from the temple?" Vicente asked. "You tried to take my mystic abilities."

Eloy swallowed hard and averted his gaze. "Sorry about that."

"It didn't work because it wasn't the real one." In a haze, Vicente put the vial of his blood on the table between them. The real one that Iver had taken before Eloy had had the chance. "I have come to let you drink my blood." Distancing himself from his actions, refusing to reflect on them in the moment, was the only way he could go through with it.

He needed his powers gone. He couldn't trust himself to not relapse, he no longer wanted the ability to do so—because no matter how much he regretted what he had done, no matter how much he had hurt Iver and Marcia and *Daiyu*, no matter how sick he felt while going through withdrawals… he still missed it. The high of opening a tunnel could not compare to any other feeling or sensation. Nothing even came close. And perhaps people were not meant to experience such euphoria, perhaps no one could handle it. Perhaps no one was created for that sort of suffering, to endure it.

Eloy didn't hesitate before drinking it.

Something in Vicente changed. The embers nesting deep in his chest, that he would tap into with his mind to access his powers, disappeared. He took a breath of freedom, he let his shoulders droop. It had been done. Any regret he would feel would be futile. There was no going back now.

"Wow." Eloy stood, looking at his hands, eyes darting, eyebrows furrowed. "How do I use it?"

Vicente stood too, stretching his aching back. "You need training from other mystics. Perhaps the quorum will take you in, though I doubt it. They won't be allowed to train another mystic as long as there are people alive to remember my failures."

Despair found its way into Eloy's face. "You can't mean that. You can teach me."

Vicente shook his head. "I don't have the powers: you took them from me. I no longer have a connection to the Stag: it's yours now."

Vicente left Eloy sputtering, then took his cloak and stepped out into the chill spring air.

Perhaps he should've made another attempt at getting the Stag, instead of giving up his powers to Eloy, but he was afraid his conviction would've faltered before he reached the cave—and that was if he could have even located it again without the map. He also didn't want anything to do with that world again: it was too late. If the quorum ever were able to recuperate, they would need to try again with some other mystic. Bonding the Stag, giving his powers to it, wasn't an option. If he was to deliver it to the quorum and avoid getting killed by the queen's guard as soon as he set his foot in the capital, he would need Stormwater to evade them. He would rather die, would rather the realm succumb to war, than to go through withdrawals again.

Llyr stood in the distance, its aqueducts arching against the azure sky, but he couldn't yet return to face Marcia—not before he had made things right. He needed to find Iver, but he had no idea where to look. He wouldn't be in Llyr. Perhaps he had gone to the closest village, Naka-Toda. On foot, it would take Vicente weeks to get there, but he needed the time to think anyway.

His boots left prints in the dew of the grass, and some of it kicked up onto the backs of his legs when he walked. He trekked over hills, through the lowland woods. Vicente knew he was the one in the wrong, and it hurt so badly to realize it. Iver had done the right thing in leaving him. Vicente had hurt him. He would never stop regretting that. It was a painful thought, and he recoiled from it, but he forced himself to let it grind in his mind. He had been angry with Iver for leaving, and now he was ashamed for ever having blamed him. Iver didn't deserve what Vicente had done to him, and he knew that.

Three days into the journey, Vicente regretted not bringing food or tools with him. He didn't even have water, and he hadn't come across a stream since he'd left.

Dehydration made his throat ache and the world span around him. He stopped in a clearing in the woods, trying to steady his ragged breaths. Now, he was no longer a mystic: he was just a person, as vulnerable as everyone else. The ground trembled beneath his feet, of his mind's own making.

He laughed out loud as his first knee struck the ground, then the other. He would die there. If he had just been able to apologize to Iver, he wouldn't have minded it, but Iver deserved a better goodbye. Vicente loved him more than he had ever loved anyone else before. He longed for him more than the trees longed to reach the sun.

The surge of grief took his breath away, it shrunk and tightened around his chest until he couldn't draw air into his lungs, no matter how hard he gasped for it.

They had only had *months* together, not even a full year. He hadn't even known Iver for an entire year. It was hard to comprehend that during his lifetime, he had spent more mornings waking up without him than with him. And now, his opportunity to change that, was squandered.

He caught himself and braced his hands against the approaching earth. He would die there. Would the wolves find his body before his mind had left him? Would they see the vile creature he had been in life? Or would they be gentle when they picked apart his bones, would they recognize a small life clinging to the ones he loved with all his might, would they see the love his heart bore and perhaps leave it intact?

The hard, solid earth caught his back as he lay down. He looked up at the lacework of leaves above. Sunlight dappled through the trees, like fingers of light, stretching downward. Particles of dust sparkled within the sunbeams, suspended in midair as if caught in a moment. They glimmered like fleeting stars. In the haze of Stormwater, his mind couldn't discern the details, and it scared him to know he couldn't remember when he had last noticed them. But now he could, and it was beautiful.

"That's all you had in you?"

Vicente lolled his head to the side.

Iver came walking between the trees. Vicente could barely make out the shape of him due to the camouflage of his clothes. Had it not been that Vicente had learned every curve and angle of him, traced the outline of his body with his hands, he wouldn't have been able to tell his body apart from the forest around him.

Iver held his rifle with both hands, close to his chest. "Travelling without water—really, Vic? You can be such a dumb cunt sometimes."

Vicente opened his mouth to speak, lips so dry they were close to cracking. "How did you find me?"

Iver scoffed. "I've been following you for months, dumbass. What, you think you survived all on your own? Please." Iver crouched down next to him, set down his backpack and placed his canteen beside his head. "Get the fuck up, you're embarrassing yourself."

Vicente pushed himself up. "I am so sorry, Iver." He clambered to his feet and stood before the man he loved.

Iver looked up at him. "Piece of shit. I know you are. You don't need to apologize."

Vicente knew Iver wanted to help shoulder his pain, he would've taken it from him if he could. Vicente would never again allow him to do so. "I am aware of the pain I have caused, the boundaries I have trespassed, the fear I have instilled. Acting like shit. I love you. I will love you forever, Iver. My affection for you will never die, and if you allow it, I'll dedicate my entire existence to you." Every breath he took, he realized, was searching for Iver's exhale. It hit him with full force that Iver was here with him, when he very nearly wasn't. After all Vicente had done, had put him through. Vicente didn't deserve him, but he could change that. He would.

Iver turned his head away momentarily, and when he looked at him again, his eyes were tearing up. "I love you too, Vic." He tried to blink away the tears. "Fuck." He dragged his wrist across his eyes. "You can't do it anymore, right? That's why you went to Eloy Errani's house?"

Vicente cupped Iver's face in his hands, feeling his warm skin and letting it seep into his core. "That's right. It's gone. I can never open another tunnel again."

"Good. You really scared me, you know."

"I know." Vicente brushed his thumbs over his cheeks, below his eyes as if to wipe away the tears that had not yet fallen. "May I kiss you?"

Iver grabbed the collar of his shirt and pulled him down, in, pressing his lips to his. He kissed him with something like passion, something like commitment. Then Iver broke it to look into his eyes, so close his breath still ghosted over his lips. "You better kiss me: I saved your life. You would've starved to death without me."

Iver still gripped Vicente's collar, and he wanted to turn his head into it, to touch his face to the inside of his wrist, to feel his pulse intimately. "You were the one who shot the deer I found in the mountains?"

"Of course. You know I got your back."

Vicente shoulders dropped as he let go of his breath. The smile that curved his lips was one of fondness. "You've got my six."

"Always."

ABOUT THE AUTHOR

ISABELLE TÖRNQVIST grew up on Sweden's windswept west coast. By day, she's a software developer; by night, a fantasy and horror writer conjuring strange worlds and stranger gods. She lives in a countryside cottage with her parrot, Ava, who insists on being part of the creative process.

INSTAGRAM: author.isabelletornqvist
TIKTOK: @chaoticAuthor